THE HAUNTING OF KARLIK

The Chronicles of the Blind:
BOOK 1

G.W. LÜCKE

With Distinction Publishing

Published in Australia by With Distinction Consultants
PO Box 97, St Marys, Tasmania 7215
https://withdistinctionconsultants.wordpress.com/
First published in Australia in 2025

A catalogue record for this work is available from the National Library of Australia

National Library of Australia Cataloguing-in-Publication Entry:
Creator: Lücke, G. W., author
Title: *The Haunting of Karlik.*
ISBN: 978-0-6488207-8-9 (Paperback)
ISBN: 978-0-6488207-7-2 (ePub)

BISAC Codes: FIC009020 FICTION/Fantasy/Epic; FIC009100 FICTION/Fantasy/Action and Adventure

The Chronicles of the Blind is a series of five books,
each with a stand-alone story connected by recurring characters
and plot threads.

Also by G. W. Lücke

The Relevation Trilogy

Book 1: When Darkness Descends

Book 2: At the End of Everything

Book 3: She Will Rise

For Hannah
A better world awaits

Ostamp
N
Nordargen Sea
Occidian Sea
elephai Bay
Ephesus
Afonwee
Germalia
Mons Harena
Disputed Territory
Slyencia Bay
Portum
Pordillo Territory
Gadhang

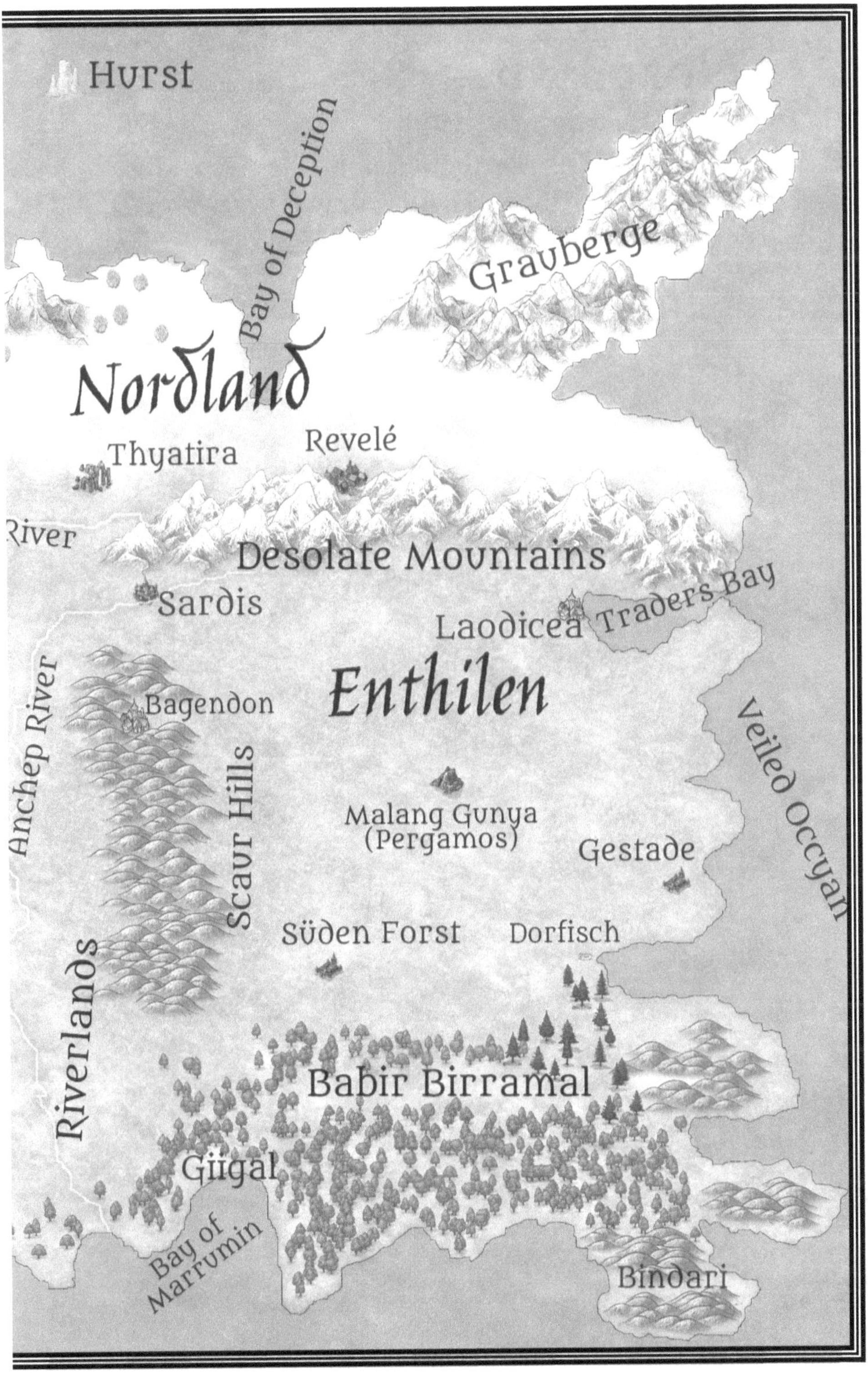

Hurst
Bay of Deception
Grauberge
Nordland
Thyatira
Revelé
River
Desolate Mountains
Sardis
Laodicea
Traders Bay
Anchep River
Bagendon
Enthilen
Scaur Hills
Malang Gunya
(Pergamos)
Gestade
Veiled Occyan
Riverlands
Süden Forst
Dorfisch
Babir Birramal
Giigal
Bay of
Marrumin
Bindari

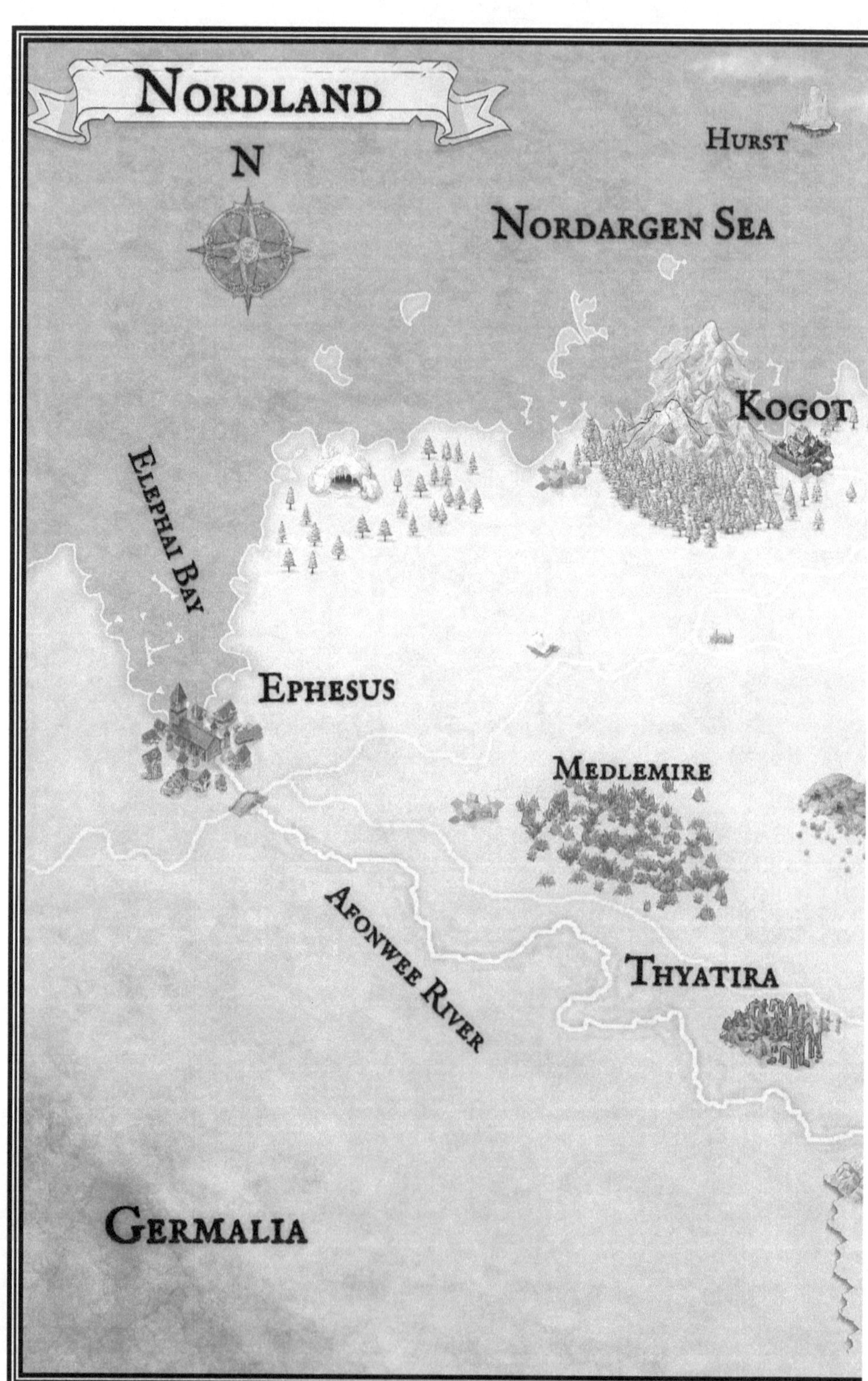

NORDLAND
N
HURST
NORDARGEN SEA
KOGOT
ELEPHAI BAY
EPHESUS
MEDLEMIRE
AFONWEE RIVER
THYATIRA
GERMALIA

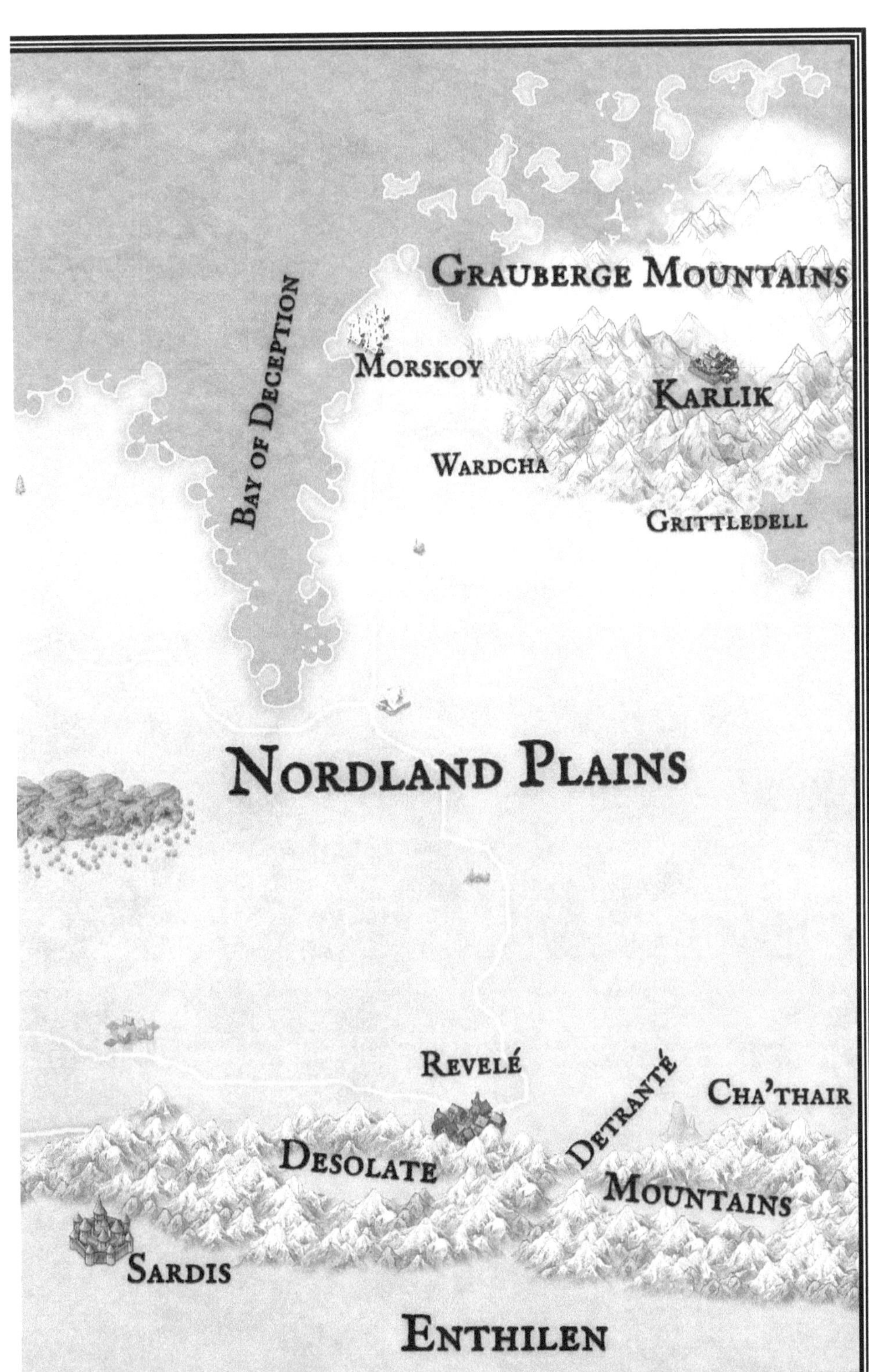

GRAUBERGE MOUNTAINS
BAY OF DECEPTION
MORSKOY
KARLIK
WARDCHA
GRITTLEDELL
NORDLAND PLAINS
REVELÉ
DÉTRANTÉ
CHA'THAIR
DESOLATE
MOUNTAINS
SARDIS
ENTHILEN

Silveny

The Devil's Prayer

Abandon logic and reason

For ghosts of former selves

Abandon faith in kindness

Let hatred rule your creed

Embrace the haunting temptation

Of power, vengeance and greed

Chapter 1

On the brink

Greed extinguishes the last flaming vent of serpent gas, and darkness consumes Karlik for the first time in generations. Eyes failing to adjust in time, I thud into Yula's back. She'd stopped without warning. The stretcher poles I carry behind me shunt forward.

"Steady, Silveny," snaps Barick as he yanks on the other end of the poles.

Lying on the stretcher, Gallan's fading life chronicles its last moments with frail inhalations of death. Without him, we'd move faster. But without him, I'd already be lost.

"Does the lantern still have oil?" asks Barick.

"Yes," I reply. "Yula, take my end of the stretcher."

She grunts as her rough hands reach down my arms, then to my sides to grasp the stretcher poles. I pull away, unshoulder my rucksack and fumble for one of the buckles that cinch the straps.

"Hurry," urges Barick. "They'll find us soon."

I undo the first buckle. The second. "I'm trying."

Tossing open the pack flap, I reach in and retrieve the lantern. As I crouch and place the lantern on the ground, the brass base clangs against the road bricks, ringing out our location. Yula hisses at me. We're sisters, but her impatient desperation doesn't make concessions for family. I shrug for forgiveness, then open a drawer in the lantern's base and pull out a thumb-sized box of firesticks and a fold of strike paper. Pushing open the box, I search for a firestick. Yula's irritation presses on my neck. Barick's fearful urgency sets my fingers trembling. I can't drop the firesticks or lose the paper. Not in this blackness. Not with vengeance in pursuit.

I pinch a firestick between my thumb and forefinger and drag the bulbous end across the strike paper. It lights first time. I lift the lava-glass cylinder protecting the lantern's wick and brush the burning firestick against the oil-soaked, braided cotton. Flames spring to life, spreading a tangerine halo across the road bricks.

I lower the opaque cylinder, extinguish the firestick, return the box and strike paper to the drawer, and click it shut. After cinching and shouldering my rucksack, I stand, holding the lantern, and push past Yula to the front of the group.

"Not far to the workshop," I say over my shoulder.

"Are you certain your invention will fly?" asks Barick.

"Not sure it's finished. But...." *...there's no other choice.*

As I stride ahead, I fiddle with the pack's buckles with my left hand. *Loosen, tighten. Loosen, tighten.* Yula mutters and follows, stretchering Gallan and pulling Barick along with her, his wimpish body struggling with Gallan's weight. The lantern casts an ever-diminishing pool of light, devoured by the dark, abandoned buildings that line the empty alleyway and lean in like hungry ghosts. Shadows jump and swirl in the misty freeze.

Oh, the chill. With all the venting fires extinguished, Karlik's true, cold heart is revealed. Thin prison rags and bare feet can't protect me from the city's biting core.

Rocks tumble from a building. I stop, jerking my head up. A murky shape, too small to be a threat, creeps along a window ledge. *Probably too small.*

"Silveny," croaks Gallan, lifting his head from the stretcher. He pulls a notebook from his inside coat pocket with a bloodied hand. "Take this." Then holds the book towards me. "I've written it down. All that happened."

I grab the notebook and nod in thanks.

Barick sniffs the unsettling air. "Does anyone else smell smoke?"

From where? No venting fires. Houses all abandoned in this quarter. But he's right.

A clamorous pursuit fills the silence. Behind us, flaming torches bob along the alley.

I grit my teeth. "Shit."

Barick throws panic over his shoulder. "Voldari?"

I shake my head. "Worse. Curmudgles hunting traitors."

The lantern will draw them in like moths. We duck into another alleyway, but it's too late. Vengeful calls hail our presence. Yula shoves past me, dragging her fellow stretcher-bearer with her. They lunge and lurch into the night. I run after them, trying to cast light ahead. We're almost at the workshop.

"Left, then right," I gasp. "We might lose them."

Yula turns left, then sharp right, scraping the edge of the stretcher along the cornerstone of a dilapidated millinery. Gallan's body rocks sideways. The alley narrows. *Good place for an ambush.* We jog faster. The thud of pursuing boots drifts away.

We squeeze out the other end of the backstreet. Across a deserted market square that hasn't heard a trader spruik in yarles, squashed between a tavern and a butchery, is the workshop. The steel portcullis door, wider than two wagons abreast, has been raised to waist height. I sprint through the market, then slow. Strewn across the street in front of the door are hundreds of dead bodies. Not mudgles or Voldari. Sewer cats, rats and snerguls.

"What happened here?" asks Yula as she catches up with me.

"Casca," says Barick. "He called them to their death."

I step through the massacre as if creeping past a haunted cemetery, then duck under the door, squeezing my breasts up against my thighs. Barick follows. Yula pushes the stretcher underneath, and we drag Gallan inside along the ground. He's passed out again, his feeble breaths whistling through a strange smile.

Inside. No skycart. More dead animals.

"Hello?" I loudly but stupidly whisper. No-one inside will hear, but I don't want to attract our pursuers.

I place the lantern on the floorstones and rush to the winch, unlocking it and turning the handle to lower the door. The steel, as thick as my arm, groans displeasure at being disturbed. Outside, boot soles slap the road bricks like lashes from a whip. They run to beat the door closing. *Knee height now.* A fist holding a knife thrusts underneath the door. Barick pulls a mining pick from his belt and buries the point between clenched knuckles.

"*Argh!*" The hand disappears, leaving the knife behind.

Might come in useful. Door at ankle height. Yula grabs the knife. *Door closed.*

Beside the main entrance, a smaller timber door shudders from the pummel of fists and boots. Yula slams an iron rod across the door and down into brackets fixed to either jamb. As she does, someone outside spews curses of vexation. Yula's shoulder muscles tense, preparing to fight. We have few weapons, but I'm willing my sister to challenge whatever comes with a frightful fury.

"Help!" My defenceless plea echoes unanswered around the cavernous workshop. Other than the animal corpses, the building appears empty. *Building or tomb?*

Barick drags Gallan's stretcher further inside as pursuers pound the timber door.

"Open up!" demands one of the monsters outside, followed by a thunderous bang that shakes the wall.

"We're trapped in here," cries Barick.

'CRACK!'

A timber panel splinters, and shards explode into the workshop. Yula pushes frantic hands against the panel, trying to hold the fracturing wood together with her fingers.

'CRACK!'

Another part of the door splinters, and an axe head slams through the wound.

"You can't escape!" a monster yells.

"Yula!" I scream. "Get away from the door."

She steps back as the axe smashes through the timber door again and retreats. A bloodshot, ravenous eye presses up to the axe hole. Yula collects a wood splinter from the floor and rams it into the hole. A monster screams, then a wolf howls.

A wolf? Shit. Without the venting fires to keep them at bay, nothing can stop horned wolves from overrunning the city.

Yula marches over, grabs my shoulder and squeezes.

"We can hide," I say. "Out the back."

"They've got wolves!" cries Barick.

I already know that.

More timber is ripped from the door, leaving a hole large enough for....

A horned wolf thrusts its snarling head inside. Yula steps towards the door, brandishing her inadequate knife. With unusual courage, Barick raises his mining pick and stumbles after her. I grope around in the half-light cast by the lantern, searching for a weapon. I pick up a wrench and join my friends. *Too late to hide.*

Yula yanks the wrench from my trembling hand. She lunges at the door and swings the tool down onto the wolf, smashing a horn clean from its head. The beast squeals but pushes further inside, driven by unimaginable madness. Its shoulders ram through the hole. Its groping fangs snap at my sister. Mudgles outside, my fellow citizens, scream with filthy, misguided retribution.

Yula swings again, cracking the wolf's skull. It exhales a pitiful snarl, and its head falls limp, shoulders blocking the door hole. Mudgles try to pull the carcass back outside to unblock the hole. Strangely...well, not strange for my sister, Yula drops the wrench and knife, grabs the wolf's head and yanks forward in a bizarre, grisly tug of war. Barick tucks his mining pick under his belt and helps, wrapping fingers around the wolf's intact horn and pulling.

What happens if they drag the wolf inside? What happens if they fail?

The door hole is big enough for mudgles to clamber through. An impasse is the only thing protecting us.

The wolf's neck stretches, then cracks. Barick loses his grip. The mudgles pull the carcass outside, almost taking Yula with it. An arrow flies through the hole and hits my sister in the thigh.

"Block the hole!" I yell, paralysed from doing much else.

Barick rolls a steel drum up to the door, and a limping, bleeding Yula lifts it from the ground and forces the end into the hole. Another arrow pings on the metal. Another axe smashes through the door. Yula braces her back against the drum, arrow fletching jutting from her thigh and blood seeping down her shin.

Barick stares at me with affrighted eyes.

Breaking the deathly trance, the squeal of an unoiled hinge wails above us. From the workshop roof, a staircase attached to chains lowers towards the floor.

"This way!" someone yells.

Not a monster. We heed the call.

Chapter 2

The Inventoria

The Inventoria Lab hummed with expectation as I hooked my shoulder satchel across the back of a chair and sat at my workbench. Around me, a dozen Curmudgles sought inventive illumination among the varicoloured shards of light cast by the flames of serpent-oil lamps from behind lava-glass cylinders. The glass, a by-product of the fiery pits found in serpent oil mines, ranged in colour from beige, honey or tangerine to as dark as mahogany. Oil lamps used the lighter coloured lava-glass, dark glass reserved for buildings hiding secrets.

Hearthed in the blocky stone wall, a gas fireplace, the gas another by-product of oil mining, attempted to ward off the chill of the windowless room. Our lab supervisor, Eminent Drudan, once said, 'Windows stifle ingenuity. Vistas spawn daydreams, not critical calculations.' I disliked his philosophy. Inspiration could be found anywhere, even in the bleak, snow-capped Grauberge Mountains surrounding Karlik.

To brighten my path to discovery, I opened a box of firesticks, struck one alight on a square of strike paper and lifted the lava-glass cylinder of my oil lamp before pressing the burning stick against the wick. A flame spluttered to life, its sepia reflection dancing across the polished steel of my benchtop. I snuffed out the stick and placed it in a tin cup full of half-burned firelighters. Then I pushed the cylinder back in place, the coarse lava-glass, a barely transparent rust colour, scraping against the lamp's brass base loud enough to cause the inventors nearest me to look up from their workbenches and glare.

I half-smiled at them as I arranged my drawing pencils from shortest to longest along the benchtop. Rather than use the shortest pencil until it became an unworkable nub, I preferred to sharpen a new pencil to add to the collection. My workmates teased that I did this to remind everyone that the crank-handle pencil sharpener was my first invention. However, rigid, logical order offered me a security others failed to grasp. I called it my 'compulsion.' Nine pencils in regimental alignment along the top edge of the bench fed the compulsion, but it always hungered for more.

I uncinched my satchel, withdrew a ruler, and measured one quotent – about a thumb width – between each pair of pencils. Then, I retrieved further drafting items from a bench drawer: wooden set squares and compasses of various types and sizes, templates, and an eraser. I placed each one inside the outlined shape I'd traced onto the benchtop.

'Everything must have its place,' my ma'one would say. 'How else will you know when something is out of place?'

From the shoulder satchel, I retrieved my most recent and important drawings and notes, untied the cinching ribbon, and, after checking for theftful glances from nosy inventors, unrolled the six parchments across the bench. But I couldn't thwart the burrowing, beady eyes directly opposite.

Sitting at his workbench, Vyrin Durk leaned forward in faux inquisitive innocence as a smile slimed from his mouth and crept over my skin.

"Presentation day tomorrow," said Vyrin, his words barely escaping from between the painful braids of a ruddy beard.

I stiffened upright. "I'm ready."

"You'd want to be. Presentation of your first major invention to Eminent Drudan. If you don't get it right...." Vyrin ran a finger across his bearded throat.

I imagined the digit transforming into a razor-sharp knife, slicing off the waist-long braids of his prized beard until the ruddy hair entangled in an emasculated, blood-splattered heap on the floorstones.

I growled, "Why are you such an arseho...."

"*Sssh!*" hissed Rula, sitting at the workbench beside me.

Vyrin smirked. "Rula believes silence is the cradle of invention, lest speech cause calamity."

Rula glared at Vyrin, then returned to her inventive hush. Vyrin continued his work, but his derision haunted my thoughts. We'd started working in the Inventoria at the same time, but he already had three minor and one major invention approved by Eminent Drudan. I had only two minor inventions, and my apprentice yarle was almost over. Without a major invention approved in my first yarle, I could lose my job and might have to join the mine crews, spending sunless days pinched tight underground in gas-filled tunnels that could explode at any moment.

"Ignore him," whispered Jolia in my ear.

I turned to smile at her standing behind me.

"You'll be fine," she said. "Don't stress."

"*Sssh!*" whined Rula again.

"Oh, you *shoosh*," snapped Jolia. "Your farts are louder than a herd of snow-deer with glass hooves."

I tried not to laugh, but a chuckle snuck out. A bit like one of Rula's farts.

"Meal date?" asked Jolia. "Governant food court at high sun?"

"Sure." I smiled and nodded.

She rested her hands on my shoulders and leaned into my ear. "You've got a wonderful invention. It could save a lot of mudgle lives."

Or kill even more. It was one of those things. We wouldn't know until we tried.

Jolia patted my shoulders, then returned to her desk, flipping unfettered blonde hair from her face. She didn't braid her hair like most Curmudgles, instead letting it grow free. I, on the other hand, contorted my tawny hair into knots of intricately woven braids until not even air could pass through. It was lumpy and uncomfortable to sleep on, but my compulsion wouldn't tolerate unruly hair.

I measured the distance between the pencils again, grabbed the middle pencil – *four either side; even, regimented* – and noted an important detail about my invention on a parchment. One of the drawings didn't meet acceptable exactness, so I erased half of it, redrew, erased some more, and redrew again.

"Careful," said Vyrin. "Late changes cause recent mistakes."

I hope your hair falls out. All of it. But he was right. A change now could lead to a big mistake, and with my presentation to Drudan booked for tomorrow morning, nerves might impair my judgement.

Make a list, Silveny. Everything you need to check.

I began a numbered list on a sheet of recycled parchment, my second minor invention, made by breaking down old parchments into a wet paper mash, filtering the mash through a sieve and remoulding it into new parchments using a watery glue made from woollydon fat. The recycled parchments deteriorated with each re-mash, so the process could be used only three or four times. Because it eventually stopped working, Vyrin hated that Eminent Drudan approved this invention. Honestly, Vyrin disliked most inventions, except his own.

The list made, but likely to be remade a dozen times, and notes and drawings pored over with liquid efficiency, meal break at high sun arrived and Jolia flashed a craving smile. I rolled the parchments together, tied them with ribbon and unlocked the bottom drawer of my workbench. After placing the parchments inside, I slid the drawer closed and turned the key in the lock, tugging on the drawer handle to confirm its security. I then unlocked the drawer, locked it again, and tugged a second time.

Secure. Safe. But do it again. Third time lucky. A fourth to be sure.

"Silveny," said Jolia, standing beside my bench with her fur-lined coat already buttoned, a woollen scarf draped around her neck, and a shaggy hat covering her unlawful blonde hair.

I nodded, stood, donned my coat and dropped the keys into the pocket before pulling on gloves and shouldering my satchel.

We walked out the Inventoria's front door together.

The three-storey Inventoria building sat in the centre of Karlik city, squeezed between the Extractory (Jolia called it 'The Office for Digging Big Holes') and the Statutoria ('The Office for Punishing Naughty Mudgles'). The seven buildings of the Ionad Precinct formed a broken circle around a central hub – the Governant ('The Office of Bumbling Inefficiencies'). Walkways covered with tiled roofs joined each building to the hub. From above, the complex resembled a wagon wheel with an incomplete rim. My compulsion approved of Ionad's austere, logical neatness as much as it fretted over the disordered, labyrinthine nature of the rest of Karlik.

Jolia and I marched beneath the covered walkway that led to the Governant building. Grey clouds blanketed Wyrm Valley where Karlik nestled. Often they brought pure snow, but only ash-snow fell today, a by-product of the flaring of vented serpent gas. The raining pollutant always shadowed the city, precipitation dependent on wind direction and extent of flaring. Once, I'd forgotten to close my mouth, and a dose of sickly, leaden ash-snow landed on my tongue. It tasted like gritty flour and sucked all the moisture from inside my cheeks.

Today I remembered to keep my mouth closed, but with no walls protecting the walkway I worried ash-snow would blow onto my hair and weave its way into the almost impenetrable braids. So, I pulled on my fur-lined hat and quickened my pace, hoping Jolia would keep up.

On either side of the walkway, workers dressed in ankle-length coats and headscarves shovelled the ash-snow into wheelbarrows. They laboured day and night to clean the city, a relentless, eternal chore that would drive my compulsion to madness. Despite the workers' efforts, drifts of ash-snow blew into the walkway. I kicked a pile aside with my boot, then wondered if I should have done it. My friend, Barick, was allergic to the stuff, coughing and wheezing whenever ash-snow fell heavily. The dozens of venting fires around Karlik also generated a pall of thin grey smoke with a smell resembling burning, oil-soaked hair. Acrid, confronting and worrisome. The combined effects of ash-snow and smoke threatened Curmudgle health as much as the sale of serpent oil filled our coffers. But we couldn't build roofed walkways everywhere, so an unpleasant dressing of ash-snow had become a mudgle rite of passage.

We passed the final pillars supporting the walkway's tiled roof. An open, perilous space waited between us and the Governant's front steps. A cold north wind gusted off the ice- and snow-capped mountains, sending eddies of ash-snow twirling above the cobblestones.

I jogged across the hostile space to the steps, dodging the eddies.

"What's the rush?" asked Jolia, risking an ash-snow morsel.

I prised a single word from pursed lips: "Hungry." Then skipped up the steps two at a time and pushed through the Governant's double doors.

Inside the reception hallway, doorkeepers accosted us with horsehair brushes, sweeping remnants of ash-snow from our hair, coats, leather skirts and boots down into grates embedded in the stone floor.

The cleansing complete, we strolled along a corridor lined with paintings, following other groups of workers to the food court, a circular room with a pitched roof and crimson, lava-glass skylights. As we stepped into the court, the skylights bathed us in a drowsy, blushing glow warmed by the largest gas heater in Karlik that dominated the room. Vented gas pulsed through an arboriform of copper tubes resembling a tree stump with exposed roots. Fingerlings of flame burned green in the unnatural light, shimmering through hundreds of holes pecked in the roots, in mockery of the treeless valley where our ancestors built Karlik.

At least, no ash-snow. Mudgle inventors had devised a way to 'clean' the gas before being burned inside. Unfortunately, the process couldn't be scaled up and applied to venting fires. One day, my inventive ambition planned to tackle the problem.

Jolia and I pocketed our gloves and stood with our backs to the heater, surveying the handful of vending stalls lining the hall's perimeter.

"What do you feel like today?" she asked.

"I'm not hungry."

"I thought you said you were. You need more fat on those bones, or you'll freeze to death. How about a hearty soup with rye bread?"

"Do we know what's in the soup?"

She laughed. "Do you want to know? Yesterday, I had woollydon shank with new season yams and marrows from Revelé."

"New season? Probably took a whole season to get here."

"You're such a pessimist."

"I'm a realist."

"Soup it is then. Warm rye bread. Ale?"

"Not during work. We'll drink later."

"Boring. Anything else?"

"Do you think anyone has fruit?"

"Fruit! You're getting exotic. I'll see. You find a table." Jolia smiled, then left before I could offer her tokens.

After scrubbing my hands at one of the two washbasins built into the granite walls, I navigated through dozens of empty tables to find a perfectly square one beside the heater and under a skylight. I shifted the four iron chairs into the centre of their respective side of the table, as best as I could estimate, then pulled out two chairs opposite each other to a distance equal to the length of my forearm. I draped my coat over one and sat down, leaving the other chair for Jolia.

The food court started to fill, but it wouldn't reach capacity. According to Eminent Drudan, the oldest mudgle I knew, that hadn't happened in a generation. Nothing to do with the food on offer. Everything to do with Karlik's shrinking population.

A handful of peace officers from the Statutoria, dressed in warning-red jackets with silver buttons, marched into the food court and cast a stern, impropriety-quashing glare. I smiled at them, knowing their casts rarely landed criminal fish. A peace officer's life was dull; the Statutoria gaol used mostly to sober up drunken mudgles. The officers sat near the door, clanking their truncheons onto the table as if they might use the thudding black batons to bash some taste into their meal.

Next came a harry of administrators from the Governant, simultaneously looking pompous and stressed. They plonked around the oval table beside me, with chairs for a dozen, slamming their satchels onto the wooden tabletop, undoing the buckles and pulling out parchments with the fussiness of someone trivial who longed to be important. Two male members wore plaited leather skirts and short-sleeved tunics, relying on body hair to warm their arms and legs. They represented the traditionalists of Karlik, who refused to cover all of their skin with fabric or don headwear, believing it caused hair loss. The traditionalists were determined to reverse this trend, even if it meant freezing to death.

Three managers from the Extractory shuffled into the room; all female mudgles with grey hair braided around their heads and necks. Like the peace officers, they had a distinct uniform. A drab-brown coat extending down to the knee, worn over an equally drab, beige long shirt cinched at the waist with a leather belt. Unlike traditionalists, they favoured headwear, donning a fur-rimmed ushka hat with a red flame badge sewn on the front, made from the hide of floe bears that hunted on the sea ice rimming Grauberge's northern coast.

With the food court quarter full, a murmur of conversation and laughter filtered through the rosewood light. The sun poked a hole in the smothering clouds and bathed us in uncommon radiance, approving of the peaceful companionship found in Karlik.

"Did you see?" said Jolia as she placed a tray on the table. She sat down, pulled her chair in and leaned forward. "That gorgeous Peace Officer Crooshka is here. Near the door."

I humoured my friend by glancing in Crooshka's direction. He was tall for a mudgle, the top of his head likely reaching a Nordman's chest, and he had such luscious caramel hair and skin that he resembled a giant walking toffee. But his blue-green eyes glimmered with an aloofness that dulled my thoughts of romantic opportunity.

"Don't stare," said Jolia, leaning back and placing the bowls and plates on the table.

She shunted an empty chair away from the table and balanced the tray on the seat, skewing the chair's position to an unequal distance from each table corner and offending my compulsion. I almost got up to correct the mistake, but distracted myself by moving the soup bowl and plate of rye bread to a hand's distance from the table's edge.

"Out of yams and marrows," said Jolia. "Woollydon shanks with onion and beans."

"What would we do without woollydons?" I asked. "Wear them, ride them, harness them to a cart. Or chop 'em up and stick 'em in a stew."

She chuckled. "Sounds like the makings of a song."

I leaned forward. "Why don't you ask the dreamy Crooshka out for drinks?"

"The only time I've seen him in one of the taverns is to break up a fight, and every time I run a message to the Statutoria, he's on patrol."

I smiled. "So that's why you always volunteer to go there."

"Would he make a good first husband?" Jolia asked.

"I've never met him."

"But does he *look* like first husband material?"

"He's handsome, I guess. Go over there. Ask him out."

Jolia sighed. "Not while he's working. I will one day."

I returned my attention to the food. "What, allegedly, is in this soup?"

"Sceptic," Jolia grinned. "A shank each from our own mountain-loving, shaggy pig-horses, fresh onions from Revelé, dried plantabeans from somewhere in Nordland, seasoned with sea salt from Morskoy. Accompanied by a half-loaf of rye bread with a chunk of thick butter." She reached under the table and revealed a surprise.

"An apple!" I exclaimed.

"We'll share it. Cost me a morning's wages."

I reached into my coat pocket and pulled out a handful of tokens. "Let me pay half."

She pushed my hand away. "You can get tomorrow's meal."

"How much was it?"

"A silver and three copper tokens."

I placed eight copper tokens on the table. More than half the cost. "Please, take it."

"Keep your wealth."

She shunted the coins towards me and put the prized apple in the middle of the table. I pondered if it was the exact middle.

I lifted a spoon and tapped the edge of the tin soup bowl four times.

"Why do you do that?" asked Jolia.

I shrugged. "Habit." I dipped the spoon in, brought the broth to my mouth and blew off steam.

"It's good," said Jolia.

I tipped the soup onto my tongue, the taste overwhelmed with salt such I couldn't discern any other flavours. I smiled at Jolia, not wanting her to think she'd made a bad choice, then nodded. "*Hmmm.* Good."

She pulled off a chunk of rye, cut a wedge of hard butter out of the pottery dish and squashed the butter to the bread.

The butter fell off, and I giggled. "You must be hungry. Can't wait for the butter to soften."

"Didn't have morning meal."

"You're working too hard."

She leaned in. "Don't tell anyone, but I'm planning another major invention."

My curiosity was piqued. "What is it?"

"I won't say, yet. The plans aren't well developed. You'll be the first to know when my ideas are better formed. I wanted something to complement your wonderful cloud wagon."

"I hope Eminent Drudan thinks it's wonderful. I doubt he's going to approve it."

"Don't say that."

I tried to cut a corner off the bread with the butter knife, but tore the crust. I placed the torn corner on the table and trimmed the edges to a perfect cube.

Jolia squinted at the knife screeching against the steel tabletop. "You'll blunt it further."

I dropped the knife and held the pottery dish above the steam wafting from my soup to soften the butter.

"Will Gallan be at *The Dragon Bellows* tonight?" asked Jolia.

"I expect so."

"Don't be coy. Did you ask him to go?"

"He's always at the tavern, whether I ask him or not. We're just friends."

"You want more, though?"

"Romance can wait. I'm too busy inventing things."

"What about Barick? You find him attractive, don't you?"

"We studied together at the Seminaria. He's like my brother."

"We don't have the luxury of dalliance," said Jolia. "I'm planning on three husbands by the end of next yarle."

"Three!?"

"Someone has to stop Karlik's population from melting away."

I tipped the pottery dish sideways, and the entire butter chunk slid off and splashed into my soup.

Jolia chortled. "I guess that's one way to soften it."

I fished the butter out with the spoon and plonked it dripping with soup back into the dish.

"I'm not sure I want to stay in Karlik," I said.

"Ah, so that's why you invented the cloud wagon. It's your vehicle to escape. Didn't your parents try that already?"

I flinched at Jolia's insensitivity.

"Sorry," she said. "That was stupid. I shouldn't have said that."

"It's alright. I was only an infant when it happened. Yula was older. The memories hit her hardest. I think that's why she can't forgive Popa, our da'one, for abandoning us after the accident."

Jolia reached across the table and grabbed my hand. "I really am sorry. I shouldn't have brought it up."

I half-smiled. "I guess it's true, in a way. Escaping Karlik is hard, and who knows what I'll find at the foot of the mountains. My parents believed we could build a better life down on the plains. They wanted to find it first, then return for me, Yula and Popa. They didn't make it."

"At least it'll be warmer on the plains," said Jolia, releasing my hand. "If nothing else."

"I shouldn't wallow while your da'three fights for his life in the

Restoria. Will you see him tonight?"

"I try to visit every night. He's often sleeping, but I hold his hand. It's all I can do now."

We finished our meal, savouring the juicy apple with an appetidal lust born from scarcity. Then we marched back to work, avoiding as much ash-snow as possible.

At the Inventoria, I sat with Jolia in a private meeting room, discussing the plans for my major invention, a flying machine I called the cloud wagon. I hoped it could carry barrels of serpent oil and other supplies out of Wyrm Valley, over the mountain range and down to the Nordland Plains. Possibly as far as Morskoy.

By day's end, Jolia had almost convinced me Eminent Drudan would approve the invention at tomorrow's meeting. Almost.

"That's enough for me," I said. "Everyone else has left. Time for a drink at the *Bellows*."

"I'll catch up with you," Jolia replied. "I want to finish some work here."

I shook my head, trying to convince her to change her mind. "Barick, Gallan and Yula will be there. We could start a fight and see if the delectable Crooshka arrives to break it up."

"Come and get me if he does," smiled Jolia. "I won't be here long. Save me a seat."

Jolia left the meeting room. I stood, buttoned my coat, rolled up my plans, tied them with ribbon and put the parchment cylinder inside my satchel before flinging it over my shoulder. I slipped on my fur-lined hat and gloves and strode out the Inventoria's rear door, ready for a merciless walk in an uncovered evening polluted by ash-snow. To my surprise, the concocted snowfall had lightened, a north wind pushing the worst of it south of Karlik. But the wind stung my face, carrying freezing air from across an icy Nordargen Sea. I buried my chin and cheeks in the woollydon fur lining the coat collar, focussed on the road bricks and ploughed ahead.

Night never truly fell in Karlik. The dozens of venting fires surrounding the city set a sky of flickering amber over the maze of spired rooftops. Some fires looked like bouquets of flaming marigolds sprouting from the rocks. Others resembled orange-yellow flags, tattered and torn symbols of untrammelled patriotism, as they flew atop hollow copper tubes bringing gas from the mines below. On cloudless nights, the rusting glow dulled the stars and moons. Only during the Dragon Festival, when the venting fires were temporarily extinguished, could Curmudgles appreciate the beauty of the sky above them.

I joined a pair of mudgles also heading for *The Dragon Bellows*. We walked in silence, none of us prepared to risk the chance of swallowing a mouthful of ash-snow. The hardy soles of our knee-high boots barely made a sound as we navigated patches of real and fabricated snow. Embarrassing myself in front of fellow citizens stopped me from running from one veranda to another to avoid the intermittent snowfall. But my compulsion nagged about it.

As we approached Karlik's largest and most popular alehouse, my mudgle companions nodded a farewell and scooted ahead, obviously keen for a drink, warmth or both. After they disappeared inside, a young boy near the entrance clambered to his feet and stood under a verandaed window, holding his gloved palm towards me.

"Spare a token?" he asked.

I stopped in front of him. "It's warm inside."

The boy looked up, his face darkened by the cresting wave of a hooded cloak large enough to drown in, and his eyes masked by bone-rimmed glasses with obsidian lenses.

"The world's warmth will soon disappear," he rasped, "if you don't stop the haunting of Karlik." Cracked lips peeled away a sliver of darkness, offering a smile of yellowed teeth stained with mockery.

I stumbled back, almost knocked over by my thudding chest, and then scurried inside, forgetting to leave a token in his palm.

Chapter 3

The Dragon Bellows

As I entered *The Dragon Bellows*, blazing gas fires thawed the coldness of the boy's prediction. The doorkeeper blocked my path, pulling off my hat and gloves and tossing them into a woven basket. They'd be cleaned, ready for me to collect when I left. He picked at my braided hair, looking for ash-snow passengers, then attacked my coat with a horsehair brush, determined to remove every flake of contamination, sweeping it down into the grate beneath my boots.

Satisfied with his work, he removed the coat, shook it, and hung it on a rack inside a garderobe adjacent to the *Bellows'* entrance. I brushed my woollen shirt and leather-panelled skirt, hoping to hasten the cleansing, but he pushed my hand away and swept his ash-snow remover down my front – chest to shins – then down my back – shoulders to calves.

"I was careful," I pleaded. "Snow isn't heavy tonight."

"*Hmph*," said the doorkeeper. "Do your boots."

I shoved my left foot into a close-fitting tube and cranked a handle protruding from the foyer wall. Inside the tube, dozens of brushes tickled around the boot made from snow hare pelts, flicking dirt and snow into a container beneath the tube. I fizzed an annoyed sigh. Irritated not at the inconvenience, which had been purposely minimised, but because this was one of Vyrin's inventions.

I repeated the process with my right foot, then scrubbed my hands with lye soap at a wash basin in the foyer and wiped them dry on my shirt. *Better than using the wreaths of drying rags hanging from the wall.*

Damp and filthy, the clusters of torn fabric could harbour any number of unwelcome surprises.

I stamped snowless boots on the flagstone floor of the *Bellows'* main room – *Xeni*, named after Xenignatious Crutter, the first Curmudgle to discover serpent oil in the Grauberge Mountains – and marched past the mudgles seated on iron stools along a bar made from slabs of precisely-cut stone, layered without mortar. Forty mudgles along, tucked away in the room's back corner beside a gas-fuelled fireplace, I found my favourite timber round table with wooden seats and plush cushions. *Xeni* had only two timber tables, the precious commodity, rare this high in the Grauberge Mountains, mostly reserved for making oil barrels.

I slung my work satchel over the back of a chair, pulled out the parchments, sat, and shifted a burning candle to the other side of the table lest it devour all evidence of my most important invention. As I untied the cinching ribbon, the first of the evening's miners stumbled through the front door, their leather coats and overshirts covered in black dirt, soot and ash-snow. Three doorkeepers attended to them, pushing the miners into an alcove beside the main entrance. There, the miners disrobed, tossing clothes into growing piles of filth while the doorkeepers brushed and combed the braided hair and beards twisted around the miners' heads, necks and torsos to remove any flecks of dirt. A stranger might consider the procedure overly fastidious. But with hundreds of mudgles filling *The Dragon Bellows* and Karlik's other three alehouses each night, a pleasant watering hole would soon become a fetid pond without the doorkeepers' devotion to cleanliness.

With the miners ending work for the day, I hoped Barick would arrive soon. It'd save me stressing over the invention notes and drawings. But he wasn't in the first group of ten, and my fingers had already unrolled the parchments before I realised.

"Will you be ordering a drink, or will you scribble on your papers all night? Again."

I cursed and fumbled, turning the parchments face down.

Horu, the waiter, smirked. "I'm not interested in your invention, Silveny. Unless it's a mechanical servant to relieve me of this dreary job."

"It's n-not that," I stuttered. "I'm waiting for my friends. I'll order when they arrive."

Horu twitched as the feet of iron chairs squealed across the floorstones behind him, the first mine team plonking weary arses around a long stone table that could seat two dozen.

"They'll keep me busy," he said, wandering off to take a slew of orders.

The mine team's snergul-warden dropped her pet's cage in the middle of the table, and the raven-like ermine barked in protest before the warden slotted a piece of dried meat through the cage bars. Mine teams always kept their snerguls close, possibly thinking the furred and feathered sentinel could warn of any threat, not only undiscovered gas leaks. But danger from outside rarely came to Karlik, despite the enticement of Ostamp's largest known serpent oil reserves. No invading army had attempted to scale the ruinous, ice-capped mountains that fortified the Wyrm Valley, or commandeered the balloon line that carried supplies and mudgles into and out of Karlik. The city's greatest asset was its greatest threat. Perched on a vast field of highly volatile gas and oil.

An old miner, Kolac, sitting with his back to me, doubled over in a hacking fit. He herked up a glob of mucus and spat it onto the floor, showering Horu's shoes with a black, gritty slime. I covered my mouth to stem the nausea.

Horu frowned and faced the bar. "Rosy! I need help here."

Rosy sauntered over, one hand on her swinging hips, the other clasping a clutter of empty mugs. "What are ye mudgles doing to me poor Horu?"

"He got slow reflexes," said Kolac before coughing up another glob.

"I'll get the slop bucket," said Horu as he marched off.

"Yur tainted sputum goes in the bucket," said Rosy. "Not on the floor or me feet. Now, what are ye drinking?"

Kolac herked and swallowed, then smiled at Rosy. "Do you have any nectar as sweet as you?"

She rolled her eyes. "One sip o'nectar that sweet and an old fella like ye would drop dead."

The miners around the table chuckled.

Rosy continued, "Anyways, I thought ye were one o'them rare mudgles devoted to a single wife. Not looking for another one, are ye?"

"One's enough for me," said Kolac. "And from Mulena came Patuki, our beautiful daughter." He fondled the braids hanging down to the snergul-warden's waist.

"But Mulena probably wants more husbands," said another miner. "Since she done so poorly with the first one."

While the miners laughed, anger flashed in Kolac's eyes before it faded to a wry smile. "You're a funny bugger, Arhe, but not a productive one. Four wives and no pucks."

"Alright," said Rosy, "let's not start a bar fight. What's ye order?"

"Black ale?" said Arhe, surveying the agreement of nods around the table. "Jugs of black ale for everyone. My treat."

The miners cheered. The caged snergul howled its approval, and Rosy smiled and waddled off.

Arhe quieted the miners and leaned forward. "Had a run-in with the pit boss today. Twenty yarles I been working the mines. Means I'm due a reward. A recompense for loyal service."

Kolac nodded. "They gave me a gold-plated hand shovel."

"Them were the days," said Arhe. "Not anymore. Pit boss offered me a cheap bottle of serp-rum."

"What?" cried another miner. "That's an insult."

Arhe inhaled a whistling enticement. "Well, know what I said to her? You can take y'bottle of serp-rum and SHOVE IT UP YOUR ARSE!"

The miners exploded in laughter, slapping the stone tabletop in appreciation, causing the snergul to bark and screech in a ruffle of fur and feathers.

"That pit boss' heart's so cold," said Kolac, "the bottle would freeze in place, and she wouldn't be able to shit for days."

"Or she'd have to shit in the bottle," squeaked Patuki.

"That'd make the serp-rum taste better!" said Arhe.

The mine team bellowed its approval.

"At least we still got work," said one miner over the din. "At least that."

Two others nodded as the group quieted down.

"They closed another mine," said Arhe. "That's four now."

"We need more serpent oil orders," said Kolac. "Otherwise, Arhe's twenty-yarle service will be the last this mine team sees."

"Might be for the best," said Patuki. "Way things are going; the next anniversary gift will be tin-plated snergul shit."

The miners chortled and nodded. Rosy and Horu arrived with ceramic jugs brimming with frothy black ale as my friend, Gallan, limped through the door, the broad smile from his ruddy face lightening *The Dragon Bellows'* dusky interior. Even without the limp, caused by one leg being shorter than the other, he'd take ages to reach me, stopping at most of the tables to exchange a laugh or a story. As one of Karlik's four scribes, he knew a lot of mudgles, publishing their stories in the *Karlik Chronicle*. And being the only offspring of Eminent Stretten, the Governant head, many mudgles sought Gallan out, hoping to influence governance policy to their benefit.

I rolled the parchments, then checked the handclock in my satchel: seven hours after high sun. *Jolia should be here. She's either working late or went to visit her da' three before coming to the tavern.*

Gallan waved an acknowledgement my way before an ambition of administrators from the Governant pulled him aside. More mine teams arrived, and *The Dragon Bellows* pulsed with a raucous hum of shouts and laughter, the enticing aroma of black ale replaced by a smothering scent of serpent oil mixed with dirt. The most common smell in Karlik.

As *Xeni* filled, I worried about keeping seats free for my friends. My compulsion fixated on moving the seats around the table equidistance apart.

A chorus and band set up on stage.

"Play *Folly's Den!*" shouted Kolac to the band. "Or *The Icebreaker.*"

The band leader smiled at him and nodded. Rosy turned off one of *Xeni's* six gas fires as the room heated up. Sweat dripped into my braids. I picked at the hair and checked my fingertips, thinking the doorkeeper may have missed some ash-snow. The rolled parchments called to me. Teased me. Begged for attention.

As my fingers went to untie the cinching ribbon, Gallan sat down.

"Are you drawing again?" he asked, stretching out his shorter leg, shod with a boot sole as thick as my arm. Designed to correct his gait, the clumpy boot could sometimes be more a hindrance than help.

I shoved the parchments into my satchel and smiled at him. "A new invention."

"Do you inventors ever stop...you know...inventing?"

"Do scribes ever stop writing?"

He smiled through a short-cropped, ginger beard, braided so tightly it stretched his skin. "Only when it's time to drink. Seriously, Silveny, you work much harder than I do."

"Inspiration can come anytime, and I need to be ready. Capture the idea on paper before it vanishes."

"The search for Silveny's missing idea. I could write a story about that."

"Don't you have enough to write?"

Gallan sighed. "Karlik's boring at the moment."

Horu returned to take our order. "So, are you ready now?"

"Still waiting on three more friends," I said.

"Let's order anyway," said Gallan. "We know what they'll drink. Yula will have honeymead to make her sweeter. Barick will have fire-rum to give him courage." He faced me. "The luscious Jolia, who rejects my advances, what will she have?"

I smiled. "She usually drinks meduz or black ale. You, Gallan, should have a glass of pride so that you can swallow it."

Gallan feigned an arrow to his chest. "And Silveny of Tork will have a blood wine. You can drain the blood from my wounded heart."

Horu rolled his eyes. "Honeymead, fire-rum, meduz, blood wine. I don't have any pride."

Gallan chuckled. "Don't be so hard on yourself, Horu. Waiting is an honourable profession."

"To drink," said a deadpan Horu, either not getting the joke or refusing to join in.

"Black ale," said Gallan. "No better drink in Karlik."

Horu nodded and walked off.

"So," said Gallan, "what's this new invention of yours?"

"Don't want to say yet, in case it's rejected. I'm presenting to Eminent Drudan tomorrow."

"Sure. But what will it do?"

"If it works, it'll make the balloon line obsolete."

"That'll put your sister out of work."

I nodded. *But Yula will adapt. She always does.*

On cue, my sister pushed through the bustling crowd, stumbling on tired legs. I'd ask about her day later. In a quiet moment. She wasn't one for excessive conversation.

"Yula of Tork," announced Gallan as she sat down.

Yula raised her eyebrows at him.

"You look exhausted," I said.

She shrugged, then raised her hand for the waiter.

"We've already ordered," said Gallan. "Honeymead for you."

Yula lowered her hand and slumped in the chair.

Another line worker, Korta, walked over to our table. "She saved a life today," he said, pointing at Yula. "Ask her about it."

I faced my sister, but she didn't meet my eyes. "Is this true?"

"It's true, alright," said Korta. "Poor sod would have died if Yula didn't save him." He turned and walked to the bar.

"What happened?" I asked Yula, but her eyes continued to evade me.

"You're a hero," said Gallan to Yula. "I'll need a story for the *Karlik Chronicle*. Can I interview you tomorrow?"

She frowned at him.

Good luck, I thought. *It'll be a short interview.*

Barick finally arrived with his mine team, waiting in the foyer as the doorkeepers removed his coat and overshirt and combed his black hair braids. His eyes flashed with nervous uncertainty, his clean-shaven face, a mudgle rarity, riven with a worry more intense than usual. He glanced at me momentarily, then turned his troubled gaze down, fiddling with the top of the snergul cage he carried in his left hand.

Being his first day as an apprentice, Barick should have joined the mine team for a drink. Instead, he left them to find a table and walked over to us.

"Barick of Donharue," said Gallan. "They made you snergul-warden on your first day?"

Barick wavered as he placed the caged snergul on the table, then mumbled, "Less likely to get lost."

"Did you get lost?" I asked.

Gallan shook his head and grinned. "I've always said dark-skinned mudgles shouldn't be miners. Too hard to find you underground."

"Very funny," sneered Barick.

Horu interrupted, arriving with a tray of goblets and mugs. "Honeymead?"

Yula took the drink from Horu's hand, downed it in a single swig, and then returned the empty mug to the tray.

Horu gawked. "*Hmmm.* Thirsty, I see. Another one?"

She nodded.

"I should have brought two drinks for each of you," he said. "Now, black ale?"

"Mine," said Gallan. "I'll savour it. Don't want you rushed off your feet, Horu."

"So exceedingly kind. Blood wine for Silveny," he said, putting the goblet in front of me. "Which means fire-rum for...."

"Barick," I said.

"And meduz for...."

"Jolia isn't here yet. But she will be soon."

Horu gave Barick his cup of fire-rum and placed the mug of meduz on the table. He then waited in silence, balancing the tray on the palm of his left hand. Gallan sighed, reached into his shirt pocket, withdrew an amber token and tossed the coin to Horu, who caught it in Yula's empty mug.

"I'll be back with another honeymead as soon as possible," said Horu. "It's busy tonight."

Gallan raised his mug of black ale. "Silveny and Yula of Tork. Barick of Donharue."

"Gallan of Fordun," I completed the salutation. "To us."

"To us," Gallan and Barick replied as we tapped our drinks together.

Barick sipped, then lowered the tin cup, trying to hide trembling hands beneath the table.

"Sit down, Barick," said Gallan.

"I should return to my team," he said. "Apprentices have to buy a round of drinks."

"At least finish your fire-rum first."

Barick stared absently but remained standing, his dark skin bubbling with beads of sweat.

I pushed my goblet aside, then pulled a ruler from my satchel to measure the distance between the table edge and the perimeter of a faded circle drawn on the tabletop. Confirming the correct distance, one delicant, about the length of my hand, I placed the goblet inside the circle, grabbed a pencil from the satchel pocket and drew a new perimeter around the goblet's base.

Yula shook her head.

"Somebody rubbed out the circle," I said. "Need to know exactly where to put the goblet."

Gallan faced Barick. "Please sit. You're making me nervous. How was your first day as a miner?"

Barick frowned, shrugged and sat, his snergul slumping on its perch in sympathy for its new master.

"They must have made you snergul-warden for a reason," said Gallan.

"Means I have to be at the head of the team," said Barick. "Walk out in front."

"You *did* get lost," I said.

Barick reached for his drink and clamped twitching fingers around the tin cup.

"Yula saved someone's life today," I said, trying to divert attention from Barick. "She won't tell us anymore."

"Well," said Gallan, "this will be a brilliant evening. We have Yula the unspeaking, our tongue-tied hero, Silveny the secretive inventor, unable to share her ideas with her closest friends, Barick the apprentice miner who'd rather forget his first day at work, and Jolia the absent. I'm starting to realise now why she didn't bother coming."

"She's coming," I snapped. "Had to finish something at work."

"I'll tell you about my day," Barick said. "After I've bought my team a drink."

The snergul squawked and bit at the bars of its cage with a pointed snout full of pin teeth.

"Is it hungry?" I asked.

Barick reached into his pants pocket and withdrew a leather purse. Opening the purse, he tipped flakes of dried meat into his hand. "Hoi up, Sneckle," he said.

The snergul pricked up its round, batty ears at Barick's voice, then emitted a sharp, high-pitched bark resembling a dog's yelp. Brown eyes, squinting with the light inside *The Dragon Bellows*, opened to the size of the circle drawn around the base of my goblet as Barick poked a sliver of dried meat into the cage. The snergul snatched at it with spidery fingers, then tossed the meat into its mouth.

Gallan chuckled. "Sneckle the snergul."

"As long as she warns me of any gas leaks," said Barick, "I don't care what she's called."

"Can they fly?"

"They can glide."

"That's what the feathers along their arms and legs are for," I said.

"Never seen one out of a cage," said Gallan.

"They live among the cliffs on the western edge of the Grauberge

Mountains. Nest in caves."

Sneckle barked as Horu arrived with Yula's second honeymead and placed it on the table before her.

"Slower, this time," I said.

She glared at me and drained half the mug.

"Almost forgot," said Gallan. "I have news if no-one else is willing to share. Big meeting tomorrow between emissaries from Kogot and Eminent Stretten. I've been asked to scribe."

"Of course you have," said Barick. "Your ma'one is the Eminent."

"And it's his job," I said, defending Gallan.

"I saw them," said Yula, lifting her eyes. "The visitors from Kogot. They walked *Death's Pass* into the city."

"Didn't take the balloons?"

"Too big," said Gallan. "Least that's what I heard. *Giants.*"

Yula shook her head. "No taller than an average Nordman."

"What do they want?" I asked Gallan.

"Rumour is, they're here to negotiate a delivery of serpent oil."

"Why not do it at our trading post in Morskoy?"

Gallan shrugged.

"We need orders," said Barick. "Mines are closing."

I groaned as Vyrin from the Inventoria approached our table and placed his clammy hands on the empty chair. "Can I take this?"

"I'm saving it for Jolia," I said. "She's working late."

"You two are so desperate to impress Eminent Drudan. It's pathetic."

"At least they can impress someone," said Gallan. "I find you exceptionally unimpressive."

Vyrin flared his lip, then took the chair before I could protest.

Gallan patted the back of my hand. "Jolia will arrive soon. Don't worry."

'Don't' and 'worry', two words I rarely used in a sentence together.

Barick left to join his mine team for a drink. The band played, the shrill of whistles and flutes, the haunting pluck of a lute, and the tappity-tap of drums drowning out much of the room's conversation. A handful of workers from the Governant joined others from the Extractory in a twirling and clapping frolicsome dance in front of the band stage. Stripped to the waist owing to the simmering heat in *Xeni*, dangling hair braids, cinched at the ends by gold or silver circlets, slapped the sweat away from naked backs and chests. Another mudgle wearing only a skirt tried to join the dance, but his drunken stagger stumbled him towards a hearth. Before he could right himself, a vent of gas shot across the fireplace and licked the flaming pilot light. The hearth exploded with fire, and the artistry of braids circling the mudgle's neck and chest caught alight. He slapped his burning hair while his friends laughed. They gathered their mugs and tipped frothy ale over their smouldering companion, dousing the flames. Dripping wet, he smiled at them, then sluiced the ale from his forehead and into his mouth.

Xeni had reached capacity. Mudgles crammed into the room and along the bar, filling all the tables. I'd have to get up soon to look for Jolia. She could be on the other side of the room, and I wouldn't see her.

A commotion came from the main entrance. Above the heads of all the mudgles towered a dozen strange-looking men and women.

Gallan leaned towards me. "Emissaries from Kogot. Voldari."

The Voldari, a devout religious group that preached in Kogot. I'd read about them in Karlik's Literati. They hunched into *Xeni*, ducking under the beams supporting a ceiling accommodating mudgle stature. The crown of the tallest mudgle would only just reach a Voldari chest, despite Yula's claim that the visitors were the same height as an average Nordman. The owner of *The Dragon Bellows*, Lukal, pushed through the crowd to reach the visitors, bowing her head and holding her arms out in welcome. She ushered them to an empty table, getting Rosy the waiter to clear away the goblets, mugs and plates of the previous occupants who busied themselves on the dance floor.

The Voldari removed frost-blue silken robes from over pearl shirts, folding and draping the robes on the back of the chairs. They sat, taking off fleece-lined hats to expose heads decorated in an array of animal adornments: feathers, fur, teeth and bones.

Gallan tapped his forehead. "A form of totem."

"Amuell," I corrected. "Every initiated Voldari is bestowed a unique animal talisman, and their headwear and facial decorations, often grafted into their skin, represent this animal. They call it their 'amuell.' Supposedly gives the wearer good fortune and power. How come the doorkeepers didn't take the hats?"

Gallan shrugged. "Or robes."

"One of them has tusks," mumbled Yula.

Gallan laughed. "Will be a challenge to get a mug of black ale between those chompers."

"Don't stare," I bit.

Lukal seconded Horu and another waiter to help Rosy serve the Voldari.

"Be a while before we see a waiter again," said Gallan, finishing his drink. "I'll go to the bar."

"No, I will," I said. "You'll take forever to return. Watch my satchel."

I left Gallan with Yula and the empty cups on the table and jostled through the crowd towards the bar, searching for Jolia. Even if she visited her da'three in the Restoria, she should be here by now. But I couldn't find her.

Leaning with his back against the bar, sipping a mug of ale, a grey-haired mudgle with pale skin stared at me and nodded a hello.

I smiled at him. "Silveny of Tork."

He belched, "Sven of Cha'thair," then scratched his bare belly below a waterfall of beard braids.

"That's the gateway to the road under the Desolate Mountains."

He nodded. "Sven was the road-watcher, then Karlik forgot about him, and Sven walked home."

"No-one's watching the road now?"

"Don't need to. Germalians brought peace to Enthilen. They were the first to use the road on Sven's watch. Been little trouble since. Sven got bored. Very bored. And Sven is old. Wants to die here in Karlik. Not alone underground."

The bartender approached and shouted over the music and laughter, "What do you want?"

"Honeymead," I said. "Actually, make it two honeymeads and a black ale." *I should order for Jolia. Yula had drunk her mug of meduz. Wait until Jolia gets here.*

Sven faced me, a waft of black ale washing into my nose. "Look around you, Silveny of Tork. What do you see?"

"Mudgles enjoying themselves."

"How many old Curmudgles like me?"

"Not many."

"I bet Sven is the oldest here. It's because he's lived most of his life away from Karlik. This city is bad for mudgles. Our ancestors grew to a ripe old age." Sven shook his head. "Not anymore." He faced the crowd and craned his neck towards the door. "What's the Voldari doing here?"

I shrugged. "Apparently, they want serpent oil."

"No good will come of that."

"I'm sure Eminent Stretten will negotiate favourable terms."

Sven belched, then frowned. "Sven won't be bettin' on Stretten. Decisions made behind a smoke screen means we all get burnt." He leaned in towards me and lowered his voice such I could barely hear. "A Voldari tried to use the road once. Sven confronted her. Not at all friendly. Travelling to Laodicea, she claimed. I didn't let her pass."

"Why go that way?"

"Didn't say." Sven tapped his temple. "Voldari are shrewd. You pucks need to be careful."

The bartender arrived with the drinks balanced on a tray. I paid for what we'd drunk so far, farewelled Sven and carried the tray back to our table, dodging upending threats as I went.

Barick had returned, talking with Gallan while Yula watched the dancers. There was still no Jolia. I placed the drinks in front of my friends. Barick had brought his cup of fire-rum, sipping at the warming spirit as if it would give him the bravery he craved.

I sat and balanced the empty tray atop the snergul cage. The creature inside snarled at me.

"Sneckle," said Barick. "Enough." He tugged at his braids, exposing a patch of singed hair on the side of his head.

"Barick is ready to tell his story," said Gallan, pulling out his notebook and pencil.

Barick groaned. "You're not taking notes."

"It might be important. Publishable, even."

"Please. Keep this between us."

Gallan sighed and pushed his notebook into the table's centre.

Barick's shoulders relaxed. "Alright. This is what happened."

Chapter 4

Barick's encounter
with darkness

"Keep close," urged Sternn. "Worst thing you can do down here is get lost."

Worse than being burned alive? thought Barick. He trailed at the rear of six apprentice miners, following the pit boss further into a tunnel that twisted and turned like contorted bowels, leading into the Grauberge Mountains' anal depths.

According to Curmudgle legend, the caves surrounding Karlik had once been home to dragons, drakes and wyverns. Barick crept through the dragons' lair, pretending the beasts still lived, though they'd died out generations ago. The folktales claimed that thousands, possibly millions of yarles of dragon bodies rotting and festering away underground resulted in the deposits of serpent oil and gas so prized by mudgles. Miners laughingly called gas expulsions 'dragon farts.'

But the pit boss, Sternn, didn't see the humour. Blotches of shadowy, tawny light from the lantern he carried poked and prised at his disfigured face, a ghoulish mash of angry red skin with tufts of blonde hair sticking out. Yarles ago, an undiscovered gas pocket had built up behind a pilot light in this very mine. Eventually, the enormous pressure fissured the rock, enveloping the pilot flame in a spew of gas and creating a fireball that raced down the tunnel as if the mine had become a fire-breathing dragon and the tunnel a rocky throat. Working an oil pit alone at the time, Sternn took the full brunt of the explosion, his body engulfed in scorching death. The pit boss' survival became as legendary as caves full of dragons. Other miners told Barick that a mesh of stinging scars, like the den of a hundred spiders, covered Sternn's torso.

Being burned alive is much worse than getting lost, thought Barick.

The lantern's half-light seeped across the mine tunnel's sliced walls, cut jagged and rough by generations of mudgles searching for the prized serpent oil. Next to Sternn walked the snergul-warden carrying her caged snergul, Sneckle. The animal should warn of a gas leak by squealing or passing out. Unfortunately, the latter caused false alarms, snerguls prone to falling asleep in mines simply from tiredness.

Sternn stopped and raised his disfigured hand. In the mines' russet light, it resembled a dragon claw. "Look at the lantern," he said. "Now look at the snergul."

The lantern flame flared bluish and pulsed a threatening jig. The snergul's saucer-like eyes drooped, the creature threatening to pass out or fall asleep at any moment.

"Thoughts?" asked the pit boss.

Barick cleared his throat. "If changes in the lantern flame suggest a gas leak, why do we need the snergul?"

"Can anyone help our naïve apprentice?" retorted Sternn.

"Snerguls detect other toxic gases," said another young miner. "Less flammable than serpent gas, or not flammable at all."

"Exactly. If we vent and burn off the serpent gas, and our snergul passes out anyway or goes batty, we got other problems to worry about." Sternn walked on, then stopped at one of the pilot lights that burned along the tunnel's length. "See here. The flame's tip extends beyond this line scratched into the wall."

Barick crowded around with his fellow trainees and nodded.

"It's a sure sign serpent gas is escaping somewhere," said Sternn. "Might be a build-up behind the walls. Could be an explosion any time."

Barick pictured the pointed stone buckling and cracking before a cannon of flame shot out. He turned away and traced an unsteady finger along a cold copper pipe that carried gas from the mines into Karlik, feeding light and heat to the city, thinking he might feel a leak. Although mudgles couldn't detect serpent gas odour, Barick sniffed at the air with desperate vigilance. The snergul had almost passed out.

"Fire is our friend down here," said Sternn, "as well as our enemy." He placed the lantern on a rock shelf and wrapped his dragon-claw hand around a lever attached to a vent pipe beside the pilot light. "I'm going to open this valve and vent some gas."

Barick and the other five miners stepped back.

"Further," said Sternn. "Half-a-dozen steps at least. The flame could fill the tunnel."

The young mudgles complied. The apprentice snergul-warden tapped the cage bars, but Sneckle didn't stir, curled up on the floor with her eyes closed.

"Get ready," said Sternn. "VENT FIRE!"

He counted to three, pulled the lever and opened the valve. A hiss exploded from the open end of a copper tube. As it wafted past the pilot light, a streak of flame resembling a fiery sword shot across the tunnel, illuminating dozens of copper pipes, vents, cables and steel columns bracing the tunnel roof. The expulsion sucked air from Barick's lungs like he'd been punched in the chest. His next breath burned, choked by a pall of black smoke. The other apprentices coughed and gagged. Sneckle woke and screeched, wrapping her hands around the cage bars and shaking so hard the snergul-warden almost dropped her responsibility.

At that moment, Barick lamented failing the peace officer exams. *Should have studied harder. Or applied for a job in the Inventoria like Silveny. Or become an administrator. Even working the balloon line would be safer than this.*

The gas expulsion fizzed to a gentle but unnerving waft, and the pilot light shrank. While unburnt serpent gas had almost no aroma, the burnt remains smelled like pickled eggs left in the sun for days.

"Not much to it," said Sternn as he closed the lever. "Never vent gas by yourself. Always in teams of at least four. If one gets injured, a workmate treats the injuries while the other two go for help. Then no-one is left by themselves. Understand? Don't get caught in the mines alone."

The group nodded as one, and Barick wondered who he could trust in an emergency.

They walked on. Around a corner, an oil cart emerged from the shadows, the rub of the wheel's metal flange against the hub setting a squealing ache in Barick's ear. *Needs more oil,* he thought, smiling to himself.

A miner tugged on the reins of a harfhorse harnessed to the cart, the animal's sagging head blackened with soot, its eyes listless and dull. The creature trudged along, barely able to lift hooves too weary for the burden they bore. Full-sized horses couldn't fit down the mines, and woollydons refused to go underground. Mudgles selectively bred the smallest horses available to obtain a creature strong enough to pull a cart laden with six oil barrels but diminutive enough to squeeze into tight tunnels. Their existence filled Barick's soul with misery. The animals rarely saw daylight, forced to work until they could no longer pull a cart. Mudgles then released the harfhorses into the mountains to fend for themselves. Most would die within days, the creatures without thick coats to protect them from the brutal Grauberge storms and without the intelligence to outwit the cunning and deadly horned wolves.

The harfhorse passed, and Barick patted it on the flank, hoping the affectionate touch may help relieve the animal's suffering for a moment. Another mudgle pushing the cart grunted as she lumbered by, her golden-brown hair smeared with globs of soiled black resembling wet ash.

As the heat in the tunnel grew, the mine team came upon their first oil pit, sealed by an iron dome bolted onto the rocky floor. The team removed their coats and hung them on hooks as Sternn gathered them around.

"Apprentices don't work this pit," said Sternn. "Too volatile. See all the pipes." He pointed to a tentacled cluster of copper pipes protruding from the dome's roof. "Venting gas. Lots of gas. There's a certain expertise required to gather oil from this pit."

Two mudgles, naked from the waist up, stood beside the dome, their braided hair drenched in sweat. They clamped a canvas hose to an outlet near the dome base, a third mudgle fixing the hose's open end to the inlet of a wooden oil barrel.

"Pressure inside the dome is enough to move the oil to the barrel," said Sternn. "But danger comes from heat and pockets of gas."

Barick stepped closer to a lava-glass thermobulb filled with water fixed to the dome outlet, thinking he spotted bubbles forming in the liquid trapped inside the opaque instrument. When the water began to boil, the temperature inside the dome became too dangerous to work the pit. But a mudgle miner checked the thermobulb and nodded a go-ahead. The other miner opened the valve at the outlet, and the third supervised the connection between the hose and barrel. Barick pondered who had the most dangerous job, making a mental note to avoid that task.

The canvas hose swelled, oil seeping along its length, creating a moving bulge like a python that had swallowed a rabbit. A fiery cough herked inside the barrel, and the apprentices shuddered their concern. The three miners chuckled with the complacency of experience. Or nerves.

"Grab your coats," said Sternn. "Next stop is the pit you'll be working today."

The miners pulled their coats from the hooks, but Barick stalled, mesmerised by the pulse of oil through the canvas hose. He tightened his tool belt and did a quick inventory, embarrassed he might have forgotten a tool on his first day. *Clawed hammer. Mining pick. Wrench. Leather gloves. Rope. Hooks.*

By the time he'd finished, the light from Sternn's lantern had faded in the distance. *Worst thing you can do down here is get lost. Don't get caught in the mines alone.* Barick tugged his coat from the hook and stumbled after the pit boss and the other apprentices. As he rounded a corner, there was no sign of the group, the only light coming from a pilot flame embedded in the tunnel wall and a spluttering lantern hanging from the roof. He should have called out. Or gone back to the other miners and admitted his mistake. But embarrassment stayed his hand and clouded his judgement. He pushed on, jogging down the tunnel, sure he would reach the group soon. But the passage forked left and right.

Which way? he wondered.

Warm air wafted from the left passage as if it led to an oil pit, and a dull light illuminated its depths. Darkness masked the right passage, but it had a broader entrance, large enough to accommodate two oil carts side by side. Right seemed logical, but Barick swore voices echoed from the left passage, so he chose that one, following an amber glow up ahead, certain it came from Sternn's lantern.

The passage forked again.

Damn. "Follow the light," he mumbled as he veered right, squeezing sideways through a narrow entrance. *Much too narrow for an oil cart. Even a barrel. Appears we'll be moving oil by hand buckets.*

He marched on, expecting to rejoin the group at any moment. But the light ahead never brightened.

"Hello?" he called into the tunnel; his plea met with a listless echo.

He tried again, yelling, "Hello!"

"Help," came a faint voice ahead.

"Hello?"

"Help me," repeated the voice. Drifting. Pained. Urgent.

"I'm coming."

Barick jogged ahead. He rounded a bend, then stopped beside a pilot light, straining to hear further cries of distress. As he stepped forward, a hiss of gas exploded from the wall. Then a sweep of fire shot across the cave, Barick tumbling backwards onto the tunnel floor. The smell of burnt hair punched his nose. He rolled in the dirt, trying to extinguish any fires that might have set on his body by slapping his arms, legs and chest. The image of Sternn's web of blistering scars fuelled his panic.

Barick doused a couple of smoulders but nothing more, then lay there, trembling, wondering when the next flush of gas might come. Thinking the entire tunnel could explode from an undiscovered gas build-up. Wishing he had the snergul with him. Wishing he was elsewhere.

The gas flow abated, and the pilot light wavered small and listless, looking as innocent as a tapering candle.

Welcome to mining. He stood, dusted himself off and gathered his courage, striding to the pilot light to check the copper pipes carrying gas from the tunnel. Strangely, he didn't find a single pipe, the little flame appearing to emanate from a hole in the rock wall.

A natural gas vent? Who would put a pilot light here?

He wavered as the tunnel darkened around him, questioning whether he should go on or back. Someone ahead of him was in distress. Another miner. He couldn't leave them.

In the indecisive silence, a shuffle of boots echoed down the tunnel from where he'd heard the voice.

"Is anyone there?" Barick asked.

The shuffling stopped. The cave stilled to a menacing shadow.

"Hello?" he whispered.

The shuffling exploded. Slapping, urgent footfalls raced towards Barick. Boots with metal soles slammed against the tunnel floor. The pounding menace shattered the tunnel's warmth as if a hole had been ripped in the roof to expose Barick to the frozen wastes outside. He shivered and cried. The footsteps hungered to eat his fear.

Barick tried to run, but his legs tangled in a rope lying in the dust. The type of rope pit bosses tied across passages to ward off foolish apprentices.

As Barick untangled the rope, the perilous, predatory boots slowed. A shadow emerged from the darkness, blacker than serpent oil. A shape swallowing every hopeful shard of light. It took the form of a man, tall and broad like a Nordman, almost twice as big as a Curmudgle. The man made a noise. A hissing, gurgling, yearning noise. He'd captured his prey and now prepared for the kill.

Shadow Man, thought Barick. *Shadow Man has come for me.*

The gas vented again, grasping flames vomiting across the cave.

On the other side of the fire, Barick caught a glimpse of the true terror he faced. He tossed the rope aside and sprinted back down the tunnel.

Chapter 5

The blind boy

"Shadow Man?" I asked Barick. "What exactly *did* you see?"

Nervous twitches skipped around his brown eyes as they stared with the blankness of the incomprehensible. "A face, but not a face. A contortion of beauty. Ever shifting. Ever changing its mask. It's hard to describe what I saw, but I know how I felt. Utter despair. Every cherished dream stolen from me."

Barick fell silent. Yula, Gallan and I joined our friend in a vigil of quiet dismay.

We spoke little for the remainder of the night. Didn't dance, sing with the chorus, or join other frivolities. Jolia didn't show. I assumed she spent the evening in the Restoria beside her ailing da'three. I should have worried more. Gone looking for her. But Barick's story distracted my concern.

Each of us mulling our thoughts, we stepped from the warmth of *The Dragon Bellows* into Karlik's cold streets. I tugged my furred hat over braided tawny hair and pulled on woollen gloves as the wind grieved and ash-snow tumbled. *Or is it real snow?* I sometimes couldn't tell the difference until the ash-snow had accumulated in crusted grey lumps on the ground.

Lost in the brittle, threatening squall, I tripped over someone's legs and stumbled forward.

"Amber token?" said the boy, rubbing his shin. The same boy I'd met earlier in the evening.

Has he been out here all night?

A hooded cloak and the veranda above the tavern window protected him from the snowfall, but the wind had pushed drifts of ash-snow across his laceless, tattered boots, which were lashed to his ankles with fraying cord.

Gallan and Barick stood beside me. Yula walked on. Stopped. Glared at me, then walked back.

"Sorry," I said to the boy. "About tripping over you."

He peeled open his left hand, warmed by a knitted fingerless glove, and offered a hopeful palm. "Amber or two, for eyes of blue."

I knelt to face him and stifled a gasp. From under the furrowed hood peered broken eyes, not blue. A scar blighted the left side of his face, running from his forehead through an eyeless, red-raw socket and ending at his cheek. Like a lump of curdled milk, the right eyeball floated aimlessly in a cloud of opaque white. I waved my hand before his face, and he didn't flinch.

Not eyes of blue. Dead eyes. Blind.

Ash-snow settled on his open palm while he fumbled with his right hand inside the top of his hooded cloak. He pulled out the bone-rimmed glasses I'd seen before and pushed them onto his face.

"You saw me naked," he muttered. "I apologise for the offence."

"No offence," I said. "Why are you still out here in this cold?"

"Do you – *cough* – do you know him?" wheezed Barick, the ash-snow starting to affect his breathing.

"No. He was here when I arrived. Didn't you see him?"

The others shook their heads.

"Can't remember the last time we had a beggar in Karlik," said Gallan. "He's not a mudgle."

The boy tucked his exposed fingertips back into his gloved palm to form a fist, crushing the handful of ash-snow. "It's killing you," he said. "This trauma falling from the sky. It's killing all of you."

Gallan clucked, "What a cheerful soul."

"Maybe he's from Morskoy," said Barick. "Or – *cough, cough* – Kogot."

"Cough, cough, Kogot," teased Gallan.

"If he can stand this cold without complaint." A rasping Barick crouched beside me, placed the caged snergul on the road bricks and faced the blind boy. "Where are you from?"

The boy sniffed. "Always a street under my feet."

"If you keep rhyming," said Gallan, "it's going to become annoying."

"I've not – *hack* – seen you around here before," said Barick. "But you speak our language like a native born."

"Where's your family?"

The boy turned the obsidian lenses of his glasses towards Gallan, catching a fiery reflection from a streetlamp. "Blood red. *Dead*."

Gallan sighed. The boy hunched back into the cloak draped over a filthy woollen jumper and trousers. He stamped his corded boots on the road bricks, squashing tiny drifts of ash-snow like roaches. Sneckle the snergul barked.

"Has the sentinel warned you?" asked the boy.

"About what?" I said.

"The haunting."

"What's he talking about?" croaked Barick, his allergy to ash-snow sticking his words with globs of mucus.

I faced my friend, thinking he should go back inside until the snowfall abated. "Stop the haunting of Karlik. He said it to me before."

"This is stupid," snapped Yula. She pulled me to standing and tried to drag me away.

I yanked back. "We can't leave him here."

She groaned.

"He looks Nordmen," said Barick. "Possibly Erstürmen."

The boy pushed his head between his knees, wrapped his arms around his legs and sobbed.

"How did he get up here?" asked Gallan. "Blind."

"Doesn't matter," I said, crouching back down. "He needs somewhere safe and warm to stay."

"You take him, Silveny," said Barick, standing. "My mothers – *cough*

- won't – *cough* – won't want another mouth to feed."

"And my ma'one would dehair me alive if I adopted an orphan," said Gallan.

Yula rolled her eyes at me. She knew what would happen next.

"That settles it; you come with us." I stupidly held my open hand towards the blind boy, but he did something I didn't expect, unwrapping an arm from his protective self-hug and latching a gloved hand onto mine.

We stood together, still holding hands. Despite his age, I guessed around ten yarles old, we were the same height.

"I'm going," said Barick, cinching his coat hood tight. "Need to get out of this damn ash-snow, and I have to buy a new clawhammer in the morning. Lost mine – *cough* – in the tunnel when I – *hack* – fell over." He picked up Sneckle's cage and ambled off, wheezing over his shoulder, "Good luck with the cloud wagon, Silveny. I'm sure Eminent Drudan will be impressed."

"What wagon?" asked Gallan.

"My invention," I replied.

"Wait. You told Barick about it, but not me?"

"You talk to everyone. Barick hardly talks to anyone. Yula...well, Yula hardly talks."

"You told Yula, too?"

I nodded.

Gallan sighed. "At least tell me what it does."

"It's a flying machine, able to haul larger loads than line balloons. A scaled-up version could carry dozens of oil barrels or mudgles."

"Dozens!?"

"*Sssh,*" I urged as a pair of mudgles walked past. "It must be approved first, then built. If I invest too much hope at this early stage, something is bound to go wrong."

Gallan smiled, "Superstitious Silveny," then faced Yula. "I've got an important meeting tomorrow, but I'll interview you the day after. To record your heroic deed for prosperity and the *Karlik Chronicle.*" He slapped her on the back and walked off into a night rusted by venting fires, leaving Yula and me with the boy, still holding my hand.

"What's your name?" I asked the blind boy.

He faced me with opaque black lenses that mirrored my concern. "Casca."

"How long have you been begging?"

"Longer than time can remember," he whispered, in a voice echoing the ages.

"We have a spare bed."

"Food?" asked Casca, squeezing my hand, then letting it free.

I smiled and nodded, then realised I needed to speak. "Yes, food."

"Not much," grumped Yula and marched off without waiting.

I tried to grab Casca's hand again to guide him, but he strode after Yula, possibly following the slap of her boot soles on the shivery road bricks. I trotted beside him, a calamity of questions swirling in my head. We approached a group of mudgles traipsing back towards *The Dragon Bellows*. I worried Casca would be confused by the noisy shuffle of a dozen feet, but he appeared to single Yula out, following her around the group and along the street. Even when she walked through drifts of ash-snow, her boots making no more sound than an owl's wings, Casca never wavered in his pursuit.

Further from the tavern, the streets grew quiet, other than the sputtering from oil-fuelled lampposts firing their orangey light out from under copper-lined caps. Sometimes, within these warm halos, a brave, hardy plant would attempt to take root in the cold depths. But snowfall soon buried the coloniser, resigning the living green to an icy death. Only during the season of Wildflower Flush, after The Melt, when flowering meadows replaced the ice and snow on the lower slopes of the Five Peaks, could plants grow in Karlik. Sadly, it was a short season.

We crossed a town square, decorated with life-sized tree silhouettes cut from tin and shading stone statues of famous mudgles, and arrived in Tork, the city quarter where Yula and I had lived all our lives. Our two-storey house bordered the square, joining others in a ramshackle row of dwellings with pointed, tiled roofs pitched askew, many topped with spires or weathervanes. The larger houses had stone turrets or grand porticos guarded by granite statues of hunched gargoyles or fire-breathing drakes. But all appeared grey, uninviting and a little *unhinged*. My compulsion abhorred the disarrangement of Karlik's residential neighbourhoods and preferred I'd been born in a place with plumb lines and disciplined construction.

Yula waited for us on the front porch of our home, sheltering under a pitched roof, as we climbed the stairs. I moved past Casca and withdrew a smooth, marble-sized stone from my coat pocket. I placed the stone on a slide, and it rolled down into a hole in the wall the same size.

'*Click.*'

From a larger hole, the marble-stone and a compartmentalised brass square the size of my fist dropped into a pail on the doorstep. I returned the stone to my pocket and gathered the square, deconstructing and reconstructing the various odd-shaped compartments in a sequence practised over many yarles.

Yula grunted. "This isn't normal."

With the reconstruction complete, I'd transformed the brass square into a six-pointed star, each point a different length. I slotted the star into a similar-shaped hole in the middle of our front door and turned.

'*Click.*' Door unlocked.

Casca smiled. "Very inventive."

"You saw that...." I started. "I mean, you could tell what was happening?"

"A unique way to open a door."

I offered a confused nod.

Yula turned the door handle and stepped inside, a waft of warm air escaping into the night. Casca followed, peeling off his gloves and shoving them into the front pocket of his trousers. Thankfully, at mudgle height, he didn't risk hitting his head on the ceiling beams.

"Wipe your boots and dust off your coats," I said.

But Yula retreated to her bedroom and pulled the privacy curtain across.

"The Curmudgles' feeble attempts at hygiene won't save you from the terrors of ash-snow," said Casca as he strolled around the ground floor of our house, head tilted to the side and inhaling his surrounds.

I longed to grab his hand and guide him to the timber bench seat in the living area where I could contain any spillage of ash-snow. But I held back, curious about how Casca sensed the world. He approached the cutting block in the cookery and stepped around it, tracing a finger along each edge. He then moved across to the coat rack. After feeling the fabric of the garments hanging there, he untied the cord cinching the hood of his cloak under his chin, shrugged the cloak off and hung it from an empty hook on the rack.

When he faced me, the gas fire burning in our stone hearth danced shadows and light across weathered and blotched skin. Wrinkled skin. *Old* skin. Much older than the ten yarles I guessed him to be.

"There's a seat over here," I said.

But Casca veered the wrong way, brushing his shoulder against the wall and knocking a prized family heirloom from its mount to the floor. He went to pick it up. I tried to stop him.

"Wait. No. It's sharp."

Casca knelt, pushed his glasses up against the bridge of his nose, and then ran his fingers over the bone handle of a long knife.

"It's a knife," I said.

"Karlik is such a peaceful city," crooned Casca. "Why do you need this weapon?"

"It belonged to Philomine Belarose. My great, great grandmother."

"Her name is etched into the handle."

"Yes." I walked over to Casca, crouched beside him, picked up the long knife, stood and placed it back in the mounting rack. "She used it in the battle against King Faramund."

Casca stood. "*Ah,* the Battle of the Under-road."

"You know about it?"

"A little. After the barbarians had invaded Nordland, Faramund wanted to lead the vanquished Erstürmen war refugees to Enthilen using the road under the Desolate Mountains. But a band of Curmudgles stood in his way."

"Mudgles have always been the under-road guardians. We built a city, Cha'thair, into the mountainside, next to the Three Sisters. When explorers found serpent oil in the Grauberge Mountains, many mudgles abandoned Cha'thair to make their fortune. But a few dozen remained to guard the under-road. They were no match for the Erstürmen when Faramund arrived. Philomine Belarose was the only one to survive and tell the tale."

Casca found the timber bench seat and sat on a cushion, humming softly. I hung my coat and shoulder satchel in the entranceway and brushed off the ash-snow before rubbing my boots against a coarse-hair floormat. I opened the front door and swept the invading filth outside.

After closing the door, I returned the broom to its rightful place, equidistant between the door and the coat rack. I walked to the cookery, trying to guess the tune Casca hummed, then checked the pantry, bringing out rye bread, cured woollydon meat, hard cheese and pickled beets. Not much, but I expected the impoverished blind boy would be thankful for anything.

I withdrew a serrated knife from the cutting block and sliced the bread. "Where *are* you from?"

"Most recently, Kogot."

"Visitors came from there today. Twelve Voldari."

"They've arrived already?"

"You didn't come with them?"

Casca shook his head.

But you were expecting them. "How long have you been in Karlik? How did you get here?"

"So blind," sighed Casca. "So pitifully blind. How do you cope? Poor little boy."

"I didn't mean to offend." I evenly divided six slices of bread across three plates, laying the slices perpendicular to the plate centre. I swapped the serrated knife for a cheese knife, cutting equisized wedges from the cheese wheel.

"A merchant brought me along the old path," said Casca. "*Death's Pass*, is that what you call it?"

"Yes."

"Unfortunate name. I sat in the cart while Snugs pulled."

"Snugs?"

"A shaggy bear-pig. Broad feet. Flat nose at the end of a truncated snout. Ears no bigger than my hand. Smelled awful. Like a stagnant swamp."

"Oh, you mean a woollydon." I placed the cheese wedges beside the bread, the sharp point facing the plate centre, and then used the same knife to slice the meat slivers. "We're eating some tonight."

"Poor Snugs," said Casca.

"Wait. How do you know what it looked like?"

"The merchant made me brush and feed Snugs every evening. In exchange for the ride here."

"Why come to Karlik? I mean, there are other, better places to beg. Warmer places."

"Those places are full of beggars. How many beggars have you seen in this city?"

You're the first. I pulled the cork from the jar of pickled beets.

"And Curmudgles have serpent oil," said Casca. "Rivers of it. A treasure the other peoples of Ostamp are willing to pay a hefty price for. The residents of Karlik are rich, are they not?"

I sighed. "I'm not sure for how much longer. Enthilen's using carborupem now instead of oil. Our markets are shrinking."

"The Voldari's arrival is fortuitous, then."

"How do you know they want oil?"

"What else *could* they want?"

I rolled the meat slices into cylinders, stabbed them with a toothpick, and trimmed the ends to make the cylinders the same size. I placed a pickled beet, cut in half, in the centre of the plate. On the opposite side to the bread and cheese, I laid three meat cylinders each.

I carried one plate to Yula's bedroom and placed it on the floor outside her privacy curtain. "Food if you want it."

As I returned to the cutting block, the bottom right corner of the curtain pulled aside and out came a hand. It grabbed the plate and vanished back behind the fabric wall that protected my sister from the rest of the world.

I sat on the bench seat beside Casca and put the plates on the knee-high table in front of us.

He inhaled. "Smells good."

I expected him to lean forward, grab the plate, and shovel food into his mouth. But he reached his fingers out front, walking them along the table until he found the plate edge. He then fingered each piece of food, moving things around. Misaligning them. Creating disorder. I wanted to put them back into place.

The blind boy won't notice. Will he?

He plucked a meat cylinder between his thumb and forefinger and lifted it to his mouth. Before I could warn him about the toothpick, he'd grasped the sharpness between his dulled incisors, pulled it from the meat and spat it onto the floorstones. He then tossed the meat roll into his mouth.

"*Hmmm.* Salty but appetising. I would never have guessed my malodorous friend, Snugs, would taste so good."

"There's not much choice up here."

"I don't take food for granted," said Casca. "I've learned to appreciate the flavours."

"How old are you?"

A hint of a smile lighted Casca's boyish but weathered face as he broke a corner of the hard cheese from the wedge and placed it on his tongue. "Where is this cheese from? It has more bite than a horned wolf."

"Ephesus. How old are you?"

"Older than the cheese. Does it matter, Silveny?"

"I can't...I mean, I need to...."

"Have an ordered life. You need everything in its rightful place. Neat and tidy. You need perplexing things explained so you can make sense of them. If you roll a stone down a slide, you need to know it will release the puzzle and that when complete, the puzzle will form a star to fit the lock in your door. You need to make order from chaos. Create inventions that make less efficient things obsolete. You need certainty, structure, sequence, harmony."

"Yes," I whispered. *I need those things.*

"This world must be frustrating for you. With its ambiguity and instability. With its ever changes. But fear not, Silveny, I've learned that there's a pattern. You cannot see it yet – being so young and isolated – but the pattern will reveal itself if you live long enough and seek broad horizons. There is always a pattern. There is always certainty and order, even if that order manifests in wars or famines. A single event may seem chaotic at the time, but the pattern emerges when placed against all other events."

Casca smiled at me as he bit-tore a bread slice in half, then proceeded to pile meat, cheese and pickled beet on it before shoving it in his mouth.

Trading food for answers hadn't gone so well. I now had more questions than ever, but I expected not to have them answered tonight. Not easily, at least. This was no boy. Not in the way I thought of a boy. I had another puzzle to solve. Another challenge to make sense of the ambiguity. If I could decipher the riddle, I might unlock the door to the mystery of Casca, the blind beggar.

Yula pulled her curtain across and walked an empty plate to the sink. She gulped water straight from the pitcher, and I glared at her. For the first time tonight and one of the rare times generally, she smiled and mopped the bread and cheese crumbs from the bench.

"Surprised these weren't tidied away," she said to me. "That boy must have you flummoxed."

"His name's Casca," I said.

"Where do the stairs lead?" asked Casca.

"Mind your business," snapped Yula.

"Second floor," I replied. "We don't use those quarters anymore."

Yula marched towards the washroom.

Casca faced her. "Sit with us, Yula. Tell us about your day."

She stopped dead, wide-eyed. Then she walked over to us as if Casca had a leash tied around her neck and pulled her in. She sat on the floor opposite, legs crossed.

"Yula doesn't talk much," I said.

"I'm sure with our coaxing," said Casca, "she'll concoct a worthy tale."

Chapter 6

Yula saves a life

The bitter northeast wind stung Yula's face despite the fringe of snow hare fur sewn into the inside of her hood. She slapped her arms across her body to keep warm and cursed the exposure of *Line Station 3*, perched on a ledge overlooking Karlik. Damaged in a rock fall and yet to be re-mortared, the teetering north wall offered little protection from the cutting crosswind, and the portable heater provided by station manager Fretal had already run out of oil before high sun. Not that the sun would make an appearance today. Leaden, snow-bearing clouds blanketed the sky, and flakes as big as Yula's hand floated down in slow poetry.

Line Station 2, at the bottom of a scree slope below station three, raised a blue flag, signalling they had an outgoing balloon ready to send. Yula slapped her arms in a last attempt to warm up, removed her coat, and then braced two hands wrapped in fur-lined leather gloves around the winch handle. The winch-master, Korta, checked the gothmeter for wind direction and speed, then nodded at Yula. She heaved and turned the handle, reeling in the rope connected to the balloon basket that would pull the whole thing up the mountainside. Differential cogs on the winch eased the physical strain, but operators needed strength and stamina to haul up a balloon and basket carrying six barrels of serpent oil.

The wind gusted, whipping across the ridge face squeezed between the twin peaks of Mt Neasa and her husband, Mt Fachtna. Korta squinted into the wind and tapped on the gothmeter needle. Yula imagined it pointed to 'deathly gale', but the winch-master simply smiled at her.

Not deathly enough to shut down the balloon line, thought Yula. As the lowest-ranked station employee, she had no authority to stop a balloon, and most station managers, including Fretal, hated shipping disruptions.

The wind eased, and Yula spun her ice-brittle arms around and around, hands locked on the winch handle, hoping to pull the lead rope in before another gust. Her mind drifted to block out the fire in her shoulders, scanning the horizons of rock, ice and snow. She pictured herself hiking up *Death's Pass*, the treacherous mountain track that led away from the bleak Wyrm Valley and to undiscovered lands full of wonder and promise. But the crack of breaking ice on the valley's opposite side shattered the dream, and she shuddered as a wave of barrelling snow fell onto the track, smothering her desire like the avalanche that killed her parents. After the accident, Curmudgles renamed the track *Death's Pass*, a cruel reminder to Yula and Silveny of the loss they experienced when their loved ones failed to escape Karlik.

A whistle blasted from atop the stone turret lookout as the balloon approached *Line Station 3*.

The wicker basket harnessed beneath the balloon clattered into the docking post, and Korta raised his hand. Yula stopped turning the winch as a stepped platform swung out to the station's left, Quoil the rope jockey balancing atop the platform. He unhitched the lead rope from the basket, then immediately hitched the basket to the rope that would pull the balloon up the mountainside to *Line Station 4*. Quoil then unhitched the trailing rope from station two and attached the metal ring at the end of Yula's rope to that carabiner. It would trail behind the balloon up to station four, then could be used by Yula to pull an incoming balloon down to station three.

Quoil wouldn't tackle the last and most important rope, which connected the balloon basket to the steel cable bolted to the rockface extending from Karlik to *Line Station 16* at the top of the ridge. Korta, the winch-master, was responsible for handling the cable rope.

After Quoil's signal, Korta laced crampons around his boots and stamped along the icy boardwalk out to the steel cable. He unhitched the rope from the cable, then re-hitched the rope above the looped bolt driven into the rock that fixed the cable. The balloon could now be pulled up to *Line Station 4* and eventually on to station sixteen, where mudgles traded the outgoing cargo, mostly barrels of serpent oil, for vital supplies of food, fibre, building materials, tools and whatever else merchants from the Nordland Plains had to offer.

Korta faced the turret and gave Fretal the thumbs up. She raised the blue flag, signalling to station four to begin winching. The lead rope tensed, and the basket full of oil barrels shunted forward, leaving station three behind.

Yula shuffled across to the down winch, ready for the next balloon travelling into Karlik. Korta clumped into the station, flecked in snow and shivering. He unlaced his crampons and knocked them against a stone in the north wall to clear the ice.

Careful, thought Yula, *or the rest of the wall will collapse.*

"Do you want a break, Yula?" Korta asked. "I can handle the next balloon."

She shook her head. *Better to be active and warm than still and frozen.*

"Have it your way." The winch-master slapped gloved hands together and pulled his fur-rimmed hood around his bearded face. "Bloody cold today. I'll bring another heater up tomorrow. Damn stupid we're transportin' all this oil and don't have a full barrel at the station."

Nobody here is the full barrel, thought Yula, pulling on her coat and cinching the hood over the hair braids looped around her throat.

Without a balloon to winch, her eyes drifted across to *Death's Pass* again, rarely used by anyone with sense. Yet, it seemed the senseless had arrived. A dozen people marched along the path down into Karlik, ignoring the threat of avalanche or falling over the sheer cliff a step to their right. Twice the height of mudgles, they wore frost-blue robes, fleece-lined hats and face masks.

"Don't see that every day," said Korta. "Who are they?"

Yula shrugged. "Strangers."

"Definitely strangers. Should have used the balloons to travel into Karlik. Safer than that damn path during The Melt. You know that better than anyone."

Yes, I know it. Can't escape it.

"Is that...," started Korta. "Is that a...."

"Floe bear."

Trailing the strangers and harnessed to a cart lumbered a bear with dirty white fur ridged along the spine, a furless, blush-coloured face and tusks curling up from the sides of its mouth.

"How do you tame a floe bear?" asked Korta.

Yula didn't attempt an answer, huddling with Quoil around the pointless heater out of habit, teeth chattering more than their voices. Fretal stayed in her covered lookout, waiting for the blue flag to be raised at station four. The station manager rarely graced the winch floor, and everyone expected she kept another heater up there all to herself. Yula bowed her head, staring at the rocky floor to avoid any chance for casual conversation. Not that Korta or Quoil spoke much at work. In line stations, all the energy went to moving balloons or keeping warm. Despite station three's bleakness, Yula took solace in the fact that she could walk home in the evening. Mudgles working at higher stations had to sleep there. Ten days on, two days off. But they had better facilities.

Trade-offs, thought Yula. *Life is full of them.*

Three sharp whistle bursts came from the turret, Fretal's signal that *Line Station 4* had raised its blue flag. Yula removed her coat and took control of the down winch to reel in the incoming balloon. Korta checked the gothmeter and smiled a go-ahead. The gusting wind had moderated to a stiff breeze. Still freezing, but less deadly. Yula turned the winch handle, and an ache set in her muscles from the weight of the supplies dragging on the balloon. Korta could help, working the handle on the winch's opposite side, but Yula's pride refused to ask him.

She strained harder as the wind buffeted breaths white with angst and exertion from her mouth. The howl of a horned wolf drifted across the ridge face like a wisp of fading fog. The animals rarely approached Karlik, avoiding the ring of venting fires surrounding the city.

Quoil climbed the platform to the station's right, preparing for the balloon's arrival. Korta tested the laces on his crampons. Yula groaned as the balloon's cargo came into view. Not a basket full of food or ale, or mudgle travellers returning home, but planks of timber laced at each end. Timber destined to be turned into oil barrels.

The flukey, remorseless wind picked up again, and the unruly timber spun around and around.

Korta cursed, "Damn it," then checked the gothmeter and frowned. "Better get it here quick, Yula."

The balloon and its cargo jolted closer. Quoil swung his platform out sooner than he should. The cargo hadn't reached the docking post.

A brutal gust of wind knocked Korta sideways. "Shit." He grasped the winch handle opposite Yula and turned. "As fast as we can now."

Yula and Korta spun the handles at a feverish pace. Sweat beaded on Yula's forehead and dripped into her eyes. Quoil's platform swayed about in the wind. The brass cups atop the gothmeter twirled with manic speed. Yula's gloved hands burned and blistered as she fought with the winch handle. Korta's pale face flared red, and he sucked in breaths with a wheeze louder than the raging wind.

"Lock the winch," called Korta.

Safest thing. In case the rope feeds back out.

They held the winch handles steady, and Yula engaged the lock. The rope strained as the wind pushed the balloon back up the hill. Then, unexpectedly, it went limp.

Don't panic. Balloon must be close enough for Quoil to remove our rope and hitch the rope from station two to the cargo.

She turned right, but the wind had brought fog, masking the platform's summit. Her rope should tense again as Quoil moved it to the trailing rope position. The clutch of timber planks dangling beneath the balloon swirled from the fog, shunting into Quoil's platform and knocking it sideways. Yula's rope remained limp. She looked for Korta, but he'd already left, clamping along the boardwalk to unhitch the rope from the steel cable.

"Wait!" yelled Yula. "Something's not right." But the wind snatched her words away.

A howling gust slammed into the station. The timber planks careered from the fog and smashed into Quoil's platform at the same time Korta unhitched the balloon from the cable. The rope from station two flew upwards. Yula jumped on it, wrapping a loop around a cleat embedded in station three's south wall. The stronger wall. The rope tensed with a scream that put the wind's bawl to shame. But it wasn't the rope wailing. Above Yula, Quoil had been yanked from the platform, suspended in midair with his lower leg tangled in the rope and being crushed as the balloon fought for freedom.

Yula grabbed a handsaw from the tool rack and sprinted onto the rock and up the platform stairs. At the platform's summit, the bundled timber moaned and twisted. Upside down, Quoil screamed, his face riven with torment, his leg like a wet rag being wrung dry.

Fretal raised an orange flag – danger – thinking that might help. Korta fought to re-hitch the balloon to the steel cable, but the rope ripped from his hands. Yula gritted the handsaw between her teeth, judging the distance from the top of the platform to a suspended Quoil, then she crouched and sprang across, grabbing the rope above him.

She pulled the saw from her teeth. "Get ready to fall!"

The fall could kill them, especially if they hit rock or ice. But drifts of soft snow surrounded the station. Yula would aim for one of those.

She sawed at the rope, hoping the wall cleat held. Otherwise, they'd both be carried off into the unknown sky. Quoil sobbed, folding himself upwards to clutch at his withering leg. Fibres untwisted, and the rope snapped. The timber cargo unravelled and fell to earth, Quoil and Yula plummeting after it. They clipped the station roof, bounced into the wind, and then landed in a snow drift.

Yula lay there, watching the balloon float off to a freedom she would never know. She wiggled her toes and fingers. Slowly turned her head one way, then the other.

Nothing broken.

Quoil bawled beside her.

"Shut up," said Yula. "At least you're not dead."

She untangled his mangled leg and carried him into the station.

Chapter 7

Silveny's invention

"**Y**ula? Are you sure you're alright?" I sprang from my seat, knelt on the floorstones, and rubbed at the dirt on her face, looking for bruises. Then I pulled at her undergarment. "Take this off. I'll check for wounds."

She yanked her arm away from me, "No," and glared at Casca.

"He's blind," I said.

"Your modesty is safe with me," said Casca, smiling.

"I'm alright," said Yula. "This is why I don't tell you these things. You overreact."

"But...I'm...you're my sister."

"Look." Yula stood and waved her arms around. "No broken bones." She marched to her bedroom and swung the curtain across.

"Is Quoil?" I asked after her.

"In the Restoria," she replied. "Might lose his leg. He'll be replaced tomorrow."

"At least wash. You're filthy."

"When the blind beggar goes to sleep."

"I truly am blind," said Casca. "It's not a ruse."

It feels like...well, not a trick, but something isn't right. "Are you sure you're alright, Yula?"

"Yes," she sighed from behind the privacy curtain.

I slumped back onto the bench seat. "Guess we should sleep," I said to Casca. "I have a big day tomorrow."

"Presentation of your invention."

"And I need to check on my friend, Jolia."

"You're worried about her?"

I nodded. "You can use the spare bed."

"Is it upstairs?"

"No, down here. I told you we don't use the second storey."

"Why not?"

"My parents used to sleep there."

"Where do they sleep now?"

"They don't…I mean…they're dead. Killed on *Death's Pass* by an avalanche. All four of them."

"Four?"

"Our da'two and da'three. Ma'one and ma'two. Travelling to Morskoy in search of a better life. For all of us."

Casca bowed his head. "I'm sorry they're no longer with you. Da'two means second father?"

I tapped my foot on the floorstones, annoyed at all of Casca's questions. Yula would be listening. She wouldn't want me talking about our family with a stranger. "Yes," I spat out. "Da'two second. Da'three third. Ma'one first mother. Ma'two second. It's quite straightforward."

Casca chuckled, which annoyed me further. "You Curmudgles have a very *communal* approach to relationships. Where is your first father? Your da'one?"

The hem of Yula's privacy curtain fluttered, and I expected her to storm out and throw the blind boy onto the street.

"Look," I growled at Casca, "do you want to sleep here or not?"

He turned to me and pushed his obsidian glasses closer to his face. "I've pried too much. Your offer of a bed is generous and one I accept. Where is your washroom?"

"Behind the cookery is a bath, basin and privy. Hot water flows in the bath and basin."

"How luxurious. Do you mind if I take a bath?"

"No." I softened my anger. "Do you need me to help?"

"I can find my way. The spare bedroom?"

"I'll leave the curtain open. It's beside the cookery."

Casca stood and ambled off with little trouble. I wondered how a boy could feign blindness or the advantage such a subterfuge would offer. But that story was as unbelievable as Casca's proffered truth that he'd acquired the skill to live as if blindness carried no burden. As if eyes were expendable without consequence.

I stood and opened the curtain to the spare bedroom, then cleaned the dishes in the sink, conscious of not using hot water when Casca might need it. After I finished, I grabbed the shoulder satchel from its hook and retired to my bedroom, tugging the curtain closed. Sitting on the bed, I opened the satchel and pulled out the parchments detailing my invention, planning to go through the presentation one more time. With Yula's accident, an impetus pressed down on my shoulders. A desire, stronger than ever, to succeed in my presentation to Eminent Drudan so line accidents never happen again. But tiredness and thoughts of Jolia made it impossible to concentrate.

After Casca closed the curtain to the spare bedroom, I went to the washroom, cleaned my face, used the privy and returned to bed, packing the parchments away for tomorrow. I had a fitful sleep. Half-waking dreams of wagon-carrying balloons full of serpent gas bursting into flames and frying mudgle crews alive.

I woke early, tipped everything out of my satchel, and laid it on the unmade bed. *Parchments tied securely. Five pencils. Two set squares. A ruler and compass. Full waterskin. Spare pair of gloves and fur-lined hat. Handkerchief.* I packed it back into the satchel, pulled it out again, and re-packed.

Stepping from behind the bedroom curtain, I laid the satchel on the bench seat. Yula had already left for work. It took two hours to walk to *Line Station 3*, but at least she'd be home tonight, barring further accidents. In the cookery, I opened the stove's gas valve and struck a firestick to light the flame. Then I grabbed a saucepan, tipped in a cup of cut oats and two cups of woollydon milk, and warmed my favourite morning meal.

The curtain walling off Casca's room was closed, but I called out to him, "Do you want food?" No response.

With the oats done to a stodgy clump, as I liked them, I walked across to Casca's curtain. "I've cooked porridge. Are you hungry?"

Still no response and no sound of movement. I peeked around the curtain edge. The empty bed had been made or never slept in.

A flush of guilty relief washed over me. Although a blind boy should be taken care of by someone, I didn't know what to do with Casca. In between nightmares of burning mudgles, I had spent most of the night worrying how I'd feed and house him. Wherever he'd gone, I hoped he stayed there. Warm and fed, of course, but not inclined to return here.

I ate the porridge, dressed, grabbed my satchel, locked the door with the puzzle key, scrambled the puzzle and put it in the drawer released by the stone marble. While the systematic, compulsive ceremony annoyed Yula, she also considered it pointless. Most mudgles in Karlik didn't lock their doors. Buildings were rarely burgled. Crime almost non-existent. Serpent oil bestowed wealth on everyone. *Material* wealth. The collateral of mining serpent oil, however, eroded our *natural* wealth. The beauty and vigour of our nature. The facets of our wellbeing unconnected to monetary gain. I called it the 'Karlik Paradox.' I hoped one day to be free of it.

To reinforce the paradox, a fluttering of ash-snow joined me on my walk to the Inventoria. Today's presentation could be the first step in building the cloud wagon. If Eminent Drudan approved my plans, they'd be sent to the model-maker, Zurta, who'd build a working scale model. If that went well, Drudan would approve building a full-sized prototype. This would be subject to many tests to ensure the invention didn't kill anyone. At least, not if operated properly.

I walked into the Inventoria Lab, keen to find Jolia.

Vyrin offered a measly token of excitement. "What a momentous day this could be," he smiled. "The legendary inventor, Silveny Belarose, has arrived, plans at the ready to dazzle the doddery Eminent Drudan with her mastery."

I pulled the chair out from my workbench. "Do you ever get bored with your smugness?"

"I'm the most exciting person I know. At least in this place."

"Where's Jolia?"

"Ah, well, *there* is a mystery. Not at *The Dragon Bellows* last night. Not in this morning. Last I recall, you two were locked away in the meeting room. Did you keep her there until everyone else had left?"

"What?" I snapped. "Why would I do that?"

Vyrin rubbed his ruddy, braided beard. "*Hmmm.* So you could knock her on the head and steal the plans for her new invention."

"Don't be stupid," said Rula to Vyrin.

How does he know about Jolia's invention? I thought. *Where is she? Slept in? She never sleeps in.*

"Silveny *was* the last mudgle to see Jolia," smirked Vyrin.

I wanted to scream at him. *Shut up. Shut up! SHUT UP!*

As I went to sit down, Eminent Drudan's voice boomed from his office, "Silveny! Now."

Already? No time to worry about Jolia. I fumbled with the satchel buckles. The flap opened, and the rolled parchments fell onto the floorstones.

Vyrin scoffed. "Hope that flying machine of yours doesn't go to ground so easily."

He also knows about the cloud wagon. I didn't have time to ask how. I gathered my drawings and notes, shoved them back into the satchel and trotted to Drudan's office.

Closing the panalope door behind me, the squealing hinges protesting the burden of weighty timber, I walked into a room flanked by floor-to-ceiling shelves along both side walls. The books and model inventions commanding the shelf space had been stored with a precise neatness that satisfied my compulsion. *'Everything must have its place.'* But the random placement of a drawing or painting, breaking the regimental order of book spines, set a thought gnawing on how I'd alter the arrangement. I squashed the thought and refocussed on the argument that sat waiting behind a timber desk larger than my bed.

Eminent Drudan, the head inventor, lounged on a plush chair in front of an arched window made from blue lava-glass, the rarest colour. Our leader enjoyed the inspirational pleasures of a view outside, however tinted, even as he derided the opportunity to his workers. Drudan fixed eyes of youthful inquisitiveness on my approach, but the scraggly mane of greying hair and weathered furrows of black skin betrayed his many yarles in Karlik. Nevertheless, age hadn't dimmed the pride he took in the presentation of a black beard, likely dyed from grey, braided in a dozen, pencil-thin lengths and cinched at the end with gold circlets.

"Ready?" asked Drudan, drumming his stubby fingers on the desktop.

"Hope so," I said, trembling in the middle of the office, a kitten about to be crushed by a falling bookshelf.

He pointed at the chair set opposite him. "Well, come on. Don't stand there all day doing a jig. Sit down and show me."

I sat, untied the ribbon from the six parchments and rolled them out across his desk. "I've done double the required number of drawings and written a page of notes for each one."

"Of course you have." Eminent Drudan sat back in the chair, his mahogany linen coat falling open to reveal an ivory-coloured woollen waistcoat with silver buttons. He placed his hands on his head, knitting his fingers together to tame the unruly grey, and sighed. "I've never questioned your attention to detail, Silveny. But I'm looking for that creative spark."

I nodded, pulled my chair to the desk, and arranged the parchments in two rows of three. Using my ruler, I measured two quotents between each pair of parchments and lined them up square to the table edge.

"We don't have time for your fussing," said Drudan.

"It's not fussing," I started. "I'm...I'm...arranging my thoughts." But my mind trembled like my hands. I tapped my boot soles on the flagstone floor. Circled a tongue around a dry mouth. *Needed a last meeting with Jolia. Weed out any problems.* I blurted, "Do you know where Jolia is?"

Drudan sat forward. "Jolia?"

"She's not at work yet. Didn't come to the tavern last night."

"If you're more worried about your friend than your invention...."

"No. It's not...I'm not. Well, I am worried. But there'll be a simple explanation. Her da'three is in the Restoria, sick." *Probably going to die.* "She visits him every evening. Might have stayed late. Slept in."

"If you're distracted, this might be a bad time for your presentation."

I shook my head and remeasured the distance between the parchments. "Parchment number one. This is the overview." I lifted the drawing so Eminent Drudan could see. "I call it a cloud wagon."

"Change the name," spurted Drudan.

I stalled.

"Hate the name," he reasserted. "Change it."

"Right now?"

"No. Not right now. Eventually. Continue."

The rough paper quivered in my fingers, the fibres threatening to unravel across the desk. I thought of Jolia's encouragement and swallowed my nerves. "It's a free-flying balloon with a carriage underneath to transport serpent oil, supplies, mudgles, anything really, in and out of Karlik."

Drudan raised his palm. "You're not the first to think of something like this. Some wouldn't fly. Couldn't steer others. One inventor tried hot air. The balloon had to be enormous to carry anything worthwhile, and he couldn't keep the air warm without burning the whole thing to ash. All inventions that made prototype eventually crashed."

"This won't," I jumped in. "Crash. This won't crash. I promise."

"Promises are no match for proof. How do you steer?"

I dropped parchment one and pointed to parchment two. "Wings fixed to the carriage's side provide stability."

"Didn't ask about stability. Asked about steering."

Parchment number three. "Sails and a rudder. At the rear of the carriage. Rudder. Moveable and collapsible sails to catch the wind. Sails and a rudder." *Already said that. You're rambling.*

"The balloon will catch the wind," said Eminent Drudan. "Sails might not work."

"Well…they're…."

"I can guess how it goes up," he interrupted. "How do you get it down again?"

I pointed to a drawing on parchment three. "Vents. Vents in the balloon. Operated from the carriage by cords. They can be opened to expel serpent gas. Closed again to stop the flow."

"But once a certain amount of gas is vented, the balloon deflates, falls to the ground and can't fly again until refilled."

I bit my cheek. My thighs hammered the metal studs lining the hem of my panelled leather skirt into the chair. I forced a swollen tongue between cracked lips. "Well, no. *Ahhh*…but there will be enough gas to get the cloud wagon, no, *um*, flying machine yet to be named, over the ridge at *Line Station 16*. Once there, the pilots slowly release the gas through the vents, descending to the western foothills or the Nordland Plains. We will build a refuelling station at Wardcha where there's a gas vent, then the flying machine can return to Karlik."

Drudan raised a bushy grey eyebrow. "We *will* build one, will we? Don't get ahead of yourself, Silveny Belarose."

I shoved my hands under my thighs to stifle the hammering. "Sorry, Eminent Drudan. We *could* build a refuelling station. Here, too, in Karlik. The balloon line is dangerous. My sister, Yula, almost got killed yesterday. Another mudgle, Quoil, is in the Restoria. Might lose his leg. It got tangled in ropes. Yula saved him. They fell off the platform…and the winching and cables…every station is dangerous…and…."

"Deep breath," said Drudan. "Take a deep breath." He stood, clasped his hands behind his linen coat in the small of his back and strolled over to the blue window. "Your flying machine will be dangerous, too. But nothing in life is risk-free. Jolia told me you were ready to present your first major invention, and she told me it was a good one."

"It is. I am. Ready, that is. I'm ready. The invention is ready. It will work."

The Inventoria head, the old mudgle with my fate in his hands, ambled back to his desk and hovered over the parchments. "I can't see a scale on your drawings. How big is this thing?" He picked up parchment number six and held it towards those deceptively youthful, piercing brown eyes, ready to find flaws in the most detailed plans.

"I put a scale on every parchment. Lefthand side."

"*Ah,* yes, there it is."

"This version of the cloud...flying machine can...*could* carry twelve full oil barrels and a flight team of two mudgles. We could build them bigger...or smaller," I quickly added. "I don't want to be too ambitious." *Or not ambitious enough.* "At this size, if we build ten, we can cover all the outgoing loads carried by the line balloons on a normal workday. Moving supplies using the balloons is limited by rope and cable strength, and the physical capacity of station teams. It's a strenuous job."

"I'm aware of the balloon line's limitations. But it's served us well for over ten yarles." Drudan rubbed his wizened face and leaned forward until the manacled tips of his beard braids brushed the parchments. He picked up another drawing.

"That one has detailed notes," I said.

"I can read," said Drudan.

"If we made the carriage bigger, we'd need a bigger balloon. More fabric. More serpent gas. There's an inflection point where build components become too heavy for the vessel to fly."

"If we could transport gas in a compressed form and pump it into the balloon to raise its height, that would solve the problem. But no inventor has conquered this challenge." Durdan looked up at me. "Only two crew members needed?"

I nodded. "Yes, Eminent. Two. You might squeeze a third in if you wanted backup. But at a cost of two oil barrels."

"You're confident these balloon vents will get the vessel down again? I'm not sending mudgles to the moons."

"Yes, definitely will get them down."

"Steering? No crashing into jagged mountain cliffs."

"Confident in the steering."

"The line *is* dangerous, but the balloons are easy to manoeuvre when fixed in place. Yesterday was a bad day, and we've lost mudgles before." He dropped the parchment onto the desk and sat back in his chair, staring at me. "Build materials will be an issue; they always are."

"The carriage can be made of...."

Drudan raised his hand and cut me off again. I waited. I'd planned my presentation to be clear, concise and thorough. But the words became jumbled between my brain and my mouth. Yula's accident. Jolia's absence. Barick's brush with...with...whatever he saw. Casca's appearance. All of it weighed on my mind until the words I wanted to say had been crushed under a mountain of confusion and worry. I couldn't have picked a worse day to give my presentation.

I breathed deeply to still my anxiety and release the tension coiled inside my chest. *There'll be other inventions. Other presentations. I'll do better at those.* 'Time running out,' snickered Vyrin among my thoughts. 'Won't have a job here much longer.'

Drudan stared past me as he contemplated dismissing my failed idea. I arranged items on his desk, lining them up along the left side: a scale model of the Inventoria building, a cup with a clatter of pencils, and a framed charcoal drawing of his husbands, wives and son.

Then I collected my parchments, rolling them together and tying them with ribbon. *Jolia will be disappointed. Yula heard a horned wolf. Stop the haunting of Karlik.*

My thoughts almost drowned out Eminent Drudan when he finally spoke. "Build the model."

I sat frozen in silence, holding the cylinder of papers, ready to put them back in my satchel.

"I'll have those," said Drudan, reaching out his hand. "Your invention is approved for model building. I'll send your plans to Zurta."

With my mouth hanging open, waiting for a word – any word – to fill it, I gave Eminent Drudan my plans.

Finally, my mouth captured the word. "Approved?"

Drudan nodded. "The plans are excellent. I hope the thing flies. It would make up for all the failures. You must thank Jolia for her help."

Yes. Thank Jolia.

Eminent Drudan waved me away. "Off you go. I'm busy."

I stood. Bowed and fawned. Collected my satchel and stumbled backwards, away from the arched blue window and between the literary regiments. I flung the door open, forgetting to close it again, then ran down the hallway as if fleeing a horned wolf. But I ran towards my ambition.

Back at my workbench, Vyrin sneered at me, acting like he already knew I'd been approved for model building. I wanted to celebrate the moment with Jolia, but she still hadn't arrived at work. I distracted my worry by writing notes for the model-builder, Zurta. Not necessary, but exaggeration of detail was my thing. *Why stop now?*

Rula offered a pained smile, like an infant dealing with wind. "Congratulations."

"Does everyone know?" I asked.

"It's written all over your face. So, what exactly will this invention do?"

"It's a flying machine. Designed to carry supplies out of Wyrm Valley and down to the Nordland Plains."

"We have a balloon line for that," interrupted Vyrin.

"Will your flying machine come back again?" asked Rula.

I nodded. "After refilling the balloon at Wardcha."

"It's been tried before," scoffed Vyrin. "Never worked."

Rula glared at him. "Leave her alone. Why do you find female mudgles so intimidating?" Then smiled at me. "Well done, Silveny. I hope it works."

I tried to smile back, wishing Jolia could share in the accolades. Gallan's arrival at the Inventoria distracted my worry.

His long leg dragged his short leg with its burdensome, clumpy boot up to my workbench. "It was today, wasn't it? Your presentation?"

"Yes," I said.

"Did it get approved?"

I beamed.

Gallan pulled me up from the chair, almost toppling over, and hugged me. "That's brilliant."

"Why are you so excited about it?"

"Can we talk? Somewhere private."

I led him to the key cabinet and took the key for the storage room. We walked down the hall. I unlocked the iron door and stepped into a chaotic room full of discarded inventions or their scale models. Nothing in this room had been successful. It reminded all inventors that a single success is built from many failures.

Gallan bumped into a plinth and a model of a drill designed to clear rocks from mines almost crashed to the floor.

"Watch it," I hissed. "If you break anything, Eminent Drudan will revoke my approval."

"These are the failed inventions, aren't they? I don't know why you keep them."

"Slight modifications can turn a failed invention into a successful one. An improved version of the drill you almost knocked over is currently being used in the mines. We keep these inventions as a record of what's already been tried. A benchmark for future progress." I straightened the drill model, took the ruler from my shirt pocket and measured the distance from each edge of the plinth to position the model in the middle of the pedestal.

We sat at the table where inventors sometimes held meetings surrounded by models to gain inspiration.

"What do you want to talk about?" I asked Gallan.

"We had an early morning meeting with the emissaries from Kogot. The Voldari. Your flying machine could be more important than you realise."

Chapter 8

The Voldari strike a deal

"Gallan. Sit here." Gallan's ma'one, Eminent Jilomain Stretten, pointed to a three-legged stool in the room's corner. "You'll be out of the way. Trotter and Hildor, you sit opposite me. Are three chairs enough for the Voldari?"

"We don't know how many are coming," said Morry, Eminent Stretten's assistant. "A dozen arrived yesterday."

"My office is too small for a dozen," fussed Jilomain. "Should we adjourn to the Governant meeting hall? And there's the low ceiling." She paced around the room, raising her hand to try to touch the roof. "They're tall, aren't they? They might feel, you know, squashed."

"We could cut the chair legs shorter," said Morry.

"Sitting isn't the problem. It's when they stand. Oh goodness, if they believe the ceiling is higher than it is...."

"Why all this fretting, Ma'one?" asked Gallan.

"Because! This could be the most important meeting in recent memory. Rumours spread across Karlik. They've come for serpent oil. A colossal order. And I've told you, don't call me Ma'one at work."

Gallan jotted in his notebook: *Ma'one wants to be called Eminent Stretten.*

"If the rumours about oil are true," said Hildor Graben, Extractory Eminent, "how are we going to supply it? Our population thins. Karlik is waning. Not enough pucks willing to risk the mines."

"I won't have talk of *thinning* or *waning*," snapped Jilomain. "You hear me? None. If all of us have to go down the mines to get the damn oil, we will."

Gallan squatted on the inadequate stool, knees pressed up to his chest, hopeful it wouldn't come to that. He wasn't miner material; tall for a mudgle, uneven legs and a lumbering boot, and a dislike for dark places. Not to mention claustrophobia and the chance of being blown to pieces. Scribing, while an unaspiring profession, had the advantage of being relatively safe. Gallan considered avoiding danger his most important ambition.

And Barick had unsettled him with the story about 'Shadow Man'. *What evil lurks beneath the mountains?* He shuddered.

Jilomain scowled at him. "Stop daydreaming. Get ready to write everything down. Don't interrupt. Don't say anything. Sit there and write."

Gallan clutched the notebook and pencil tighter, preparing to race the words across the page.

"We need this order," muttered Vice Eminent Trotter Borke. "Other markets are wan...*drying* up. Since the Germalians liberated Enthilen, the Dobunni and Erstürmen have used carborupem. It's slower-burning and less volatile. They found a big seam of it in the Scaur Hills."

"The Scaur Hills!" cried Jilomain. "That's all we need, a self-sufficient Enthilen. Don't tell the Voldari any of this. They'll twig we're desperate. They can't know we're desperate." She glared at Eminent Graben who nodded.

"But we're caught between a floe bear and its den," said Hildor. "If we must mine more oil, we don't have the mudgle power. I should know."

"Not enough workers," sniped Jilomain. "Markets drying up. It can't be both at once. We'll find more miners, even if we have to import them. Better that than closing mines."

Hildor's eyes flared in defence. "I'll close mines if we don't have the teams to work them. Using smaller teams puts miners in danger. I won't have that. You can bluster all you want."

Hildor Graben won't yield to ~~Ma'one's~~ Eminent Stretten's bluster, scribbled Gallan in his notebook. *Unlike my two fathers,* he thought.

Morry glided around the office desk, red-brown mahogany with carved legs resembling griffin wings, moving a bust of Wilhorace Mittle, one of Karlik's founders, to the corner beside a fruit bowl. She sighed, "I wish we had flowers. Something pretty. Anything that can grow."

"Nearly broke the treasury buying all that fruit," grumbled Borke.

"Nonsense," said Jilomain. "We have to impress our guests."

Need to impress the Voldari, Gallan wrote, as someone knocked on the office door.

"Yes," said Jilomain.

The door opened, and the Governant Secretary poked his head inside. "They're here."

Jilomain flattened her hands down regal garments: a black silk robe with silver stitching and a white-furred fringe that brushed the rugged floorstones, worn over a crisp, butter-yellow shirt with sapphire buttons that reflected the light from the oil lanterns hanging from the ceiling.

Gallan panicked. *What if they knock their heads on the lanterns?*

"Alright," said Jilomain. "Places, everyone."

Morry left the room. Trotter Borke and Hildor Graben stood in front of their chairs; ornate, plated silver fashioned as unfurling fronds with plush cushions made from woollydon fur. Jilomain strode to the opposite side of the desk, standing before a grand cathedra of gold-plated iron, the backrest and seat stitched with tapestries of Karlik's early days emerging from the hard cold of the Wyrm Valley.

She snapped at her son, "Stand Gallan," then her ruddy face flushed scarlet. "What's the greeting again?"

"Fingers to forehead and then to heart," replied Borke.

"Which fingers?"

"All four."

Four fingers to forehead then heart, wrote Gallan before standing.

The mudgles waited in silence. The mounted heads of a horned wolf, woollydon and cliff deer fixed their lifeless, glassy eyes on Gallan, daring him to disappoint his ma'one by uttering some nonsense during the meeting. He squashed a ridge in the floor rug with his short leg before disappearing into the tapestry of green fields, trees and flowers. Outside the office's arched windows, a pewter-grey sky offered no hint of sun. A typical Karlik day. But Gallan loved the city, almost as much as he loved his ma'one. Both could be hard taskmasters, but he failed to imagine another life. And at least he'd done better than his two fathers. They'd be outside now, shovelling ash-snow into barrows.

Morry opened the office door, and the room chilled. Gallan worried the hearthed gas fire waned, giving the visitors from Kogot a bad impression. *No talk of waning.*

In walked four Voldari, stooping through the doorway and standing until their head coverings brushed the ceiling. Jilomain's eyes bulged. She rushed over to Gallan, pulling the stool from behind him and placing it next to the chairs.

She smiled at the visitors. "Welcome. Welcome." Flustered, she slapped herself on the forehead with the palm of her hand, the whacking assault bouncing from the stone walls, then placed her hand on her heart, leaving it there.

Trotter Borke, Hildor and Gallan mastered the formal greeting with more aplomb, placing the tips of four fingers to their forehead and then heart. The Voldari repeated the gesture but showed no emotion that Gallan could discern. Long, thin arms with pale skin extended beyond the fringed cuffs of frost-blue robes like daggers poking through the bottom of sheaths. But the head and face adornments stunned Gallan the most. He'd never seen such elaborate masking.

"Please, sit," said Jilomain, waving her hand across the empty chairs.

The Voldari glanced at each other.

"You understand mudgle?" asked Borke.

"Yuh-es," said the shortest of the four, a female with black rings tattooed around her eyes and the shafts of more than a dozen owl feathers grafted under her forehead skin, their snow-white vanes extending beyond the crown of her bald head and tickling the room's ceiling.

"Yuh-or lan-gu-age, hard on us," said Snow Owl.

The three male Voldari sat on the chairs. Snow Owl hesitated before kneeling on the stool.

"This isn't right," fretted Jilomain. "Morry. Another chair. Quickly."

The Eminent's assistant nodded, disappeared, and reappeared a moment later, carrying a chair into the room. With awkward sign language, she got Snow Owl to swap her stool for the chair.

Gallan slouched against the wall as Morry left the room, taking the stool with her. He wrote in his notebook: *Voldari twice mudgle height. Speak in a mechanical, halting way. All have ~~bizarre head coverings~~ animal amuells.*

Jilomain stubbed her toe on a table leg as she danced to the desk's opposite side and plonked down onto her dramatic chair. She glared at Gallan, who sighed and stood up straight. Trotter and Hildor sat beside the Voldari.

"I'm Eminent Jilomain Stretten, leader of Karlik's Governant. This is my second in command, Vice Eminent Trotter Borke, and Eminent Hildor Graben, head of the Extractory."

The oldest Voldari man, with skin resembling crumpled paper and the clawed foot of a floe bear covering his bald crown, faced Gallan and pointed. "Him?"

"Oh, he's nobody," dismissed Jilomain. "The Governant scribe. It's his job to record our meeting. For prosperity's sake."

Nobody. Gallan stabbed the word into his notebook.

Snow Owl covered her mouth and whispered to her colleagues.

"What was that?" asked Jilomain.

She faced Eminent Stretten. "I Urn-hasa. In yuh-or tongue 'White Owl.' My f-ar-ends, Fal-ursa 'Floe Bear', Run-targa 'Wave Lion', and Hor-gnasher 'Black Griffin'."

White Owl, wrote Gallan. *Not Snow Owl.* He jotted the other names into the notebook: Voldari and their translation.

"Griffins," said Hildor. "Who'd have thought any still lived until...."

"Welcome," interrupted Jilomain, clearing her throat. "Fruit?" She held the bowl towards the guests.

Trotter Borke stumbled from his seat, grabbed the bowl and offered it to the Voldari. They shook their heads in unison, the animal adornments swinging with the refusal.

Borke sucking up, jotted Gallan, before scribbling over the top of it.

"Rare in Karlik," said Jilomain. "Fruit, that is. Not serpent oil." She chuckled.

"Pa-lenty in Kogot," said Urn-hasa. "F-ar-oot."

Plenty of fruit in Kogot, wrote Gallan. *Trade for serpent oil?*

"Of course," said Jilomain, waving at Borke to put the bowl down. "How was your journey here? You travelled the old path?"

"Long way," said Urn-hasa.

"*Death's Pass,* we call it," said Borke, proud of the fact.

Jilomain scowls at Borke. Ignored.

The Vice Eminent continued, "Who rules Kogot now? I remember when Emperor Wenloch governed. It was a marvellous city then. I was a puck, of course, full of vim and...."

Jilomain interrupted, "Shall we get straight to business?"

Urn-hasa nodded.

The room fell silent again, so quiet that Gallan swore he could hear the ash-snow falling outside. The rub of the carbon pencil tip across paper sounded like chalk on slate as he tried to capture every detail of the meeting. The Voldari sucked wheezing breaths through pursed lips, likely not used to the altitude. Run-targa, who had tusks protruding down from the sides of his mouth as if they'd been fused to the jawbone, struggled the most. With no hemleaf in the room, Gallan thought about asking Morry for some. A drink of hemleaf steeped in warm water lessened altitude sickness. He dismissed fetching Morry when Hildor Graben broke the silence.

"Serpent oil?" she asked, facing Urn-hasa.

The Voldari replied, "Yuh-es. Fa-erst, we need help."

"Of course," said Jilomain.

"Cur-a-mudgles good rulers."

Jilomain fake smiled. "You're too kind."

"Kogot need help for ba-etter. Be ba-etter leader. Understand? Difficult ta-imes. We la-earn from yuh-oo."

Trotter Borke coughed. "We haven't had any problems in Karlik for generations. Nothing to learn...."

Jilomain cut him off. "Vice Eminent Borke is trying to say we'd be delighted to help in any way we can."

Voldari having trouble with leadership, wrote Gallan. *Asking mudgles for help. Mudgles??*

"What help are you after?" asked Hildor.

"Observe only," said Urn-hasa. "La-earn from yuh-or leaders."

"Well," said Jilomain, "that sounds manageable."

"Observe for how long?" asked Borke before Jilomain launched a glare that pinned him to his seat.

"Not long," said Urn-hasa. "Build ba-etter life for Kogot."

Voldari not here for long, scribbled Gallan. *Appear more interested in learning mudgle management techniques than serpent oil. What is happening in Kogot?*

"Emperor Wenloch would have sorted out any problems," said Borke.

"Will you understand what we're doing?" asked Jilomain. "I don't mean offence, but as you said, our language is difficult."

Urn-hasa whispered to her colleagues, then faced Jilomain. "Understand. Nar-uth-ing to fear."

Nothing to fear from the Voldari, wrote Gallan.

Hildor sat forward. "This is all good, but what about the serpent oil?"

Urn-hasa faced the Eminent and nodded. "Yuh-es. Oil."

"Well," stammered Jilomain. "There are rumours."

"Rumours can be truths yet fulfilled," said Fal-ursa, in a voice that sounded like stone rubbing on glass. "Or lies yet exposed." His faced turned hard.

Shit, scribbled Gallan. *Floe Bear speaks fluent mudgle. Do they even want serpent oil?*

Jilomain smiled at Fal-ursa. "You speak well."

"Is this a ruse?" blustered Borke. "I won't be taken for a fool."

Fal-ursa turned to Urn-hasa, who nodded, then he smiled at Borke. "You must understand. We follow a strict hierarchy. Urn-hasa is our leader. She had the right to speak with you first. But I may speak now. We do not wish to deceive."

Borke crossed his arms and leaned back in the chair with a glare of dissatisfaction. Jilomain pushed parchments around her desk as if she'd been caught napping during work hours. Eminent Graben sat forward, likely keen to know if she'd have enough miners to fulfil the yet-to-materialise order.

Not all is what it seems, wrote Gallan before thinking he should cross it out. While knowing almost everything that happened in Karlik, he knew very little about the world outside the Wyrm Valley. He'd never travelled and had only spoken with a handful of traders who brought stories from the rest of Ostamp with their wares.

"How much oil is in your mines?" asked Fal-ursa, staring out the beige-tinted, lava-glass window, its sill piled with ash-snow.

"Impossible to say," said Hildor. "Mudgles have been mining these mountains for generations."

"Plenty more to come," cut in Jilomain, deciding she'd shuffled the parchments enough.

"Enthilen now uses carborupem," said Fal-ursa. "Your customers are thinning."

We won't talk of thinning!

"Nordmen still use it," said Borke. "And we have other...*ah*...other options."

There was a knock on the door.

Jilomain scrunched up her face. "Enter."

Morry came in carrying a tray with eight cups. "Hemleaf tea. It helps with the altitude sickness."

"Put it on my desk, Morry," said Jilomain before waving her away.

Hemleaf finally arrives, noted Gallan.

Trotter Borke took a cup but didn't offer the drink to the guests. Jilomain reached across her desk, wrapped her fingers around a cup, nodded to the Voldari, then drank. Urn-hasa leaned forward and grabbed a cup. The other Voldari followed. Hildor and Gallan declined the drink. For Gallan, the hemleaf effects could often be worse than altitude sickness.

Hor-gnasher, the black griffin, sniffed at the liquid, the hooked beak fused to the end of his nose scraping against the cup's side. He screwed up his face, ruffling the tight black feathers grafted onto his forehead that ceded to a swatch of lion pelt adorning his crown, and placed the cup back on the tray. Urn-hasa took a sip and nodded to Fal-ursa and Run-targa, who also drank, the tusked Voldari dribbling most of the tea onto the front of his robe.

Fal-ursa cradled the cup in his lap. "The hemleaf is flavoursome."

"Should stop the headaches," said Jilomain. "The air is so thin up here."

Borke huffed on his seat, expressing his discomfort at the exchange's current opacity.

He's busting to ask about oil again, wrote Gallan.

"We'll take three barrels," said Fal-ursa.

Borke spat a mouthful of tea back into his cup. "Three barrels! Is that all? We're wasting our time...."

Fal-ursa raised his hand. "Of hemleaf tea. Three barrels of tea."

"Oh," said Jilomain, chuckling.

Fal-ursa drained his cup, then returned it to the tray. "Now, to the real business." He stared at Jilomain. "Serpent oil. We wish to order one thousand barrels."

Hildor Graben nodded. "Reasonable. We can supply that easily enough. Could have that much in storage."

"One thousand barrels per season," clarified Fal-ursa.

Jilomain placed a hand over her gasping mouth.

A thousand barrels a season!! wrote Gallan.

"Well," blustered Jilomain, "that is a generous offer...."

"We have not offered anything yet," said Fal-ursa.

"*Uh...um....no,* of course. But there will be a price to negotiate."

"Yes," said Fal-ursa in his gravel-cut voice. "We must decide the price."

"That's four thousand barrels a yarle," said Borke.

"*Ahhh*, I forgot you have four seasons here. We actually need six thousand barrels per yarle. For as long as you can supply it."

Trotter Borke almost fell from his chair with excitement. Hildor Graben looked distraught, wondering how she might oversee the mining of so much oil, while Jilomain Stretten appeared to be already counting the coin in her head.

Fal-ursa continued, "When we travelled along *Death's Pass*, the balloon line was quiet. Not much oil being carried from Karlik."

Borke snapped out of his internal exultation. "Temporary lull. Things will pick up again. Enthilen's tryst with carborupem won't last. They'll be back once they miss the convenience and reliability of serpent oil for their energy needs."

"Are you certain you can meet our needs? Your city is less than it once was."

"It's true that...." started Hildor.

"We'll manage," interrupted Jilomain. "Let us worry about mining the oil. Eminent Graben is most adept at getting the best out of her miners. She won't let us down."

"How much can suh-ply na-ow?" halted Urn-hasa.

"Wait a moment," said Borke. "We haven't discussed price."

Run-targa reached inside his frost-blue robe and plonked a bag of coin on the table. "Gold moynes," he said. "Three hundred gold moynes for the first one hundred barrels, and we want exclusive access." He emphasised 'exclusive' with a suck of spit through his tusks.

"There'd have to be a meeting of all the Eminents to approve such a condition," said Hildor, casting a side glance at Jilomain, daring to be contradicted.

All the ditherers in one room, scrawled Gallan. But it's a <u>lot</u> of oil.

"This is most unusual," said Borke. "A recurring large order with exclusivity. It means cutting off our other loyal customers."

As if there'd been a secret signal, the Voldari stood as one.

"We're sure you will carefully consider our offer," said Fal-ursa. "We go to prepare observers for your offices."

The Voldari placed four fingers on the forehead, then on the heart.

Eminent Jilomain Stretten stood and returned the gesture. "We'll call a meeting for tomorrow. It's only a formality. I expect full support."

The Voldari walked from the room, the lion's tail stitched to the back of Hor-gnasher's head swaggering with authority and menace.

Trotter Borke fingered his braided beard, calculating profits. "Three gold moynes per barrel. Eighteen thousand moynes per yarle. Eighteen! That's twice the price we get from Nordland or anywhere else."

"Did you get all that?" Jilomain asked Gallan.

He nodded.

Morry entered the room. "They've gone."

"Why do they want so much?" asked Gallan. "Can we supply it?"

"No," said Hildor.

"We must," countered Jilomain. "It could mean wealth beyond imagine."

Wealth beyond imagine, wrote Gallan. *We're rich!*

Chapter 9

Losing a friend

"To ship all that oil," said Gallan, "we're going to need a fleet of cloud wagons."

"I'm not calling it that anymore," I said.

"What are you calling it?"

I shrugged. "Haven't decided."

"Let me know when you do. I have to get back. Write up my notes from today's meeting."

He limped from the Inventoria storage room before I could protest. It would be days before Zurta finished a model of my yet-to-be-named flying machine and many more days to build a full-sized prototype. Karlik's future couldn't rest on my invention. Yet, the balloon line would struggle to meet the Voldari order. Station managers would take more risks. Yula would face more danger.

I must protect my sister.

I stood and tidied the shelves of failed inventions, my compulsion putting chaos into order. Large models on the bottom shelf, working my way up to the smallest on the top shelf. I measured one delicant between each adjacent pair of models. That required re-sorting. I ran out of space and panicked. I couldn't get them to fit. Couldn't arrange it all.

Why should I be expected to!? Why did the ordering of Karlik fall to me?

I slapped my arms across my chest and stumbled backwards. Behind me, a plinth rocked then fell, smashing onto the floorstones and shattering into dozens of pieces. Underneath the rubble was the model invention that once had pride of place on the plinth. One of

Eminent Drudan's inventions. *One of his!* I knelt and swept the rubble away, picking up the gas heater model, the same type they used in the Governant food court, between my thumb and forefinger. I held it to the light of the oil lamps and blew off the grey dust and flecks of sandstone, trying to convince myself the model hadn't been damaged.

This isn't a failed invention. It works. It's been stored in the wrong place. Will Drudan notice? Should I move it? No. Find a new plinth. Leave it here. No-one will know.

I knelt as tears welled in my eyes. I needed a calm hand. A comforting word. I needed Jolia. Where *was* she?

"What a mess."

I spun around to find Vyrin lounging against the door jamb, arms crossed with simpering satisfaction.

"Accident," I muttered, standing and moving another plinthed model to the shelves and putting the heater model in its place.

"That's Drudan's invention, isn't it?" Vyrin purred, content at having recognised the fact.

"Model isn't damaged," I snipped.

"The plinth will cost a few tokens to replace."

"I'll pay for it." I took a broom and pail from the corner and swept up the stone fragments.

"Don't worry," said Vyrin, "I won't tell anyone. You can owe me the favour."

Don't worry? Don't worry? He doesn't know me at all, does he?

Vyrin slunk away. I left the pail full of stone pieces behind a chest. A cleaner would find it eventually, but I didn't care. I needed to talk to Jolia.

I returned to the lab. My friend still hadn't come to work. Knowing I wouldn't concentrate, I grabbed my satchel and coat and walked out.

Standing on the Inventoria's front steps, I pulled on my hat and woollen gloves and planned how to reach Jolia's apartment while avoiding as much ash-snow as possible. I scooted down the steps, dashed between the covered walkways leading to the Governant, then turned sharp right into an alley. I collided with Casca, almost knocking the blind boy over.

"You're still here?" I blurted.

Casca smiled. "Wonderful not to see you also, Silveny."

"I thought when you disappeared...where have you been?"

His grin broadened. "I've been to Sardis to visit...well, there's no queen anymore. No king either, so that doesn't work."

I shook my head. "You're playing games again. Sardis is many days' journey away."

"You're right," said Casca. "I wouldn't even reach it in your flying machine."

"How do you know about that?" *Peeked at the drawings? No, stupid, he's blind.*

"When we first met, you mentioned it to your friends."

Overheard a conversation. I've been too loose-lipped. I walked off, determined to get to Jolia's place and not caring if Casca followed.

He called after me, "If you're looking for your friend, you're going the wrong way."

I turned on my heel and marched up to him. "What are you talking about?"

"Jolia isn't home. The apartment is empty."

"How do you know?"

He clasped his left hand onto my wrist. "The worst thing you can do to someone with a disability is to underestimate them." He released me. "Yula took me there this morning."

Yula? She doesn't like you. "Since you know so much, where *is* Jolia?"

"Missing," said Casca.

"Genius," I replied, not masking my sarcasm. "Her da'three will know. I'm going to the Restoria."

I strode off towards the Fordun Quarter, and Casca skipped after me. I didn't care if I lost him or not. He wasn't my responsibility. I shouldn't have to look after him. I had my own worries. Karlik needed my invention. I didn't have the luxury of failure.

I hope Gallan doesn't publish anything yet. He's not supposed to. Not until the prototype is approved. But the promise of shipping more oil, combined with the Voldari order...he won't be able to contain his excitement about my invention. Gallan, please. Don't. I'm not ready.

The dozens of venting fires surrounding Karlik burned fiercely, whooshing and flapping in fiery streams buffeted by the north wind blowing in off the Nordargen Sea. We couldn't avoid the ash-snow. It stormed around us, swirling in a depressive grey haze and catching on every thread of my hat, coat and skirt. I sought cover under a store veranda, but the wind pushed the torment into my face.

Despite pronouncing the pollutant's murderous intent, Casca didn't seem to care. He stood in the middle of the street, the hood of his cloak pulled back and ash-snow piling on his wispy hair. He must have felt it. But he did nothing to cleanse his body of the threat.

Two mudgles scooted past him, veering further away than they needed, acting like the strange boy with the bone-rimmed, obsidian spectacles was the menace, not the ash-snow. I wanted to rush out and grab his hand. Pull him under cover and sweep the toxic manna off his face and clothes. But he didn't need me. He simply stood and waited like a faithful dog.

"Come on," I called out to him before marching up the street.

He jumped at my voice and followed. *My footsteps? Another sound?* I couldn't tell. He never stumbled. Never bumped into anything, even when the street narrowed to a single lane bordered by disordered, ghoulish townhouses whose front steps spilled onto the road bricks. If I didn't know better, I would have said he'd been blind for a hundred yarles. Possibly two hundred. But he was a boy, ten yarles old at the most. *Right?*

The narrow lane opened to a city square, grey and barren with stone plinths covered in ash-snow resembling frozen ghosts. Three peace officers from the Statutoria huddled around a flaming gas vent under a slate-roofed rotunda barely large enough to shelter them. They rubbed bare hands above a pale orange fire that couldn't outshine their smart red jackets adorned with silver buttons and crisp white lapels. Flecks of snow clung to furred hats that resembled pails turned upside down, and smaller flecks weaved in among the beards and moustaches plaited together with head hair. Truncheons hung from their belts, still shiny black amid the ash-snow storm and decorated with painted scenes I couldn't make out.

Do they hope for a crime to happen? Something to vitalise a dull day. Or are they happy beside the fire in an uneventful city?

Casca and I strode across the square as if the peace officers had begun a pursuit, dodging through a forest of sculptures with no recognisable shape. Abstract art insulted my compulsion and served no practical or aesthetic purpose I could discern. I dismissed it as Artary pretentiousness. Contributions from artists with too much time to dabble in the meaningless.

The Restoria in Fordun Quarter lined one boundary of the square. The long, single-storey building with two dozen shuttered windows built into the stone had a sharply peaked, slated roof. Ash-snow and real snow slid off, collecting in drifts under the windows. Four mudges cleared the affliction, shovelling the snow into barrows and wheeling it off to carts that would dump it in disused mines.

Oh, for ash-snow to act like real snow and simply melt away.

A grand portico of twisted granite columns capped with sculptures of sniggering gargoyles holding up the slated roof awaited us. We climbed three steps and pushed through a honey-coloured, lava-glass door framed in brass. Casca followed me into a reception hall with polished tiled floors interspersed with mosaiced patterns of mudge life, and an oil fire that resembled a waterspout surrounded by circular stone seats.

Casca stopped and leaned into me. "It smells of death."

"Sssh," I hissed.

"Clothes," said a doorkeeper as he marched towards us.

"Coats? Hats?"

"Everything except undergarments."

"Everything?"

"This is a place of healing. Can't have visitors infected with ash-snow roaming the corridors. You'll be given gowns and slippers. You can collect your clothes when you leave."

I disrobed, wondering what Casca had on under his ragged jumper and pants. I didn't have to wait long. *Nothing.*

He stood naked in the foyer, offering his gaunt, withered body to the world. The doorkeeper yanked a gown from a garderobe and threw it at him. It hit Casca in the face, knocking his glasses askew, then fell to the floor.

"Put on the gown," I said, picking it up and handing it to him.

"I'm not known for my modesty," he replied, straightening his glasses.

"Put it on anyway."

I cinched a gown over my undergarments, then retrieved two pairs of slippers from beside the garderobe. We walked across the hall to where a mudgle in a mauve dress sat behind a granite reception bench.

"I'm here to see Da'three Sircom," I announced.

"Miners' ward," she said, not looking up. "Along the south corridor. First turn left."

I smiled a thank you and turned on my heel. Casca was already on his way.

I skipped up to him. "How do you know where to go?"

"Unpleasant mix of serpent oil and impending demise. The place reeks of it, and the source of the offence is down this passage. Left, then right."

I trailed Casca as he marched down the corridor, his slippers spanking the tiled floor. I couldn't smell serpent oil, but sweetly worrisome aromas of crushed herbs and blood filled my nostrils, and ruthless fits of coughing grew louder as we approached the ward. Most miners became patients in the Restoria at least once in their lives. For some, it would be their first and last visit, carried out in a burial shroud and taken to the catacombs to be shoved into one of the empty holes excavated by their fellow miners. I dreaded the day I'd have to visit

Barick in the Restoria because he'd had a terrible accident in the mines. Given his fretfulness, I imagined that day would come sooner rather than later.

We walked into the miners' ward. Dozens of patients lined the walls, lying or sitting on narrow cots with soiled alabaster bedding that accentuated the foul desperation in the room. Some miners coughed and spluttered as if a witch had cursed every breath they took. Others clung to sheets with frail hands, holding them tight over chests shadowed by bulging, corpulent necks threatening to burst with an ooze of seeping pus. Many patients had lost their hair; the occasional random tuft left clinging to their faces and scalps.

As I wandered down the line of beds, hollow, dark eyes watched me expectantly, hoping I'd come to visit or bring gifts. But I let them all down, reluctant to offer even a faint smile as consolation.

What comfort would such a feeble token be to these workers? Most appear younger than thirty yarles, their lives stolen away and buried in the darkening soot of the mine tunnels.

As I passed an older miner, she sat up and surrendered to a ferocious coughing fit. Thick blood sprayed from her mouth and across the quilt, turning alabaster to garnet. Rivulets of the oily-dark sludge dripped from the sheets and onto the floor. An attendant rushed over and placed an arm across the miner's chest, trying to hold her upright. A healer arrived and rubbed the miner's back as if healing magic would flow from the palm of her hand into the patient's spine. With his free hand, the attendant reached across to the bedside table and tipped a honey-coloured liquid from a pitcher into a cup. He held the cup to the old miner's lips. She sipped at the elixir like a nursing puck pursing for a mother's teat.

But the sweet, nectaral healing failed to stem another fit of explosive coughing, so violent I swore a lump of flesh cannoned from the miner's mouth.

"Won't last the night," Casca whispered into my ear.

I turned away and approached an attendant carrying a bedpan. "I'm looking for Da'three Sircom."

He pointed to a bed at the far end of the ward.

I walked over and checked the name written on a parchment clipped to a board at the bed's foot. Jolia's da'three lay there, eyes closed, every slow, shallow breath inhaled with a painful wheeze as if the air had to be sucked from a rock. He appeared to be the oldest patient in the ward, with thatches of braided, greying hair on his face and crown refusing to surrender to the bane of a serpent oil miner. But the entangled mess of hair on his naked chest couldn't muffle the deathly warning rattling beneath.

"We better hurry," said Casca. "Death won't take long with this one, either."

I glared at him. *Waste of time. Remember?*

I didn't want to wake Da'three Sircom, but I needed to find Jolia. I moved to the bedside and began rearranging the items on his table, lining them up along the edge closest to the bed. A framed charcoal drawing of Jolia, his sole offspring. A handclock. A cup of water. A bowl of dried petals. A clay figurine of a female mudgle.

I almost dropped the figurine when Da'three Sircom sat upright and hacked a glob into his mouth. Wide-eyed, he looked at me and pointed to a tin pail on the floor beside the bed. I grabbed the handle and lifted, straining my arm with the weight and trying not to glance inside.

After resting the pail on the bed, Da'three Sircom leaned over and spat out a black-red clump of bile that resembled a chunk of seared meat. A piece of it teetered on his bottom lip before sliding away and falling into the receptacle. He coughed again, blood dribbling from the corner of his mouth and down into his matting grey beard.

"Makes for a new twist on the phrase 'deathly pail,'" mumbled Casca.

Instead of scolding him, I called for a healer. But they ignored me, engrossed in their burdens of dispensing potions, cleaning bedpans and pails, or replacing bedding.

Da'three Sircom held up his hand, indicating for me to wait. I stood there, pail at the ready. He spat out another vile lump, sipped water, then slumped back into his bed.

Casca wandered off, strolling along the aisle and pausing at the foot of each bed, likely trying to guess who'd die next.

"S..s..sit," stammered Da'three Sircom. "Please. Sit with me for a while."

I returned the pail to the floor and sat on an iron stool beside the bed. "We've met before," I said. "I'm Silveny."

He nodded. "You're Jolia's friend. From the Inventoria."

"I thought she might be here, Da'three Sircom. Visiting."

"Call me Yohane. I haven't seen her for a while. She didn't visit last night. Or today. There's still time."

"She wasn't at *The Dragon Bellows* and didn't come into work this morning." *Idiot. Don't feed the worry of a dying mudgle.*

Yohane propped himself up on two pillows. "Kyra."

A passing attendant stopped her busyness and faced us.

"When did Jolia last visit?" asked Yohane.

"Two nights ago," said Kyra, before busying away.

Yohane smiled at me. "We can wait together. She'll visit today after work. She often brings food. Sometimes ale." He winked.

But she wasn't at work. "She works hard," I said instead.

"Trying to make life better for Karlik's citizens is important to her."

"She's an excellent inventor. She's been helping me."

He nodded and coughed. I reached for the pail. *Deathly pail.* But he waved it away.

"She...*cough*...is fond of you. Impressed with your inventions. Who is he?" Yohane pointed at Casca with a wavering finger.

The blind boy had opened a cabinet brimming with medical implements. He withdrew a razor-knife, wooden handle with a polished steel blade, and held it to his nose before running his finger along the sharp edge. I pictured him slicing his hand open and almost yelled a reprimand. A healer cooled my parental scold as she raced over to Casca, took the razor-knife from his grasp, pushed him away from the cabinet and shut and locked the door.

Casca ignored the healer, shuffled across to a table and picked up an ointment bottle, popping the cork and tipping a drop onto his tongue.

"I found him begging in the streets," I told Yohane. "I think he's an orphan."

"Jolia will be orphaned soon. When the hógdubh, the black lung, takes me." He coughed again, reinforcing the point, then clutched my hand. "Sorry. That was insensitive. Jolia told me you lost your parents."

"Not all," I said, the words catching in my throat. "Da'one still lives. In a cabin in the mountains."

"If that boy was a mudgle puck, we'd find a home for him. He looks Nordman."

"Not sure what he is." *Other than blind, and I'm not sure of that either.*

"On the streets. In this...*cough*...cold. No place for a young'un, no matter where he comes from."

Yes. No place for a young'un. I leaned forward on the stool, tucked in the crumpled bedsheet, then shunted the brimming pail under the bed with my foot. The clipboard at the end of the bed hung skewwhiff, so I stood, stepped across and straightened it before Kyra approached with a tray of potions.

I sat back down.

"Who's this?" said Kyra to Yohane.

"This is Jolia's friend," he replied. "Silveny. She's a famous inventor."

"Really?" Kyra raised her eyebrows, and a blush warmed my tawny cheeks before I smiled at her.

"Do you have any sleep potions?" asked Yohane.

"How's your chest today?"

"No better. But I...*herk*...need to sleep."

Kyra nodded, walked behind me and placed two thumb-sized vials on the bedside table. "Take the red one first. It will clear your chest. Take the blue one when you want to sleep. That's all the healer has prescribed for tonight."

She walked off, and I moved the vials closer to the bedside table's edge, in perfect alignment with the other items.

"The red one doesn't work," said Yohane, folding his arms across his chest to smother the rattle.

"Why don't you tell a healer?" I asked.

He shook his head. "No point. Tried other potions. None work, except the blue one."

Casca shuffled over and stood at the foot of Yohane's bed. I clenched my teeth, hoping he wouldn't continue with his insensitive statements about death.

But Yohane blurted an insensitivity of his own. "Never seen glasses like those before. What are you trying to hide?"

Casca reached for the clipboard and tilted it up as if reading. "I'm hiding the bitter cruelty that took one of my eyes and the selfishness that took the other."

Yohane looked at me with confusion.

"He often talks in riddles," I said.

"Where are your parents?" Yohane asked Casca.

"My father, I hope never to see again. My mother, I never saw at all."

"How...*cough*...terrible. Jolia could adopt you. She's always wanted a puck." Yohane craned his neck around me and stared at the doorway, hoping his daughter had walked in. But she wasn't there, and he slumped back into his bed, pulling the sheet under his chin.

We sat in silence, Casca's unspoken impatience binding my nerves. Yohane closed his eyes again, and his cough settled. Healers and attendants moved about the ward, delivering potions, poultices and soothing words or removing bedpans, pails and soiled bedding. I checked the handclock on Yohane's bedside table: five hours after high sun.

Casca wavered in place like a stalk of grass in a changing breeze.

"I'll find you a seat," I said to him.

"No need. We must move on."

Move on to where?

The next hour went with painful slowness. I didn't have the energy to read or talk to Casca, so I retreated into my thoughts and waited there as they swirled about and tugged my mind one way, then the other.

At six hours past high sun, Yohane opened his eyes. "Jolia?"

I shook my head.

His whole body sank into the mattress, and glistening eyes trapped me with a resigned desire. "The blue vial," he said, pointing to the tiny bottle.

I picked up the vial, popped the cork and leaned over Yohane. He opened his mouth, and I turned away for fear of gagging at the wafting stench. I regained my courage and faced a shrivelled, bruised tongue poking out over rotting teeth that resembled blackened stumps scorched by wildfire. I tipped the potion onto a violet wound, the blue liquid disappearing amid the camouflage in an instant.

"We should go," said Casca.

I placed the empty vial on the bedside table and stood.

Yohane grabbed my hand. "Jolia will visit soon." He released me, lay back down and closed his eyes.

We retrieved our clothes and my shoulder satchel from the Restoria doorkeeper and stepped outside. Night had taken hold, a rusty darkness stained by the ever-present venting fires. Between the clouds and wisps of smoke, two moons floated over the Wyrm Valley. In Enthilen, they had names for the moons: Seena and Bargan. But in Karlik, clouds often masked the moons' presence, and when they did appear, the leaden pall of venting fire smoke dulled their sheen. Consequently, Curmudgles never considered the moons worthy of names.

"Where are we going?" asked Casca.

I faced him. "I thought you'd know."

He smiled. "I'm not a soothsayer."

"We'll go to the Statutoria. I want to register Jolia as a missing person. Are you sure she wasn't home?"

"Not when Yula and I visited. We made quite a racket."

"Why are you helping me? I mean, why do you care?"

"You were worried about your friend. Yula was worried about you. I worry about everyone."

I rolled my eyes at Casca, then strode towards Karlik's Ionad Precinct, the broken wagon wheel of buildings surrounding the Governant.

* * * * *

While the Restoria façade radiated a unique, eccentric warmth, the Statutoria projected hard, angular impost. In Karlik's early days, when settlers battled over the mining rights to serpent oil pits, peace officers had their hands full. Owing to the wildness of colonisation, our ancestors built the Statutoria before any other major construction. It had five floors with a standing line of twelve phallic columns running the length of the sandstone building to the top of the second floor. Nowadays, the upper floors were vacant, and the windowless, airless gaol in the basement rarely used. Barick told me it hadn't been full in more than a generation.

I climbed the Statutoria's front steps, Casca in tow, and offered a hesitant, hopefully unsuspicious nod to the peace officer guarding the steel doors. She didn't acknowledge me, staring off into the city's muted hues as if crime might spring from the shadows.

I pulled on the door handle and almost broke a finger as my hand yanked back, and the door didn't budge. I gripped the handle tighter, braced my feet on the steps and pulled again. Unoiled hinges groaned at me, a comical irony in Karlik, and the door heaved open.

As soon as we entered, we stood in front of a timber counter half a body taller than me. Behind iron bars embedded into the countertop sat a male peace officer, scowling down at us with judgement already passed.

"Where are the doorkeepers?" I asked.

"Gone home," the peace officer grumped. "It's late. Are you infected?"

"No," I said, brushing flecks of ash-snow off my coat, then shaking out my hat and gloves and shoving them in a coat pocket. I pulled a horsehair brush from my satchel and swept it over Casca's filthy clothes.

"I'll have to clean that floor," complained the peace officer.

"We're here to see Warden Mulburat," I called up to him.

He sat in silent contemplation for a moment, then turned his gaze to Casca before returning to me.

"Appointment?" he asked.

"*Ah, no,*" I stumbled. "I'm a friend of his son, Barick Pulson."

"Still need an appointment."

"Well, can I make an appointment?"

"Not for today."

"When?"

The officer opened the leather-bound cover of a ledger thicker than my forearm. As he flicked through the pages, the scrunch of parchment echoed around the entrance hall.

He stopped flicking and ran his eyes down the page. "Fourteen days."

My hope sagged. "Why so long?"

The officer ignored my distress. "Reason for the appointment?"

"It'll be too late then. My friend is missing."

"Missing mudgles is a different department. Go through that door, down the hall, second door on the left."

He closed the ledger and pointed to a doorway on our right. I stormed off, and Casca followed, down a corridor and into another office with seating in the reception area for five mudgles. Behind the chest-high counter sat Peace Officer Crooshka, the dreamy, caramel-haired prince that Jolia often swooned over.

This is good. He'll want to find Jolia.

Hovering behind Crooshka stood a female Voldari, the first time I'd seen a visitor up close. She wore the same frost-blue robes and pearl undershirt as her companions, her head covered in rats' tails grafted onto her skin. The tall, gangly visitor stared at me with an unsettling intensity, her snow-white complexion glistening like porcelain under the flicker of oil lamps.

I shuddered as I walked up to the desk, fixing my gaze on Crooshka. "I want to report a missing person."

"Another one?" he replied.

"What do you mean? I haven't reported one before."

"This will be our third today. Haven't had any for two yarles and now...."

The Voldari stepped forward, leaning over Crooshka's shoulder until the bizarre hairpiece dangled its tapering rats' tails down past her eyebrows. Her raisin eyes glazed with an obsidian transparency, resembling shadowed holes drilled into the skull, as she tilted her head towards Casca standing behind me.

Her eyes, the same colour as Casca's glasses.

"You a relative?" asked Crooshka.

I shook my shoulders to cast away the cloaking spell. "What? No. A friend. I'm her friend. You've seen us, haven't you? In the Governant food court. We often eat together at high sun. Jolia...." *Dreams about you. No, say something else.* "Jolia thinks highly of you."

"Who?"

"Jolia Sojule, the mudgle who's missing."

"You didn't tell me she was missing."

"That's what I'm here for. You know her, right? Blonde hair. Pale skin. Blue eyes."

The self-absorbed Crooshka shook his head. "We've never met, and I don't remember seeing her in the food court."

Jolia will be devastated. "It's not that important. She's missing. We need to find her."

Crooshka sighed, opened a drawer, pulled out a form, and slipped it over the counter to me. "Fill this in," he said, pulling a pencil from a tin cup and placing it on the form. "As much detail as you can. We'll investigate in coming days."

"Coming days? She's missing now."

"Expediting the process requires a submission from a family member. Does she have any family?"

"Her da'three. But he's in the Restoria." *Waiting to die.*

"You'll have to do." Officer Crooshka pushed the form closer to me.

I took it and walked back into the reception area. The Voldari observer stepped away from the counter but continued her silent inspection of our presence.

With all five seats occupied by mudgles, I leaned against the wall and flicked through the pages of the missing person's form. It would take an hour to complete, if not longer. Casca wandered around the room, navigating the gaps between the seated mudgles. He stopped in front of an open cabinet, reached up and grasped the handle of a rusted sword slotted into a display rack.

The blind boy pirouetted in place and pointed the sword's tip at the Voldari.

"Hoi!" called Crooshka. "Put that back. It's an antique."

Casca smiled and returned the weapon before wandering over to me and turning his back to the counter. "Do you know where the warden's office is?" he whispered.

"I've been there with Barick," I whispered back.

"We're wasting time here. These peace officers couldn't find a snowflake in a blizzard. And that Voldari is making me uncomfortable."

"How do you know she's there?"

"I can hear her breath. Rasps of vile intent."

"You have the most morose outlook of anybody I've met."

"If you'd experienced what I've experienced, you'd consider me optimistic."

I shook my head at Casca and returned to completing the form. Crooshka and his Voldari companion left the reception area.

"Come on," I whispered, tucking the form into my satchel and pulling Casca through another doorway.

As we walked down the corridor holding hands, I tried not to step too quickly, balancing the need to appear confident in our purpose, but not linger in a place we didn't belong. A warden approached, dressed in admiral blue with gold buttons, but she passed by without so much as a blink.

We came to Warden Mulburat's closed office door. I released Casca's hand and knocked.

"Enter."

I opened the door and walked in with Casca.

Seated behind his desk, Warden Mulburat looked up and squinted with suspicion or confusion. The black hair on his cheeks and head had been trimmed, accentuating a drooping moustache and plaited beard that reached his chest.

"Pipe," said the warden.

"Sorry," I started. "I don't...."

"Pipe," Warden Mulburat said again. "Behind you."

I turned to face a set of shelves.

"Third shelf from the bottom," directed Mulburat. "Pipe and pouch of bunbili leaf."

On the shelf, I found a clay pipe the length of my hand beside a leather pouch. I squeezed the leather, feeling the soft crunch of leaf through my fingertips, then picked up the pouch and pipe and carried them to Barick's da'one.

"I'm Silveny," I said as I held the smoking implements towards him.

"I know who you are," replied the warden.

Sleepy brown eyes widened, raising unruly eyebrows as he snatched the pipe and leaf from me. Thick, dark-skinned fingers fumbled with the pouch's drawstring until he pulled it open, took out a pinch of leaf and dropped it into the pipe's bowl. He discarded the pouch, grabbed a pencil nub, and pressed the leaf down.

"Not too tight, not too loose," he mumbled before pinching another fall of leaf and repeating the process. He dropped the pencil and patted the pockets of his blue jacket. "Firesticks?"

"I don't have any," I said.

"Must be here somewhere." He opened a desk drawer, then slammed it shut. Opened another one. Slammed shut. "Damn firesticks. Where are they?"

Casca forced a box of firesticks into my hand.

"I have some," I said, placing the box on the desk.

Warden Mulburat squinted again. "Thought you said you didn't?"

He took a firestick from the box and dragged it across a piece of strike paper on his desk. It lit the first time, and he smiled before holding the flame to the bunbili leaf packed into his pipe. He sucked on the mouthpiece until wisps of smoke drifted between the needle-like braids at the edges of his moustache. Shaking the firestick out, he dropped it in a tin, leaned back in his chair and took a deep drag.

"Nothing better than a good pipe to finish the day," said Mulburat through an exhale of smoke. "Now," he pointed the pipe's tip at us, "who in damnation are you?"

"I'm Silven...."

"Wait. What's wrong with that boy?"

I turned to Casca, then back to Mulburat. "*Ah*, nothing."

"Take off those glasses," ordered the warden.

"It's not necessary," I started, but couldn't finish before Casca removed his obsidian lenses.

"Mountain spirits save us from abomination," exclaimed Mulburat. "What happened to you?"

Casca stood exposed, the crimson savagery of his eyeless left socket screaming terror, and the fogged whiteness of his right eye masking all those secrets I knew waited to be discovered.

"An unfortunate accident," said Casca.

"He's blind," I interrupted. "Well, I think he is."

"You *think*?" queried Mulburat.

"No, yes, he is. Blind. And he's homeless and without family here."

"Where are you from?" the warden asked Casca, blowing smoke in the boy's face as if it carried the question to his ears.

Casca coughed at the affront. "Everywhere and nowhere, and everywhere in between. That weed you're smoking will kill you."

I kicked Casca in the shin. "Sorry. His manners are lacking. I'm looking after him for now. His name's Casca. I'm putting him on the next caravan to leave for Morskoy."

"You can try," Casca whispered under his breath.

Warden Mulburat sighed. "Bunbili leaf or ash-snow. One of them will kill me. I know which one is more pleasurable." He waved the pipe at Casca. "Put the glasses back on; you look hideous. Why are you in my office without an appointment?"

"A friend of mine is missing," I said. "Jolia Sojule."

"So-jul-a, So-jul-a. That name sounds familiar."

"Barick knows her."

"Barick doesn't know squat. But he is my son. My burden." He trailed off, then pointed the tip of his pipe at the door. "There's a missing person's dept...."

"We've come from there," interrupted Casca. "They couldn't find the haystack, let alone the needle."

The warden coughed up a clump of phlegm and swallowed it. "What's he talking about?"

"They'll take too long to find Jolia," I said. "Days, and we don't have days. I hoped you could speed things along."

"I'm not Eminent Gardia," blustered Mulburat. "I'm not even a chief-warden, though it's damn long past time I should be."

"You should definitely be a chief-warden," cooed Casca. "Your insight is remarkable."

Mulburat squinted again.

I changed the subject before the squint became wide-eyed recognition. "Jolia is my friend and Barick's friend. Her da'three is a patient in the Restoria. Jolia hasn't visited him in two days, and she never misses work."

The warden coughed and waved smoke from his face. "Hasn't been gone long. Nowhere else she might go?"

I shook my head.

"She's been taken," said Casca. "Abducted."

"That's a serious accusation," spluttered Mulburat. "Abducted by who?"

Casca shrugged.

"Don't need to be talking about abductions. That's a mess of extra work no-one wants. There could be many explanations for her absence. Had enough of Karlik, for one. Tired of this infernal cold. Wanted to see a tree. Smell the ocean. Maybe someone saw her leave on a balloon?"

"She'd never abandon her da'three," I said. "Or quit the Inventoria without telling me."

"There have been others," said Casca. "Three reported missing today, according to the fools working in your Department of Irrecovery."

Warden Mulburat sat forward and relit his waning pipe. He puffed a waft of stale smoke, pierced by brown eyes that had set hard. "Not only three," he rumbled with an unexpected seriousness. "Five so far. Six, if we count your friend...."

"Jolia," I said. "Jolia Sojule."

"All taken," said Casca.

"But where?" asked the warden. "Why and by whom?"

"Barick heard calls for help in the mine," I said. "But he saw only the shadow of a man."

Mulburat squinted again. "A man shadow?"

"Tall, dark...."

"Not handsome," interrupted Casca.

"Frightening," I finished.

"He didn't speak to me about this," said the warden.

"He's embarrassed he got lost. Thinks he imagined it all. What if he didn't? What if someone is holding mudgles prisoner in the mine?"

"This man shadow? Why would he do that?"

Shadow Man. I don't know.

The heat from the oil fire in the warden's office sent rivers of sweat down between my breasts, and I thought I'd pass out. I bowed my head and fiddled with the buttons on my coat, twisting a button one way and then the other. I moved my sleeve down and up, up and down, down and up, up and down. Casca clutched my fidgeting hand and held it still.

Warden Mulburat tapped the open bowl of his pipe on the cedar desk until flecks of blackened, expired leaf collected in a pile. He swept the pile into his palm, pressed a finger against the left nostril and snorted the remnants up his right.

"Did he...?" asked Casca.

I couldn't comprehend an answer.

The warden herked more mucus and spat it into the oil fire. The globule sizzled on the perforated pipes, and I wanted to vomit.

"Look," said Mulburat, "I'll ask a chief-warden to prioritise your friend. What's her name?"

I've told you twice already. "Jolia Sojule."

"And you are?"

"Silveny," I sighed. "Silveny Belarose."

"The one and only Casca," said Casca.

The warden glared at the blind boy. *Pointless*, I wanted to say.

"Return to the missing mudgle department," said Mulburat. "Fill out the form and hand it over. I'll follow up on it personally. Now, it's time for my fire-rum."

Casca and I returned to complete the missing mudgle form, but my confidence in the Statutoria finding Jolia had been sapped. No missing mudgles in two yarles and now a flood of them. I doubted the peace officers would know where to start.

I convinced myself of something, then Casca spoke my thought aloud.

"The answer lies in the mine," he said.

I nodded. "You're right. We need Barick to show us where he got lost."

Chapter 10

Another venture into darkness

"**S**ilveny! Look at the wildflowers."

Jolia skipped across the foot of Mt Neasa, dancing among the quilt of flowers like an alpenbee skimming blooms for nectar. Lugging a basket of food, I jogged after her, trying to keep up.

She stopped and faced me with a beaming smile, holding her hand aloft. A meander butterfly had alighted on her finger, opening and closing its wings of golden toffee to flash the whites of fake eyes designed to deter would-be predators.

"It's beautiful," Jolia announced, then laughed when the butterfly flew and landed on the tip of her nose.

I laughed, too, giddy with the wonder around us. Grass-pipits flitted from one clump of rabbet-sedge to another. Fluffy, round alpenbees bumbled among the flowers, trying to beat the butterflies to the sweetest treasures. A finger-long heath snake slithered under a rock, possibly a tiny ancestor of the enormous serpents who once called the Wyrm Valley home.

As I stepped over a rivulet of meltwater that ran like a vein into Karlik, supplying water not polluted with ash-snow, a bearded bullfrog called, heralding a welcome or warning. Jolia had moved on, walking towards a ridge framed by an iridescent blue sky brushed with wisps of clouds that vanished across the mountains like escaped dreams.

"Will this do?" she called over her shoulder.

I trotted up to her. She'd found a flat ledge cushioned with moss patchworked in green, yellow and tangerine.

"It's perfect," I said, putting the basket down.

Jolia unshouldered a blanket roll, untied the cinching cord and laid the blanket over the moss. "It's a shame to squash this lovely underlay."

"Better than sore butts." I began to unpack the food from the basket.

Jolia wandered off, then hovered above a mountain pool. "There's a fish! How did it get all the way up here?"

I stopped unpacking and walked over to her. At the bottom of a crystal pool sat a hand-sized creature with silvery skin, fins at the front and bowed legs at the rear.

"It's an alpen-glaxia," I announced.

"A what?"

"Cross between a fish and frog."

"Can we eat it?"

"It's too small."

"I'm going to catch it." Jolia crouched down and sprang forward like a giant glaxia. She plunged her hand into the pool, then cried, "It's freezing!"

I chuckled. "Are you surprised?"

The alpen-glaxia swam to the surface, climbed on a rock and jumped from the pool, landing under the gnarled branches of a hemleaf bush.

Jolia lay on her front and prised the branches apart. She reached in and grabbed, then stood, triumphantly raising her hand. "I got it!" But the glaxia squirmed from her grip and dropped down the front of her tunic. "Ahhh, it's inside me." Jolia danced in place, patting her clothes.

"Careful," I laughed, "you'll squash it."

She removed the tunic, the glaxia clinging to the bottom of her undergarment. I went to catch it, but it sprang into another pool.

"You win, little frog-fish," said Jolia.

"I was never going to eat a raw glaxia, anyway. Raw anything."

"Not even a leg each?"

I shook my head and returned to the blanket, sitting down and emptying the basket.

Jolia sat beside me. "I should have brought something."

"I wanted to do this as a thank you for welcoming me to the Inventoria."

"Vyrin or Rula weren't going to do it. Drudan is always busy, and the

others are consumed by their next invention."

"I hope I can invent something."

She reached across and clasped my hand. "You will, soon. Don't pressure yourself."

I blushed at her touch, trying not to stare at the nipples pushing against the thin cotton undergarment.

"Aren't you cold?" I asked.

Jolia shrugged. "On days like this, I only need the warmth of the sun and good company."

She took her hand away, and I nearly grabbed for it. Nearly.

"What did you bring?" she asked.

"The bread was a disaster. I rushed this morning."

Jolia heaved the loaf from the basket like it was a rock. "I see what you mean."

We laughed together.

"I'm sure it's not that bad." She placed the bread on the blanket. "You've brought fruit. Blomgarnet. Apples. Raisin-berries. Where did you get this from?"

"A trader from Wardcha braved Death's Pass to bring his cart laden with fruit down into Karlik. Sold out in a day. I got in early."

Jolia plucked raisin-berries from the bunch and tossed them into her mouth. "Hmmm. Almost fresh. He must have hiked up those mountains at a cracking pace."

"Used a harfhorse to pull his cart, not a woollydon. Said it was quicker."

"Cheese. Pickled pargus. What's in the bottle?"

"Meduz."

"Are you trying to get me drunk?"

"N-n-no," I stammered, then flicked nervous fingers across the studs of my leather skirt. "It's probably flat anyway."

"I'll still drink it. We could forage for finberries. They'd be ripe now."

I screwed up my face. "They're so sour."

"Wash them down with meduz, and you won't notice."

Jolia took a paring knife and hacked a corner off the cheese wedge. "Ow," she cried, dropping the knife and jamming her finger in her mouth. "Cut myphself."

"Is it deep?"

She pulled the finger out and held it towards me.

"Looks alright. Might bleed a little."

"I always cut myself when sharpening pencils at work."

"Hmm." My mind turned, thinking how I could invent a safer way to sharpen pencils. A trivial thing, but best to start there rather than try to solve all of Karlik's problems in a day.

"Stop working," scolded Jolia. "It's a rest day. Let's enjoy the view."

She sucked on her finger while I took a cutting board from the basket and used the paring knife to slice cheese. Then I uncorked the jar of pickled pargus, ripped off chunks of bread and squashed cheese and pargus into bite-sized, doughy saddles.

Jolia removed her finger and scooped up a bread chunk. "Tastes good," she mumbled. "Better than my finger, at least."

I poured two cups of meduz – flat as expected. Jolia didn't complain, washing the bread down with a gulp. I chewed a cheese-pargus saddle, the sweet pickle making up for my failed baking.

Jolia inhaled. "Wildflower Flush is amazing. So many perfumes. So many colours. Like a rainbow fallen to earth."

"It's my favourite season."

"But there's another world outside this valley, one I've never seen." She faced me and smiled. "We could explore it together. A visit to see what it's like. Catch a balloon to the ridgetop and hitch a ride with a merchant to Morskoy or Revelé. Buy a horse…or, or a tufted goliath and ride to Ephesus."

I chuckled. "That would take forever, and we can't afford a tufted goliath or a horse. Or pay for lodging and food."

"You'd like to go, though, wouldn't you? You'd like to see what the rest of Ostamp has to offer? Then there are all those lands across the oceans. Ones we've never heard of."

"If you've never heard of them, how do you know they exist?"

"Your da'one was in the Literati. He'd know."

I nodded. "You're right. Beyond Ostamp's borders are other lands. The barbarians that settled Nordland came from some of them."

"Doesn't your imagination run wild thinking about what we'll discover?"

"I haven't even discovered my first invention. I need to stay here and focus. Make the most of my current life, not dream of another life elsewhere."

"Fun spoiler."

Jolia sat up and tickled my ribs. I laughed and tried to push her hand away, but she dodged my deflection and continued her tickle attack. We laughed together. Fell backwards and rolled on the blanket, knocking over the cups of meduz. Jolia's pale skin felt like a silk sheet, and her hair smelled of rosemary and vervain. She'd braided it today, a hasty effort of loose plaits.

We untangled ourselves and mopped up the drinks with a handcloth. After eating most of the food, we lay together in the sun and dozed. Jolia rolled closer to me and draped her arm across my waist. Warm and secure, I let my dreams explore landscapes my waking self may never see.

When I woke, Jolia had gone. I sat up to scan the wildflower meadows. On the western ridge of Mt Neasa, Jolia's silhouette walked into the setting sun.

"Where are you going!?" I yelled after her. She kept walking.

I pulled on my boots, stood and chased after her. The pursuit burned my muscles as every footfall felt like a brick tied to my sole. The landscape dulled, the flowers turning their faces inwards and bowing closed heads. The low heath and prickly grass scratched at bare shins.

"Jolia!" I called out, but she disappeared over the ridge with the sinking sun.

* * * * *

The night after our visit to the Statutoria, another day gone when Jolia hadn't come to work despite the pleading hope of the memory of wildflower meadows, Yula, Barick, Gallan, Casca, and I hid behind an icy boulder, watching the entrance to the mine where Barick had seen Shadow Man. Although mudgles called it a mine, it resembled the mouth of a cave. Barick said it led to a maze of tunnels; some natural, others excavated by miners in search of serpent oil. Half-a-dozen workers stood outside the entrance, warming themselves near a flaming gas vent. They smoked bunbili leaf rolled in fine paper and drank black ale, passing a small wooden barrel among themselves and opening the tap directly above their mouths.

"This is a bad idea," moaned Barick. "If they catch us breaking into the mine, I'll lose my job."

"We're not breaking in," I said. "We're visiting."

Barick's caged snergul, Sneckle, turned its pointed snout to the clear, frosty night sky and barked at the two moons floating overhead.

"*Sssh*," admonished Barick. "You'll give us away." His boyish eyes whimpered at me. "Why did I let you talk me into this?"

"I'm wondering the same thing," said Gallan. "There better be a story here."

"Jolia is still missing," I said. "So are other mudgles. And Barick heard calls for help in the mine."

"That could have been anyone," said Barick.

"What about Shadow Man?"

Barick averted his eyes and fiddled with the cage's handle. "I don't know. I could have imagined it all."

Gallan scoffed. "*Now* you're having second thoughts. I should be in *The Dragon Bellows*, drinking ale and trying my chances with Rosy the waiter."

"You'd have better luck with Horu," said Yula.

Gallan smiled. "I'm not picky."

"Concentrate," I snapped. "How do we get into the mine?"

"You're fixated on this one explanation, Silveny, like you fixate on other things. There might be another reason for Jolia's absence."

I squeezed the handle of Philomine Belarose's long knife tucked under a belt that cinched my coat tight around my waist. My great, great grandmother would agree that I shouldn't stab Gallan with the knife, but his casual doubt and penetrating, honest observation about my compulsion taunted me.

I pierced him with words instead. "This is the only lead I have. If you don't want to help, if you don't want to find Jolia, then go home."

Gallan raised his gloved hands in deference.

Barick pointed at Casca. "Why do we have the blind boy with us?"

"You'll be glad I'm here if we get lost in a dark tunnel," said Casca.

"None of you have to be here," I grumbled. "I'll find my own way in and search for Jolia."

"You won't get past the miners," said Barick.

"Are they *guarding* the entrance?" asked Gallan.

"Sort of. They're entrance attendants, checking who enters and leaves the mine. Since the Eminents accepted the Voldari order for serpent oil, pit bosses have become stricter, ensuring all extracted oil is accounted for. And they've rostered on extra night shifts. I'm not meant to be here tonight, and you're not miners, so we look suspicious." Barick's whimpering eyes turned doubtful. "I'm not sure I can find the correct tunnel again."

"Great," huffed Yula. "We should let Casca lead us. He can probably hear Jolia's heartbeat."

"If she's in that mine," said Casca, "I'll find her."

A stout harfhorse, the saddle of its back no taller than a mudgle, lumbered from the mine. Steam wafted from its sweat-drenched skin as the chill night air took hold. The poor creature staggered forward, muzzle almost touching the ground, harnessed to a cart laden with six wooden barrels full of oil. Behind the cart stalked a Voldari, her crown masked by a furred hat.

"Why is that Voldari here?" asked Gallan.

"To control Karlik," said Casca.

Barick shook his head. "They're keeping an eye on their investment."

"Don't be fooled," said Casca. "The Voldari seek more than oil. They're a zealous religious cult with limited influence in Kogot."

"Are they planning rebellion?" I asked. "An invasion of Karlik?"

"I don't know. But we should find out."

"Is Kogot a big city?" asked Gallan.

"Once, it was the largest in Ostamp," said Casca. "And the most powerful, even more than Pergamos in its prime. But the climate changed. The north grew colder. Kogot withered like the last flower in a snow-covered meadow."

"We don't have time for a history lesson," grumped Yula. "If we can't enter the mine, I'm going home."

"There's a side entrance," said Barick. "A barred gate. Padlocked."

My shoulders slumped. "You didn't mention a padlock."

"You said, 'Take me to the mine,' so here we are. I didn't expect to be breaking in."

"These mines must all be connected," said Gallan. "If we enter another one, we'll find our way to the right tunnel eventually."

"We'll get lost," said Barick.

"I brought this," said Yula, pulling a bolt cutter from her rucksack.

My sister, always prepared. "Will that do it?" I asked Barick.

He shrugged. "Probably."

"Let's at least try."

"This is the blind leading the blind," said Casca.

Barick snuck ahead, and I followed. Gallan clumped behind me, and Yula slouched at the back, Casca following her. We made little noise traipsing through shin-high snow. A cliff owl hooted in the distance, a wail on the far wind.

Yula pushed up to me. "How long are we keeping the boy?"

"We don't own him," I replied.

"Ask him to leave. We can't afford to feed him."

"He doesn't eat much and appears to know more than all of us combined about...."

"About what? What exactly is *this*?"

"First, we have to find Jolia."

"It won't be your last challenge," said Casca, who'd sidled up to us. "Certainly not your hardest. And I don't require your food. I can look after myself."

Hiking above the venting fires at night, we risked attack from a horned wolf. I'd never seen one, other than a sculpture in the Artary and pictures in books. I tapped my fingers against the long knife's bulbous pommel, wondering if Philomine Belarose's weapon could slay a wolf.

Across snow drifts, shifted and shaped by the wind, we approached a jagged rockface of grey slate and granite, illuminated by the nearly full two moons. At the cliff's foot, a barred gate no larger than a house door, with snow piled up to half its height, had been bolted into the stone.

"Why is this here?" I asked Barick.

"Emergency exit."

"But it's padlocked from the outside."

He glanced at me and shrugged.

When we reached the gate, I began to clear away the snow. Yula helped while Gallan whistled to himself. Barick stood shivering, the caged Sneckle trembling along with her keeper's cold. Or fear. Casca looked to the moons.

Well, not 'looked,' I guess. Honestly, I don't know what he's doing.

With the snow cleared, Yula placed the blades of her bolt cutter around the padlock's shackle and squeezed. She strained and cursed and barely made a mark, retreating to catch her breath.

I yanked at the padlock. "This won't work."

Yula pushed me away and tried again, her olive face turning redder than a venting fire. But the padlock wouldn't yield.

"Well," said Gallan, "tavern time."

"Wait," said Casca. "I have something given to me by a mouldewerp."

"A what?" asked Barick.

"*Moulde*-werp. They live in Enthilen. Little furry creatures no taller than my thigh. But very intelligent. One gave me a special key."

"Why didn't you tell us before?" I asked.

"I wanted to see how strong Yula was."

"Give me the key."

"Please. Let me do it. It's important to continually test my mind's acuity. Otherwise, I truly will be blind."

I guided Casca to the padlock. He removed a glove and brushed the lock with his fingers, then felt the key's bit. "Should work." He inserted the key, turned, and the lock popped open. "*Voila!*"

"Vo-what?" asked Gallan.

"Word from another language."

We opened the gate and followed Casca into a pitch-dark cave. Barick put Sneckle on the ground and unshouldered and uncinched his rucksack. He brought out an oil lantern, box of firesticks and strike paper. After lighting the lantern, he shouldered his pack and led us down a tunnel, carrying the caged snergul in the opposite hand. I expected the mines to be better lit, then questioned when this emergency exit was last used. The suffocating blackness set my compulsion yearning for a task. Yula gasped, and I wanted to tell her to shut up. Gallan tramped along, dragging his shorter leg with the thick-soled boot. Sneckle growled warily. Only Casca made no noise.

We turned a corner.

"*Aah,*" I cried, swiping at my head. "Something flew at me."

"Cave moth," said Barick. "Probably."

"Moth? It was as big as a bird."

"Are there spiders in these tunnels?" asked Yula. "I hate spiders."

"Don't worry," said Barick, "Sneckle will eat them. The non-poisonous ones, at least."

"I'm worried about the other ones."

A muffled clang of metal on metal echoed down the tunnel, followed by the whinny of a harfhorse. A miner shouted, "Vent fire!" and an amber glow lit up ahead.

Barick stopped dead. "Hold back. We'll wait until the night-workers pass. Halfway down the main tunnel is where I got lost. I think."

"Think?" said Gallan.

"I can't remember exactly."

We stayed silent, the noises of the mine crew moving their harfhorse and oil cart down another tunnel keeping us company, along with a raft of questions floating around my head. *What's up ahead? Is Jolia being held prisoner? Why? Is she here at all? Gallan's right. I've fixated on this explanation for Jolia's absence. I've decided she's in the mines and needs saving, and only we can do it. I could be wrong. All this could be wrong.*

The mine's stifling gloom sent beads of sweat dripping into my eyes. We all pocketed our furred hats and gloves. I wanted to stash my coat, but worried I'd lose it.

Barick waved us forward, and we followed him into another tunnel lit by lanterns hung from steel braces holding up the roof.

"This is the main tunnel," he said.

We crept down the passage, shuffling boots across a stone floor layered with dirt and soot. Lanterns above us swung with a cloying waft of air, their fiery light skittering across the rockface like the spiders Yula hated. The walls and roof closed in around me. I'd been caught in a web of my own making. Snared by my compulsion.

We passed an oil pit the size of a dining table. The iron dome fixed over the pit creaked and groaned, the rivets that kept it whole threatening to pop, one by one, letting metal sheets peel back before an explosion of boiling black sludge burned us to death.

Trapped underground, with threats around every corner, I thought about my lost parents. *Did they die straight away? Or were they buried under ice and snow, still able to breathe? Still alive with hope that rescuers might find them, until the hope slowly suffocated.*

Barick hurried past the oil pit as if he also expected an explosion at any moment. We followed. The tunnel forked, and he took the left passage. We still followed, but I worried he'd get us lost.

At another fork, Barick turned right.

Casca tugged on my sleeve. "Can you smell it?"

I shook off the doubt. "I smell musty dirt and oil."

"No. Something else. Very unusual."

He pushed ahead, brushing Barick aside and feeling along the left-hand tunnel wall. He turned a corner. We scampered after him, but when we rounded the corner, Casca had vanished. I backtracked, investigating the same wall as Casca until my arm disappeared into space.

"There's a crevice," I said.

I squeezed through the narrow gap and tripped over Casca lying on the ground.

"Stepped on a rock," he mumbled, getting up and brushing himself off.

"This can't be the entrance," said Gallan, standing on the other side of the crevice. "I'll struggle to get through. Yula definitely won't. Barick, is this right? You didn't say anything about such a narrow opening."

Barick wavered in his boots, pushed back and forth by indecision. Perched on an iron rod spanning the cage, Sneckle rocked to and fro in time with her warden.

"I think...." started Barick. "I don't remember such a narrow entrance, but the rock has shifted. Wait...." On the ground, he kicked up a frayed length of rope. "I remember getting tangled in rope like this."

"Come on," I said. "You'll fit, Barick."

He handed me Sneckle and the lantern, then turned sideways, squeezing his body through the crack. Gallan tried next, thrusting one arm into the crevice and driving his legs forward. But he stumbled, his chest jamming between the rocks.

Barick grabbed Gallan's arm and pulled. "Push with your feet."

"I'm trying," said Gallan, his face turning redder than his hair. He groaned until a hole tore across his woollen coat, and he fell forward, almost taking Barick down with him.

Alone on the other side of the gap, Yula glanced up and down the tunnel, fearful someone might come.

"Try Yula," I said.

She shook her head. "I'll never get through. I'm too big."

"You'll have to stay in the tunnel," said Gallan.

"I'm not staying here by myself."

Barick took the snergul from me and handed the cage to Yula. "Take Sneckle. She'll keep you company and warn of any gas leaks."

"How?"

"By passing out. Or worse."

"What if there's a leak?"

"Get out. As quick as you can."

We left Yula in the main tunnel. Barick held his lantern high, and we walked on into the dimness, Casca leading the way, sniffing as he went. The air in the passage warmed, cloaking us in a sickly sweet smell like burnt toffee. Sweat trickled from my armpits. Gallan's breaths laboured, his throat rasping along with the drag of his clumpy boot on the dirt floor.

Around a corner, shadows peeled from grey to tangerine, and a slap of hot air hit my face. Casca stopped and raised his hand. He turned to us and put an index finger to his lips. *Silence.* Then he waved us forward.

We joined the blind boy on a ledge overlooking a cave with a pool of bubbling lava, explosions of red-orange and yellow-white bursting through a black crust. If the fall from the ledge didn't kill us, the scalding lava would. A tripod had been positioned above the pool, a pulley hanging from its apex, and a steel cable running off to the side and connected to a metal harness fixed to the cave wall. It resembled a strange and inefficient way to mine serpent oil.

We ducked behind a boulder when someone walked from the shadow of a passage leading into the cave. A man, tall and gaunt with a slick, leaden coat down to his shins and cinched at the waist, and thick, unruly hair masking his face.

Shadow Man?

I spun around to ask Barick, but he'd retreated into the passageway, keeping the lantern light from spilling over the ledge. Gallan clutched my shoulder, the tremble of his hand forcing my eyes forward.

Shadow Man, I concluded with some doubt, stopped beside the lava pool and faced the passage from where he'd come. Out walked a Voldari, almost naked except for a skirt around his waist and black feathers and fur attached to his head. He tugged on a chain, pulling behind him a shackled mudgle, who staggered forward as if her legs had been beaten with a hammer.

Jolia? I wanted to cry out. I wanted to jump from the ledge, swoop down and save her. I wanted to do something.

But Casca squeezed my arm. "No," he said. Simple. Stern. Effective. *It's not Jolia.*

"I recognise that Voldari," whispered Gallan. "His name's Hor-gnasher. Black Griffin."

"What's going on?" asked Barick behind us.

"Quiet," I hissed at him.

The Voldari led the mudgle like a butcher leads an animal to slaughter. He stopped at the metal harness and unlocked the chain and shackles.

Run, I urged the prisoner. *Now's your chance.* But she collapsed to her knees and bowed her head.

"What do you see?" whispered Casca.

"A man," I said. "I can't see his face, even when he turns this way. A Voldari with a beaked nose."

"A beak, grafted to his nose," interrupted Gallan.

"And a mudgle. I don't recognise her. The Voldari is lifting her into a harness. Strapping her in."

Hor-gnasher walked the compliant mudgle to the edge of the lava pool, bowed to Shadow Man and stepped back. The man turned the handle of a winch, and the steel cable tightened, the harnessed mudgle swinging out over the pool.

"No," I whimpered. "She's suspended above the lava."

"Are there others?" asked Casca. "Other mudgles. Alive or dead."

"I can't see...wait...." In the dusk of the passage leading into the cave stood another stout figure of mudgle height. "At least one other. We have to save them."

"You can't."

Shadow Man locked the winch and reached for the suspended mudgle, grabbing her by the ankle. He pulled her leg out and bent it backwards until it snapped. Gallan gasped. I bit my tongue, and blood seeped into my mouth, flowing as freely as the tears down Gallan's cheeks.

"He knows we're here," sobbed Gallan. "He knows."

"What?" cried Barick. "What's happening?"

Shadow Man took the other leg and bent it the same way.

'Snap!'

The horrid facture echoed around the cave. Vomit burned my throat. The Voldari chanted in his strange, merciless language. Shadow Man grasped the winch handle, unlocked the teeth and lowered the naked, broken mudgle towards the lava pit. He paused, suspending her a fraction above boiling death and seeming to enjoy the expectation, then dunked her in.

From that point, everything happened so fast I can't remember it all.

I jumped from behind the boulder and yelled, "NO!"

Shadow Man winched the mudgle from the lava, her body covered in a grey ash that had set like stone. The Voldari stopped chanting and looked up, the feathers fixed to his forehead twitching, ready to take flight. The other mudgle stumbled out into the cave, and the shock wrenched the air from my lungs.

Jolia? Yes, it is. Jolia. "JOLIA!" I screamed.

Shadow Man glared at me with blazing eyes that laid waste to my soul.

Gallan pulled me away from the edge. "Don't let him inside."

Behind me, Barick wept.

I fell to my knees, sobbing. "Fight, Jolia. Please."

She didn't look at me. Instead, she faced Shadow Man and bowed her head. He locked the winch, leaving his macabre trophy in suspended animation, then pushed Jolia back into the passage. I considered jumping down to the cave. Calculating how I could miss the lava pool and not break any bones. Gallan held me tight, stopping my stupidity.

From another passage beside the ledge, footsteps pounded rock and dirt. A flaming torch peeled away the darkness, exposing Hor-gnasher in fearful flight.

"Run," ordered Casca. "If you value your life, run."

Gallan lifted me to my feet. The long knife tucked under my belt fell to the ground with a useless clang. I wanted to wield the weapon. I wanted to channel Philomine Belrose's ancestral strength and stab the Voldari monster in the chest. But the others ran. So, I ran with them.

Down the passage, Barick dropped the lantern, plunging us into darkness. But we kept running, crashing into tunnel walls and tripping over rocks. I greeted the bruises. They'd remind me of the betrayal. Abandoning Jolia. Leaving her to the demented whims of a demon.

I stumbled and staggered. Ran and fell. Steadied my feet and ran again. Somewhere in that black space, I lost touch with the others. Too frightened to call out. Too frightened Hor-gnasher would catch me. I couldn't think about Barick, Gallan or Casca now. I thought of survival. My own selfish life. Pushing ahead, running towards a welcoming guilt.

"Don't let my cripple kill you," called Gallan from behind me. "Keep going."

But I stopped at Gallan's plea.

"Silveny," shrilled Barick's voice up ahead. "Are you there?"

"I'm here," I replied. "Where's Casca?"

"I don't know."

A hand reached out and grabbed mine. "I've got you," said Barick.

Gallan's gasping, limping fear bumped into us.

"Hold hands," I said. "We go together."

Behind us, a flaming, searching light melted the darkness.

"Hor-gnasher is still coming," said Gallan.

We turned and stumbled forward, joined together by sweaty, clutching fingers. Up ahead, lantern light from the main tunnel pierced the crevice we'd squeezed through. The evil, gangling Voldari couldn't follow us through the narrow gap.

"Yula!" I called out.

We staggered on. The pursuing flame lessened. Safety beckoned. Yula stood in the tunnel, holding Sneckle.

Sneckle. What a stupid name. I almost laughed from the delirium.

Yula's strength pulled Gallan through the crack. I followed, then Barick. We had no time to explain things to my sister. No time to wait for Casca to appear. We told Yula to run as fast as she could.

We all ran.

Chapter 11

Roadblocks abound

paced around our home in manic circles. Once, twice, thrice. Stopped and pulled a washcloth from the basin and wrung it out above the drain. Twisted tight. Folded in quarters. Unfolded it. Wrung it out again. Five drops of water. Four. Three. *Mudgle broken and burned alive. Jolia next.* Folded the washcloth. Draped it over the basin. Uncorked the tea canister. Tipped the tea leaves on the bench. Took a spoon. Measured each spoonful exactly, sluicing the mounded tea by running a knife across the spoon's edges, and spooned the tea back into the canister. *Six spoonsful. Ten. Sixteen. Twenty-three. Shadow Man. Voldari. Evil. Run. If you value your life, run.*

Bed curtain bunched at one end. Pulled it across. Flattened the pleats with my hand. Made it straight. Neat. Ordered. Took a ruler and measured the distance between each pair of curtain rings. One delicant. Exact. Won't be even all the way. *Make it even! Silveny, make it right!* Bed sheet untucked. Pushed the sheet beneath the mattress with the ruler. Tight under. Flattened the creases. Paced the distance from the wall to the bedhead. From the wall to the foot of the bed. *Make it exact. Square. Casca missing. Jolia? Jolia's dead. Mudgles dead. Evil. Run.*

"Stop."

Noise. Disorder. Fear.

"Silveny. Please, stop."

Noise.

Yula pulled me to her chest. "Stop. You're delirious."

Delirious. Frenzied. Furious. Petrified, like the burned mudgle. I'm all those things.

Yula hugged like she wouldn't let go. She never hugged. Rarely made any physical contact.

"Jolia," I whispered before going limp in her arms.

I cried, Yula's strength carrying the burden of my distress. She lowered me to the bench seat and sat beside me, holding my hand. We leaned on each other. Sisters from different mothers. But blood sisters, nonetheless.

"Go to bed," I mumbled. "You have work."

"I won't sleep," said Yula.

My eyes drifted out of focus. "I don't know what I saw. In that mine. I don't know what it was."

"You saw Jolia in trouble. That's enough."

But Barick and Gallan said they didn't see her, and Casca is blind. And missing.

"They'll kill her," I sobbed. "She may be dead already."

"Barick will tell his father, Warden Mulburat. The Statutoria will investigate."

I shook my head. "Barick didn't see. Gallan...when we parted, he seemed *peculiar.*"

"I believe you, Silveny. About Jolia."

"I have to go," I said, releasing Yula's hand and standing. "To see Da'three Sircom."

"What good will that do?"

"I have to tell him about Jolia." I pulled my coat from the hook. "Why?"

Yula stood as if she'd block my path. As if she *didn't* believe me.

I buttoned my coat. Pulled on boots. "He should know about his daughter. About why she doesn't visit him."

As I laced my boots, Yula stepped in front of the door. "It will cause him more grief."

"I have to do it," I growled, pulling my laces as tight as they would go. Squeezing my feet to welcome the pain of life. "Please understand."

I stood, donned my furred hat, and then readied to push Yula aside.

Her broad shoulders relaxed. "At least let me come with you."

Two hours before sunrise, we left our house and entered an empty street void of answers. Karlik's venting fires had dimmed, freeing us from the ash-snow peril for at least a moment. On every street corner, I expected to see a Voldari waiting, ready to silence my voice lest someone believe the strangeness I held inside. But no-one braved the city in this chill hour, not even a Statutoria peace officer.

We arrived at the Restoria, changed into gowns and slippers, and approached the reception attendant. He ignored us, engrossed in a book about Germalian wind riders. We trudged down the corridor to the miners' ward, the misery of the news I had to deliver dragging on my feet. *What should I say to Jolia's only remaining parent? Will he believe the unbelievable?*

A single oil lamp lit the dark of the miners' ward, the stillness punctured by the ever-present coughs and groans. I sat on a stool beside Yohane Sircom's bed as he snored a rasping lullaby. Yula propped a chair against the wall and slumped into it, arms crossed, head dipped to her chest.

While I accepted the old miner lay on his deathbed, I wrestled with the idea of inflicting more distress with a wild story about shadow men scorching mudgles. About his daughter in peril. No doubt, he hoped to die before Jolia. No parent wishes to outlive their offspring. But life had cruelled Yohane Sircom, and I was life's messenger, about to explain how it had cheated him again.

I opened the bedside table's top drawer, finding charcoal sketches of Jolia and her mothers and fathers inside. I pulled out the parchments and arranged them on the bed, one hand-width apart and square to the bedside. *Five drawings.*

I tucked in the bed quilt, and Yohane stirred.

"I don't need more potions," he groaned.

"It's me. Silveny Belarose. Jolia's friend."

"Silveny?" He tried to sit up but slumped back down with a cough. "Why are you here?"

I placed my hand over his. He faced me with eyes glistening in a half-light ambivalent to condolence. I worried he'd feel the racing blood pulse through my fingers. Recoil at the guilty cold of my skin. Jolia remained lost to him. I'd come to confirm it. I'd come to admit I didn't save her.

Yohane nestled my hand between both of his, a warming comfort I didn't deserve. "You're not here this late to convey welcome news," he said. "Welcome news can always wait. Unwelcome news must be delivered immediately."

I slumped forward and wept. He rubbed the back of my hand. Yula carried her chair over and sat beside me. Da'three Sircom, Yohane, didn't seem to notice her, fixing his unyielding eyes on me.

"Jolia?" he whispered in an almost imperceptible, aching wheeze.

I nodded and cried, unable to put my emotions in order.

"She is dead," said Yohane.

I jolted upright. "We d-d-don't know. They...they had her in the mine."

"They?"

"Voldari," said Yula.

Yohane's face creased with confusion. "Who? What do they want with my daughter?"

"Nothing," I slobbered, hoping Yula wouldn't tell Yohane what I'd seen. He didn't need to hear that. *What* *does* *he need to hear? Silveny?*

"We couldn't save her," said Yula in a dispassionate, stony voice that'd be enough to quell Yohane's hopes.

I tried to rekindle the dying flame with a feverish splutter of words. "She was in danger. It's true, we couldn't save her right then in the mine. But there's still a chance. The Statutoria know. My friend, Gallan, will tell his ma'one, Eminent Stretten. The Governant will investigate. Hold the Voldari to account. Seek answers and...."

Yohane released my hand and sank back into the feather mattress.

"Jolia said you're a good friend. Kind. There's no need to protect my feelings. The hógdubh will take me soon. I'm almost gone. I didn't expect my daughter to leave first, but life's poetry is sometimes tragedy." He pulled the soiled quilt up under his chin. "Jolia was always a curious puck. But you can be too curious. Want to know too much. Protect yourself against curiosity, Silveny."

I shrivelled on the stool, head bowed, rocking back and forth between sadness and anger. My compulsion tapped the side of the chair. Fingers drumming in bursts of four. Feet shuffling. Four taps. Shuffle feet. Four taps. Shuffle. Four.

"Where is she?" rasped Yohane. "My Jolia."

Trapped. Dead. Killed by Shadow Man and the Voldari. Scorched alive in lava. Turned into a shell of rock-hard ash.

I lied to give him hope. "I'll go back for her. Search the mine and bring her home."

"Take her to Reilig Mountain," said Yohane. "Not the catacombs. That's for miners. Wrap her in a cerement and leave her at the funeral altar for the horned wolves and cliff vultures to return her to an earth that's given Curmudgles so much."

"Ye-y-yes," I bawled.

"I lost wives and husbands, and now my only daughter. I'm alone, but you're not, Silveny. You have a family." He glanced at Yula.

She nodded. "I'm Silveny's sister."

Yohane smiled. "Your da'one still lives?"

"Yes. But...."

"He l-l-lives in the mountains," I interrupted. "Away from Karlik."

"Go and see him," said Yohane. "Don't stay absent. One day, you will have no choice."

He descended into a coughing fit, rolling to the other side of the bed and leaning over to hack up another piece of his insides and donate it to the insatiable death pail. A healer entered the ward and bustled us away. I had no final words for Yohane. No last lie of hope. Nothing to ease his torment. He died that day, not long after we had spoken with him.

* * * * *

We arrived home at sunrise. Yula went to work on the balloon line, already late, leaving me alone in the house. I sat on the bench seat, clutching my hands together to stop them from fidgeting. But nothing could stop my compulsion. It sifted through the bedlam, trying to place my thoughts in a logical sequence. An unattainable alignment of perfection. One thought, words from the absent Casca, kept returning.

'If you value your life, run.' *Run where? All I know is here.*

I needed a distraction, but couldn't face Vyrin at the Inventoria Lab or Eminent Drudan to explain why Jolia wasn't at work again. I'd leave all the explaining to Warden Mulburat and the peace officers. Instead, I decided to go to the Inventoria basement to check on the model-maker's progress with my flying machine. If we had to escape Karlik, flying would be better than running.

I entered a basement room that looked like a whirlwind had hit it. Half-finished models were scattered across tables, discarded parts littering the floorstones like rocks after a landslide. Books spilled from shelves, a few clinging to the edge with broken spines. Tools rested in strange places. A hammer clung to a ceiling lantern by its claw. A drill stood upright on a table because its bit had been drilled into the sheet metal. A chisel protruded from a mouldy cake as if it would be used to cut a slice. Dust layered across the floor recorded the model-maker's footsteps, marking her paths of endeavour. Half-eaten food served as an enticement for sewer rats, their black, seed-like droppings advertising frequent and recent visits.

I stepped further into the room, knocking my head against the basket of a deflated model balloon hanging from the ceiling. It kick-started my thoughts on how to make order out of the mess. But the scene overwhelmed my compulsion. A rare defeat.

Zurta, the model-maker, rushed in from another room. "Hold this," she said, handing me a palm-sized wheel before disappearing into the bedlam.

"Eminent Drudan gave you my plans," I called out to her.

"Eminent who?" she called back.

"Eminent Drudan."

I think she muttered 'stiff old fool', but I couldn't grasp it. While Drudan *was* old, Zurta was the oldest female mudgle I knew. Inventors called her 'Granma'one', a rare title in Karlik because most females died before seeing grandpucks. Lately, an increasing number of females died during childbirth.

Zurta returned carrying a brass cylinder the size of her finger. "Hold this," she said and scampered off into another room.

"I can't...." I started. "What are you making?"

"Baking? No time for baking. Barely have time to eat."

"No, *ma-king*. Are you building a model?"

I followed her, hesitant to peer into the other room for fear of what I'd see.

Zurta met me at the doorway, carrying six cogs. "Always making models. It never ends. If you mudgles upstairs stop inventing things, I can have a rest. Hold these." She dumped the cogs into my hands, and I almost dropped the wheel and cylinder.

I joined her, necessity trumping worry, in a room almost as dark as the first. I cleared space on a workbench and put everything down, arranging the cogs in order of size. Then I gathered a dustpan, its handle jammed into the centre of a stale pie, preparing to clean house.

"What are you doing?" asked Zurta as she emerged from the dullness holding a bucket.

"Do you have a broom?" I said.

"Of course I have a womb. Never been used, though. Likely why I'm still here. Pucks are dangerous."

I sighed. "I said...oh, forget it."

Zurta swept her hand across the table, dumping everything she'd given me into the bucket before marching to another room.

I strode after her. "I've come about my flying machine. I was going to call it a cloud wagon, but Eminent Drudan told me to change the name. He should have given you the plans."

"Stiff old fool. Wait." Zurta stopped, and I almost ran into her. "*Crowd flagon.* That's a good idea. A flagon big enough to quench the thirst of an entire crowd." She put the bucket on the ground, pulled paper and pencil from her pocket and scribbled.

"Isn't that a barrel?" I asked.

She shook her head. "You're right. Stupid idea." She screwed up the paper and threw it on the ground. "Why did you invent it?"

"I didn't. I invented the cloud wagon."

Zurta squinted at me, grey eyes twinkling under bushy eyebrows that knitted into messy, unbraided brown hair at the sides of her face. "A wagon to carry clouds?" She picked up the bucket and walked off. "That's an even stupider idea."

"Not carry clouds," I said, scurrying after her. "It carries barrels of serpent oil. Or mudgles. Or any other supplies. Flies through the clouds without being attached to the balloon line."

"Call it something else. Less confusion."

"That's what Drudan said. But I haven't had time to...."

She stopped and rubbed her chin. "Sky wagon. No. Fly wagon. No. Wind carriage. I like that one. Sky ship? The amazing levitating dray? Flycart. Skycart! Call it that. Less confusion."

"Whatever we call it, you're supposed to be making a model. Eminent Drudan sent the plans."

"Stiff old fool," she said as we walked into yet another room.

This appeared to be the space where Zurta did most of her work, and it looked unexpectedly organised, with clear benchtops, tools in racks, and a roaring gas fire in the hearth. A snergul scuttled into the corner, and I jumped.

"Don't mind Willamay," said Zurta. "She finds parts for me in Karlik in exchange for spiders, roaches and other insects. Don't much like dealing with mudgles unless I have to."

In the middle of a bench sat a half-finished....

Skycart. I agree with Zurta. It's a better name. "It's here," I said.

She waved her hand dismissively. "Oh, that ridiculous thing. It's not going to work. Can't make a balloon big enough to accommodate carriage size, and if you don't have a good-sized carriage, what's the point?"

"You're making the carriage, the cart, out of metal. It's supposed to be timber. Meladoor, the light and pliable wood the barbarians use for their ships."

She dropped the bucket on the floor, the contents spilling onto the flagstones with a rattle and clang. Willamay shrieked and disappeared into a hole in the wall.

"Barbarians!?" cried Zurta. "Are they here? Have they finally come for me?"

"What? No. The plans clearly say meladoor timber. Did you read them?"

"Plans?"

"Eminent Drudan...."

Zurta flared her upper lip.

"I know," I said. "Stiff old fool. But I drew the plans. Put many days of work into them."

"I skimmed through them. But intuition is better than plans. Once I've seen the drawings, I know what to do."

I found my compulsively drawn and detailed plans rolled up and tossed in a waste basket. "They're here. You can't ignore them."

"Meladoor tree, did you say?"

I nodded.

"Rare timber in the mountains. How am I supposed to find that?"

"Can't you order it? From Morskoy or Revelé?"

"Would take half a yarle to arrive. How soon do you need this wagon for harvesting clouds?"

If you value your life, run. "The sooner, the better."

"Meladoor timber," said Zurta. "Mel-a-door. Wait here." She disappeared, back from where we'd come.

The snergul poked her head from the hole in the stone wall and sniffed. I found a jar of pickled spiders on the bench; palm-sized ones that live in caves. I uncorked the jar, grabbed a spider and held it towards Willamay. She sniffed again and crept from the hole, inching over to me. I crouched and held the spider closer. The snergul grasped a leg with its pin-like front teeth and tugged the arachnid from my fingers.

"Don't feed Willamay too much," said Zurta. "She'll get fat and lazy." She heaved a dust-covered model ship, as long as her torso, onto the workbench, the ship's broken masts and torn sails shuddering with the thud. "This is an ancient invention. Older even than that fool, Drudan. Built by mudgles who used to live in Morskoy before the lure of serpent oil trapped us here." She pointed to the bow. "Iron casing and prongs. *Icebreaker*. The real one could navigate a Nordargen Sea crusted with ice sheets. Before it sank."

As I marvelled at the model's detail, every square of rigging, every deck plank, cabins, holds, railings and windows in place, Zurta took a chisel and began prising it apart.

I cried, "You can't do that. That's our heritage. It should be on display in the Historium."

"Histor-ee-um, bore-*dum*. You need meladoor wood. This ship is made from meladoor."

She tore the sails, cut off the rigging and yanked out the masts, pulling the ship apart.

"Will it work?" I asked.

"Not after I've dismantled it."

"I meant the skycart."

"I can't smell anything."

"I said 'cart', not...oh, never mind. Will the model work with meladoor?"

"It might," said Zurta. "Won't know until we try."

I grabbed her hand. "We need this quickly."

She nodded. "As quick as a snergul sliding down a melting glacier to catch a spider."

* * * * *

After high sun, I sat at home thinking on nothing and everything. I couldn't face the lab – Vyrin, Rula and the others – although I knew I had to tell Eminent Drudan about Jolia soon. Casca hadn't appeared. *Why do I expect him to?* But the same voice declaring Jolia's death also affirmed Casca's survival.

As if I'd magicked the blind boy into existence, someone knocked on the front door. I jumped up and opened it to find Gallan listing on the front step.

He smiled with empathetic hazel eyes. "How are you?"

"Scared," I replied. "Sad. Angry. Unsure what to do."

"Grab your coat. We've been called to a meeting in the Governant. Eminent Stretten and Warden Mulburat want to discuss what we saw."

An irritation scratched my sense of justice. "Talk? Haven't they talked already? Peace officers should be storming the mine, looking for Jolia and any other mudgles left to the mercy of Shadow Man and his lackeys."

Gallan turned away to deflect my angst. "It's a delicate matter. We can't jeopardise the Voldari serpent oil order."

"Damn the Voldari! Mudgles are being killed. Jolia is probably dead. I don't care about bloody oil."

Gallan grabbed my wrist and clenched with desperate and unnecessary force. "Calm down. If we lose our composure, things won't go well. I know my ma'one. While she wants to placate the Voldari, her generosity rarely extends towards me or my friends. I don't fall within her circle of grace."

I twisted out of Gallan's grip. "She's your ma'one."

"She's Karlik's protector. I'm but one of her many pucks." He stepped inside, and I began to dress for the cold reception awaiting us.

"Where's Barick?" I asked.

"Already there. If we present a united front, we'll receive a fair hearing."

"We're not on trial. The truth should be enough for authorities to act."

"My ma'one says, 'Truth without proof may be no truth at all.'"

After lacing my boots, I pulled on a hat and gloves. "Why would the three of us make up such a story?"

He shrugged. "Stranger things have happened, I guess. Those in power want certainty before acting."

"When we were in the mine, at the lava pool, you said, 'Don't let him inside.' What did you mean?"

Gallan averted his eyes, staring out the open front door. "I didn't want us to get caught," he mumbled. "We were going to get caught."

*   *   *   *   *

After the doorkeepers cleaned us of ash-snow and took our coats, we walked into the Governant foyer. Barick sat alone, his hands squashed between his buttocks and a granite bench. With brown eyes already pleading for compassion, he glanced at every administrator who walked past and offered a feeble smile of innocence. They ignored him. I hoped it wasn't a sign of things to come.

Barick relaxed as we approached. "They'll call us when ready," he said.

"What did your da'one say?" I asked.

"Be patient."

Not my strongest trait.

Removing our hats and gloves, Gallan and I sat beside Barick, the nip of the cold polished stone biting through the leather panels of my skirt. A young female mudgle, about my age, sat behind a desk, sifting through parchments and greeting visitors. Dressed in a hoitary of silk and linen robes, an endless stream of administrators trickled past looking important, harried or bored. Their gowns' glarish colours of tangerine, lilac, lemon or chartreuse, with gold or silver stitching, caught the light from the oil lamps bracketed to the walls and threw it back into the faces of the unworthy. Brown leather boots, polished to a commanding sheen, smacked the tiled floor. Braided hair of black, blonde, red or brown had been contorted into an inventory of designs and plaits, the loose ends tied up with political neatness by silver or gold bracelets. Some administrators had hair down to their waists or twirled into mounds on top of their heads. Others had split beards saddling their shoulders like coils of rope draped over harfhorses. The most garish had set gems into their braids or used hairpins of finely sharpened bone that sometimes extended into earlobes or through noses.

Regardless of their dress, all took no notice of the three insignificant visitors perched on the granite bench. We warranted not a whisper among the grand murmurings echoing through Governant halls. More warmth came from the life-sized marble statues of famous mudgles standing watch along the foyer walls. I'd learned their names when studying at the Seminaria but had forgotten most, except the inventors.

As my compulsion fixated on the uneven length of my boot laces, a handclock on the receptionist's desk chimed two hours after high sun. She stood, crossed the foyer, smiled at us, then knocked on a carved cedar door.

She entered, then returned almost immediately. "They're ready for you."

We stood as one. I clutched my hat and gloves and pushed forward, wanting to confront political apathy head-on. Gallan and Barick trailed behind, ceding to my determination. I expected to walk into a warm, congenial office with Eminent Stretten and Warden Mulburat greeting us with the requisite smile and comforting hello. But we entered a cold, cavernous room, sparsely decorated with no fire or window to let in the sun. I doubted Stretten used this as her office.

The trudge of our boots echoed on the tiled floor as the receptionist guided us to three seats set before a long table in the room's middle. Behind the table sat a grim Eminent Stretten. On her left sat Eminent Drudan and Warden Mulburat smoking his pipe, and on her right sat Eminent Graben from the Extractory and two Voldari, one with black circles tattooed around her eyes and white feathers swept back over her crown, the other with tusks protruding from the top of his mouth.

Our hosts had organised themselves into an unbending line of judgement. I wanted to ask Gallan or Barick if they knew all these mudgles and the Voldari would be here. If they knew *why* they were here. But my friends kept their eyes downcast, and Eminent Drudan offered no response to my silent plea. No word of welcome or explanation.

"Thank you, Morry," said Eminent Stretten to the receptionist. "That will be all."

Morry left the discomfort behind. Stretten waved her hand at the chairs. We sat, nursing our hats and gloves in our laps. Gallan pulled his notebook out.

Eminent Stretten scowled at him. "Put that away. You won't be scribing today's meeting."

Gallan looked to me, possibly hoping I could change his ma'one's mind, then tucked the notebook back into his pocket.

Stretten scanned a parchment while her colleagues watched us with an accusational intensity that set my compulsion on edge. I fondled the cuff of my long-sleeved shirt, tucking it under against my wrist and then pulling it out over my thumb. *Tuck back, pull over.* Other hand. *Tuck back, pull over.*

Eminent Drudan cleared his throat. "You weren't in the lab this morning, Silveny."

Stretten raised her eyebrows. "I'll add that to the list."

List? What list? "I went to see Zurta...." I started.

Stretten raised her hand to stop me. "You'll get your turn." She lifted her eyes from the parchment. "Last night, my son raised some serious issues with me. I understand Warden Mulburat's son did the same. But the stories are littered with inconsistencies. We hope to clear those up today."

"Jolia's missing," I blurted. "Eminent Drudan, she's missing. She might be dead."

"Order," snapped Stretten. "We won't get to the heart of the matter with fragments of truths or lies thrown out like yesterday's garbage."

"It's all true," I said, refusing to let Stretten roll over me like she did Gallan.

"Is it true you broke into a mine through a locked gate?" asked Eminent Graben.

I didn't know the Extractory head well. I couldn't remember ever speaking with her. She wore the same drab-brown coat and shirt as her underlings, ironed with a crease-devouring exactness that impressed my compulsion. And she hadn't removed the fur-rimmed ushka hat from her head, the red flame badge at the front the only attempt to thaw the room's chill.

"We saw mudgles in there," I said, ignoring the question about the gate. "Jolia included. A mudgle was burned alive in a lava pool."

"Thought you said Jolia was missing," puffed Mulburat, blowing smoke over my explanation.

"She was. Is. Could already be dead."

"Was, is," muttered Stretten.

I blushed with anger. "The Voldari, Hor-gnasher, sacrificed a mudgle."

The tusked Voldari whispered to the feathered one. She scoffed. He stared at me, droplets of saliva trickling down his tusks like tears, as if the burden of his adornment always pained him.

"Why are you here?" I asked the Voldari.

Gallan stepped on my toes, trying to squash the boldness.

"Not that it's any of your concern," started Stretten, "we're joined by welcome guests Urn-hasa, White Owl, and Run-targa, Wave Lion. You will show them the same courtesy you show us. Now, if your friend Jolia is truly missing," she faced Drudan and rolled her eyes, "why didn't you go to the Statutoria?"

"We did," I snapped. "I spoke with Warden Mulburat."

Stretten faced Mulburat.

"It's true," he said, leaning back in the chair and drawing on his pipe. "But young Silveny only wanted to report a missing mudgle. She didn't say anything outlandish about sacrifices or breaking into mines, and

Barick and Gallan weren't there. Just an odd blind boy. Not Curmudgle, mind you."

"Who's this boy?" asked Stretten.

Run-targa whispered to his companion again. Her eyes widened such that the combination of raisin irises, white sclerae and black circle tattoos resembled a bizarre archery target.

Wish I had a bow and arrow.

At this point, I hoped Gallan or Barick would intervene. I'd done all the arguing. Taken all the risk. But they sat in repressed silence, scared to utter a word of support.

"A beggar," I said, answering Stretten's question. "No-one important. We went to the mine to find Jolia. The Statutoria wasn't…."

"One thing at a time," interrupted Stretten.

Left shirt-sleeve cuff. Tuck back. Pull over. Tuck back. Pull over. Right shirt-sleeve cuff. Repeat.

"Silveny," sighed Stretten, "you're an inventor. Eminent Drudan tells me a bright one. He says you've invented a wonderful flying machine that could transport many barrels of serpent oil."

I faced Drudan. "I'm calling it a skycart."

He nodded his approval. The Voldari sat forward, appearing keen to hear more. I resisted offering further information.

Stretten continued, "Because of your value as an inventor, the mine break-in is a misstep we're willing to overlook. But we must agree to the other fragments of your story. We don't want to start a panic. Not at this delicate stage of negotiations." She nodded to the Voldari.

Delicate stage? Mudgles are being abducted and killed. The Voldari are involved. Gallan. Barick. Say something!

"Other than you three, did anyone else enter the mine illegally?" asked Eminent Graben.

"Yula," said Barick. "Silveny's sister."

I glared at him. *Now you speak up and say that?* Gallan joined the confession.

"And Casca," he said. "The blind boy."

"You took *him* into the mines?" asked Mulburat, eyebrows raised and fogged with smoke.

"It wasn't like that," spurted Barick, finally finding his courage. "He can almost see."

"How can someone blind *almost* see?" asked Graben.

"He has other senses," said Gallan. "Acute senses."

"Where is he?" asked Stretten.

"Missing," I said. "Possibly lost in the mine."

Stretten groaned. "You went into the mine to find your missing friend, but lost a boy instead."

My hat and gloves fell from my lap, tumbling to the floor with the futility of a failed argument. I didn't see the point in collecting them.

"Where's this Yula?" asked Mulburat.

"Probably missing," chortled Drudan, folding his arms over his chest.

I'd hoped that at least he would support me. He would care. But he barely spoke, acting like I'd shamed him and the Inventoria with my delusions.

"Yula works the balloon line," said Gallan.

Mulburat nodded to Stretten. "I'll have a peace officer speak with her."

"We're not criminals," growled Barick. "Da'one, I told you last night what happened. Why are you treating us like this?"

"Son, the world is a complicated...."

"You've made serious accusations," interrupted Stretten. "The most outlandish against our distinguished visitors. Urn-hasa and Run-targa strongly refute any charges of wrongdoing."

White Owl had not shifted her gaze from me the entire time, her dark eyes searching my soul, probing for weaknesses. When Gallan and Barick spoke about Casca, the pulse in her neck quickened, pushing hard against her pale porcelain skin.

"Why go to the mine in the first place?" asked Drudan. "I mean, what led you there?"

"I saw something," said Barick. "While I was working, I lost my way and someone cried for help."

"Barick heard a mudgle in distress," said Gallan. "Silveny's friend, Jolia, went missing along with other mudgles. The mine was the obvious place to look."

Mulburat shook his head and banged the bowl of his clay pipe on the table until dregs of bunbili leaf scattered across the floor. "This is Statutoria business. We can't have pucks running around mines brandishing shovels and picks like vigilantes fuelled by rampant imaginations."

"We're not pucks," I growled. "You were dithering. Nothing's happened in Karlik for yarles. Peace officers aren't used to solving serious crime."

"Listen here," blustered Mulburat.

"It's all my fault," said Barick. "Don't punish my friends. I led them into this."

"We'll discuss punishment later," said Eminent Stretten. "Now, we need to get the story straight."

Punishment? For trying to save mudgle lives? I stiffened my jaw. "Barick took us to where he heard cries for help. Off the main mine tunnel, we squeezed through a crevice. Except Yula. She couldn't fit. It was dark, so we followed Casca."

"This blind boy led the way?" queried Graben.

"I know it sounds implausible."

"According to my son," Stretten read from a parchment, "you were also searching for a shadowy man who Barick saw previously."

"Shadow Man," corrected Gallan.

"Shadow Man?" asked Graben. "This story is getting stranger than a naked mudgle riding a woollydon through an ash-snow storm."

"You found him?" queried Stretten.

"Silveny and I saw him," said Gallan.

"What about Barick?" Stretten turned her eyes of judgement on him.

He shook his head. "That first time...when I heard the call for help, I saw...something. Someone. But when we returned, I couldn't look."

He faced me, tears welling. "I'm sorry, Silveny. I knew something was happening down in that cave, but I was too scared to get closer."

I clutched his hand.

Stretten remained cold. "So, you saw nothing?"

Barick nodded.

"I'll assume this blind boy saw nothing either, or had he already gone missing?"

"He was there," I said.

"There, but unsighted, and Yula back in the main tunnel, which leaves you and Gallan."

I returned to the night in the cave. The beaked Voldari leading a chained mudgle to slaughter. Shadow Man snapping bones like twigs. The prisoner being dunked in lava. The scream. *No. She didn't scream. Why didn't she scream?*

I yanked my hand free and sprang from the seat, wanting to find the privy, but the vomit couldn't wait, spewing all over my hat and gloves on the floor.

"Oh my," said Stretten. "Morry!" she called out.

The door opened.

"Bucket and mop, please, Morry. One of our guests has vomited."

Gallan stood and wrapped his arm around me. "Are you up to this?"

I nodded, sat back down and wiped vomit from my chin. But the nausea of the memory still churned in my stomach.

Gallan sat beside me. "Silveny's right, Hor-gnasher was there. I remember him from our first meeting. He chased us from the mine."

"Maybe he was coming to help you?" said Graben. "The Voldari have two observers in the mines, recording how we manage things."

"No," snapped Urn-hasa. "Hor-gnasher not in mine."

As Morry returned with a bucket and mop, I squashed vomit chunks between gritted teeth. "He *was* there, helping Shadow Man murder a Curmudgle."

"That's preposterous," spluttered Stretten. "Our guests arrived three days ago. How could they know anything about what was happening in the mines when this is the first we've heard of it? Is this Shadow Man a Voldari?"

I shook my head.

"*Hmph,*" said Stretten. "I thought not. The Voldari are not murderers. They're here to learn from us and buy our oil. A *lot* of oil."

"Did Hor-gnasher kill any mudgles?" asked Warden Mulburat.

"No," said Gallan. "But Shadow Man...he...he...." Gallan fought to release the words from his mouth.

"Shadow Man killed the mudgle," I said. "Burned her alive."

"Sounds disturbing," said Mulburat, dropping pinches of bunbili leaf into his pipe. "Something that definitely needs investigating."

"We're doing that," said Stretten. "I think we've almost cleared the matter up."

"What about Jolia?" asked Eminent Drudan. "She's one of my best inventors."

"The next victim," I said. "If not already dead."

His black face turned queasy as he pieced together our story. "Oh. How horrid."

"Did *you* see Jolia, Gallan?" asked Stretten.

My friend squirmed under his ma'one's glare. "Well, *um*, Silveny did, and I believe her."

What? You were right beside me. You must have seen her. "She was there," I cried.

"But only *you* saw her. Your recollection may be nothing more than another imaginative invention. Jolia has been missing for a few days. You're worried, of course. You broke into the mine expecting to find her, and you believe you did, though no-one else saw her. It makes perfect sense. Urn-hasa confirms that her companion has never stepped inside a mine, and this Shadow Man was probably nothing more than a tall mudgle mining serpent oil from the lava. Your story is a concoction born from the worry of missing your friend."

"And she's just had her first major invention approved," said Drudan. "That can be stressful."

"Then where's Jolia?" I blurted.

"We went to ask her da'three," said Mulburat, "but he died early this morning."

"A shame," said Stretten as the others nodded their agreement.

At that moment, I wanted to kill them all. I wanted to punish their casual indifference.

Morry picked up my hat and gloves. "I'll have these washed and returned to you."

The receptionist left us to our bitter fate. The faces of the judgement panel offered no consolation. No hint they'd take anything we said seriously. Jolia would die for nothing, and no-one would be held to account.

"Let's end this," said Stretten. "All we know for certain is that Jolia Sojule is missing. Warden Mulburat assures me the Statutoria are looking into it, along with some other *unfortunate* absences. Everything else you claim must be forgotten and never spoken of again. Do that, and you'll not be charged with breaking into a mine. The Dragon Festival starts tomorrow. Use the two days off to help you recuperate from your misadventure. You're dismissed."

We trudged from the cold room, through the foyer, collected our coats and stepped outside, the falling ash-snow poisoning my hair and the cold wind biting my fingertips. I wouldn't forget what I saw, despite Eminent Stretten's demand, and my compulsion needed answers, or it would never let me rest.

"I'm going to see my da'one," I said. "He was Literati Reader. He'll help us unravel this mystery."

"Leave it," said Gallan. "You heard my ma'one. Best we forget everything."

"I don't expect you to come."

"I'll come," said Barick with welcome bravery. "You...*cough*...can't hike those mountains alone. Horned wolves roam beyond the venting fires."

Gallan groaned. "Dammit. I guess I'm coming too. I'd rather be celebrating the Dragon Festival."

"We'll return for the final display," I said. "I promise."

Morry rushed down the Governant steps and handed over my hat and gloves. Still wet, but at least clean. I said goodbye to Barick and Gallan, lacking the energy to talk more about what happened in the meeting, and went home to bed. Late in the night, someone opened the front door. I got up and peeked from behind the privacy curtain, expecting to see Yula home from work. But Casca strolled past like he'd always lived here.

I should have locked the door. He could have been Hor-gnasher.

As Casca disappeared into the spare bedroom, I wanted to confront him, hug him, ask him what happened, but I was exhausted. It could wait until the morning. Unless he went missing again.

Chapter 12

A trek into the mountains

The next morning, I pulled my curtain across to find Casca sitting on the bench seat. Yula made breakfast in the cookery; fried eggs and hog rashers by the smell.

Not wearing his glasses, Casca faced me with broken eyes that hid so much. "Good morning, Silveny."

I sat beside him. "You vanished again. You keep doing that."

"I underestimated the disorientation of those mine tunnels. You shouldn't worry about the wanderings of an impoverished blind boy."

I screamed, "I thought you were dead!"

Yula dropped a plate, and it smashed on the floorstones.

I stood, heaving air into my lungs as I paced around the house. "I thought Shadow Man or the Voldari had taken you. I thought they'd do to you what they did to that poor mudgle. What they were...what they *have* done to Jolia." I stopped and pushed my hands into my thighs, forcing them up and down to inflict a different kind of pain. Redirect my mind. "What does it matter?" I muttered. "No-one cares. Stretten, Mulburat, Eminent Drudan. I thought he'd support me, but none of them care. *You* don't seem to care."

"I care, Silveny," said Casca with infuriating calmness. "I may not show it often, but I care."

"Tell me what happened to you." I sat again, fighting to still my exasperation.

He lifted his glasses from the seat beside him and placed them on his nose. "I tried to follow you from the tunnel, but the Voldari was upon me. The smell of burning oil from his flaming torch seeped closer. The vibrations of his footsteps set a shudder in my soul. To thwart capture, I squeezed into a crevice in the tunnel wall. I can avoid being seen as the world avoids being seen by me. I waited until he'd abandoned his search before pressing on. But those mine tunnels are torturous, and miners are everywhere, working day and night."

Yula put a plate of eggs and rashers on the table in front of us, with slices of dark rye to mop up the yolks and fat.

"You're angry with me, Silveny," said Casca.

"She's frustrated," said Yula. "Sad. She lost her friend."

"Do you wish Jolia came back instead of me?" he asked.

Yes. I do.

"She's not coming back," said Yula with biting apathy.

Casca leaned forward, waved his hand to waft the smells of the cooked food into his nostrils, then plucked a hog rasher with his fingers and tossed it into his mouth.

"*Hmmm*," he cooed. "Long time since I've had this."

Yula perched an egg and rasher on a slice of bread, folded it over so the yolk squeezed out the edges, then sucked it into her mouth. The whole scene reeked of ludicrous banality. My sister and our adopted boy enjoyed breakfast while mudgles were being cooked alive in lava pits. As if Jolia hadn't joined them. As if those in authority, addled by their greed, weren't letting the Voldari infiltrate our community and direct our actions.

"How can you do this?" I asked. "How can you do nothing?" I clutched Casca's hand before he could take another rasher. "In the mine, you said, 'If you value your life, run.' You understood what was happening there. You were terrified. Despite all that you hide from us, you couldn't hide that."

Casca shook his hand free and heaved his chest. "There are two types of fear. The first is rational fear. If you're trapped by a boulder lion or horned wolf, you fear being eaten. If a man runs at you with a knife or sword, you fear being stabbed. These are rational fears. The second type is primeval fear. Some might call it *irrational*. A visceral terror stretching back to the roots of our origin. This is the type of fear that can drive people mad. Force them to turn on each other until whole communities are torn apart." Casca drew in another deep breath. "In that mine, the moment we came upon your Shadow Man, is when I felt primeval fear."

"Do you know who he is?" asked Yula.

"I'm going to find out. I'll follow the Voldari. Listen to their conversations, hoping they offer clues to his identity and more information about their plans for Karlik. I learned to speak their language long ago, but if I'm discovered, they'll not expect it. I will pretend to be nothing more than an orphaned, blind beggar."

"So," I said, "you admit it's a ruse."

"Not the blindness. The rest, well...." Casca shrugged and smiled.

"Then you can pay for food and lodging," grumbled Yula through a mouthful of bread.

Casca removed his laceless boot, which should have been left by the front door, untied the cord holding the upper to the sole, then knocked the heel against the table edge. The heel slid across, and coins tumbled onto the floor. "Take what you want," he said. "I can't remember all I have or where they came from. Some coins feel the same to me. Very inconvenient."

I picked up a gold coin and held it to the lamplight. "This one has a woman's head on the back and a building on the front with a domed roof."

"Germalian," said Casca. "The woman would be the Sella of the Conventus."

"Sella?"

"Conventus chairperson."

"This silver one has a hole in the middle," said Yula.

"*Ah*, barbarian coin."

"You don't have any mudgle tokens," I said. "We can't use foreign currency."

"You can exchange them. A well-connected merchant would be more than happy to swap these precious coins for your tokens."

"Merchants rarely come into the city. Most trading is done at *Line Station 16.*"

"So, you get a balloon ride into the bargain."

Yula sighed and dropped a handful of coins onto the table.

"We'll arrange something," I said. "Your lodging is not such a burden. I mean, you're often not here. And before you risk being caught by the Voldari, we should visit my da'one, Ardgal Courtan."

At the mention of Popa, Yula jumped up and strode to the cookery, dumping her plate in the sink. She wanted to avoid the invitation to Popa's cabin, but I'd ask her anyway, then plea for a change of heart when she refused.

"We have two days off work for the Dragon Festival," I continued. "Everything shuts down for the celebration, even the balloon line. Gallan, Barick and me are trekking into the mountains to Popa's cabin. He was Literati Reader. Books, parchments, words and knowledge define him. He may know more about the Voldari's motives. About Shadow Man."

"He doesn't know anything," growled Yula, tossing another dirty dish in the sink before wiping the benchtop.

"I'll come," said Casca. "Da'one Courtan sounds like a wise Curmudgle."

"Gallan will take forever to hike to the cabin," complained Yula.

"He'll make it," I said.

"We all carry burdens," said Casca, before turning towards the cookery. "You must come, Yula. I'll feel safer with you there." He faced me and smiled. "She's the strongest among you. The mountains outside Karlik are dangerous. If we're trapped by a horned wolf, I want Yula by my side."

"I wish I still had my great, great grandmother's long knife. I lost it in the mine."

"It would be no use against a wolf. You need a spear, or bow and arrows. To wound or kill before it gets too close."

"Yula can use a hunting bow."

I didn't need to look at my sister's face. I knew she simmered inside at the thought of visiting our father. She hadn't seen him in yarles.

I stood and walked over to the cookery benchtop, pressing my waist into its steely edge. "Please come and see Popa, Yula. Things are changing here. I need to know...*we* need to know if it's too dangerous to stay."

"I'm not leaving Karlik."

"You may have no choice," said Casca.

Yula didn't relent, but she agreed to get a hunting bow from *Line Station 1*. I searched my garderobe for warmer clothes for Casca. The Melt had begun, but the mountains above Karlik, away from the venting fires, would be much colder than in the city. Although it seemed the boy didn't feel the cold, I couldn't recall once seeing him shiver, my compulsion needed to dress him in layers of fleece and fur. While I'd planned to send him back to the Nordland Plains at the earliest opportunity, the longer I spent in his company, the more he weaved himself into my life. He didn't need taking care of, but part of me *wanted* to care for him. Wanted to understand the link between Casca and recent events in Karlik.

I found a wrap, an old floe bear pelt. Age had turned the blotchy white fur to parchment beige, the wrap dotted with bare patches of dry, wrinkled skin where fur tufts had fallen out. Casca would swim in it, but I could use belts and cords to fashion something that would stay on his gaunt frame.

I filled two rucksacks with bags of oats, cheese, dried meat and bread, full waterskins, an oil burner and tin bowl to melt ice, rope and a compass for navigation. Despite Casca's doubt, I packed a cookery knife to use as a weapon and strapped two pairs of snowshoes to the outside of the packs. It would take about a day to hike to Popa's cabin. Most of the food I'd give to my father, and we'd wear all the clothes we needed.

Barick and Gallan arrived after breakfast.

"Casca's alive," sparked Barick as he walked through the front door.

Casca stood and placed his hand on his heart. "They say he died, but it was they who lied. And he deigned to forgive, so he could live, live, live!"

Gallan raised his eyebrows. "What's he talking about?"

I shrugged. "He survived the mine tunnel, Hor-gnasher and Shadow Man. The riddle of Casca continues."

"I love riddles," said Barick.

"Where's Sneckle?" I asked him.

"My mothers are caring for her while we're away."

Gallan faced me. "Are you still upset about the meeting?"

I bit the inside of my cheek. "Yes. But I can't dwell on it. I need to do something."

"I'm not going back in that tunnel," said Barick. "Sneckle or no Sneckle. Not to that place."

"Neither am I," said Gallan.

"I won't abandon Jolia to injustice," I snapped, then calmed my need for redress. "But I have to find another path."

My friends went silent as we organised the last of our gear. Yula returned from *Line Station 1* with a hunting bow.

"Are you coming, Yula?" asked Gallan.

She shook her head.

"Please," I urged. "I packed a bag for you. No-one else can shoot a bow as well as you."

"Don't look at me," said Casca.

"We're taking a bow?" stammered Barick.

Gallan placed his hand on Barick's shoulder. "You said yourself, horned wolves roam the mountains."

"They're coming closer to Karlik," said Yula. "I've heard them from the line."

"It's true," said Gallan. "I've interviewed miners who said wolves aren't shying from the venting fires like they used to."

"They must be hungry," said Casca. "The wolves, not the miners."

Barick shivered. "We need four bows. Yula, please."

Her shoulders slumped. "Alright." She glared at me. "But don't expect forgiveness."

I never expect too much from you.

We hiked through Karlik's streets, dressed and ready for a strenuous journey. The city exuded an expectant busyness not seen for most of the yarle. Around us, mudgles prepared for Dragon Festival events, carrying barrels of meduz and ale into taverns, hanging cloth lanterns shaped as dragons in flight, and wagoning in blocks of ice to be sculpted into creations that would be judged on the final night. A handful of my co-workers built a display outside the Inventoria showing off inventions from the previous yarle. Artisans fashioned wire and cloth creations that would be set alight and launched into the sky like flaming comets. Behind a store window, Eminent Músa, Historium Curator, cleaned and exhibited ancient relics from the abandoned mudgle city of Cha'thair. I wondered if anything belonging to Philomine Belarose had made it into the collection. Possibly something to replace the long knife I lost.

A giggle of pucks from the Seminaria dressed in rosewood uniforms and led by their tutor skipped down the street towards us waving hand-painted dragon flags. I smiled at the memory of Barick and me studying together. We enrolled and graduated from the Seminaria at the same time. Inseparable friends. Now he, Gallan and Yula would miss most of the Dragon Festival for my sake. They sacrificed so I could correct an injustice. Changed their plans to accommodate mine. My compulsion sometimes imprisoned those close to me.

On the outskirts of Donharue, Karlik's southeast quarter, I stopped the group at the eastward stables. "We should hire a woollydon and sleigh," I said. "It will be easier walking without packs."

"I won't complain," said Gallan, unshouldering his rucksack and dropping it to the ground.

"Since you're here on my behalf, I'll pay."

"Definitely no complaints," said Barick, smiling.

I walked into the stables, immediately wrapped in the fusty warmth of woollydon dung mixed with straw, and ambled down the stone corridor between two rows of six stables. At the far end, a stable-hand mucked out a stall, forking old straw mashed with dung into a wheelbarrow.

"Excuse me," I said.

The stable-hand disappeared back into the stall without acknowledging me. I walked up to the stable door and leaned in. "Where's the stable-master?"

"I'yn the master," she said, lifting another load of straw. "Out the way."

I stood to the side as she hurled the straw over the half door and into the barrow. In the corner, a woollydon lay on its side, eyes closed, breathing content in a warm bed.

"The stables seem quiet," I said.

"Nun else here. All git the day orf cos o'the Dragin Fest." She swapped the fork for a broom and swept the cobblestones.

"I want to hire a woollydon and sleigh."

"O'night?"

"Ah, yes, overnight. Return tomorrow in time for the final celebration."

"Where?"

"Sorry?"

"Where ye goin'? Not sendin' me animals to dange'russ places. Recent days, 'orned wolves killed two o'me woollies." She stopped sweeping, leaned on the broom and bowed her head in a silent remembrance.

"Oh. Sorry. We're going to see my da'one. He lives in a cabin at the foot of Mt Ciar."

"Long trek. Plenny time fa wolves to attack."

"We'll be hiking during the day, and there's a stable at the cabin where the woollydon can rest at night. Safely."

The stable-master faced the sleeping woollydon. "What ye think, Grendal? Wanna take a stroll?"

The woollydon, Grendal, opened her eyes, lifted her shaggy head, and snuffled the air with a black nose the size of a bread plate.

"Nay food," said the stable-master. "Hike. Pullin' a sled."

Grendal heaved a sigh, then dropped her head back onto a straw pillow, looking completely disinterested in any type of walking.

"My sister, Yula, has a hunting bow," I said. "She's an excellent shot."

"Wolves hunt'n packs. Might kill one, two wiff an arrow. Won't kill'em all."

"I can pay extra. For the risk."

"T'irty-five amber tokens. Back before end of festival."

I nodded, reached into my coat pocket, pulled out a leather pouch and loosened the purse string. Some of Casca's foreign coins sat on top. I considered offering a couple to the stable-master but doubted she'd view the attempt favourably. Instead, I took out three silver and five amber tokens and dropped them in her waiting palm.

"Git up, Grendal." The stable-master poked the animal in the belly with the broom handle. "We gotta 'arness ye up."

Outside, while the stable-master harnessed Grendal, we strapped our rucksacks to the sleigh, leaving room for Casca to sit. Although the floe bear pelt corded around his waist and chest would keep the wind at bay, he had no fleece-lined boots or snowshoes, and trekking through snow with laceless shoes would be nigh impossible.

"She's ready," said the stable-master, patting Grendal on the backside. "Slow'un, but she'll git ye there. Put a bag o'mixed pellets n'grain on the sled. Feed her high sun and t'night."

"We'll look after her," I said, taking the lead rope to encourage Grendal forward.

We climbed *Death's Pass* out of Karlik, the dirt road packed solid owing to generations of miners using the lower stretch to reach the eastern mines. Side tracks branched right, leading further into the mountains. On our left, a sheer cliff dropped to city rooftops, the pass soon offering a commanding view across the Wyrm Valley. The metal spokes of the sled's wheels strained and creaked over uneven ground, the composite resin bound to the rims doing little to protect a shuddering Casca from an endless parade of jolts and dips.

As the road narrowed, we stopped at a junction marked with a sandstone pillar no taller than me. A brass plaque, the size of a supper plate, had been riveted to the stone. Unassuming. Insignificant to most. But not to Yula and me. Popa commissioned the plaque, the last thing he did before leaving us behind.

Yula stood at my shoulder. The others held back. A short salutation and four names had been etched into the brass: *In memory of those who died searching for a better life. Ma'one Jora Adermont. Ma'two Selny Belarose. Da'two Porl Staner. Da'three Donray Fulbear.*

Yula stepped forward and traced her index finger over Jora's name, her birth mother. I did the same with Selny, then draped my arm around my sister's shoulder and pulled her close. We stood in silence, the flames of a nearby venting fire spluttering and gushing with the ebb and flow of serpent gas pulsing through a copper pipe. A southerly breeze wafted a warm caress around us, comforting our sorrow. Meltwater dripped from icicles hanging underneath a rocky ledge, counting down to when The Melt would cede to Wildflower Flush, and the bleak grey slopes surrounding Karlik would be washed with streams of scarlet, tangerine, indigo and mauve.

Our parents didn't die here. The avalanche happened more than a league up *Death's Pass*. Their bodies were never recovered, and Popa thought no-one would visit a memorial so far from Karlik.

He's probably right.

Grendal the woollydon snorted her impatience. We returned to the sled, finding Barick and Gallan had already wound down the waxed steel runners to below the wheel rims. I gathered Grendal's rope and took the east track, which climbed its way up the foot of Mt Sorcha. The sleigh's runners glided across compressed snow, the woollydon seeming to handle the burden of our rucksacks, and Casca, with ease. We'd climb the lower west face of Mt Sorcha before veering north, then east again through the valley between Sorcha and Mt Ailbhe. A few mudgles claimed a mountain pass could be navigated east all the way to the northern reaches of the Veiled Occyan. But I'd never met a traveller who'd completed the journey, avalanches, ice crevasses, horned wolves, floe bears or exposure likely to have taken anyone foolish enough to attempt the crossing.

As we left the Wyrm Valley and the venting fires behind, we wrapped scarves around our faces to ward off the cold. A cliff vulture glided beneath sheets of alabaster cloud that covered the sky, hopeful an early melt might yield a worthy meal. Snow hares would be active, searching for the first shoots of green pick, while cave babbits, fluffy, pudgy, stoat-like creatures, would have awakened from their hibernation and be out searching for insects and grubs. With prey came predators, and in the muted daylight, I worried a pack of hungry horned wolves might forgo the cover of darkness and brave the sun. Yula carried the bow and quiver of arrows over her shoulder, but the bulkiness of her attire would hamper an attempt at unshouldering the weapon and firing an arrow in quick time.

We stopped at mid-morning to rest and strap studded snowshoes over our boots to navigate the shin-deep snow. I fed Grendal a handful of pellets and grain and checked the base of her splayed feet, brushing out any stones that had lodged between the foot pads. While the broad, grooved feet were perfect for navigating snow, they collected material that could make walking uncomfortable. The gentle woollydon didn't complain or resist my attention, nuzzling my side with her damp, cold nose, or poking out her tongue to coax more food from me.

We ate a few mouthfuls of dry bread and took swigs from our waterskins, tied close to our bodies underneath the layers of fleece to stop freezing, then followed a mostly unmarked track due east. The summit of Mt Ciar rose in the distance, five fingers of broken rock resembling the peaks of a royal crown, marking our destination with imposing surety. I led the group, Grendal following my tugs on the lead rope, with Casca lounging among the packs and burying himself deep into the floe bear pelt. Gallan limped behind the sleigh, sometimes gripping the rear frame for balance. In times like these, the burden of his uneven legs weighed heaviest, but he never complained or asked to rest more than we needed. Barick followed Gallan, only a sliver of dark skin around his eyes visible between the peak of his hood and the top edge of his face scarf.

Yula trailed at the rear, turning her head left and right in conscientious diligence as group protector. She'd enjoy the hike the most from this trip, especially the journey home. The part in between might not be as pleasant, but I never lost hope of reconciliation.

As we approached the base of Mt Ciar, the north wind picked up, howling through the mountain passes and whipping us with snow and sleet. I re-wrapped my face scarf, trying to cover every inch of skin around my eyes. But they became almost useless when a fog, so dense I could barely see my hand held at arms-length, dropped down to blanket us. Grendal snorted in protest and pulled against the rope, the first time she'd resisted my coaxing. Gallan yelled from behind me, his outburst ripped away by the wind.

I spun around as Yula trotted up to my side. "We can't go on in this fog. I lost sight of the sled for a moment."

I stopped and shouted, "There's extra rope in my rucksack! Tie it around your waists and to the back of the sleigh."

Yula nodded and returned to the packs.

Barick trudged up to me. "We're being followed."

"What have you seen?"

"Nothing in this fog. Casca said he smelled something."

"This wind would carry scents from leagues away."

"He said it was close. Didn't know what it was."

As Yula tied a rope around the waists of Gallan then Barick, I opened my rucksack to check the handclock. We'd been hiking for four hours, Popa's cabin about two hours away. With the sun and Mt Ciar invisible, I pulled out a box-compass and checked for east.

"Not far to go," I said, trying to sound confident.

"We should shelter beside the sled until the storm passes," said Yula.

I shook my head. "Something might be stalking us."

"Not might," called Casca into the wind. "Definitely."

"If it's horned wolves, we must reach the cabin."

"I can ride for a bit on the back of the sleigh," said Gallan. "I won't slow us down."

I walked to the front, balancing the box-compass in my gloved hand. One of Rula's inventions, the steel needle wavered around the 'E' on the display, not giving an exact direction, but good enough. Mountain ranges bordered the north and south of the pass we traversed, so if we started to climb, we'd lost direction.

I tied the lead rope around my waist and dragged Grendal forward. She groaned and snorted, then shook her shaggy coat to shed the snow before plodding after me. Gallan jumped onto the back of the sleigh, with Barick and Yula trailing behind.

We walked for another hour, heaving snowshoes through drifts sometimes to my knees, the fog barely lifting. Sleet slapped our faces, the mountains punishing us for breaching their domain. I cursed my father for living out here in the wildness. For not being able to face his grief.

I kept my eyes focussed on the compass lest we get lost. When I next looked up, a shape in the distance moved towards us. I stopped and waved Yula forward.

"What is it?" she cried over the wind.

"Something up ahead."

"A wolf?"

I shrugged and pointed. She unshouldered the bow and pulled an arrow from the quiver, the wind almost wrenching it from her hand. She nocked the arrow and pulled the bowstring taut, unsure where to aim.

The shape vanished. We waited. The others hunched beside the sleigh. Grendal stamped her feet. A blur of movement on the right flashed past. Yula spun around, ready to fire. The shape disappeared again like a cruel magic trick.

Then something moved on our left. Yula turned again, desperate to find a target in the fog.

A lilting voice wailed on the wind, "Si-Si-Silveny!"

"Wait!" I yelled to Yula, grabbing her shoulder.

She lowered the bow as a ball of white hair raced towards us.

"Silveny!" it cried again.

"Rambleton?" I said.

The ball took a mudgle shape, arms and legs flailing, body covered in a mass of white hair almost invisible against the snow and fog.

Rambleton rushed out of the mist and wrapped me in a hug, lifting me from the ground. "Here you are."

"We almost killed you," I said.

He placed me back on the snow. "Why would you do that?" He turned on his heel and cried, "Yula is here also," lifting her stiff frame in another smothering hug. "Long, so very long," he sang as he jiggled Yula up and down.

"What are you doing out in this storm?" I asked him.

Rambleton returned Yula to solid ground and swept his hairy arm across the vista. "Far, far away. Over the hills I went. Far away, but back in a day."

"Do you remember Gallan and Barick?"

"As most certain as I can be." He strode towards Gallan, ready to deliver another hug.

Gallan backed away. "A hello is sufficient."

"No!" snapped Rambleton. "A hello won't do when you I can hug."

He pulled both Gallan and Barick into a white mudgle smother, his hairy, naked body surrounding them until they almost vanished.

Casca called to Gallan, "You thought I was annoying."

Rambleton pulled away from my friends and walked up to Casca still sitting on the sleigh. "Who is this shaggy, baggy thing? He looks like a baby floe bear." The white mudgle laughed aloud, lifted Casca from the sleigh and spun him around above his head.

"Put me down," said Casca. "The blind can get dizzy."

Rambleton obliged, still laughing.

"Are you well?" I asked him.

"Never ever better. Better than I've ever been." He grabbed my arm. "Come, Popa Courtan is waiting."

"He knows we're coming?"

"No. But he's always waiting. Come Silveny. Come Yula, and friends, and baby floe bear."

"Casca," said Casca. "Not a floe bear."

Rambleton prised his fingers under the rope tied around my waist and pulled me forward, dragging Grendal, the sleigh and my friends along behind. "Not far to go," he said. "I know the way. Tricking fog, not tricking me."

"How is Popa?" I asked, walking beside Rambleton.

"Ails torment Popa Courtan," he replied. "Silveny, sorry to say, soon my hunt will feed only me."

"Worse than my last visit?"

"Much worse. Forever, none of us live. But Yula's visit will soothe him."

I didn't share Rambleton's optimism. *It's clearly been a long time since you last saw Yula.* "We thought you were a horned wolf."

The broad smile lighting Rambleton's face dropped away. "Wolf numbers grow. They raid our traps. Chase me through the valleys."

We walked together in silence. The wind abated, and the fog lifted, Mt Ciar appearing as a colossus a short walk away.

"Home!" cried Rambleton. "King Ciar, with his rocky crown, calls to me."

We untied the ropes from around our waists and tossed everything onto the sleigh. Rambleton insisted on leading us to the cabin, singing an ancient song about the mountain kings and queens as he went.

"Queen Neasa
Kind, Queen Neasa
Mountain ma'one of our town
Meadowed skirt and icy crown
Mudgle pucks dance the ground.
King Fachtna

Strong, King Fachtna
Boulders slip and tumble down
Danger scatters all around
While mudgle miners dig underground.
Queen Ailbhe
Veiled, Queen Ailbhe
Honeycomb ice brings water pure
But beware the soft allure
Mists can lead to thoughts impure.
King Ciar
Brave, King Ciar
None reach further to the sky
Arresting slopes, the danger belie
Because death awaits those who try."

Soon after Rambleton finished his song, we trod a worn path cleared of snow and ice. Gravel crunched under our studded snowshoes as a stone cabin came into view, set into the rock at the foot of Mt Ciar. *Brave, King Ciar.* Smoke rose from a chimney above a slated roof, and a window teased a flicker of life inside.

We stopped at the front door and removed our snowshoes. Rambleton unclipped the sleigh's harness and led Grendal to a stable built onto the side of the house.

"Fire warms both," he called over his shoulder. "She'll be well cared for."

Casca climbed off the sled, and we untied our rucksacks. Rambleton returned, opened the front door and led us inside.

A fire smouldered in the hearth, fed by sticks that sat bundled up against the stone wall. Rambleton must have traded for the firewood, a rarity this high in the mountains. A candle melted onto a plate in the middle of the cookery table fought to peel away the cabin's dullness. We passed shelves and shelves of books stacked to the roof before stepping into the living area where Popa sat in a cushioned chair, his withered frame begging my heart for nourishment. He wore a bedtime robe, cut off at the sleeves, covered in food stains and the dirt of cabin living. Dark, puffy eyes catalogued life's bruises, and tufts of thinning hair, as white as Rambleton's, clung to brown coriaceous skin that draped from his neck like faded curtains.

I crept up and kissed him on the cheek.

His eyes opened, and he whispered with a rattling wheeze in his chest, "Silveny."

"Sorry it's taken so long to visit," I said. "Yula is here."

He grabbed the armrests and pulled himself upright, turning his head to face his first daughter. "Yula?"

She stood by the door, not stepping further into the cabin. Not offering another compromise.

Don't expect forgiveness.

Popa reached for me, and I pulled him up into a hug, shocked at the boniness hidden beneath the robe. I ached for Yula to come over. To share the family reunion. But she stepped behind Gallan and Barick to hide her stubbornness.

I wanted to grab her. Slap her. Force her to...to *love*. But force wouldn't break the unforgiving rock of her disdain.

"Barick and Gallan," I said, pulling away and letting Popa return to his chair. "You remember them?"

"Of course," he said, weathered lips cracking a frail smile.

"And Casca. We've adopted him for now. He's from...well, he's not from Karlik."

"He's a floe bear cub," said Rambleton. "With spectacles strange."

Popa laughed. "I hope Mumma-bear doesn't come calling."

"Casca's from the Nordland Plains," I said, not offering details. "He's blind."

"*Hmmm.* Rambleton, get me some water."

"Water, water, for Popa Courtan and daughter. Sorry, *daughters.* Daughters and friends and baby floe bears."

Rambleton fossicked around in the cookery.

I uncinched my rucksack. "We brought dried meat, grains, flour, fresh bread."

"You spoil me, Silveny," said Popa. "We have enough here."

"You're so thin."

Popa's eyes turned sombre. "I feel thin. Frayed rope suspending a bridge above a chasm. Each day, another strand untwines."

"Don't say that." I faced my friends. "Sit, everyone."

They removed their coats, hats, gloves and scarves, then pulled up old crates to sit beside the fire. Yula plonked herself at the dining table, and Casca sat on the dirt floor with his legs crossed.

Rambleton brought pitchers and cups. "Water, woollydon milk, tea."

"No ale?" asked Gallan.

Rambleton shook his head. "Makes Rambleton ramble."

"I knew we should have brought ale."

"I brought fire-rum," said Yula.

"Not too much," said Popa to Yula.

She scowled, and he flinched, and I wanted to slap her again.

Rambleton untied a bundle of wood and tossed some sticks on the fire. "A little, ittle bit. Otherwise, we run out. Not of the cabin – that would be silly. Out of wood. Then, Rambleton down the mountains must sleigh and heave a weary load back to Popa Courtan."

"Where do you get the wood?" asked Gallan.

"Village Grittledell. A shoe on the ranger's foot."

"At the foot of the range," corrected Popa.

Rambleton scrunched his face. "That's what I said."

Yula pulled a flask of fire-rum from her coat, almost daring Popa to scold her again. She tipped a mouthful into tin cups, and Gallan, Barick and I took the drink. Despite bringing supplies, Rambleton insisted on feeding us from the cabin's pantry, retiring to the cookery while we discussed things more worrisome than food and rum.

"Why have all of you come?" asked Popa. "I've not seen Barick and Gallan since they were pucks, and Yula never visits."

"Bad things happening in Karlik," I said.

"And the Voldari arrived," interrupted Gallan, smiling.

"Yes, the Voldari. We witnessed a murder in the mines."

"By Shadow Man," said Barick.

"Who?" asked Popa.

"We don't know who he is," I said. "But a Voldari was there, helping him murder mudgles. They...they dropped...." I closed my eyes, trying to block the image from my mind.

"A ritual sacrifice with a purpose," said Casca. "The victim, still alive, is dunked into a pool of boiling lava with a unique consistency. A sorcerous brew, you might say. When extracted, the victim's body is coated in a crust of ashen stone. Beneath the fouled skin, their soul rests, suspended."

"They're alive when they come out?" whimpered Barick, his eyes threatening tears.

"In limbo. A kind of purgatory, for want of a better description."

"That word 'purgatory' is not from this world," said Popa. "It seems our blind boy is widely read."

"How is that possible?" asked Gallan, uselessly facing Casca.

But the boy must have sensed the inquisition. He shrugged. "I wasn't always blind."

"My friend, Jolia, was the next to be sacrificed," I muttered. "We told the authorities all this, but they won't help. Their sense of justice is frozen by greed."

"You were a reader of the Literati, Da'one Courtan," said Gallan.

"Not *a* reader," called Rambleton from the cookery. "*The* Reader."

"*The* Reader. A mudgle of letters, words and books. Of knowledge."

"Still is," said Rambleton. "Every day reads and writes. Here, there, over there and everywhere, books and parchments are stacked, words are read, and thoughts are written. And knowledge is gathered."

Gallan faced Popa. "We hope you might be able to explain what's happening. But we must be careful. The Voldari want a lot of oil, an order that could benefit Karlik for yarles. We can't step on their toes."

Damn their toes. I want to step on their heads. "The Voldari want more than oil," I said. "They're infiltrating the city. Putting observers in important places."

"They want to learn from us," defended Gallan.

"I don't believe it. They have other ambitions."

"You can use only so much serpent oil," said Popa.

Rambleton sang, *"Oil is mined, and mined some more. Barrels and barrels are taken ashore. The demon delights, the innocents flee. Fire burns bright and boils the sea."*

"What on earth are you talking about?" asked Gallan.

Rambleton shrugged. "Words from a book. I made the melody."

"Not any book," said Popa. "A book of augury. Omens." He sighed and sank into his chair. "Tell me more about this sacrifice."

I steeled myself. "Before the mudgle was dropped into the lava, Shadow Man snapped the victim's leg bones. Bent them backwards to shape them a certain way, creating a macabre sculpture."

Popa stroked the furrows on his brow, flattening the loose skin. "Voldari, shadowed men and boiled mudgles. This is extremely concerning. Rambleton, after our meal, you must fetch the Book of Leaves. You know the one."

The white mudgle nodded. "There is dust. Generations of dust. Ingrained in the wooden binds. But words, too. Faded words. Written long, long ago. Before anyone was born."

"Then who wrote them?" asked Barick. "I mean if no-one was born yet."

"We don't know who wrote them," said Popa. "But the words tell of a time long ago when Ostamp was a vastly different place. When dark and shadow ruled."

Rambleton served us an austere meal of salted snow hare that sucked all the moisture from my mouth, a sudsa of mashed grain and beans, and dried mushrooms soaked in slitherweed broth. I convinced Popa and Rambleton to eat the bread before it went stale.

After the meal, the white mudgle placed a stool in front of a tower of shelves, climbed on the chair and searched the highest shelf. He pulled out a timber box as large as his chest and almost toppled backwards with the effort.

"Why must it be so high?" he said as he stepped back down.

"Safer there," muttered Popa.

Rambleton thudded the box onto the table, and dust exploded from its joins.

"Careful," admonished Popa. "Get my thin gloves, Rambleton."

In all my visits to the cabin, I'd never seen this box before. The dark wooden sides, hickory coloured, had been carved with delicate, intricate creations of people, animals and plants intertwined with abstract symbols of lines and loops, ellipses and half-circles forming designs with unknown meaning, at least to me. A triangle with a cross below it and a lidded eye with a sideways 's' beneath had been carved into the handled lid.

Popa pulled a handkerchief from his robe pocket and wiped the outside of the box before unclasping four latches at the top and lifting the lid off. Inside, timber squares fit together perfectly like mosaic tiles, each with a letter engraved on them. Rambleton handed Popa a pair of thin, white cotton gloves. He tugged them over bulbous fingers gnarled by old age, then plucked a square with the letter 'V' from the arrangement. Except it wasn't a square but one end of two lengths of wood about as long as my forearm and as wide as two fingers. Popa unclipped the hinged 'V' square and pulled the lengths of wood apart. Inside, opening like a concertina, pieces of parchment as long as my torso unfolded, held in place by lengths of twine running through holes in the parchment and connected to each wooden runner.

"Can't be too careful," mumbled Popa. "Skin is decaying."

"Skin?" queried Barick.

Popa nodded. "Everything in the Book of Leaves is written on skin. What skin? Whose? I don't wish to consider. The threads running through each leaf, holding them together, are sinew." With the tips of gloved fingers, slow and gentle, he tugged a leaf of skin from the top wooden runner and folded it down to the bottom. He repeated the action with three more leaves before stopping. "*Ah*, here it is. This parchment provides a short history of the Voldari."

"They're that old?" exclaimed Gallan.

"Oh yes. They're an ancient religious group. Though they live in Kogot now, they resided in Thyatira before that and originated from a place much older and long forgotten. The secrets of their faith are known only by those accepted into the order. They build no places of worship, at least not that I've read, and each initiated member adopts an animal talisman. Their amuell."

"Same as grells," said Rambleton.

Popa shook his head. "No, quite different. The Stone- and Weald-grells *protect* their totem. The Voldari claim to gain strength and knowledge from theirs. If they find one in the wild, they'll kill it and drink its blood."

Barick placed a hand over his mouth. "Disgusting."

"Do they hunt their amuells?" I asked.

"It's more complex than that," said Popa. "They believe an unseen force will bring them together, and when it occurs, a battle must be fought to prove dominance. A battle of physical strength or willpower. It can end in death or subservience. Amuells may be tamed rather than killed."

"One has a rat amuell," scoffed Gallan. "Hardly much of a battle."

Popa smiled. "Voldari of higher status have more, shall we say, *challenging* amuells."

"Did Black Griffin, Hor-gnasher, kill a griffin?"

"Maybe," I said. "Or made one his servant."

"Not only size or ferociousness prove challenging," said Popa. "Some animals are cryptic. Hard to find in the wild."

"Like a snow owl."

"Definitely," perked Rambleton. "Rare in the wild. And hard to see or hear."

"Other animals are difficult to tame," said Popa.

"Like a floe bear," mumbled Yula.

"Most definitely," smiled Popa.

"This is a disturbing conversation," said Barick. "Do we know anything else about the Voldari?"

"Although they are powerful," said Popa, "they don't rule Kogot. Last I heard, Emperor Urlack ruled, but I've lost touch with current events."

"Now rules Empress Orleni," said Rambleton. "Traders tell me."

Popa nodded. "Urlack's daughter."

"Why did the Voldari come to Karlik to purchase serpent oil?" I asked. "Why didn't Empress Orleni send someone else?"

"I don't know," said Popa. "But you're right, Silveny, it is strange."

"They might be trying to recruit converts," joked Gallan. "It would take a lot to shave a mudgle and keep the hair off, but I wouldn't mind trying it. Have animal fur, feathers or teeth grafted to my skin. Wonder what my amuell would be?"

"A goose," grumped Yula.

"Would you drink its blood?" asked Barick.

Gallan shrugged. "How bad can it be?"

How bad? How bad can any of it be? With no concern for antiquity, I placed a naked fingertip on a lettered wooden square and moved it to make the space between it and the other squares even. I did the same for the adjoining squares.

"You must be worried, Silveny. Your compulsion doesn't usually follow you to the cabin."

I pulled my finger away. "Sorry, Popa. I lost myself."

"But we found you," smiled Rambleton.

The white fingertips of Popa's gloves soiled with dust, he continued to collapse the skin leaves from top to bottom, the twine rubbing flakes from the holes along each edge.

I stopped him at a leaf. "What is that?" I asked, pointing to a thumbnail sketch drawn in the middle of the leaf and surrounded by barely visible text.

Popa guided my hand away. "Not too close. The sweat and oil in your fingers will fade the ink."

Barick and Gallan shifted their crate-seats to crowd around me. Yula remained at the dining table, and Casca sat on the floor in silent contemplation. Rambleton threw more sticks on a waning fire, then wandered around the cabin humming to himself and wiping dust from the shelves.

"It's a chair," said Barick. "Made of...of bodies?"

"Petrified bodies," said Popa. "Fitted together in a grim puzzle to form...."

"A throne," whispered Casca.

I glared at him. "What did you say?"

"He's right," said Popa. "The obsidian lenses worn by our mysterious boy may mask his blindness, but his intellect is there for all to see. This is the Throne of the Dead," announced Popa, placing a gloved fingertip on the sketch. "Volerdie's throne."

"That throne was destroyed over thirty yarles ago," said Barick. "Atop the great pyramid in Malang Gunya. Turned to ash by Tom Anderson and Adalwolf Heine."

Popa nodded. "True. The Book of Leaves is ancient. The text written generations before that event, in a language long dead. It has taken me many yarles of study to learn it." He held the concertina of leaves up towards his face, leaned over and squinted. "Hard to read, but these words seem to describe the throne in Pergamos."

"The city of Pergamos is older than the text," I said.

"Pergamos was not always a city. It began as a circle of stones. A place of simple worship. The Book of Leaves may refer to this time." Popa heaved a tired sigh, then collapsed all the parchments, pushing the wooden runners together and flipping the 'V' cap, hinged to the top runner, closed.

"Wait," said Gallan. "Is there more?"

"What more do you want to know? Barick is right; the Throne of the Dead was destroyed. Another cannot be made unless...."

"Unless what?"

"Volerdie returns to this world," said Casca.

"But he didn't return," squeaked Barick. "Volerdie was foiled. That's what the stories say. He didn't return, and a new throne can't be made."

Popa nodded a sleepy head. "Right again, Barick. Malphas sacrificed his immortal brother, Widukind, on the dead throne to lure Volerdie back to Enthilen. But the sacrifice failed, and Malphas was defeated when the throne was destroyed. Volerdie didn't return, leaving Widukind dead on the summit of Malang Gunya's pyramid. You shouldn't worry about these distractions. About things that won't come to pass. The Voldari are your biggest concern."

"The Voldari want nothing more than our oil and knowledge," snapped Gallan. "I'm sure there's an explanation for what happened in the mine. One bad Voldari acting alone."

"Murder!" I snarled at Gallan. "Abduction. Sacrifice. That's what happened in the mine. And Hor-gnasher wasn't alone. They killed my friend."

"We don't know that. Only you saw Jolia."

I boiled inside. I wanted to jump up and shake Gallan until the truth fell out. Instead, I ran my thumbnail along the edges of each fingernail. Both hands. Back and forth. Back and forth.

Rambleton wandered over to Casca sitting on the floor and circled him, sniffing at the boy's hair. The white mudgle crouched before the boy and waved his hand in front of his glasses, then leaned forward and blew in his ear. Casca remained motionless.

"He can't see," Yula said to Rambleton. "He's blind."

Rambleton stared at Casca. "Oh, no. He can see. Remove the spectacles."

"Stop making nonsense," muttered Popa. "Tend the fire, Rambleton."

The white mudgle left Casca to his thoughts and knelt by the fire, shoving an iron poker into the scattering of twiggy coals and letting it rest there. Yula kept her distance at the table while Barick and Gallan went outside to the sleigh to retrieve the bedrolls, their tiredness trumping further curiosity about the Book of Leaves.

I sat beside Popa. "Do your parchments say anything about shadow men?"

He chuckled. "I need more information than that. Shadows abound in all the dark corners of this world. Light and love can cast them away. Did you see his face?"

"Yes, and no. He turned to me, but it was like a veil dropped between us. A blurring of lines that might offer explanation. Barick said something similar. A face, but not a face. A contortion of beauty."

"Maybe he's another Voldari?"

No. He's worse than that.

Popa let me wear the gloves. I pulled out the wooden runners labelled with the letter 'M.' After opening them, the parchments told stories about Morskoy during a time when the city, then only a village, wasn't icebound. And showed a drawing, the size of my fingernail, of a mouldewerp.

Popa soon tired of our exploration and shut the box. He gazed longingly at Yula with an ache that pleaded for reconciliation. "How is your work?" he asked her. "On the balloon line."

She shrugged.

"Still dangerous," I said. "But I've invented something to make it less so."

Popa smiled. "How wonderful, Silveny. Tell me about it."

"That's right," rumbled Yula. "Return your attention to her."

"You have my attention, Yula. You've always had it."

"Liar," snapped Yula. "We didn't have it when we most needed it. When our other parents died."

Popa's eyes glistened. "I gave it to you for as long as I could bear. Until the grief...."

"Made you slink away like a coward. Run up here to the mountains to hide in your squalid cabin."

"You could have visited. Silveny visited."

"Why should I chase you?" Yula stood, bunching her fists.

Barick and Gallan walked back inside carrying the bedrolls, then stopped in the doorway. A cold wind blew snow into the cabin. But it melted with Yula's anger.

"You're pathetic," growled Yula. "You have more time for a simpleton mudgle than your offspring. More love for your books and words than for me."

"That's not true," wept Popa, curling over with grief.

It didn't dampen Yula's need for reckoning. She stepped towards Popa with blood dripping from her palms where the nails had dug in. I stood, ready to protect my father from an assault. An attack I couldn't believe might happen. Barick and Gallan dropped the bedrolls on the floor and closed the door behind them.

Popa held a trembling hand towards his first daughter. "Yula, please."

"I hate you," she sobbed. "I wish you were dead. I wish you died in the avalanche."

As she took another step towards Popa, Rambleton cried out, "No hurting," then stood and spun away from the fire, still holding the iron poker.

Despite all of Casca's seeming intuition, he didn't sense the hot poker coming. It smacked into the side of his face, smashing his glasses and searing his skin. The boy reeled back and cried out. A shocked Rambleton pulled the iron away. Casca rolled on the floor, his hand on his cheek, screaming.

Rambleton dropped the poker and lurched around the room, moaning, "I'm sorry. I'm sorry. Didn't mean. Stupid mistake. Stupid white mudgle." He slapped his forehead, over and over.

Popa lifted himself from the chair and wrapped his arms around his companion. Barick dropped to his knees to help Casca. But the boy had already stopped reacting to the pain. He sat up and pulled his hand away from his face. I gasped. Gallan and Yula stared in disbelief. Where the poker had hit, where the iron surely burned his cheek flesh, there wasn't a mark. Not a scald or a blackness or blistered skin. Rambleton was strong. A big, beefy mudgle. And he was frightened and protective when he swung the poker. The blow shattered Casca's bone-rimmed, obsidian glasses to pieces. Most normal people would have been knocked out. But Casca wasn't normal.

Rambleton pulled away from Popa, knelt on the floor and crawled over to Casca. He poked his finger out, gentle, shaking, a hair's breadth from Casca's cheek, ready to caress the skin.

"No hurt," said Rambleton. "How no hurt?" He lifted the boy and set him on a timber crate.

Casca faced me with his naked, scarred eyes, daring an explanation.

"Your skin should be burnt," I said.

"At least seared or red," said Gallan.

"But there's nothing," said Barick.

Yula moved before any of us could stop her. She loomed behind Casca, then thrust a cookery knife into his left hand resting on the crate. The blade stabbed him between the knuckles and pinned his hand to the timber. But there was no blood. No screams from Casca this time. He groped for the knife, yanked it from his hand, and the wound healed itself.

"You can't be harmed," I said.

"Not in the way you think," replied Casca.

"There's an explanation for this," said Popa.

"Casca is immortal," said Gallan.

I faced him, agape.

"Yes," said Popa. "That is the only explanation."

Chapter 13

The Dragon Festival

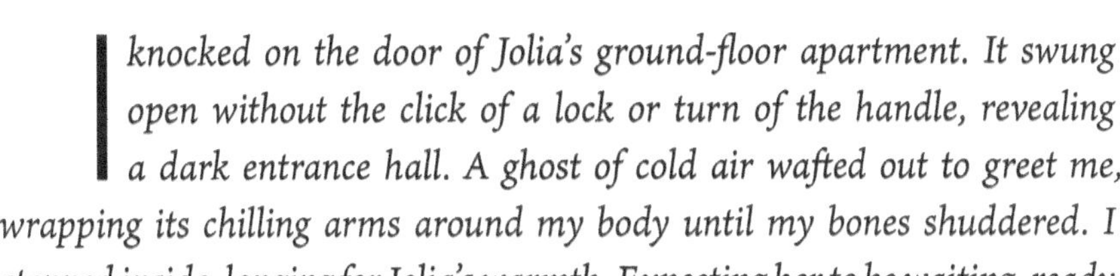

knocked on the door of Jolia's ground-floor apartment. It swung open without the click of a lock or turn of the handle, revealing a dark entrance hall. A ghost of cold air wafted out to greet me, wrapping its chilling arms around my body until my bones shuddered. I stepped inside, longing for Jolia's warmth. Expecting her to be waiting, ready to pull me from the ghostly embrace. Only emptiness was the doorkeeper, its welcome a dull ache setting in my chest.

"Jolia?"

A rusting flicker answered, creeping out the doorway to another room and washing the darkness with an auburn half-light.

"Are you there?"

Through a cloud of misty breaths, I brushed the ash-snow from my coat.

"Leave it," came Jolia's voice.

I stumbled further inside, drawn by the promise of her companionship, and stepped into the other room. Jolia sat at a table, her bowed head covered in a black veil. A candle hung above the table, tied horizontally and dripping wax onto a plate. I sat in the chair opposite Jolia, the room's shadows crowding around us, eager to hear their fortune.

Jolia raised her head and pulled up the veil, revealing blighted eyes like Casca's. Milky. Vacant. Blind. Dead.

"What happened...," I started, too dismayed to finish.

"Our world is melting," she said. "Can you read the signs?"

Confused, I shook my head.

Jolia waved her hand over the wooden tabletop etched with a

checkerboard of pictures of Karlik: dragons, mines, serpent oil, balloons, mountains, and many other things contributing to Curmudgle life. Tiny, intricate representations carved into the wood.

"Our history and future," she said.

Jolia removed the wax-covered plate and swung the suspended candle in an arc. It flew above the table, dripping wax onto random pictures. Random, I thought. But not random, I learned.

The candle's flight cast a spell over my logic. Swept away reason and judgement. The room's chill ached in my core, trapped there by the leering shadows that pressed closer as the prophecy took shape. I wanted to beg for warmth, but expectation had frozen my mouth shut.

The swinging candle halted. Jolia broke the strings suspending it in place and fixed it to the plate.

"What do you see?" she asked.

I chipped the ice from my lips. "The wax has fallen on...dragons...mine... barrels of serpent oil...."

She bowed her head and ran her fingers over the tabletop, feeling for every lump of cold wax. Her ruined face offered no hint of understanding. No trace of what she read.

Shivers crept through my body as if Jolia's fingers tried to read Karlik's future in the fractures of my bones.

Then she stopped. Statue-still. Fingers pressed against a wax lump.

The shadows leaned in such that their breaths almost snuffed the candle's flame. The silent anticipation gnawed. I screamed inside for it to be filled.

Jolia looked up with blue eyes as clear as a cloudless sky at high sun. "Danger ahead," she warned. "Karlik will fall. You must escape."

"What danger?"

She grasped my hands, pushing the palms together in an urgent prayer. "Don't let the promise of my discovery trap you here. It's too late for me, Silveny. My life is lost. Save yourself."

*   *   *   *   *

The rising sun formed a halo around Yula, who stood like a sculptured sentinel on the rocky lookout above Popa's cabin. Although she'd wrapped herself in thick furs, she looked small and distant. Our begging had forced her to come to the cabin. Bent her will against her own desire. Nevertheless, after not seeing Popa for yarles, I had hoped she'd bring compromise, but the events of last night offered no hint of it.

I wanted someone to talk to about the premonition in my dream. About Jolia's warning. About Casca's immortality. It would take me an hour to reach Yula, slogging through knee-deep snow, and I expected my sister wouldn't offer the counsel I desired. Instead, I appreciated the sunrise from the cabin's porch as it melted away the storm clouds and offered the promise of untainted blue, something I longed for. Karlik's venting fires turned everything a stained amber, and the ash-snow fell, clouds or no clouds, peckering the air with its bone-coloured poison.

Oh, to be free of it.

I strapped a pair of snowshoes over my boots and shunted through the snow, not planning to go anywhere particular. Needing time and space to think. On the upper slopes, away from Karlik's unnatural atmosphere masking subtle seasonal changes, nature offered convincing evidence of The Melt taking over from Snowfall. Icicles clinging to rock ledges dripped their thaw with the first sunlight. Animal tracks, meadow mice by the looks, dotted the snow near boulder shelters as the creatures awoke from their cold-induced slumber. After last night's storm, the wind had abated to a teasing breath. Overhead, a stone falcon circled, searching for a sign of snow hare among the vast white.

I passed a frozen waterfall, stepping across the top of its iced pool with the lightness of a flower petal falling from the stem lest the ice crack, plunging me to unknown depths. A maze of snow-covered boulders dotted the other side of the waterfall, a good place for animals to den. It reminded me that horned wolves had been spotted close to the cabin. I shouldn't wander further. I should've brought the hunting bow, though I had no skill in using it.

As I turned to go back, a voice called out from behind, "Sil-Sil-Silveny. Better than gold!"

Rambleton bustled around a boulder outcrop, pulling a sled. Against the backrest sat a bundle wrapped in animal skins and furs with a weathered face peeking out.

"Popa?" I asked.

"It's him," said Rambleton as he stopped beside me.

"He should be in the cabin. It's cold out here."

"Nonsense," said Popa. "I like to do the trap rounds every once and a while."

"Snare down there," said Rambleton, stepping from the sled harness and pushing past me to a den under a boulder with black dirt showing through the snow.

"Caught anything?" called Popa.

"Another empty one," said Rambleton.

Popa sighed. "We'll do better in coming days. The Melt is early this yarle." He pointed to the lookout. "Is Yula up there?"

I nodded.

"What is she doing way up there?" asked Rambleton, returning to the sled.

"Getting away from me," said Popa.

"Don't say that."

"It's true, Silveny. It's been five yarles since her last visit. She'll never forgive me for leaving both of you in Karlik. But every day, your little faces reminded me of what I'd lost."

"No, Popa Courtan," said Rambleton. "No time for sad."

He smiled. "No time for sad."

Rambleton perked up. "I see another snare good place." He grabbed a roll of wire and sticks from the sled and scooted off to a distant boulder.

"I dreamed of Jolia last night," I said to Popa. "She begged me to leave Karlik. Warned of danger ahead."

"Danger forever stalks. We can't let it rule our lives."

"Our family sought a better future elsewhere. And you abandoned Karlik; why shouldn't I?"

Popa looked again at Yula, a glisten of tears sparkling in the sunlight.

I stepped closer to him. "Sorry. I didn't mean...."

"I don't want you or Yula to face danger. Your safety is more important to me than anything."

"What do you make of Casca?" I asked.

"Those who endure endless lives have many secrets. Casca will keep his close."

"I expect he's involved with the Voldari."

"Involved?"

"He claims he wants to uncover their plans. But how did he know they'd be in Karlik? How long has he been following them?"

Popa turned to me, his sad face hardening. "Immortality can do strange things to those who have it. Turn good people bad. Cause them to devalue mortal life. Be careful with Casca. His motivations may never be clear to you."

"Immortals *can* die," I said. "Athalee Stansfield killed the immortal Malphas when the dead throne was destroyed. Malphas sacrificed his immortal brother."

Popa offered a faint smile. "You remember the Seminaria history lessons."

"The Literati Reader's daughter was always going to be a dutiful student."

Popa's smiling face turned serious again. "*One birth twin, immortal no more.* When the dead throne was destroyed, all immortals in this world should have become mortal. Their immortality was tied to the throne's power. How did Casca escape this fate?"

I shook my head in confusion. "We learn something new about him, and it raises more questions."

Popa's eyes drifted to the lookout. "Rambleton could pull the sled to Yula."

"She won't talk to you."

"I'll keep trying. Rambleton!" Popa called to his companion, who jumped up and trudged through the snow, almost disappearing in a shroud of white.

"You're going to lose him one day," I chuckled. "We might need to dye his hair black."

"What would I do without him?" lamented Popa. "He's been my carer for so long. When I'm gone, Silveny, will you...."

"Don't say that," I stumbled.

"But you won't leave him here alone, will you? You'll take him back to Karlik to live with you and Yula."

"Will he want to go? They treated him like an aberration. An oddity to be ridiculed and tormented."

"You can look after him."

"Another snare set," said the white mudgle as he arrived.

"Can you take me to Yula?" asked Popa.

Rambleton stared at the rocky outcrop and scrunched his face. "A long way she's walked. Up, up, up steep hills. We can try."

"Return to the cabin, Silveny," said Popa. "It's dangerous out here alone."

"We leave after high sun," I said. "Barick and Gallan don't want to miss the end of the Dragon Festival."

"We'll be back in time."

Rambleton strapped himself into the sled harness and tramped off through the snow, barefoot and without a care, dragging Popa behind him.

He won't make it to Yula. Even if he does, what will she and Popa talk about? At least she doesn't have the hunting bow.

When I returned to the cabin, Casca sat cross-legged on the floor by the fire while Gallan and Barick ate bread and porridge at the table. I pulled a stool up beside Casca.

"Did you sleep, Silveny?" he asked.

"Not much. Do immortals need to sleep?"

He smiled. "I'm immortally tired. I hope, one day, for an eternal sleep."

"Popa said you should be mortal. Lost your immortality when the dead throne was destroyed."

"Yes, it seems I've outlasted all the other immortals. Crown me the 'Immortalised Immortal.' What a wondrous but depressing mantle."

"What's it like? Knowing you won't die."

His smile faded, and he faced me with unmasked, lifeless eyes. "Awful. Death creates life's urgency. Its *vitality*. A reason to get things done, knowing such an opportunity will never come again. I lost that vitality long ago and replaced it with a sullen wandering occasionally enlivened by an unexpected ray of light. You, Silveny, are such a ray."

I blushed and instinctively turned away as if Casca wasn't blind. No-one had called me a ray of light. Not even Popa. "The fire poker and knife blade left no mark," I said, changing the subject. "Yet you have scars."

"I got those as a mortal. The process of becoming immortal made me blind. My birth twin slashed my face before I took her soul."

"We learned a little about birth twins at Seminaria."

"Some of us have one. They live in another world. If we travel there, or they travel here, the opportunity may arise for one to take the other's soul."

"How?"

"Using the eyes of lost souls. Obsidian glass balls that fit into the palm of your hand. If you hold both in your right hand and press your fist against your birth twin's heart, you can steal their soul. You become immortal, they become a draughoul – one of the living dead."

Obsidian. Like the lenses of your glasses. "Why would you steal a soul?" I asked, horrified at the thought.

"I was young and naïve, and I was forced."

"By whom?"

Casca turned away and went quiet.

I changed focus. "Why did you travel to Karlik?"

"I followed the Voldari. I have a bad feeling about what they want. But then, in the mines...."

"You're more worried about that, aren't you? About what Shadow Man did."

"My worry won't help you. The advice I give you now is the same advice I would offer if I knew more. Flee Karlik. Leave the city as soon as you can."

Casca gave the same warning as Jolia in my dream. *I can't ignore both, can I?*

Barick and Gallan peppered the blind boy with questions, but he had little else to offer other than his birth twin, a ten-yarle old girl, had travelled to Ostamp from another world using the eyes of lost souls. While he said she was terrified, he showed no mercy and took her soul anyway, a harrowing immortality his penance.

Popa and Rambleton returned without Yula, unable to make it to the lookout with the sled. We packed our belongings and waited for my sister. She arrived at high sun, sitting beside Popa at the dining table while we ate. But they didn't speak, Yula making the only concession of being physically close to her father.

The azure sky offered hope as we stood outside the cabin, packed and ready to leave. I didn't get all the answers I sought, and received some I didn't expect. I shouldn't trust the Voldari, but hadn't decided if I could trust Casca, and still we knew nothing about Shadow Man or why mudgles were being sacrificed in such a horrid way.

"You're fretting," said Popa as he approached. "You've checked the strapping on your snowshoes a dozen times."

I stood from a crouch and smiled. "Now I'm going home, my compulsion will exploit the familiar complacency."

"You're always welcome to call the cabin home, Silveny. If you think it will help."

We hugged, and I whispered in his ear, "We could make a home together. Somewhere safe. You, me, Yula and Rambleton."

He pulled away. "I look forward to the day."

Popa approached Yula, but she turned away and walked off, slinging the hunting bow over her shoulder. He retreated to his cottage sanctuary, the thick stone walls dulling his heartache at losing those he loved.

Rambleton insisted on joining us for part of the journey. "Braver horned wolves," he said. "More dangerous mountains."

We left the cabin behind, Yula marching in front carrying the hunting bow, Barick leading Grendal pulling the sleigh with Casca on top, bundled up like a floe bear cub, and Gallan, Rambleton and me bringing up the rear.

Despite the warm, clear day, the trek was long, slow, bitter and silent. When Rambleton turned for home, I held him tight and cried. A weight returned to my shoulders, and the burden pressed with an ache I struggled to endure.

* * * * *

We arrived in Karlik as the sun set and a dusk light free of sepia stains settled over the city. After returning Grendal and the sleigh to the stables, we walked to the *Drake Amphitheatre*, the best place to watch the closing display. Thousands of mudgles had already crowded into its stone terraces overlooking the city. Set on a southeast ridgeline, the height of the amphitheatre meant we'd avoid the ash-snow generated by the display. But it wasn't snowing now, real or otherwise. Most venting fires had been temporarily extinguished to heighten the spectacle's visual impact.

At the bottom of the amphitheatre, an orchestra played on a stage, plucking strings, blowing horns and trumpets, and tapping drums. The lilting chorus hinted a hopeful rebirth. The bleak cold of Snowfall had ended, and The Melt heralded a flush of new growth soon to blanket our lonesome valley. Mudgle legend claimed that The Melt began when dragons awoke from their chill-induced hibernation and filled the Grauberge Mountains' caves with fiery breath.

To honour the legend, today's mudgles had built ice sculptures of dragons, drakes, serpents and wyrms on the amphitheatre's periphery.

Pucks played in the snow, building castles with bucket-formed turrets or launching snowballs at each other from behind icy merlons while their parents wandered past canvas pavilions surveying the choices of food and ale. The amphitheatre bustled with the jovial energy I'd always associated with Karlik, but the still, clear night brought a sense of unease.

Mingling with the crowd, like horned wolves in disguise creeping through a woollydon herd, Voldari 'observers' fired my nerves. Dressed in their frost-blue robes fringed with fur, the visitors towered above everyone else, casting raisin-dark eyes down on their hosts. Dispensing judgement and disdain, decorated with the fanciful head and face adornments of the animal amuells they sought to control.

A terrible thought came to me. *Would a Voldari take a Curmudgle as an amuell? Cover their depraved mind with braided mudgle locks in a murderous acknowledgement of the vow to kill or tame every mudgle they encounter.* I shook the stomach-churning thought away.

The orchestra stilled for a moment until the conductor waved her hand, and they struck up the *Eminent March*. Onto the stage paraded the ten Eminents from each mudgle office of power, led by Eminent Stretten dressed in a finery of scarlet robes fringed with snow hare fur. Eminent Graben, the Extractory head, followed, then Eminent Gardia, the Statutoria's Cardinal-warden, walking beside Eminent Drudan and leading Eminent Leabaran from the Literati and the other five Eminents, E'alin, Ospid, Tradal, Músa and O'Deach, the Seminaria head.

Walking behind them came four Voldari, each with unique and elaborate head coverings. I recognised Urn-hasa and Run-targa from my meeting with Eminent Stretten. The third Voldari had a floe bear claw fixed to his bald head. *And the fourth.* The fourth was my nightmare incarnate. Hor-gnasher, the black griffin, marched onto the stage with an authority that said he could cut down the mudgle Eminents there and then, and not a single Karlik citizen would lift a finger to stop him. He turned and fixed his dark eyes on me, smiling with a malice that froze my soul quicker than a water droplet in the death of Snowfall.

The orchestra finished its prelude. Eminent Stretten stepped to the front of the stage, taking the lectern from the conductor, while the other Eminents and guests sat on gilded chairs facing the crowd. Gallan pulled out his notebook and pencil, preparing to record the events for a story in the *Karlik Chronicle*.

Casca nudged me in the side. "Who has arrived?"

"All the Eminents and four Voldari."

The crowd's murmurs stilled as Eminent Stretten swept her arm across the gathering of eager faces. "It's delightful to see so many of you here!" she cried. "Welcome to the culmination of our event. The 66th anniversary of Karlik's Dragon Festival."

The crowd clapped, cheered and whistled.

"This is a special anniversary," said Stretten before pausing to let the crowd settle. "A special anniversary because our honoured guests from Kogot have agreed to join us." She faced the Voldari and placed four fingers to her forehead, then her heart. The visitors repeated the gesture, then Stretten returned her attention to us. "I'm certain they'll enjoy the spectacle, as we always do. Everything driven by the wonders of serpent oil!"

The crowd cheered again.

Stretten quieted them with pressing hands. "Never have I been so optimistic about Karlik's future. Old mines will soon be reopened. More balloons will travel the line, carrying oil to our valued customers and floating back down with all the treasures that make our city a joyous place to live."

Joyous place. For how long?

"In days to come," continued Stretten, "the Eminents may call on you to devote your energy to securing valuable oil supplies. To make sure the opportunity before us is not lost. I know I can rely on the tenacity of Karlik's citizens. It's enshrined in legend!"

"What she means," mumbled Barick, "is that all of you will be down the mines digging for oil with me."

"I've spoken enough," said Stretten, one thing we agreed on. "Without further waiting, let the finale begin!"

She stepped down from the stage, and an attendant handed her a flaming torch. The Eminents and Voldari turned their chairs around to face the city. Stretten lit a fuse. The crowd stilled to expectant silence, then jumped when a fire rocket launched and exploded into the night sky with a shower of sparks that resembled amber diamonds trying to outshine the stars.

The conductor returned to her lectern and raised a baton. With a gentle sweep, she directed a solitary viola in a mournful tune that floated above the crowd, drawing their eyes to a single venting fire set alight on the other side of the valley near the balloon line. Another viola and another venting fire beside the first sprang to life, flames entwining and dancing like lovers in a ballroom trying to suspend time. A lantern floated up from the city, the first of many that would be released. It resembled a wyvern, one of the smaller dragons, with a fire glowing in its golden belly. As it drifted over our heads, an archer shot an arrow into its chest, and the lantern exploded in a ball of flame.

The bass drummer started a menacing, rhythmic thump. Through the crowd ran a dozen mudgles, each with a pole lifted above their head supporting a winding, twisting serpent. When the fabric beast opened its mouth and spat a flame, the pucks screamed and cowered behind adult skirts. But this was only the prologue. Rising from the mines to our right came a larger serpent, floating from a belly full of serpent gas. It drifted towards us. The drummer increased the tempo of his beats. The serpent loomed, thicker than a house and longer than a laneway. A symbol crashed, and a ring of venting fires near the east mines burst to life. A mechanical dragon flew between the flames, paper-thin metal and fabric held aloft by gas-filled balloons painted black, so it appeared the dragon soared on its own. A stilted flap of wings, driven by coiled springs, enhanced the charade as the dragon bore down on the serpent. The winged beast opened its craving mouth. I expected to see a bolt of flame shoot out. But something faltered. The dragon collided with the serpent, and fire exploded across the night, consuming the fabric serpent and a dragon balloon.

The crowd cheered regardless, welcoming the calamity. The dragon spiralled towards the ground, crashing into the cliff marking the western edge of *Death's Pass*.

The orchestra strings took the baton from the drummer and offered a sombre chorus of heraldry. Hundreds of hand-sized lanterns drifted up from the city below, carrying little tealights to the stars. The night sky filled with speckles of flickering light, dancing behind curtains of coloured paper. Some crowded together, jostling for ascension to the realm of mountain spirits, while others floated off on their own, beginning a journey of solitude to destinations unknown.

Each lantern represented a lost mudgle still remembered, and the number grew with every passing yarle. Yula and I had made lanterns for our departed parents. Standing beside me, Yula shed tears as the lanterns floated off into the night. I wrapped my arm around her, promising to make a lantern for Jolia and her da'three next yarle.

The orchestra increased tempo again, horns, trumpets and drums joining the strings as venting fires sprang up across the mountains in a synchronised dance. A few set fire sculptures alight, and burning wolves, bears and dragons invaded the ridgelines. Fire rockets exploded from the roofs of city buildings, showering Karlik with sparkling fountains. Balloons shaped as dragons, drakes, wyverns, wyrms and lindwyrms filled the sky. One caught fire from the rocket sparkle and exploded in flame, setting the crowd to rapturous applause.

I considered describing the spectacle to Casca, but he appeared content offering his blind face to the stars.

In a flash of golden scales, a mechanical dragon larger than six houses glided from a ridgeline. Too heavy for balloons to hold it aloft, sweeping, fabric-covered wings helped it fly, at least until it had passed the adoring crowd. It opened its cavernous mouth, and the fire worked this time, shooting a searching flame into the darkness.

The crowd stood in gaping awe. Even the Voldari seemed impressed, fixing their judgemental eyes skyward. I smiled. *Best Dragon Festival ever.*

Then, something awful happened.

A rumble came from the amphitheatre's eastern edge. At first, I thought it was part of the finale. Another spectacular display. But then, a wall of rock exploded from the mountainside, hurling boulders into the air. Some brought down the balloons. A flying, tumbling boulder as large as a wagon cannoned into the mechanical dragon and shattered it. A ball of flame bigger than a house erupted with a fiery scream, followed by a spew of rock and ash. The calamity landed on the amphitheatre crowd. Chaos ensued. Mudgles on fire stumbled into their companions. Others cowered beneath rocks. More detritus burst from the mountainside. Another vent of uncontrolled fire followed. Screams burst my ears. Terror filled my soul. On stage, the orchestra wrestled with their instruments and ran for cover. The Eminents and Voldari had already disappeared. Gallan and Barick cowered beside me. Yula sprinted into the chaos, wrapping her coat around a burning mudgle to extinguish the flames. Casca joined my sister, grabbing for a dying infant and cradling her in his arms.

I pulled Barick and Gallan to their feet. "We have to help!"

They followed me into the unforgiving night, and the horror engulfed us.

Chapter 14

Clearing away the rubble

The Restoria bulged with the frightful pain of the injured and dying. Lying on the reception floor, dozens of mudgles moaned and writhed like a bloody, disjointed serpent. Barick and I tried not to slip on the blood as we carried an unconscious mudgle into the carnage and laid him on the tiled floor, the final moments of his life pulsing through the holes of a shredded coat.

Barick rocked his head in quavering hands. "What do we do? What do we do?" He yelled into the madness, "Healer…healer!"

"There won't be enough healers," I said, crouching beside our victim. "Or enough beds."

I pried apart the mudgle's coat and torn undershirt and turned away, biting my tongue. Barick whimpered. Shards of rock like shattered lava-glass had embedded in the victim's chest. Circlets of blood seeped around each shard in threatening pools, then overflowed with scarlet tears mourning a fading life.

"We need to get the rock out," I said, steeling myself to face the affront.

"How?" asked Barick. "I'm not a healer."

"None of us are," I snapped. "But we have to help."

Yula strode into the Restoria with a mudgle slung over her shoulder. She dropped the victim to the floor and then marched back out the door.

Look after one, Yula. Don't keep bringing more in.

Gallan stumbled around the room, searching for a face he recognised.

As if only willing to offer care to those he knew. Casca sat in the corner, still cradling the same mudgle infant he'd found in the amphitheatre immediately after the explosion. Most of her hair had been burnt off, and a bruise of violent purple spread across her skull and neck.

"Find tweezers," I said to Barick. "And padding and bandages."

He nodded and staggered away, trancing across the tiles in a nightmare he couldn't escape.

I reached fingers towards a rock shard about the size of my thumb. As I pinched its end, the seeping blood pool encircling the shard bubbled a deathly threat. I cringed, then paused, uncertain of my action. *I'm not a healer. I don't know what I'm doing. Leave it alone. Leave it alone. Don't….*

The victim spasmed, arching his back. My fingers squeezed before I pulled my hand away, taking the rock with me. Blood seethed from the rockless wound, angered by my stupidity. I tossed the shard behind me.

"Healer!" I screamed. *None here. You're on your own.* "Barick!" I cried instead, hoping he'd arrive with bandages to cover my error.

Casca laid his adoption on the floor, then crawled over to me. "Silveny. Can I help?"

"Go back to your patient," I said.

"She's dead."

Damn, damn, damn, damn. "Can you see Barick anywhere?" *Of course, he can't. Idiot, idiot, idiot.*

"I hear him coming," said Casca.

"I should have left the rock. Should have left it alone. Should have…." I pressed my hand onto the unforgiving floor tiles, trying to glue my fingers in place to avoid another stupid mistake. Lifted them – *not stuck* – pressed them down – *stick!* Lifted them – *not stuck* – pressed them down again – *stick! Stick! Stick! Stick!*

Casca grasped my wrist. "You did the right thing, but we should wait for bandages before you try anything else."

Barick arrived, tripping over the legs of a prostrate mudgle and spilling padding and bandages on the floor. I crawled after them, clutching the dressings to my chest as tears soaked into the cotton.

Casca covered the seeping wound with his crimson hand. "I'll hold a swatch of padding here." He reached his other hand towards me, and I squeezed a square of padded cloth into his palm.

"Tweezers?" I said to Barick, frozen above us.

He shrugged with clueless eyes.

"Help me," I pleaded.

Barick knelt beside the victim – *nameless, impersonal* – and I shoved dressings into my friend's hands. I hesitated above another rock shard, smaller than the first, then gritted my teeth and pinched its protruding end. I tugged, but my fingers slipped from the end. The victim – *what's his name?* – moaned.

I tried again, holding tighter. But when I pulled, the bloodied skin around the wound bulged.

"It's buried deep," said Barick.

"Knife?" I snapped. "Do you have a knife?"

He shook his head. "I can go find one."

"No. I need you here."

Blood tears streamed again as I probed a finger between the rock's edge and the skin, searching deeper into the wound, trying to find the buried end of the shard. Drowning my fingertip in a stranger's flesh. Violating his creation.

I found the bulbous end – *hope I found it* – pressed my thumb into the tip of the protrusion, tensed, then, without thought or fear or concern, I pulled my hand away. The skin tore, the blood pulsed, and the gruesome shard of rock relinquished its burrowing threat.

Barick pressed padding against the wound. "Another six to go. We'll run out of padding, but we can wrap bandages around his body."

That's what we did. I found a knife on another victim, now a corpse, and pried the remaining rock shards from their wounds. We padded and bandaged the best we could. I didn't know if our patient would survive. I didn't even know his name.

Finally, a healer rushed into the reception area and helped us treat the neediest victims. But there were so many – too many – hundreds, at least. Nevertheless, we worked together, the blind boy, the daunted Barick, and the obsessive me, into the night and the next morning.

In the end, we could barely move from exhaustion, with only enough energy to stagger home.

*　*　*　*　*

A knock on the door woke me. I stumbled from bed into a dark, cold house, the gas fire unlit.

The knock came again. "Wait," I called out, fumbling with a box of firesticks on the cookery bench. I pulled a firestick out and scraped it against the strike paper. Then I lit a lantern and walked half-asleep to the door.

"Who is it?" I asked. Not something I'd normally do, but Karlik had veered from the normality I recognised.

"Gallan," came the reply.

I opened the door to find my smiling friend.

But his smile soon faded. "Silveny. Are you alright? You're covered in blood."

I squeezed the braids of my blood-mattered hair, rubbing dry flakes between my fingers until crimson snow tumbled down the front of my naked body.

Oh, I'm naked. "It's not mine," I said with dismissive absence. "At least…I don't think it's mine. I didn't have the energy to wash."

Gallan guided me back inside and shut the door. "You'll freeze. I'll light a fire while you put on clothes."

"Clothes? Yes, clothes."

I drifted back to my bedroom to find a shirt, skirt, and coat thrown on the floorstones. The assaulting smell of dried blood punched my nose. I opened the garderobe and took out a nightgown. It would do for now. I'd wash everything tomorrow. *Tomorrow? Today?*

"What time is it?" I called out to Gallan.

"The night after the explosion. Ten hours from high sun."

"It's late," I said, slipping on the gown and joining him beside the gas fire.

"I wanted to make sure you were alright."

I nodded, then peeked behind Yula's bedroom curtain. "She's not here."

"All the line workers got called out. The explosion damaged the balloon line."

"She can't work now. She hasn't slept."

"They're working in shifts. Sleeping at the stations."

I shivered and held my hands over the fire to dispel chilling thoughts.

"Do you have any ale?" asked Gallan as he stepped into the cookery.

I shook my head. "How can you? How can you think about that?"

He shrugged and began his search for fermented courage.

I shuffled over to the spare bedroom and pulled back the curtain. Casca slept under the bedcovers. I closed the curtain and returned to the fire, slumping onto a chair.

"I found serp-rum," said Gallan.

He brought a flask and two tin cups over. I pushed the empty cup away when he offered it to me. He shrugged again, as if all this chaos was worthy only of his apathy, then placed a chair beside mine, sat and poured himself a drink.

"Still don't know how many dead," he said. "At least hundreds."

"Where were you? Barick, Yula and Casca helped the injured. But you...."

"Had to record what happened."

"Take notes? Is that what you were doing? While mudgles lay dead and dying. Buried alive. You took notes?"

Gallan swigged some bravery. "It's my job. This is the most significant event in a generation. There must be an official record."

Despite sleeping all day, I had no energy for anger. "I should return to the Restoria."

Gallan put his hand on my knee. "It's under control. The injured are being treated. Corpses are being taken to Reilig Mountain. The vultures and wolves will be feasting for days."

Maybe I imagined it, but Gallan had a hint of relish in his voice. A scribe might dream of making a name for themselves by being the herald of such a dire, earth-shattering event.

I moved my knee away. "The catacombs?"

"No room. Too many dead to allow the usual ceremony."

The thought turned my stomach. "I *will* have a drink."

Gallan poured me half a cup of serp-rum, and I downed it in a single gulp.

"Steady," he said.

Steady? I've never been more unsteady. I traced my finger around the cup's rim. *Clockwise. Anticlockwise. Clockwise. Anticlockwise. Clockwise....*

"Gas buildup," mumbled Gallan. "That's what some of the miners say. When we turned all the venting fires off for the Dragon Festival, too much gas built up close to the amphitheatre."

Clockwise. Anticlockwise. Steady.

Gallan leaned closer. "But I heard another story from a survivor. She claimed sabotage. Said she saw the Voldari carrying oil barrels into a mine near the amphitheatre. Soon after, everything exploded."

Unsteady. "What did you say?"

"Doesn't make sense. Why would the Voldari jeopardise their own oil supply?"

Dragons. Mine. Barrels of serpent oil. "The wax prophecy. Jolia warned me. In my dream."

"What are you talking about?"

I shook my head. "Nothing. Forget it."

Gallan leaned back into his chair. "*Death's Pass* is blocked. Barick will be out there tomorrow with the other miners, clearing rubble. The only way we can ship serpent oil is via the balloon line. Makes it harder for us to meet the Voldari order. I think the mudgle claiming sabotage was seeing things. Probably hit on the head by a chunk of rock." He finished his drink and poured another. "The balloon line is our sole link to the outside world. That's why poor Yula has to work tonight and likely a few more nights to come."

"They would do it," said Casca, pulling his bedroom curtain across and walking into the living area. "The Voldari would enact this sabotage if they wished to get a foothold in Karlik."

Gallan scoffed. "They're hardly an invading army. There are only twelve of them. Twelve versus a city of mudgles. Don't like their chances."

"They won't hesitate to sacrifice their own for a greater goal. Already they're favoured by the Eminents. Already they've cast a spell over the city."

"My ma'one cares about Karlik's best interests," snapped Gallan. "About mudgle prosperity."

"Prosperity comes at a cost. When wealth accumulates for some, it diminishes for others."

"Serpent oil has made all of Karlik wealthy."

"Would the miners agree with that?" asked Casca. "Those lying on their deathbeds in your infirmary? And now, it seems, oil is the cause of this most ghastly of tragedies."

Gallan sculled his serp-rum, then ground the cup's base into his thigh.

I faced Casca. "Do the Voldari even *want* oil?"

"Most certainly," said the blind boy, sitting on the bench seat. "But they want to control the means of production at minimal cost. More than the oil, they want your mines. With *Death's Pass* blocked, their next objective would be to secure the balloon line."

"*Line Station 16*, the last station on the line. If you wanted to hold Karlik to ransom and control supplies coming into the city, you'd take over station sixteen. You don't need an army for that. I must find Yula." I stood, prepared to head straight for the line.

"No," said Casca. "Forget Yula. You need to build your flying machine."

"Skycart. I'm calling it a skycart."

"If the Voldari secure the balloon line, your skycart will be the only way out of Karlik that doesn't involve days of tramping through waist-deep snow and being hunted by horned wolves."

"I don't have a model of it yet."

"You must hurry things along."

Casca's right. Damn him. I grabbed a coat from the rack beside the door. "I'm going to see Zurta, the model-builder."

"I'll come with you," said Casca.

"This late?" yawned Gallan. "I should go home to bed, but I'll return to the Governant. It's chaos there. I should be recording it for," he glared at Casca, "*prosperity.*"

Gallan stood, placed the empty flask and cup on the cookery bench, and left.

I buttoned my coat over my nightgown and pulled on a pair of furred boots.

"Are you going like that?" asked Casca.

"I don't have time...."

"You reek of blood and death."

I collected the lantern and shone it up and down Casca's body. "Where's all your blood?"

"In my veins and arteries. Where else would it be?"

"I mean the blood from the mudgles we treated. I'm covered in it."

"I washed," said Casca. "I washed, you passed out, and Yula got dragged to the balloon line. Clean yourself, Silveny. Put on fresh clothes. There's time for that. The Voldari disease is not terminal. Yet."

Casca took the lantern from me. I undressed before him, leaving my clothes on the floor, and stumbled to the washroom. Taking a cake of lye soap, I ran it under the cold-water tap, then scrubbed at my arms and legs, welcoming the cleansing graze of the embedded sand grains as they dispersed the victims' blood. I tipped a pitcher of water over my skin, the blood disappearing down the washroom drain in a final acknowledgement that a life had ended. *This* life. This life that mudgles had known for generations. Down the drain. Into the sewer.

I didn't wash my hair. *No, Casca. No time for that.* Put on a clean shirt, leather panelled skirt, furred hat and gloves. Collected my coat from the floor. Pulled on my boots.

Casca stood by the front door, wrapped in his floe bear furs. "Will the model-builder be working at night?"

"I've never known her to be anywhere else," I replied, donning my coat.

We hurried to the Inventoria, striding through quiet streets like any other Karlik night. But not like any other night. Quiet not because most mudgles had retired to their homes or gathered in the taverns for a festive beverage. Quiet because, on the eastern ridge overlooking the city, workers toiled among the rubble, searching by venting firelight for the dead or the diminishing hope of life. Quiet because healers and helpers laboured inside a Restoria burgeoning with injury. Quiet because Eminents and Governant administrators planned what to do next. At least, I hoped they did.

As we stepped into the front room of Zurta's basement complex, I stumbled over a clutter of discarded steel struts.

"Careful," I said to Casca, "there's so much rubbish here."

A lone lantern flickered on a table beside a tower of books.

"Zurta?" I called out. No response. "You wait here; I'll find her." I walked further inside, leaving Casca in the doorway. As I stepped over another pile of rubbish, cubes of broken stone, I banged my foot into a table leg. "*OW!* Damn."

"Who's there?" came a voice from under the table.

"Zurta?"

"Who else? What do you want? It's late."

I knelt and moved two timber crates aside to find Zurta on her hands and knees, surrounded by piles of rubble. "What are you doing?"

"Making debris," she quipped as if the task enthralled her. "Eminent Drudan says, 'all mudgles to the grind.' Stiff old fool. But there's been an explosion. Didn't you hear? Everyone in the Inventoria is working on machines to remove rubble. Better than spades and shovels. Or bare hands. Some poor souls might be buried alive! Got to clear the road.

Hold this." She handed me a spiralled brass cone and crawled out from under the table, brushing the rocks and stones from her leather apron when she stood.

She gawked at me with horror. "Mountain spirits, preserve us. What happened to you? You didn't trip on an invention, did you? Tumble to the ground and split your head open? It was bound to happen one day. Wait." Zurta reached out and tugged at my hair braids. "Matted with dried blood. Disgusting." She flicked her hand towards the ground, trying to dislodge the unwanted attachment.

"I was at the amphitheatre when the explosion happened. We carried injured mudgles to the Restoria."

"Damn Dragon Festival," she huffed. "I keep telling that stiff old fool Drudan it's too dangerous. Turn off the venting fires. Let gas build up for dramatic effect. Have dragons and balloons and all manner of stupidity flying across the sky. Breathing fire. Madness. You'll never get me near one of those cursed festivals. I'm surprised you're still alive. Anyone's alive. Put the rockscrew on the table so I don't forget it. Who's that?" She pointed at Casca still standing in the doorway.

"A friend," I said. *An immortal friend, but that's not important right now.*

"Blind?" she asked.

I nodded.

"Excellent. He can work with me. The sightless have an amazing sense of touch, and his fingers are fine and delicate. He can position the tiny cogs and wheels better than my gnarled hands. I'm building a model rockscrew. Transportable. Hand-operated. Will pull the rubble out. Fancy kind of auger. Blind boy! Over here."

"Casca tends to do his own thing," I said as he walked towards us, dodging the mayhem strewn across the floorstones.

"All mudgles to the grind," repeated Zurta. "Mudgles, Voldari and boy strangers."

"Do you mean, 'all hands on deck'?" said Casca when he arrived.

"This isn't a ship." Zurta raised her eyebrows at me. "He *is* blind, isn't he?"

It didn't feel right to ask, but I had to. "My skycart?"

"Piecart? Already invented. Made one yarles ago. Apple pies, marrow pies, berry pies – wheeled from street to street and kept warm by an ingenious oil burner."

Casca leaned into me and whispered, "Is she…all there?"

Zurta waved her hand in front of Casca's face. He didn't flinch. "Brilliant," she said. "Definitely blind. He'll be an immense help."

"No!" I said, slamming the rockscrew down onto the tabletop. "I want to know if you've built my skycart model. *Sky-cart.*"

"Oh, that conflummoxing annoyment. Yes, it's done. Up there." She pointed to the ceiling, where a model of my skycart floated above us.

"It works," I said.

"Of course it does," said Zurta. "I don't build nonsense down here."

"Will it come down?"

"Yes. The balloon vents operate as you designed. It will go up, come down, but then must be refilled with gas. You should work on that. Gas cylinders that can be transported in the carriage. But don't expect me to fly in it. Damn thing could explode at any moment."

I climbed onto the table, reached up and pulled down my model skycart. Zurta had fashioned the meladoor timber into a seamless carriage, the front end pointed like a ship's bow, the rear wide like a stern, and wings protruding from the sides. Hugging it to my chest, it was much lighter than I expected. She'd built a storage cabin in the deck's centre, a steering wheel, fabric rudder, propellers, pulleys, rigging, a mainsail, and a drawbridge to allow passengers to embark and disembark. Everything I'd drawn on the plans.

I pulled on the strings attached to the two balloon vents, letting a little gas escape so the skycart wouldn't fly off if I released it, and climbed down from the table.

"I'm taking it to Eminent Drudan," I announced. "He has to approve the full-scale build now."

"Don't know if a real one will work," huffed Zurta. "Anyway, that stiff old fool wants machines to clear rubble and reopen the mines. All mudgles…."

"To the grind," interrupted Casca.

"He won't be bothered with your flycart...."

"Skycart," I corrected again.

"...until we've cleaned up all the mess. Could take days. Many, many days."

My shoulders slumped. I had to get this invention made. If Casca's guesses about the Voldari were right, it could be our sole chance of escape.

"I'll argue with him," I said.

"You can't argue with an imbecile!" screamed Zurta. "Drudan won't approve your skytart. But if you're desperate to build it, you don't need his approval."

"How?"

She leaned in and whispered, "You didn't hear this from me. There's a rogue builder. Flies off the handle, if you get my meaning."

"No," said Casca.

"*Sssh!*" hissed Zurta. "Seems you can talk alright. Now, where was I?"

"Rogue builder," I said.

"That's right. Fergutch. Crotchety old fool. You didn't get his name from me. Will build for the right price."

"I don't have a lot of tokens."

"Might want something other than tokens. He tends to make unusual requests. He's a tad...*unhinged*."

I stood on Casca's foot, hoping he'd keep his mouth shut. "How do I find him?" I asked.

"I'll tell you, but you didn't get his whereabouts from me. Understand?"

I nodded.

Zurta pulled a pencil from her apron pocket and scribbled something on a piece of parchment. She scrunched it up and shoved it into my hand. "He was an Eminent once. Don't make him grumpy."

"How do I avoid that?"

"You can't! He's always grumpy. Don't make him grumpier. Now, I've got rubble-removing inventions to build. Will the blind boy help?"

"I'd be honoured," said Casca, "but maybe another time."

Zurta clutched my shoulder. "Wait. Before you go, have you seen Willamay? My snergul."

"No," said Casca.

I rolled my eyes. "I don't see her here."

"She's gone missing," said Zurta. "Haven't spotted her in...."

A squeak came from under the table.

Zurta's olive face turned pale. "Oh, mountain spirits preserve us! I forgot. I buried her in rubble. Wanted to see how long it would take to get her out. Willamay! I'm coming!" Zurta dropped to her knees and crawled back under the table.

I retrieved my skycart plans from a shelf, already rolled and tied with ribbon, and handed them to Casca for safekeeping. We carried our treasures from the Inventoria and into the darkness. I planned to visit Fergutch in the morning. I didn't want to make him grumpier by arriving on his doorstep late at night.

Karlik had fallen stony quiet. Not a single mudgle walked the streets, and the workers on the ridgeline had thinned, likely exhausted from their gruesome chore. Ash-snow floated around us like downy feathers, in flakes as large as my hand. The venting fires surrounding the city flared with determined vigour, flaming away any chance of gas building up behind the rock and exploding with another calamity.

As we crossed into Tork, my home quarter, Casca dropped the plans.

"Careful," I admonished.

He bent down to pick them up. "It was deliberate," he muttered, placing his hand on the road bricks and holding it there momentarily before collecting the plans. "We're being followed."

I tried to spin around, but he stood and threw his free arm across my shoulder, drawing me close. "Don't look behind," he whispered. "Where is this Fergutch?"

"The workshop's location is in my pocket," I said. "Why?"

"Take it out and read it."

I balanced the skycart in one hand and shoved the other in my coat pocket, withdrawing the crumpled paper.

Fumbling with gloved fingers, I flicked the paper open and stepped under the halo of a streetlamp. "It says...."

"Not aloud," whispered Casca. "I'm trying to listen for our pursuer. They've stopped now. When we walk off, I expect them to follow. We can't go home, and we shouldn't visit Fergutch either. But we need a place to hide close to his workshop."

Casca's concern set my mind reeling. "Why would anyone follow us?"

"You've seen the Voldari sacrificing Curmudgles. You've *reported* it. And you have invented a flying machine that could ship many barrels of oil or other supplies."

"It's not built yet. I don't understand why anyone would want to...."

"*Sssh,*" hissed Casca. "Trust me. Let's walk."

I shoved the paper back into my pocket, wrapped both arms around my invention and followed Casca down the street.

He quickened his pace. "They're continuing their pursuit. Where are we going?"

"Tablease. Karlik's abandoned quarter."

"Somewhere to hide?"

"We'll find a place," I said with flickering confidence. "Close to the workshop."

"Not too close. Lead on. Don't run until I say."

Run? I ducked in front of Casca, walking as fast as possible while trying not to drop the model skycart. The pointed bow dug into my ribs, and I cursed.

We turned a corner.

"Run," said Casca. "Now."

I ran ahead, stumbling through snow drifts, clutching the invention to my chest. I couldn't turn around to check on Casca for fear of falling over. I trusted he'd be there. Or he'd disappear and then reappear in a few days.

I ducked into a side alley, turned another corner, and found another alley leading to Tablease.

"Stop," said Casca, gasping behind me. "We've lost them."

I stopped and dared to check for our pursuer, peering down a dark alley and picturing a wailing terror bolting from the shadows. "Was it the Voldari?"

Casca steadied his breath. "Don't know. Someone persistent, but unfamiliar with the city."

"We could double back to my house."

"Too risky. We should hide here."

Snow, rubble and hardy weeds of dead brown made not-so-happy families along the alleyway. The buildings on either side had broken doors and windows, and the slate or tiled roofs opened to the sky, exposing any shelter-seekers to the toxic blizzards of ash-snow. Despite our coats and furs, we'd suffer a brutal cold braving a night in the open, and we couldn't risk a fire for fear of attracting our pursuer.

I walked on to a steel bollard poking from a snow drift piled on a street corner, then measured three paces into the street.

"What are you doing?" asked Casca.

"We can hide underground," I said, brushing snow away with my boot. "There'll be a pit-lid here, leading to the city sewer."

"I'm not hiding in a sewer."

"It'll be warmer and protected from the weather."

"But exposed to whatever comes out of Curmudgle arses."

"No worse than what comes out of yours."

"I'm not so certain."

I stomped my boot on the ground, a metal clunk answering the knock. "It's here. Help me find the turnkey."

Casca squashed my rolled plans under his arm, dropped to his knees and brushed the remaining snow away from the pit-lid. He removed a glove and prised his fingers underneath the turnkey slotted flat into the pit cover. "Rusted solid. Can't budge it."

I placed the skycart on the ground and picked up a stone from the base of a crumbling wall. "Move away."

Casca crawled aside, and I knelt and bashed the turnkey's edge with the rock.

"Might as well scream *here we are*," grumbled the blind boy.

"Do you have a better idea?"

He shook his head.

I bashed again, and the turnkey budged. I dropped the rock, clutched the iron key and tensed my shoulders. Straining with fearful determination, I lifted the hinged key vertical and turned it ninety degrees. "Alright, need something to lodge under the lip of the pit-lid so I can lift it open."

"Would my special key work?" asked Casca.

"Let's try it."

He placed my squashed plans on the ground, retrieved his magic mouldewerp key, and handed it to me. I removed my gloves and shoved them in a coat pocket, lay on my chest, and slipped the key's bow under the lip of the pit-lid.

"Must be an easier way than this," said Casca.

"Sewer workers have a special handle they insert to lift the pit-lid."

"You seem to know an uncomfortable amount about poo drains."

I made a fulcrum under the key's stem from a brick splinter, then stood and smashed my boot heel down on the key's bit. The brick shattered, but the lid lifted enough to get my fingers under the lip.

"Is my key broken?" moaned Casca. "Did you break the most valuable possession I have?"

I retrieved the key and pushed it into his hand. "Feel for yourself. All in one piece."

"It's bent. It won't work like this."

"You can straighten it."

I knelt again. Hinges squealed as I breached the vault of mudgle waste. A waft of warm, putrid air stung my nostrils, and I gagged. *At least it's warm.*

"More noise," mumbled Casca. "Squealing. Gagging."

I pushed the turnkey back into its slot. "We can lock the pit-lid from the inside."

"What creature of sane mind would lock themselves in a sewer? And how do you know all this? Did you spend your childhood exploring waste drains?"

"My da'two was a sewer worker." I stood and picked up the skycart. "You go first. There's a ladder leading into the drain. I'll hand down the plans and the model."

I swore Casca glared at me with his tortured eyes before he backed down into the sewer and fumbled for the first ladder rung.

Footsteps? Getting closer? Despite my fretting mind, the night offered no clues. No hint the pursuer had found our trail. But my fretting mind wouldn't relent. It never relented.

Casca stepped from the last ladder rung and sploshed into 'whatever comes out of Curmudgle arses'. He mumbled something, then lifted his hands towards me. I lay on my front and lowered the plans down to him. He shoved them under his floe bear furs and reached up for the skycart.

"Don't drop it," I said.

"I could pass out at any moment," grumped Casca. "You realise my sense of smell is heightened. Even mouldewerps consider me an olfactory master."

"Master your concentration," I said, handing him the skycart.

I descended partway down the ladder, then pulled the pit-lid closed after me and turned the underside lock, plunging us into a black so pitch, it was like I'd turned off the sun, moons and stars, and every venting fire and lantern in Karlik. I stumbled to the bottom of the ladder, squeezing each rung lest I fall into the nauseating stench lining the bottom of the drain. *Or knock Casca into it, which would be worse because I'll have to cope with the smell **and** his complaining.*

"Are you there?" I asked.

"Did you expect me to go sightseeing?" he replied. "I assume you can smell this indescribable filth?"

"I'm trying not to vomit."

"I'm trying not to tear off my nose."

"Give me the skycart."

A sharp bow poked into my belly, and I reached forward and placed my hands on either side of the carriage, under the wings. The half-inflated balloon smacked me in the face.

"Got it," I said.

"Now what?" asked Casca.

"There'll be a ledge. Somewhere to sit."

"Sit?"

"Above the drain. Let's walk a bit."

"We're not getting lost. I'm not living for a hundred yarles in a sewer."

"We won't get lost. Follow me."

I sloshed ahead, putrefying liquid swilling against my shins and seeping into the top of my boots. Casca retched behind me. The smell numbed my nostrils. But I could still taste it. An acrid lash stinging the back of my throat.

We walked one hundred and twenty-seven steps, then my left boot toe kicked something protruding into the drain.

"I found a ledge," I said. "You lean down and feel around."

"Why me? I'm not getting my hands covered in this shit."

"I'm holding the skycart. Your sense of touch is much better than mine."

"Oh, so now I'm valued. Now Karlik's citizens welcome the blind boy with open arms."

Casca's sigh echoed down the drain. He bumped me aside and waved his hands about, nearly knocking the skycart into the drink.

"Careful," I snapped.

Casca shuffled and scraped. The shuffling stopped.

"Well?" I asked.

"There's a ledge here, and it's dry. We might be able to lie down on it."

"Alright."

I balanced the skycart in one hand, bent down and waved my opposite hand in front of me. I found flat, solid, dry stone. I hugged the skycart close, spun my bottom around and sat-tumbled into a splashing spew of mudgle bodily waste.

"Damn it!" *I missed the ledge.* The smile on Casca's face blinded my imagination.

"Sometimes," he chuckled, "my different abilities can be advantageous."

I placed the skycart on the ledge, then braced my hands on the bottom of the drain, heaving myself up to sit beside my invention. I scooched my backside away from the sludge until I hit a wall, then slumped against the bricks.

"That was beyond disgusting."

"I believe I've identified a flaw in our plan," said Casca. "How will we know when it's daylight?"

"I'll count."

"What?"

"It was around middle night when we came down here. Six more hours until sunrise. That's exactly 21,600 beats. I'll count; you rest."

"That's madness. Don't do that. You should rest, too. We'll check when we think it's safe."

"I'm not going to sleep. Not with all the drama playing out inside my head."

"You should learn to meditate."

"What?"

"Focus your mind on a quiet, peaceful emptiness. Some people find it useful to have a word they repeat over and over."

I shook my head at the darkness. "I don't have time for that."

"You seem to be in a perpetual hurry. I'm going to meditate. I also find it hard to sleep. Despite eternal weariness."

"How old *are* you?"

Casca sighed. "I stopped keeping track after one thousand yarles."

"A thousand yarles!"

"A nice even number to finish on. But I've lived many more yarles than that. I was born long before the Curmudgles built Cha'thair under the Desolate Mountains. Before the Erstürmen ruled Thyatira, or the stone-grells arrived in Enthilen, or Pergamos arose from the Dambay Plains."

"That's thousands of yarles ago."

"Is it? Yes, you're right. I might glibly ask where the time has gone. But I feel every one of those yarles more each day."

"I understand now how you can navigate this world like you weren't blind. You've had thousands of yarles to hone your other senses."

"I guess that is one advantage of my predicament."

"You said before, when we were at Popa's cabin, that you'd met other immortals. Why didn't you ask them to...you know, put you out of your misery?"

"I find it a difficult thing to do – ask someone to take a life. It's not something I would have done for them. I'm not a killer. I've rarely carried a weapon. And there's an unresolved matter to attend to."

"Unresolved?" I asked. "For how long?"

Casca shuffled his boots on the stones. "I lost count of that also. But the chance to resolve it may be soon approaching."

"What is *it*? This unresolved matter?"

"I'd like to meditate and rest," yawned Casca. "We can talk more later."

I crept my hand out into the darkness and found that Casca had laid down and rolled over, turning his back to me. I pushed the skycart up against the wall to ensure it didn't fall into the stream of waste trickling past our feet, then closed my eyes and tried to focus on the emptiness.

But my compulsion soon filled the void with an avalanche of fixations.

*   *   *   *   *

I woke to something tugging on the laces of my right boot. Casca snored beside me. I kicked out with my left foot.

'*Howwwl. Hisss.*'

Sewer cat. "Go away." I kicked again, the toe of my boot thudding into flesh and bone.

The cat mewled, then sploshed off through the waste stream.

"What?" groaned Casca, half awake.

"Sewer cat. It's gone."

"There are cats down here?"

"My ma'one used to say, 'sewer cats eat sewer rats, and sewer rats eat mudgle scats.'"

"Grotesque," said Casca before yawning.

"Did you find the emptiness?" I asked.

"It's all around us." Casca shuffled beside me. "Is it daylight yet?"

"I got to five thousand before falling asleep."

"We should check."

I heaved myself from the stone ledge, picked up the skycart model, and followed Casca back the way we came, counting out the one hundred and twenty-seven steps that I hoped would return us to the pit-lid.

As we rounded a corner, Casca called out, "Ouch!"

"Sewer cat bite you?"

"I ran into the ladder."

"One hundred and twenty-seven steps. We're back where we started."

"You could have warned me at one hundred and twenty-six."

"I'll look outside."

I gave Casca the skycart model and climbed the ladder, feeling with my hand above my head so I didn't step headfirst into the pit-lid. At the top of the ladder, I grasped the underside lock and turned. But I didn't push the lid open, waiting to catch feet shuffling above ground or any other hint the pursuer might be there, ready to spring a trap.

"We can't stay here all day," called Casca from below.

"*Sssh!*" I hissed.

Casca splashed in the drain, trying to kick the waste away. I hoped he didn't drop the skycart or the plans, then returned my attention to the sounds from outside. Failing to hear anything, I heaved the creaking pit-lid open and poked my head above street level. A rising sun blinded me.

I waited for my eyes to adjust. "Seems clear."

Casca climbed up behind me, balancing the skycart on one hand in a risky, tottering journey that threatened to turn my worry into a nightmare.

I pulled myself onto the street and reached down for the cart's balloon. "I've got hold of it."

Casca released his grip, and I lifted the model from the drain hole and onto the street. Casca followed.

"Daylight and almost blue sky," I said. "A nice welcome from Karlik."

"How far away is this workshop?" asked Casca.

I retrieved the instructions from Zurta and read aloud. "West end of the old marketplace. Between Silas Tavern and Homm's Butchery."

"A drunkard wouldn't want to walk into the wrong one. Do you know how to reach the marketplace?"

"Tablease was abandoned before I was born, but we used to play there as pucks. Best place for hide and seek, ghost stories, chasey. I know where the market is. Don't remember a workshop, but we'll find it."

I walked on, and Casca followed, into a chill air free of ash-snow, the abandoned quarter distant from most venting fires. I tried to relax, knowing Casca would hear any sounds of pursuit long before I did.

Tablease's marketplace sat lonely and silent. The canvas roofs of dilapidated stalls had long torn and shredded into fragments of bustling commerce. The ghostly echoes of merchants haunted the empty laneways, selling worthless trinkets of abandoned hope. Crumbling mortar failed to hold cracked stones in place, and shop facades tumbled to the ground, exposing a nothingness beyond. Benches that once would have been covered in food, cloth, ale, tools, books, arts or other treasures now offered rat excrement as their jewels.

The market reminded me of what Karlik used to be and heralded a presage of what the city could become. A dire prophecy that shouldn't be ignored. *Karlik will fall.*

At the market's western end, squeezed between a tavern and butchery, their identity advertised by rusted signs that wailed a haunting with a bluster of north wind, sat a building as large as six houses. From outside, it looked ready to fall, external stone walls listing to the right, a front window boarded closed with metal sheets and timber beams, and a flat roof of buckled tin. But two sturdy doors exposed the deception; one made of solid timber kept free of decay, and the other made of smooth, imposing steel, tall and wide enough to accommodate two laden wagons abreast. On this door, someone had painted: *Structure unsafe. Do not enter.*

"I've found the workshop," I said to Casca, leading him to the timber door no larger than the entry to my house.

We stopped out front, and I pulled on the door handle. It didn't budge. "Can you hold the skycart?"

Casca cradled his arms, and I placed the model in the crook of his elbows.

"You still have the plans, don't you?"

"Tucked safely inside my bear furs," he said.

I banged a fist on the timber door. "Hello?"

Casca groaned. "Noise is the enemy of those who wish to remain undetected."

"I have to let Fergutch know we're here. Wait, there's a hatch at the bottom." I knelt and slid open a small door, the size of a supper plate, built into the timber. I poked my head inside a dark hole. "Anyone here? Fergutch?" No response. I leaned back on my haunches as the wind picked up, lifting snow drifts into whirlies and racing them across the empty market square.

"I can't hear anything," said Casca. "Not over this inconvenient wind."

I picked up a forlorn road brick and banged it against the steel door. 'Clang. Clang. Clang.'

"Did I not say...." started Casca.

"I know," I interrupted. "Noise is the enemy, *blah blah blah.*"

I knelt and poked my head through the hatch again. Something bit me on the nose. "Ow!" I tumbled backwards, holding my face.

"Sewer cat?" asked Casca.

"Very funny."

"I can smell one of those creatures your friend, Barick, had in a cage."

"Snergul?" I pulled my hand from my nose. No blood.

Casca made a click at the back of his throat.

"What are you doing?"

"Communicating."

From the hatch, a snergul poked its pointed nose outside, sniffed, squealed, and disappeared back inside.

"Did you tell it to run away?" I asked.

"No. Fetch your master. Or something of that nature."

A bell rang inside the workshop, peeling and echoing through the emptiness before the wind ripped the chorus away. Casca wrestled with the skycart, trying to stop the balloon from being torn from the wooden carriage. I stood and huddled beside him, attempting to block the wind's path. Gritty snow smacked the back of my head. The taint of Karlik's sewer swirled around us, enveloping us in a putrescence that would deter the most accommodating helpers.

A voice bellowed behind the door. "What?"

"Zurta sent us!" I yelled.

"Demented old fool," came the reply. "Go away."

"Are you Fergutch?"

"No. Get lost."

"Please!" I pleaded. "We need your help."

"None here."

"A real Curmudgle, if ever there was one," said Casca.

"*Shoosh!*" I snapped, then yelled through the wooden door, "Karlik needs help!"

"Never helped me," came the reply. "Leave me alone!"

Casca pushed the skycart into my arms, crouched beside the door hatch, reached into his pants pocket, and pulled out a square of hard, mouldy cheese. He waved the enticement in front of the hole and clicked at the back of his throat.

After a short while, a furred hand appeared from the darkness and reached for the cheese. Like a striking serpent, Casca snatched at the snergul's arm with his free hand, pulling the creature outside. It squealed and wriggled before biting the cheese from Casca's fingers. The blind boy mouthed barks, clicks and trills, and the snergul relaxed in his arms.

"What are you doing with Levan?" asked the voice behind the door. "Give him back."

"Not until you let us in," said Casca, "and listen to what we have to say."

"How many of you are out there?"

"Two," I said. "I'm Silveny Belarose from the Inventoria, and my friend is Casca. I've brought an invention ready to build. We need your help."

"Ask Drudan."

"He's too busy with other things."

"Stiff old fool."

"You *are* Fergutch, aren't you?"

"Yes, but I'm not building your invention. Give Levan back before I stick a spear in your arse."

"Open the door," said Casca. "I'll deliver Levan and a pouch of gold moynes if you help us."

"Ha!" called Fergutch. "Fool's gold. You won't trick me with that."

Casca placed Levan on the ground, unwound the cord from his boot and banged the heel against the road bricks. A bevy of coins tinkled to the ground. He felt each one in turn until picking out a shiny gold piece with eight sides.

He tossed the coin through the hatch. "Plenty more of those."

Fergutch cursed and grumbled. A door latch clicked, and the door swung open. Inside, bathed in serpent gaslight, stood a stout mudgle, younger than I expected, with brown hair and brown skin like mine. Levan scampered inside and climbed Fergutch, sitting on his shoulder.

I stepped into the workshop, cradling the skycart. "Zurta sent us."

"Demented old fool," grumbled Fergutch.

"She said you could help."

"Can help? Most certainly. Will help? Most certainly not."

As Fergutch went to slam the door, Casca scrambled inside and stood behind me.

"Now, this is an invasion," said Fergutch. "I should report you...." He gagged and latched a hand across his face. "Mountain spirits blight my nose, what is that repulsive smell?"

"We had to hide in a sewer," I said.

"Criminals on the run. Should have guessed. I'll report you to the Statutoria."

"They won't help," said Casca. "They're too busy dealing with the explosion."

"Explosion? What explosion?"

"You didn't hear it?" I asked.

"I heard something. Thought it was part of that ridiculous Dragon Festival you mudgles wet yourselves over."

"A mine exploded. Collapsed half a hillside. Hundreds of mudgles were killed and injured."

"Dangerous out there," said Fergutch. "Good reason to stay here. What's that?" He removed his hand from his face, flared his nostrils, then pointed at the skycart.

"My invention. It's a free-flying airship, I call it a skycart, that doesn't have to be attached to the balloon line. We desperately need to build a full-sized one so we can escape Karlik."

"Escape? You *are* criminals. I'm not working with criminals."

"We're not criminals," said Casca.

Fergutch peered into the blind boy's face. "You look like a criminal. You have shifty eyes. What's left of them."

"He's blind," I said. "Listen, the Voldari are trying to take over Karlik. No-one wants to listen to us. If things go bad, we need a way to get out."

"So, you'd flee like cowards instead of stay and fight?"

Yes. Maybe. I don't know. Should I fight?

"There's more to this than the Voldari," said Casca. "Escaping is the smart thing to do, the only thing if you want to live."

"Well, good luck. I can't help you." Fergutch turned away and Levan barked at us.

We followed the Curmudgle further into the cavernous workshop, dodging past machines that resembled cranes, balancing scales or mechanical clocks, so unique I didn't recognise them from the Inventoria archives. Racks of steel and timber, more timber than I'd ever seen, towered above us, stacked to the tin roof. Copper tubes with brass fittings poked up from the flagstone floor. Other pipes led into hearths that blazed roaring fires. Metal cogs, pulleys and cables hung from stone walls. Cabinets full of tools stood shoulder to shoulder with shelves brimming with books and parchment rolls.

"Why are you following me?" Fergutch asked over his shoulder. "I said I can't help."

"You have no choice," said Casca. "Unless you want to die, you'll help us."

Fergutch stopped and glared. "Are you threatening me?"

Levan bared his canines.

"Not a threat," cooed Casca. "A reality."

"Will this invention of yours save *me*?"

"It will save some of us," I replied. "At least, I hope it will. *Death's Pass* is closed by the mine explosion. I worry the balloon line could be compromised. Taken over by the Voldari."

"Voldari," spat Fergutch. "Can't be trusted."

Levan bowed his head, and his big, round eyes simpered.

"Then help us," I begged.

"Where are the rest of my coins?"

"You'll get them when the job's finished," said Casca. "But you can have these as a deposit." He knelt and opened his boot heel again, letting the coins spill to the floor.

Fergutch hovered over the pile. "Don't recognise most of those." He wavered in place, thinking. The snergul scratched his chin as if also contemplating an answer. "*Hmmm*," sighed Fergutch. "Alright, explain how your flying machine works."

I placed the model skycart on a table, the half-inflated balloon sagging to the carriage deck. Casca withdrew the plans from his furs and rolled them across the tabletop. I talked through the drawings and notes with Fergutch as he walked around the model, tapping on the timber hull, flexing the wings, pushing the rudder left and right, spinning the propellers, tugging on the rigging and sails, and peering into the cabin.

"Rudder will be useless in strong wind," he said. "As will the propellers. Not going to move you in the direction you want to go."

"We can raise the mainsail."

"Ha! Can't build this thing with a large sail. No room."

"The rudder and propellers will work in calm conditions," I defended.

"Gas?"

"Filled from a copper tube. Released by vents in the balloon."

"Refill?"

"Ground station at this stage."

Fergutch vacillated again, then mumbled, "Could be built, but the carriage would have to be smaller and made of reeds. Hardly big enough to save all Karlik."

Casca grabbed my arm. "This is ludicrous. Even if he agrees to help us, it will take seasons for this curmudgeon to build the skycart on his own."

"Cur-mud-gle," growled Fergutch. "And you're wrong, I'm not on my own."

He led us into a dark room with no windows and a smell that smothered me like a blanket soaked in urine, putting to shame our sewer aroma. Fergutch lit an oil lantern hanging from a wall hook and turned up the flow until an amber halo spread across the darkness. A murmuring noise bubbled until it turned into a calamitous wail of barks and screeches. Hundreds of snerguls pressed pointed noses through the metal bars of cages stacked to head height.

"It's morning feed!" yelled Fergutch over the clamour.

He picked up two buckets from the floor and handed them to Casca and me. Inside, grubs, bugs, worms and spiders crawled and squirmed.

"A handful in each feeder!" shouted Fergutch. "Unlatch the doors. They have the run of the place. I only lock them up at night. Can't get any sleep otherwise."

I stepped up to a cage, removed my hand from my nose, dug it into the bucket and threw a handful of bugs into an empty tin cup hanging at the front. Then I opened the door. The snergul gulped down her morning feed, sprang from the cage and climbed onto my shoulder.

"She likes you," said Casca.

"Did she tell you that?" I asked.

He smiled. We continued feeding the animals and opening the cages, dozens and dozens of them.

"I gave up working with mudgles long ago," said Fergutch. "It's why they sacked me as Inventoria Eminent and put that stiff old fool Drudan in charge. But I can work with snerguls. They'll help me build anything."

"Despite all these helpers," said Casca, "you can't build the skycart. You don't have the skills."

Fergutch stopped and flared at the blind boy. "Who are *you* to tell me what I can and can't build? I have the expertise to build anything."

"The skycart is complex. You've seen the plans. You'll need balloon silk, meladoor timber, and light, pliable, strong metal."

"I've seen the plans. *You* haven't. They're rudimentary. Missing a lot of details. I'm the only one in Karlik able to fill in the blanks."

"Can snerguls read plans?"

Fergutch boiled, and Levan, still sitting on his shoulder, snarled. "They don't need to! I've trained them for yarles. They'll do what I order. Miners are idiots. Using snerguls as gas-sniffing sacrifices is a waste."

Casca wandered away from Fergutch and among the snerguls climbing from their cages. Some of the animals barked at him. Others climbed over him or nipped at his ankles. Casca's throat twitched, his mouth slightly parted, and I assumed he was 'talking' to his new acquaintances. The snerguls around him sat quietly at his feet, preparing for a story of bravery and adventure.

He faced Fergutch. "Your workers are concerned that the skycart will be too much for you."

Fergutch flared then screamed, "You don't think I can do it! I'll show you! I'll prove you wrong! Now, get out. I've got work to do."

Levan jumped from Fergutch's shoulder, took empty buckets from our hands and carried them to the table.

The snergul grabbed my hand and dragged me to the door. The other animals scattered from around Casca's feet.

"When do we come back?" I called to Fergutch over my shoulder.

"Later!" he replied. "And bring those gold moynes!"

Levan unlatched the wooden door and pushed it open. We walked outside.

"Exactly how long do you think 'later' is?" asked Casca as the door closed behind us.

I smiled. "You knew he'd argue with you, didn't you?"

"I've met many stubborn people in my lifetime. You learn how to read emotions quickly."

"Is it safe to go home?"

"You'll have to return eventually, but I'm not coming with you. I want to investigate the Voldari further. Find out how much they know about us. If you get into trouble, come back here. This seems the safest place."

"When will you be back?" I called after Casca.

He walked off without answering, me still worrying if he'd find his way. But being blind for thousands of yarles meant his eyes had become redundant. He could sense the world in ways I couldn't imagine.

I marched through Tablease, careful to keep watch of any pursuit. When a pair of mudgles approached me, I ducked into an alley to hide. I'd become paranoid. Afraid of everyone and everything. Not sure who to trust.

But as I entered the Ionad Precinct, Karlik's central hub, I couldn't avoid the dozens of mudgles gathered outside the Extractory. On the building's steps, Eminent Graben stood, addressing the crowd.

"Mines open tomorrow," said Graben.

"You can't open the mines yet," yelled a worker. "Too dangerous."

"We're not going back in," said another.

"Pit bosses assure me," said Graben, "that undamaged mines will be safe to enter once rubble is cleared from the entrances."

"Who decides if a mine is safe?" snapped the first miner. "I've seen the damage, even in the mines further from the explosion. Tunnels could collapse any moment."

The other workers called their support.

"We have orders to fill," said Graben. "Now, I'm going back to work. You should too."

She turned to walk up the steps. The miners scuttled after her, surrounding the Eminent and blocking her path. From out of the Extractory's front door, three Voldari appeared holding pikes diagonally across their chests. Other than the peace officers and their truncheons, I'd never seen anyone brandish a weapon in Karlik to threaten another citizen.

"You don't care for miners anymore," snarled a worker. "You're a Voldari puppet."

"That's preposterous," bit Graben.

"We don't trust the Voldari," called another miner. "Or the Eminents."

"Yeah!" cried others.

"We'll die if we go back into the mines."

"You'll die if you don't," snapped Graben.

The miners closed in around her. The Voldari marched down the steps, weapons poised to attack. A whistle blew from behind me, and a handful of peace officers, truncheons drawn, raced towards the confrontation. The jostling crowd shouted a surprised hatred at their fellow mudgles. But the unarmed miners dispersed. Graben pushed her way up the steps and inside, flanked by the Voldari.

Following the peace officers, trotted Barick and Gallan.

"Silveny," called Gallan. "Where have you been?"

"Hiding. I shouldn't be here."

"Hiding from who?"

I turned away from him, not wanting to linger in this place close to Voldari observers.

Standing beside me, Barick shivered. "He's inside my head, Silveny. Shadow Man entered my mind."

"You're being overly dramatic," said Gallan, before facing me. "His da'one took him into the mine to look for evidence of sabotage. He shouldn't have done that."

"It wasn't there," interrupted Barick. "He was on the road. *Death's Pass.*"

Gallan sighed. "It's been quite a morning. The Eminent Assembly in City Hall got heated. The miners followed Graben outside, threatening her with all sorts. I came after them, sniffing another story."

The crowd of miners had left, and the peace officers returned to their posts. I expected to see the Voldari burst from the Extractory and race down the stairs, ready to take me prisoner. Ready to torture me until I divulged the location of my skycart. I couldn't comprehend why else they'd be interested in me.

"I can't stay here," I said. "But I don't want to go home yet. Or back to work."

"Come with me," stuttered Barick. "I need the company. My mothers won't understand."

"We'll both go," said Gallan. "No story here after all."

*   *   *   *   *

We opened the rose-coloured, lava-glass door to Pulson Teahouse, the store that fronted Barick's home, and a bell attached to the doorframe rang out.

"Be there in a moment," called a female mudgle from a back room. "Clean off the ash-snow."

I stood over a grate in the floor and lifted a horsehair brush hanging from a hook on the wall.

"I'll do it," said Gallan.

I handed him the brush, and he swept my clothes, dislodging flecks of ash-snow and sending them down into the grate.

"Silveny," started Gallan, "when's the last time you bathed?"

"I fell into a gutter full of waste," I said, unwilling to divulge the truth at this stage.

Once Gallan had finished with me, he did the same for Barick, who fidgeted the whole time like he'd been infected with my compulsion. I brushed Gallan's clothes, then we sat at a round table, Barick pressing his fingertips into his temples, and Gallan scanning the menu. I fixed my gaze out the window, in case....

In case what, Silveny? What will you do if a Voldari comes calling?

"Barick!" snapped his ma'one as she strode to the table. "You look awful. What happened to you?"

Barick pulled his fingers away from his face. "I'm fine, Ma'one."

"Dortha! Come out here. Our son is ill."

A second female mudgle, Barick's ma'two, burst into the room. "Is it that cursed ash-snow? You know how it distresses him. Oh goodness, look at his face. Beautiful chocolate brown turned sickly gingerbread. Wilda! Come see Barick."

A third female, Barick's ma'three, walked into the room, wiping her hands on an apron that spread across her broad frame. "It don't surprise me. Always said he was a sickly boy. Never eats enough."

"He needs a good herbal tea," said Dortha, turning to Barick's ma'one. "Bletheny, get our son a slitherweed and citrus infusion."

"Yes," she nodded. "Excellent choice." She retreated behind a shop counter and pulled jars of herbs from the shelf behind her.

"I might have one of those," said Gallan, placing the menu back in its holder. "And a slice of honey-devil kuchen."

"Gallan Stretten," said Dortha. "You don't appear ill. Why is my son unwell, and you look the picture of health?"

Gallan shrugged.

Dortha screwed up her nose. "What's that stench? Barick, are you festering?"

"It's me," I said. "Small accident."

Dortha turned her mothering eyes my way. "Silveny Belarose, did our Barick get caught up in your little *accident*?"

"No. Warden Mulburat took him into the damaged mine," I said with an absence that didn't recognise the consequences.

Barick groaned.

Wilda howled from the corner, "Oh, that infernal buffoon! I knew he'd be involved somehow. Incompetent fathering."

"It's not Da'one's fault," mumbled Barick.

"It's always his fault," snapped Dortha. "Wait 'til that poor excuse for a parent gets home. He'll have a storm of explaining to do. How's that infusion going, Bletheny?"

"Done," she said, pouring boiling water into a pottery cup.

She carried the herbal tea over and placed it in front of Barick. "Let it cool. Then sip. Then, off to bed."

"Ma'one," moaned Barick.

"No argument."

"Before he goes to bed," interrupted Gallan, "can I get a slice of cake?"

"*Humph*. Tokens? Just because you're Barick's so-called friend, there's no free ride here. We're running a business."

Gallan reached into his coat pocket and placed a handful of amber tokens on the table.

Bletheny faced me. "And Silveny, is your concern for your stomach also more important than your life-long friend?"

"I'm not hungry," I said, focussing my attention on the mudgles passing the shop window lest one of them worked for the Voldari.

"I need help with the evening meal," said Wilda. "Otherwise, there'll be nothing to serve tonight's customers."

"Drink, then bed," said Dortha, glaring at each of us.

Barick's three mothers disappeared into the back room.

"They didn't take my tokens," complained Gallan.

"No cake for you." Barick blew the steam from his herbal tea and took a sip.

"So," I said, needing a distraction, "are you two going to tell me what's been happening?"

Chapter 15

Shadow Man

Hundreds of mudgles laboured like worker bees, climbing over hills of rubble and tossing rocks down slopes. Sledgehammers rang a resolute, metallic tune as boulders shattered into dozens of fragments. Shovels dug the load, moving debris from *Death's Pass* and piling it into barrows. Creaking wheels protested the weight as labourers trudged down the path to tip the rocky waste into mountain crevasses. Pit bosses roared their orders from mouths masked by beards caked in sweaty dust, and the Voldari, Run-targa, with tusks protruding from his mouth like enamelled daggers, watched the mudgle workers as a prison guard would watch for an escape.

The Melt flexed its muscles this morning, with a clear blue sky offering no impediment to a challenging sun. Barick removed his undershirt, wiped the sweat from his face, then tossed the shirt over a boulder before gathering his shovel and thrusting the blade into a mash of rock, dirt and ice. He heaved the burden aloft, swung his hips and threw the load into a waiting wheelbarrow. With the barrow full, another mudgle wheeled the unwanted cargo along *Death's Pass*. Eventually, she'd reach a precipitous edge where she could tip the debris down a cliff face and have it tumble away from any further inconvenience.

Beside Barick, a patient harfhorse harnessed to a cart waited for its burden to swell as two miners used a swivelling crane, a new contribution from the Inventoria, to load a boulder onto the tray. The animal swished its tail and whinnied, likely thankful at being aboveground for once and able to bask in the fresh mountain air. But the thud of the boulder into the cart cut the celebration short, and the harfhorse tensed thick, seasoned legs ready to begin their work.

To the east of *Death's Pass*, dozens of mudgles swung mattocks and sledgehammers to clear the entrance to the mine where Barick worked. The explosion during the Dragon Festival had collapsed the front half of two mines and blocked the road at a point where it ran through a steep ravine, making it impassable until the rubble had been cleared. Barick expected the chore to take many days, if not an entire season. While he disliked being a miner, he hated being a rubble-digger even more.

"Squark!" chirped Sneckle, also voicing her displeasure at the situation.

Barick rested his shovel against the boulder, uncorked the waterskin resting beside his undershirt, crouched and tipped a mouthful into the tin cup inside Sneckle's cage. The snergul fluffed her dust-covered fur and feathers, sniffed the water, then turned away and climbed onto her perch.

"It's all I've got for now," said Barick. "Meal break comes at high sun."

The female mudgle returned with her empty wheelbarrow. Barick groaned, gulped from the waterskin, then swapped it for his shovel. He heaved a load into the wheelbarrow, but his back eased with the sight of his da'one, Warden Mulburat, striding up the path beside Peace Officer Crooshka. Barick's muscles tensed again as a Voldari followed them, the skeleton of a tail, possibly a wild dog, grafted to the back of her bald head swinging defiantly as she cast interrogating eyes left and right.

Sternn, Barick's pit boss and supervisor, stepped in front of the new arrivals as they approached. "Only workers past this point," he said. "Debris pile too unstable for tenderfoots."

Tender*feet*? thought Barick.

"Not interested in rubble," said Mulburat, pulling a clay pipe from the top pocket of his blue warden coat. "Here to investigate the cause of the explosion."

"Gas build-up," bit Sternn. "Nothing else to it."

"We'll judge that." Mulburat tipped the pipe upside down and tapped the bowl against the back of his leather glove before forcing the stem between pursed lips. He often sucked on an empty pipe out of habit.

"Since when are peace officers mine experts?" asked Sternn.

"Eminent Gardia has tasked me with finding clues," said Mulburat, taking an imaginary puff. "We need to enter the mine."

"Ha!" cried Sternn. "Death trap in there. No access until we've braced the roof."

"We have to get in before mine teams contaminate any evidence."

Sternn bristled. "Contaminate? Contaminate? What are you talking about? Only contamination I got to worry about is removing the corpses of self-satisfied, shiny-buttoned peace officers who entered a dangerous mine when they shouldn't have."

Barick's da'one reached into his coat. "Here's the order from Eminent Gardia." He handed a rolled parchment to Sternn.

The pit boss broke the wax seal, unrolled the parchment and began reading.

The Voldari faced Barick and smiled, then fingered the vertebrae of the skeletal tail hanging down past her shoulder. Sneckle placed her snout through the cage bars and hissed. The Voldari bared her teeth and mimicked the gesture.

Concentration broken, Barick missed the wheelbarrow and tipped his shovel-load of rubble onto his co-worker's boots. She cursed. The Voldari returned to her smile.

"Can't stop stupid," grumbled Sternn, rolling the parchment and shoving it under his belt. "You'll have to use the side entrance. Gate's been blown clean off, and I'm not responsible if the mine collapses."

"Of course," said Mulburat. "We'll need a snergul and its warden. How about him?" He pointed to Barick.

"All miners are working the rubble this morning. Can't spare anyone."

"This is official Statutoria business."

"Fancy-arsed mudgles with pressed uniforms don't impress me. I've seen everything."

Mulburat withdrew the pipe from his mouth and pointed the

indictment at the pit boss. "Have you seen the inside of a gaol cell?"

Sternn grabbed a mattock and braced it across his chest. "Are you threatening me? I got an army of miners at my back."

The dog-tailed Voldari stepped forward. "Nu-eed snergul-warden."

"Can't scare me," growled Sternn. "Don't care how tall you are. I'll chop that bald head of yours clean off with this here mattock if...."

The Voldari placed her hand on Sternn's shoulder. "We su-eek only answers. For benefit of Karlik."

Sternn's body relaxed, and he dropped the mattock. "I won't interfere with an investigation."

The Voldari smiled again.

Barick's da'one walked over to him. "Bring the snergul. We're going into the mine."

"What's happening?" whispered Barick.

Warden Mulburat turned his back to the Voldari. "We're looking for evidence of sabotage. Mudgles at the amphitheatre have filed reports of suspicious activity around the time of the explosion."

"Why's she here?" said Barick, tilting his head towards the visitor.

Mulburat glanced over his shoulder, then returned his gravity to his son. "Her name's Pul-ussa. We can't do anything without the Voldari sticking their noses in. The Governant has decreed that all offices in Karlik must cooperate fully with the visitors. I don't like it, but I'm only a warden."

Barick downed his shovel, put his undershirt back on and picked up the caged snergul.

"Do you know the side entrance?" asked Mulburat, chewing on the bit of his pipe.

"Back down the path, then head east. Not far. I'll lead."

Barick walked on, leading his da'one, Officer Crooshka and Pul-ussa to the same entrance he and his friends had used to break into the mine and search for Jolia. After the explosion, he had no idea what he'd find in there now. He hoped Shadow Man had been buried in a graveyard of rubble and would never be seen again.

"What are we looking for?" Barick asked as they walked.

"Fragments of oil barrels," said Mulburat. "Wicks. Discarded firesticks. Anything that might be used to create an explosion." He leaned closer and whispered, "You can also show me where you saw this Shadow Man killing mudgles."

"I can't do that," hissed Barick. "Not with a Voldari here."

"We'll be careful."

"It could all be collapsed. I don't want to go back...."

"Be brave, son. Karlik needs bravery now more than anything."

They reached the side gate, twisted iron ripped from its hinges by the explosion and lying in the dirty snow like an entrance to a haunted underworld. After stepping inside the mine tunnel, Crooshka lit a lantern and held it aloft.

"Watch that flame," said Barick. "Could be gas leaks everywhere." He checked Sneckle, worried the snergul might not survive the journey.

They crept through the passage, its contorted steel braces resembling spider webs ripped by the wind. Rock walls had splintered, fissures spreading through them like tree roots, and slithers of dirt tumbled to the floor as Barick passed.

The main tunnel echoed with the ominous grate of shifting stone. Oil lanterns had run out of fuel and hung from the tunnel roof in listless surrender to the dark. Shovels, picks, mattocks and other mine tools lay on the floor, scattered by the blast. Barick turned a corner and stumbled onto the corpse of a harfhorse still harnessed to a wagon that had become jammed between rocks. He covered his mouth to deflect the smell. Sneckle gagged.

"What's that doing here?" asked Crooshka.

"Mines were closed for the Dragon Festival," mumbled Barick. "Only miners working the venting fires outside. And the harfhorses should have been stabled."

Mulburat shoved his pipe in his coat pocket and checked the cart tray. "Empty."

With the main tunnel blocked, they went left, then right, into the passage that led to the crevice where, if they squeezed through, would eventually take them to the lava pit and Shadow Man. This was Barick's chance to show his bravery. Lead his da'one and Crooshka straight to the monster. The Voldari would have to stay behind. She couldn't fit through the crevice.

Barick strode ahead with unexpected courage. But the passage looked nothing like he remembered. Parts of walls had collapsed. New fissures had opened. Pilot lights that should never be extinguished offered no flame. The Voldari bunched the hem of her cold-blue robes up to her knees and ducked ahead to walk beside Barick. He hoped the journey's awkwardness would wear her down and she'd have to return outside. Then he could show his da'one exactly what Shadow Man did.

Barick's bravery vanished when they stepped back into the main tunnel. He'd walked straight past the crevice. Not even noticed it. Steel braces above him creaked a threat of collapse, and handfuls of dirt spilled from the roof into his hair, showering him with mockery. He cursed being a snergul-warden. He cursed everything about the damn mines. He cursed his cowardice.

Sneckle gasped and coughed. The flame of Crooshka's lantern flared bright and turned blue.

Barick sniffed. "Gas leak somewhere. We should move on or get out."

Mulburat pulled him aside. "Where did you see the dead mudgle?"

Barick shook his head and shivered. "I think we've passed it. It's all so different. The crevice must have closed."

His da'one sighed and walked off, kicking the ground. But he stopped dead. "Crooshka, bring that lantern over here."

The peace officer trotted to Warden Mulburat, the hunched Voldari, ducking beams and extinguished lanterns, not far behind.

Mulburat crouched and ran his hand through dirt and crumbled rock. He sifted out a triangle of iron, torn and sharp, and held it to the lantern light. "Does it look like a hoop fragment from an oil barrel to you?"

Crooshka shrugged. "Could be."

Mulburat handed the fragment to Crooshka and continued the

search, uncovering another shard of iron stamped with two letters. "K–B," he said.

"Same two letters before the serial number of every oil barrel in Karlik," said Barick. He knelt beside his da'one, put Sneckle on the ground, and scuffed his hand through the dirt, finding a piece of iron with numbers stamped into it. "Definitely part of a serial number stamped into the barrel's bilge hoop. If we find the whole number, we might be able to discover where the oil barrel came from. Who had it last."

Barick kept looking. Peace Officer Crooshka held the lantern above the search area. Pul-ussa stepped closer, casting her dark raisin eyes over the ground. Sneckle sucked in wheezing breaths but hadn't passed out. Barick expected it to happen any moment. He quickened his pace, sweeping his hand through the dirt beside his boots. A sharp point poked into his palm. He grimaced, then shuffled across to block Pul-ussa's view and wrapped his fingers around a strange metal object – a golden star. He slipped the treasure into his boot, planning to show Da'one later.

Warden Mulburat found more barrel fragments, but not enough to make a complete serial number. Still, a partial number could help uncover where the barrel came from.

"Looks like someone rolled oil barrels here and blew them up," said Mulburat, standing.

"Who wa-ood do?" asked Pul-ussa.

"May never find out, but I'm going to try. Do we have to go back the way we came?"

"No," said Barick. "Further into the main tunnel, we can turn right. It will return us to the emergency exit."

"Let's get out of here. Your snergul is almost dead."

Barick picked up the cage. Sneckle lay on the floor, eyes closed. But her little, furry chest still rose and fell with hopeful breaths.

Barick marched forward, determined to escape the mine and save Sneckle. Crooshka trotted beside him, holding the lantern out front as if it might wail with any hint of danger. The gold star in Barick's boot dug into his ankle with every step, but he refused to stop and reveal his discovery to Pul-ussa.

They turned right off the main tunnel, the cloying air constricting Barick's throat, trying to choke a confession from him. The flame of Crooshka's lantern stuttered, sending grotesque shadows to explore weaknesses in the steel braces that held death above the intruders like a guillotine. Sneckle's breaths grew shallower. The tunnel faded to black, and Barick's hope became lost.

But when he turned left, a shard of sunlight from the emergency exit lifted his spirits. He trotted ahead, eager for an embrace from the arms of daylight.

Outside, Sneckle stirred and yawned, then climbed back onto her perch.

"Glad to be out of there," said Mulburat. "Let's go home before this whole damn mountain comes crashing down."

They weaved through a cluster of boulders, heading for *Death's Pass*. The star in Barick's boot burrowed like a flesh-eating parasite, and his foot squelched inside his sock as he marched on. Scree shifted under his feet, and he stumbled into a rock.

"Dammit," he cursed.

Sneckle barked her displeasure.

"Quiet," snapped Barick. "I'll feed you when we get back." He pushed away from the rock, and a razored edge cut into his palm. "Damn!" He punched his thigh in frustration.

"Calm yourself," said Mulburat.

"I'm not one of your peace officers," growled Barick. "Direct your orders elsewhere."

Mulburat raised his eyebrows. "What's wrong with you?"

Nothing, thought Barick. *Nothing and everything.*

They approached a narrow ravine, two mudgles wide, between sheer cliffs. A man stepped from behind a boulder and blocked their path. He wore a slick, almost shiny grey coat with a belt cinched at the waist and a hood shadowing his face. As he raised his eyes to meet them, Pul-ussa stopped and stepped back as if preparing to flee. But the man held her in place with a captive glare.

The stranger wasn't Voldari. He could have been a Nordman, but they rarely visited Karlik, and he looked poor, not like the well-heeled merchants who sometimes came to the city to trade. Dreds of mattered hair poked out from under his hood, framing a cruel face plagued by an unruly beard full of disordered knots.

The man locked eyes with Barick, and a fearful anger strangled his soul.

Shadow Man. A contortion of beauty.

But as soon as the recognition came, as soon as the chill mountain air stabbed an ice dagger into Barick's chest, the malignity of Shadow Man's face vanished, replaced by mirrored calm that stilled Barick's dread.

Warden Mulburat stepped in front of his son and faced the stranger. "Are you lost?"

"I almost lost my life," said the man, "when the mountainside tumbled down."

"You were here when the mine exploded?"

"I was bringing wares for trade down *Death's Pass* when the earth spewed its anger. My horse was killed, and my wagon shattered to pieces. All my life's treasures are strewn among these stones. I'm here to reclaim them."

"Mudgles sometimes use the pass to transport serpent oil, but traders seldom come down it. Most wares are transported in line balloons."

The stranger glanced across to an empty balloon line. "Nothing is moving now. And I have no interest in being suspended above the ground in one of those flying baskets."

"There's a trading post at *Line Station 16*," said Crooshka. "Top of the ridge. You would have passed it on your way here."

The stranger smiled. "I would have missed seeing Karlik's wonders."

"Well, you're trapped here until the pass is cleared," said Mulburat. "You'll be able to experience the city's wonders until you're sick of them."

"Yes, this has come to my attention. Hopefully, I can find a few precious trinkets to trade for accommodation."

"There's plenty of work going. Rubble to be cleared and buildings and mines to repair. Your Curmudgle is near perfect."

"The trappings of wanderlust. If you're going to travel, Warden Mulburat, best to learn the lingo."

"If you were here when the mine exploded, did you see anything suspicious?"

The stranger leaned back against the boulder and crossed his arms. "What would be suspicious to you?"

"Anyone carrying barrels of serpent oil into the mine. They might have had other items like...."

As Mulburat began his description, the stranger moved his mirroring eyes to Barick, who stepped forward, drawn into the reflection like an innocent child hoping to stroke the mane of a boulder lion. The golden star inside his boot ground into bone, trying to hide under his skin. But the star point wasn't the only thing probing Barick. A presence revealed itself inside his head – an emotionless voice of requisition.

You are a thief.

No, thought Barick.

You cannot hide from me. You stole something of mine.

Sneckle growled at the stranger. Barick's ankle throbbed. His sock splodged as if saturated with water.

You will return it.

Barick fought the demand. Tried to ignore the invading voice. But it grappled and prised, and he wanted it out of his head. He needed it out.

Da'one finished talking, apparently satisfied with the trader's story.

As the rest of the group walked past the man, Barick lagged. He placed Sneckle's cage on the ground, sat on a rock and removed his boot to find a blood-soaked sock. After peeling the sock away, he revealed a blood-stained, five-pointed star, etched with a goat's head in the centre and surrounded by intricate patterns. He dug the treasure from his flesh and handed it to the stranger.

The man took it and smiled.

I remember you, Barick Pulson. We have met before.

Barick wanted to speak. Wanted to scream to his da'one, 'THIS IS SHADOW MAN!' Wanted to fight. Or run. Hide. But all his wants drowned in the impossible.

One day, we will meet again.

Barick put his sock and boot back on, then stood and collected the caged snergul. As he passed the stranger, Sneckle flared the frill of scarlet feathers around her neck, warning of her readiness to fight.

Wait.

Barick stopped.

The blind boy, what is his name?

Don't say it. Don't think it. Don't, don't, don't, don't...Casca.

Ah, I expected as much.

Chapter 16

The Eminent Assembly

Gallan squeezed into his Governant office, little bigger than a garderobe, pulling the print trolley behind him. He lined it up beside his desk and began moving button-sized metal squares, each embossed with a letter, into the top tray to spell out his story on the mine explosion before taking the trolley to the print room. Working by the light of an oil lantern, he arranged thousands of letters and blank spacers to correspond with the words inscribed in his notes. Gallan considered this the most important story he'd written in his two yarles as Governant scribe. The explosion near *Drake Amphitheatre* had upended Karlik in a way he hadn't experienced. But he didn't have the *full* story. That bothered him.

After two hours, Gallan had finished his proof, spread out over three trays stacked on the trolley. He wheeled it out of his office, shut the door, and headed for the print room in the basement.

Partway along the corridor, raised voices echoed from behind the door of a meeting room. He stopped the trolley and tilted his ear towards the conversation.

"Mudgles have died," said Jilomain Stretten. "We must respect the dead."

"We need oil," said a Voldari voice Gallan recognised as belonging to Fal-ursa.

"I'll propose the mines open tomorrow," said Jilomain. "That's the best I can do. Some miners are already refusing to return to work. Too dangerous, they say."

"Danger comes in many forms," rumbled Fal-ursa. "The unexpected is the cruellest menace."

"Are you threatening me?"

"You are the Governant Eminent. I bow to your wisdom."

Fal-ursa's words dripped like rancid honey. Gallan placed his hand on the doorknob and almost opened the door. His ma'one might be in danger, and he could be her saviour. For one of the rare times, he could make her proud. But fear overcame his need for recognition, and he held back.

"What of the balloon line?" asked Fal-ursa. "The road?"

"*Death's Pass* could be closed for a season," said Jilomain. "There's a mountain of rubble to clear. The balloon line is being repaired. Two stations were damaged. It will run soon."

Shuffling feet preceded an anguished yelp.

Then Fal-ursa spoke. "The balloon line must open tomorrow."

"Alright," moaned Jilomain, so softly that Gallan could barely hear her. "Alright. The balloon line will open."

The voices fell silent. Gallan leaned closer to the door. His knee knocked a print tray, and a clatter of letters fell to the floorstones.

The door swung open.

His ma'one glared at him with accusing, uncaring eyes. "What are you doing here?"

"N-n-nothing," stammered Gallan. "Taking my story about the explosion to the printers. Knocked a tray off the trolley."

"Fool of a puck. Your clumsiness is a burden for all."

"I'll be more careful." Gallan peered over his ma'one's shoulder, trying to glimpse Fal-ursa. She moved her body to block his view.

"This meeting room is for confidential Governant business," said Jilomain. "Lowly city scribes have no reason to be here."

Gallan flinched with the sting of his ma'one's dismissal. He knelt as if offering his undying fealty to her and gathered the metal letter-squares from the floor. She slammed the door shut as he dropped the letters into his coat pocket. Still kneeling on the floor, he considered the implications of a Voldari giving orders to the Governant Eminent. If other mudgles found out, it would look bad for his ma'one. Jeopardise her authority. She may need his protection after all.

Gallan stood and limped off, the drag of his oversized boot accentuating his disadvantage. At the end of the corridor, he put the letters back in place and wheeled the trolley into the lift that would take him to the basement. After closing the doors, he grasped a spoked wheel that protruded from the lift wall and spun it clockwise. The lift shunted down, groaning at the disturbance.

Gallan's arm ached with the effort of activating the cogs and cables that lowered the lift. While only two floors below, the journey to the basement always tortured him. The reflection in the lift's polished brass walls turned his jovial face into a twisted monstrosity. He shrank with the burden of misaligned legs and the clumpy boot that struggled to correct the injustice. But more so, he couldn't escape his lack of ambition. This 'lowly city scribe' didn't want greater things, content with his apathy. But trapped in this metal box with his inadequacies, his ma'one's taunts ricocheted around the walls. The jollity he presented to the outside world couldn't shield him here. The isolation stripped his humour away, revealing an emptiness beneath. But he could fill this emptiness if he pulled his ma'one out from under the Voldari thumb.

Gallan bowed his head and turned the wheel, sighing relief when the lift bumped to a stop. He yanked open the doors, assaulted by an attack from the raucous, chaotic clang of the printing room.

Trying to block the noise from his mind, he wheeled the trolley out and walked across the room to Uga, the print-master.

"HOI GALLAN!" she cried over the din of the printing press. "STORY FOR THE CHRONICLE?"

Gallan nodded.

"GOT TO BE APPROVED BY BUNNY EARS." She pointed to a corner where a Voldari stood, the flopped, white rabbit ears grafted to her skull peppered with printing ink.

It looked comical and menacing at the same time, and Gallan

laughed aloud, brave behind the printer's rowdy, clacking shield, then snapped his mouth shut with a clutch of fear.

He faced Uga. "WHY?"

"ORDERS FROM STRETTEN," she yelled. "BUNNY EARS READS EVERY STORY BEFORE PRINTING."

It seemed this Voldari also knew the Curmudgle language, and Gallan wondered if Urn-hasa had been bluffing all along. The only stories needing approval before printing were ones that might cause embarrassment to Governant officials. Gallan should be able to print the mine explosion story without interference. But he couldn't go against his ma'one's wishes, so he wheeled the trolley to Bunny Ears.

The towering intruder leaned over the print trays. With spidery, interfering fingers, she removed words and rearranged sentences. Gallan wanted to protest. Wanted to grasp the intruder's hand and pull it away. But he did neither. He stood in compliant silence, shamed by his indolence.

The Voldari finished her edit, then waved Gallan away, a fly shooed from a scrap of bread.

*　*　*　*　*

City Hall thrummed with a deafening murmur. Despite many citizens still clearing the rubble from *Death's Pass* or tending the injured in the Restoria, over five hundred mudgles considered this Eminent Assembly worthy of their attention. Pews full, dozens joined the handful of peace officers who stood watch along the perimeter walls. Officials from the offices of power huddled in their uniformed groups. A cluster of dour grey administrators from the Extractory. The Artary's raven black robes. Peach for the Mercher. Gold yellow of the Literati. Sage green for the Historium.

But most attendees, the beating heart of Karlik, didn't qualify to don the garb of mudgle officials. They'd left their coats and hats with the doorkeepers, stripped back to the cloth of simple folk, tunics or undershirts draping over the traditional leather-panelled skirts, or more modern woollen trousers soiled by sweat and graft. A lake of ivory, beige and brown surrounding the islands of administrative colour.

Gallan sat beside the stage, already taking notes and planning how to get this story printed without interference from Bunny Ears. Truth mattered, and Gallan, guided by his ma'one, had been the largely unimpeded gatekeeper of truth for two yarles. While Karlik had four scribes, only he reported on Governant matters. The others wrote mostly whimsical pieces about goings-on at the Seminaria or Historium. The Statutoria scribe reported on city crimes, but she'd written just a handful of stories in recent yarles.

They're the lowly city scribes, he thought. *Governant scribe matters. My truth matters.*

The anticipating shuffle and murmur of the crowd stilled as ten Eminents marched into the hall, led by Jilomain Stretten. Urn-hasa and Fal-ursa walked with the Eminents, acting like they'd become the Assembly's eleventh and twelfth members. All wore ceremonial robes, none more garish than the taffy pink and lime green concoction with swirls of silver and gold worn by Gallan's ma'one. Besides the scolding outside the meeting room, he hadn't spoken with her since the explosion and, according to his fathers, she'd not come home, apparently working day and night.

The Eminents and Voldari climbed the stairs to the stage and took their seats. Jilomain walked to the lectern at the front, then banged a gavel. Every face in the crowd turned to her. But she banged it again for good measure.

Gallan poised pencil over paper, ready to transcribe each word his ma'one uttered.

She cleared her throat. "Welcome, everyone. Thank you for coming to this particularly important Eminent Assembly. We have many issues to cover, the first being progress on *Death's Pass*. Clearing the rubble has begun, but it will take time. Eminent Drudan…," Jilomain faced the Inventoria head and nodded, "…assures me his inventors are developing new machines to move rock. But we must be wary of avalanches...."

"When will the mines open?" lobbed a stone from the crowd, starting ripples of disquiet.

"I'll get to that," glared Jilomain. "We need to conduct these proceedings in an orderly manner. The mine explosion has shaken everyone. Be patient; there'll be time for questions later." She continued, "Despite the new inventions, *Death's Pass* may not open until the end of The Melt."

The simmer of distress threatened to boil over.

Crowd getting restless, wrote Gallan.

"We can't wait that long," said a trade administrator from the Mercher, his face flushing the colour of his peach shirt. "Not with the balloon line also damaged."

"Rushing the process risks more mudgle lives," cried someone from the crowd.

"We'll starve!" yelled another citizen.

Eminent Stretten banged her gavel. "Order! The balloon line will restart soon." She turned to Eminent Tradal, Mercher head.

"A few days, hopefully," he said. "Survey team hasn't returned from *Line Station 16*. Repairs not completed on the damaged stations."

"I'm sure we can open it sooner than that," said Jilomain, turning her back to Tradal to avoid his dissent. "Tomorrow, maybe."

"What caused the explosion?" a citizen asked. "One of my wives died under the rubble."

"My son died!" yelled another, setting off a parade of grievance.

Jilomain huffed. "Eminent Gardia? Do you want to speak?"

She nodded, stood and stepped to the lectern. "It's too early to say. Warden Mulburat is investigating reports of sabotage."

"Sabotage?!" cried a few.

Urgent dread flashed across Jilomain's face. She whispered in Gardia's ear.

The Statutoria's Cardinal-warden returned her attention to the crowd, offering palms of composure. "Only reports at this stage. No evidence. No need for panic."

"Gas build-up more likely," called Eminent Graben from the rear of the stage. "We'll get the mines open soon enough. Undamaged ones can open tomorrow."

A swell of protest met Graben's assertion. At the hall's rear, a dozen miners, still filthy from clearing rubble, had started the surge, their yells and threatening gestures swirling together in a wild tide before breaking against the Eminents.

Too bloody dangerous! scribbled Gallan, trying to capture what the miners said. *Death trap. Kill us all. Not going to risk it.*

Jilomain pushed Eminent Gardia aside and banged the gavel. "Quiet! Peace officers will deal with any further interruptions. There's plenty of space in the gaol."

The miner tide withdrew, but a rogue wave still threatened.

"Undamaged mines open tomorrow," stated Jilomain with the defiance of Karlik's most powerful Eminent. "Double shifts are needed to fill the most generous order from our Voldari friends." She smiled at Urn-hasa and Fal-ursa, who returned the gesture. "Damaged mines fixed within days."

"That'll take workers away from clearing rubble," called a miner. "We can't do both."

"Wasn't gas build-up," yelled another. "Not an explosion that big."

A Mercher administrator swished her peach robe, stood at the front of the hall, then turned to the miners. "We must open the mines. Supplies don't come in unless oil goes out. We've all got families to feed."

Balloon line won't cope. Can't wait. Won't risk workers in unsafe mines. Clear the rubble first. Selfish. Lazy. Greedy. Gallan struggled to jot down all the insults flying around the hall.

A few in the crowd sprang to their feet, pointing their disdain at the nearest opposer. Others waved hands of protest or puffed out chests of defiance. The peace officers nearest Gallan wrapped tense fingers around their truncheons. But the batons would have little hope of quelling the flared animosity that threatened to engulf everyone.

Jilomain banged her gavel, yelling over the crowd, "There'll be no talk of extended mine closures."

More mudgles will die. Coward. Who's calling me a coward? Speak up!

"STOP!" screamed Jilomain, smacking the lectern with her gavel. "Mines open tomorrow. The majority of Eminents agree."

"Paid off by the Voldari," called a mudgle sitting close to Gallan.

He noted it, then considered erasing the slight. The words wouldn't get past his ma'one, or Bunny Ears.

"When the mines open," said Jilomain, still yelling, "*all* available workers, not only miners, will be tasked with filling the Voldari order."

The Voldari order, wrote Gallan, then wondered if his ma'one meant the order for serpent oil. After overhearing the conversation in the meeting room, it appeared the visitors may be issuing other orders for Eminent Stretten to follow.

A chaotic assembly continued, Gallan struggling to capture the atmosphere in City Hall. *Unsettling. Hostile. Threatening. Brink of violence.*

The mine explosion and the Voldari presence had fractured Karlik's usual calm. Stripped away a veneer of stability and exposed a pressing conundrum. Without the Voldari order for oil, Karlik would continue its slow, inevitable decline into insignificance.

But is the new path worse?

The Eminents completed their presentation and filed out of City Hall amid howls of disagreement. But Eminent Graben from the Extractory wouldn't escape further affront. The group of disgruntled miners chased after her, trying to tether the Eminent with their demands.

Gallan sniffed more to the story, so he shoved his notebook into his pocket and chased after them.

Chapter 17

An unexpected arrival

"I saw Shadow Man's true face," shuddered Barick. "For a terrifying moment. Now his voice inside my head urges me to forget."

"Barick Pulson," cried Dortha as she exploded back into the teahouse. "Bed rest for you. Silveny and Gallan, out."

We couldn't argue. Dortha pulled Barick from his seat, and they disappeared into the back room. Gallan and I stepped outside into an ash-snow blizzard.

"What if he's still there?" asked Gallan, pulling his coat hood over his braided red hair. "Inside Barick's head. Hiding. What if Shadow Man can hear everything we say?"

"Is that our biggest worry?" I said, taking Gallan's lead and donning my hat. "What happened at the Eminent Assembly scares me more than voices inside Barick's mind."

Bravado. I shouldn't dismiss the threat of Shadow Man so readily, but I couldn't deal with multiple perils at once or decide if Shadow Man had anything to do with Karlik's woes. Nevertheless, something deep in my gut told me our city was spiralling to an unfortunate end. *Escape.* Jolia and Casca's warning rang in my ears.

"Someone followed us," I said. "We had to hide in Tablease."

"Why? Who?"

"Casca suspected a Voldari."

I marched off, heading for the rotunda in the centre of Donharue Park to escape the blizzard. Gallan followed, but part of me wanted him to go away. To not have to deal with his peppering questions.

Underneath the rotunda's slate roof, I stood beside the iron railing and brushed spaces in the line of piled ash-snow with my gloved hand, a finger-width apart. I shuffled along the edge as Gallan followed.

"Why were you in Tablease anyway?" he asked.

I didn't want to tell him the truth about Fergutch's workshop and the skycart. The fewer mudgles knew, the better. Paranoia had become my compulsion. "We used to play there as pucks. I remember all the good hiding places." I stepped across. *Brush away a pile of snow. Measure a finger-width. Brush away another pile. Try not to disturb the fingers of snow left behind.* Each pile represented a worry I couldn't dispel.

"You've fixated on the Voldari," said Gallan. "Ma'one will ship the oil after payment. She's not stupid."

I spun on my heel to face him. "What if they want more than oil? What if they're trying to control Karlik?"

"This is madness! A dozen Voldari are hardly a threat."

"It's more than a dozen."

"Where did they come from?" asked Gallan. "*Death's Pass* and the balloon line are closed. The Voldari didn't spring from holes in the ground."

"They might have," I said. "They could have been hiding in old mines all this time, or the sewer, waiting for their moment to infiltrate our city."

"The sewer? Madness has turned to insanity."

"Casca said the Voldari want to build skycarts to transport oil. And for other purposes. A weapon of war. They want my plans."

"Casca said, Casca said, Casca *said*," spat Gallan. "What do we know about Casca? Three days ago, we discovered he was immortal. We don't know how long he's lived. Where his allegiances lie. You trust this blind boy more than your friends."

I know how long. But I won't tell you.

Gallan stormed off.

"Where are you going?" I asked after him.

"Back to work," he called over his shoulder. "You should do the same, Silveny. But bathe first. You stink."

I hadn't been to work in days and wasn't going now. *Paranoia has become my compulsion.* I should be helping to invent machines to move rubble and repair mines. *Paranoia stronger than guilt.* The Voldari observer at the Inventoria would report me to Urn-hasa or Run-targa. Or Hor-gnasher. *Do they even care about you? Casca said they did. Is he lying?*

I couldn't face work. But Gallan was right about one thing: I needed to wash. So, I headed home, careful to watch for a Voldari pursuit that may be nothing more than compulsive paranoia.

*   *   *   *   *

I unlocked the door and entered an empty, cold house, Yula still not home. I hadn't eaten properly in days and found a bag of mixed dried fruit in the pantry. I tipped the sticky clump into a bowl and sat on the bench seat, arranging the dried fruit in family clusters – prunes here, apricots there, sultanas over there. I plucked one from each group in turn and tossed it into my mouth, appreciating the sweetness and little burst of energy and comfort.

After turning on the gas heater, I disrobed and stepped into the washroom, running hot water into a basin. Dipping a cake of lye soap into the water, I lathered froth all over my body, scrubbing it with a damp cloth, trying to erase the sewer stench from all the creases in my skin. I drifted in a nightmare of uncertainty, the very thing that set my compulsion afire. I may never return to work. Might be on the cusp of leaving Karlik forever. I didn't know who to trust. Who my real friends were.

If the skycart flies, who comes with me? If it doesn't fly, what then?

After putting on my nightgown, I sat on the bench seat and stared into nothingness for hours, my mind drifting like an untethered balloon. Pushed by flukey winds. This way. That way. No control over its direction.

243

A knock on the front door brought me back home. I expected Casca. Or Yula may have lost her marble and couldn't unlock the door.

When I opened it, I found a huffing, puffing Rambleton, his pale skin as red as a candy-apple. Behind the white mudgle, sat Popa strapped upright to the backrest of a sled and surrounded by baggage.

"What?" I asked, trying to shake the confusion from my head.

"We had to come," scattered Rambleton. "Escape the cabin."

"What are you talking about?"

"Horned wolves attacked," said Rambleton, placing his hands on his forehead and making horns with his fingers. "Herds and herds."

"Packs," called Popa from the sled. "They roam in packs, Rambleton."

The white mudgle nodded to me. "Packs. Bulging packs. Dozens. Double dozens. Triple, even."

"They can't get into the cabin," I said.

"They tried. Smashed the window shutters. Crashed against the door. I fought them back."

I stepped past Rambleton and went to Popa. "Why would horned wolves attack the cabin?"

He shook his head. "I've never seen so many. The day you left, they came all at once, arriving at dusk and circling the house to plot their assault. Deep in the frozen dark, they attacked. Rambleton pushed bookcases against the door and windows. Without him, we would have died. The wolves vanished with sunrise."

"To die not a nice way," muttered Rambleton. "Eaten by wolves."

No. Not nice. "Come inside," I said.

Rambleton unstrapped Popa from the sled and carried him into our home, placing him on the bench seat. He returned for the sled, scraping it through the doorway.

"Where's Yula?" asked Popa, taking off his coat, hat and scarf.

I gathered his clothes, shook the ash-snow away over the grate at the front door, then hung them on the coat rack. "Working the balloon line," I said. "There was a huge explosion...."

"We saw," interrupted Rambleton as he unpacked the sled, scattering ash-snow and real snow all over the floor. "Broken rocks and boulders. A mess of rubble and death."

"Mudgles working so late," said Popa.

I grabbed the broom beside the coat rack and swept up Rambleton's mess. "They have to clear the debris to open *Death's Pass* and the mines."

Popa shook his head. "The wolves are a bad omen."

"Will they attack Karlik?"

"They're becoming bold. Something has given them an unwelcome courage."

"We saved the Book of Leaves," said Rambleton, holding up the prized crate.

"Yes," said Popa, "we saved the book. All the answers we seek are in there. Where's your immortal friend? The blind boy?"

"He's spying on the Voldari," I said.

"A dangerous business. How can you spy without sight?"

"*I don't spy with my broken eye,*" sang Rambleton.

"He's thousands of yarles old," I said. "His other senses are honed beyond our imagining."

"That's quite a life," said Popa. "Quite a life, indeed. He could write his own Book of Leaves."

"Maybe this one he wrote?" said Rambleton, tapping the crate's side with his toe.

Popa smiled. "Maybe he did."

"Food," said Rambleton as he strode into the cookery. "Haven't eaten all trip."

The white mudgle prepared a meal while I sat with Popa, both of us fighting tired eyes. A lot had happened since I left the cabin, and my stories to Popa filled him with concern. Rambleton made a stew of freshly caught snow hare and yams, but only he ate. I couldn't stomach it, and Popa soon fell asleep, slumping down on the bench seat. I put him in the spare bed, and Rambleton laid blankets on the floor beside Popa and nestled onto the hard stones. Neither would go upstairs,

Popa's grief from lost love as raw as a wound inflicted yesterday.

I retired, lying on my quilt and falling asleep immediately.

* * * * *

The next day, as we sat at the table eating porridge for morning meal, the door lock clicked, and in staggered Yula, looking like she'd hiked from the Nordland Plains to Karlik without stopping. But her weary eyes widened at the sight of Popa and Rambleton.

I stood, ready to welcome her with a hug, but Rambleton beat me to it. He sprang from his seat and trotted over to my sister.

"Yula, welcome home," he beamed, wrapping her in hairy white arms.

She stood tired and stiff, not returning the embrace.

"You've been gone for two days," I said, stepping across to Yula and reaching for her hand as Rambleton released his hold.

She squeezed my fingers and let go, leaving me to be satisfied with this small act of affection.

"Why are *they* here?" Yula asked, pointing at Popa.

"Horned wolves rampaging across the mountains," said Rambleton, returning to his bowl of porridge.

"They attacked Popa's cabin," I said.

Yula stepped away from me, towards her bedroom. Popa stood, maybe expecting his eldest daughter would offer him a moment of reunion, but she brushed past him and drew open her privacy curtain.

"Do you want porridge?" I asked her. "Food is becoming scarce, with the balloon line not moving and the road closed."

"Voldari at *Line Station 16*," mumbled Yula.

"Observing?"

"No. Taking over."

Chapter 18

Line Station 16

Yula squeezed into the corner of the wicker basket waiting to depart *Line Station 1*, the silk fabric of the balloon above her rippling with a westerly breeze. Her workmates from *Line Station 3* came next: Fretal, the station manager, and Korta, the winchmaster. Yula expected a Voldari to join the reconnaissance; the blue-robed visitors were everywhere, but Fretal insisted on a light cargo to maximise balloon speed.

At Yula's feet sat a crate of dried meat, pickled beets and cukes, fresh rye bread and a wheel of hard cheese. Enough food to last them two days in case damage to the up line delayed their journey to *Line Station 16*. Yula had also packed the hunting bow, hoping to snag fresh snow hare emerging with The Melt.

The manager of station one tapped on the basket's side. "All ready?" he asked.

"Wind?" said Fretal.

"Gentle westerly according to the gothmeter. Enough to run its fingers through your hair but not rip clumps from your scalp." The station manager chuckled to himself. "I don't expect much trouble. If you get stuck, raise the orange flag, and we'll bring you back down the way you came." He nodded and walked up the turret's stairs to his lookout.

As he disappeared, three Voldari strolled into *Line Station 1* and stood by the entrance, folding their hands across their fronts.

Korta turned his back to them and grumbled, "What do they want? Can't leave us alone for one moment."

"The functionality of the balloon line is of utmost importance to them," said Fretal. "Considering their investment in our oil."

"*Functionality,*" huffed Korta. "*Utmost.* Talk like a real mudgle."

Fretal greeted the Voldari with four fingers to the forehead, then heart. They returned the gesture.

The manager of *Line Station 1* blew the departure whistle and raised a blue flag, signalling to station two to begin winching Yula's balloon up the ridge. The lead rope tightened, and the balloon shunted forward, Fretal clutching the sides of the wicker basket until her knuckles flared red.

Korta scoffed. "Wait 'til the wind picks up."

The balloon left station one and drifted skyward as tension on the trailing line released. It climbed to its travelling height, the cable rope halting the balloon's ascent to about five storeys above the rock, ice and snow. Still certain death should anyone fall out.

Despite Korta's warning, the westerly breeze offered little threat, Yula more concerned about the utility of the line stations. Up ahead, much of the tiled roof of *Line Station 2* had been shattered by rock and debris sent flying when the mine exploded. But the turret still stood, flying a green flag to indicate their readiness to dock the balloon from station one, and a repair crew scrambled about the ruins.

We'll see, thought Yula, not convinced they'd make it all the way to *Line Station 16*.

"Station four is serviceable," said Fretal, trying to dispel Yula's worry. "No word from the other stations, though. Debris wouldn't have made it higher than station three."

"What about balloons stuck on the line?" asked Korta.

Fretal shrugged. "I expect they've all been pulled up to station sixteen. We'll find out soon enough."

"Let's hope *we* don't get stuck," he said. "Don't fancy being trapped in this basket with just one crate of food and you two clodpolls."

"You can always shimmy down the cable rope," muttered Fretal.

The crew at *Line Station 2* continued to reel in Yula's balloon. The westerly wind gusted, and she clutched the basket's side with a grim worry. Despite being a line worker, she'd rarely ridden in a balloon. She tried to dispel the concern about freak wind gusts and focussed on the rivulets of meltwater below her that glistened under the sun like diamond necklaces. Patches of melted snow revealed button plants, mounds of juniper green that would blush with pink flowers during Wildflower Flush. A snow hare sat in a huddled white clump outside its burrow, enjoying a simple life of eat, rest, reproduce. Yula envied the modesty of the ambition. Admired it so much that she wondered how she'd feel shattering the humility with an arrow to the heart.

As they approached *Line Station 2*, the basket lurched from side to side, winched down and towards the docking post by an operator who clearly needed more practice or more strength.

The docking platform swung out too early, and Fretal cursed. "Not yet. We could hit that."

But they reached the docking post without incident and looped a rope from the wicker basket over a cleat to hold the basket in place. A rope jockey trotted up the docking platform steps.

"Too damn early," snarled Fretal. "Wait until the basket is fixed to the post."

"We're filling in," said the rope jockey. "Regular team's gone to station three. We're covering for them."

"I hope you know how to handle the ropes."

The rope jockey nodded, unhitched the lead rope from station two and hitched the basket to station three's lead rope. She then unhitched the trailing rope from station one and replaced that with the rope from station two.

"Any balloons come down?" asked Korta.

The rope jockey shook her head. "Not this far down. Not seen any at station three either." She checked the ropes again, then faced Fretal. "I'll go do the cable rope, then you can be off."

"Winch-master should do that one," said Fretal.

"Don't have a winch-master. Only two of us working the line. Others are repairing the damage."

The rope jockey skipped back down the steps, then jogged along the boardwalk to the steel cable that ran from station one to station sixteen. She unhitched the rope from the cable, then re-hitched it above the looped bolt fixing the cable in place. The jockey turned to the turret and waved her hand.

The station manager pulled down the green flag and hoisted a blue one. Korta untied the rope fixing the basket to the docking pole and tossed it at his feet. The balloon swayed forward, beginning its journey to station three.

Halfway between stations, the down line's cable had been severed in two places. Four workers hiked to the first breach, their strides slow and laboured, weighted down by lengths of spare cable slung over their shoulders and a burden of tools hanging from their belts. They dug crampons into slick ice and levered themselves forward with spiked walking poles.

"Poor bastards," muttered Korta. "If they can't reconnect the line, they'll have to lay a new one. Could take days, and Karlik's pantry is bare."

"The Governant has supplies stored," said Fretal.

"How long they gonna last?"

"Supposed to be ten days for the entire city."

"*Sup*-posed," spat Korta. "Supposed to be this. Supposed to be that."

"Stop complaining," said Fretal. "We can use the up line to send balloons both ways."

Korta chortled. "That'll take forever. We'll starve first."

The group went quiet approaching *Line Station 3*, Yula's home station. She expected the north wall to have collapsed, given it had already been damaged by a previous rockfall. But it clung to vertical, a stubborn barrier that refused to yield to the gusting westerly that cut across the exposed rockface. Debris littered the walking path Yula used to climb from Karlik to the station, but the structure itself appeared undamaged, avoiding the storm of rock that thundered down after the mine explosion.

We should be down there, thought Yula, *not in this balloon.* But Eminent Tradal wanted an experienced team surveying the line, so here they were.

The replacement station team worked their posts unhindered, and the balloon transfer went smoothly. Yula and her companions continued their journey to *Line Station 4*.

"Geez," whistled Korta as they left station three behind. "More damage to the down line here. Didn't expect to see it this far up."

"Listen," said Fretal, "when we get to the upper stations, let me do the talking. Some of these teams would have been on duty for eight days straight and running low on food and heating oil."

"We could raid the Governant store," chuckled Korta, before his face turned serious. "If Karlik is runnin' out of food, don't like the chances of sendin' it *away* from the city."

Yula gritted her teeth. "We can't abandon the station crews."

"She speaks," crowed Korta.

"We're not abandoning them," said Fretal. "But I'm not making promises I can't keep. Food will need to be sent either up the line from Karlik or down from station sixteen, and tired station crews must be replaced. Otherwise, we'll have more accidents."

More accidents, thought Yula, *and angrier mudgles.*

While Karlik grew smaller as they floated up the ridge face between Mt Neasa and Mt Fachtna, the city's worries loomed larger in her mind. She understood why mudgles might want to leave and find a better life elsewhere. Station four would be the farthest she'd been up the line. Other than the rare hikes to Popa's cabin, it would also be the farthest she'd been from home. Across the mountains, *Death's Pass* sat empty, a bulge of rubble swollen across its middle like a pregnant ma'one. A league further on was the location of the avalanche that killed four of her parents. Yula estimated that once she'd passed *Line Station 6*, she would have bettered their attempt at escaping Karlik. The realisation left a bitter taste.

Line Station 4 perched on the lip of a sheer cliff, but an outcrop of rock protected it from westerlies. The balloon pulled into the docking post, and the docking platform swung out, a mudgle striding up the steps with a roiling impatience.

"About time," said the mudgle as she arrived.

Fretal raised her hand in greeting. "Morla. Good to see you're still here."

"Where else would we go? No balloons going up. No balloons coming down."

"Is the line damaged above you?"

"How would I know? All we heard was a bloody great bang. What happened down there?"

"Mine exploded. Gas build-up, most likely."

"Or sabotage," muttered Korta.

"Anyone killed?" asked Morla.

Fretal bowed her head. "Hundreds. We're still searching for survivors."

Morla softened her stance. "That's awful. Truly awful. Look, I gotta get back to the city. My husbands...."

"They're fine," said Fretal. "I checked before I left. They're helping in the Restoria."

"Thank the mountain spirits. My crew will want to know about their loved ones. Did you bring food? Our supplies will last only two days."

"You said no balloons coming down?"

"That's right. Shipping suspended during the Dragon Festival should have re-started this morning, but we ain't seen a damn thing."

Fretal stared uphill. "I'll get supplies sent down from station sixteen. The line's damaged closer to Karlik. We need to check the rest of the stations."

Morla glowered. "You got room for three mudgles but no food. We need heating oil, too. No game and no firewood on this damn clifftop. If supplies don't come, or you don't get us down, then we'll either starve or freeze to death. It was bad enough being rostered on during the festival."

"At least you missed the explosion," said Korta with casual indifference, met with a fiery stare from Fretal.

The survey team left station four and continued up the line. As they travelled higher, station crews became more desperate. For news from Karlik. For reassurance they wouldn't starve or freeze, and the line would re-open soon. For a guarantee they'd go home when their shift ended. Fretal used all her negotiating skills to avoid situations getting out of hand. Still, some mudgles refused to let the balloon leave without dispensing rations, and Yula had almost emptied the food crate they'd brought with them. At *Line Station 8*, they had to rescue the winch-master who'd taken with a fever. A protesting but, in the end, compassionate Korta replaced him.

Dusk settled over the balloon line as they approached the ridgetop between the summits of Mt Neasa and Mt Fachtna. Dozens of wagons crowded on the eastern side of *Line Station 16*, oil lanterns hanging from their tailgates and lolling horses and oxen tethered nearby. A handful of campfires burned among the wagons, surrounded by merchant traders preparing their evening meals. Yula questioned how long they'd wait for the balloon line to open before trying to sell their supplies elsewhere. A clear night and moderating wind encouraged them to stay, but the emergence of a notorious Grauberge storm would see the traders scatter.

A shout came from the station as the balloon approached, and the station manager waved an oil lantern from atop the turret flying a green flag. Winched into the landing post, Yula expected to see a mudgle climbing the steps of the platform as it swung out to greet them. Instead, a soldier stood atop the platform, dressed in armour with the sheen of blue ice. Armour of a type Yula had never seen before, made of thousands of interlocking scales no larger than her thumbnail and covering the soldier's body from neck to ankle, such that she resembled a blue snake. A smooth, open-faced helmet covered her head, and from her belt hung a scabbard with a sheathed broadsword. In her hand, she held a pike with a hooked blade.

"Is that a Voldari soldier?" asked Fretal.

Yula shrugged. "Appears so."

The soldier used her hooked pike to hold the wicker basket against the landing post as Fretal fixed the balloon in place with ropes.

"Where's the rope jockey?" asked Fretal.

The soldier looked at her but didn't reply.

Fretal disembarked. Yula picked up the feverish mudgle, cradling him in her arms. The Voldari soldier rested her pike against the landing post and held her arms out, nodding to Yula. She didn't want to, but Fretal had already descended the stairs, so she handed over her companion, resting the sick mudgle across the Voldari's forearms, then climbed from the basket.

"I'll take him," said Yula.

The Voldari smiled and gave him back. Yula heaved her companion into the crook of her arms, then lumbered down the stairs, along the boardwalk and into the station.

Inside, dozens more Voldari soldiers milled around oil fires burning in hearths. They resembled topaz statues washed with amber. In the middle of the soldiers stood a male Voldari with silver armour and hair braids as thick as fingers. As Yula got closer, the braids moved of their own accord.

Not braids, she thought. *Serpents. A knot of living snakes has been grafted to his scalp.*

Yula laid the fevered mudgle on a cot bed and covered him with animal fur.

Fretal confronted the silver soldier. "Are you in charge of these Voldari?"

The soldier offered a blank, impassive glance, but one of his snakes reared and hissed. He pulled a wriggling grub from a purse attached to his waist belt and fed it to the snake.

"They are mine," he said, placing four fingers to his forehead, then his heart. "I am San-vessa."

Fretal scanned the room. "Where's the station crew?"

"Resting. These days are long."

"Why are there soldiers here?"

"The merchants grow tense and restless. It's a long journey from the Nordland Plains to the ridge of Mt Neasa. When they arrive, they're greeted with a balloon line not in operation. They can't offload their wares or receive payment. The stores are full."

"The down line is clear to station four. Balloons must be sent to station crews with food and heating oil."

"No balloons are coming up," cooed San-vessa, "so no balloons are going down."

Fretal pushed up to the soldier. "There was a damn explosion. Killed hundreds. Balloon line is damaged."

"How unfortunate. We have no news of this."

"Why are you here at all?"

"We escorted our ambassadors this far, then let them continue to Karlik on their own. We didn't want Curmudgles thinking we'd come to attack their beautiful city."

Fretal cast her jittery eyes across the fray of blue, thumb-sized scales that surrounded her. "No-one told us about this."

"You are fortunate we are here," purred San-vessa. "My soldiers have paid for all the wares in the stores. But we have no more moynes. Unpaid merchants await the arrival of new balloons carrying coin or serpent oil. But they lose patience and must sleep in the cold. This balloon station cannot accommodate them."

Fretal shook her head and snapped, "Where's the damn station crew?"

San-vessa pointed to a back room, then fed a handful of grubs to his head snakes.

Fretal led Yula through the storage area adjoining the main room. It had been stacked to the roof with supplies, enough to feed half of Karlik for days. At the rear of the station, a dozen balloons and their baskets sat idle, connected to the cable line that looped around station sixteen before it returned to Karlik.

"Look at all this," gruffed Fretal. "Supplies waiting to be shipped. Balloons going nowhere. Useless crew doing nothing."

She marched into the back room with Yula in tow. There, the mudgle station team, all eight of them, sat around a fire feasting on roasted meats and vegetables.

The station manager, Gomhorl, beamed as he raised a rack of goat ribs in salute. "Hail, Fretal, you've come to join the feast. *Belch.*"

"All that should be going to Karlik," barked Fretal.

"Will you grow wings and fly it down yourself?" slurred Gomhorl, before throwing chewed ribs in the fire and swilling black ale from a mug. "Since station fifteen raised the black flag, we've been stuck here with no word from Karlik about what's going on. Our new Voldari friends are the only thing protecting us from a rumbling of angry merchants. When's this blasted balloon line going to open again?"

"We're working on it. Massive explosion damaged stations two and three, and severed parts of the down line. Up line is intact."

"So, when do we open? Traders are desperate for oil and tokens."

Fretal reached down, grabbed a fist of Gomhorl's blonde hair, and pulled him to standing, black ale sloshing over his boots.

"*Arrhhhh!*" he screamed. "For the...mountain...bloody spirits... what...."

"Hundreds of mudgles dead and injured," spat Fretal in Gomhorl's face. "And you sat on your fat arse feeding your fat stomach."

"Look," protested Gomhorl, shaking off his accoster, "we didn't hear about any explosion. All we saw was the black flag."

Another worker, chewing on a leg bone, raised her head. "That what blocked *Death's Pass*? A few traders tried to get through. Said there was a landslide."

"A mine exploded," said Yula.

"No-one told me about the pass," said Gomhorl, glaring at his workers.

The circle of workers glanced at each other and shrugged.

"Pass could be blocked until Wildflower Flush," said Fretal. "All the more reason to get this balloon line open." She pushed Gomhorl away. "Sober up. You and your crew. Tomorrow morning, we need balloons sent down to every station as low as four. One balloon per station, packed with food and heating oil."

Gomhorl swelled his chest. "You ain't the boss. *Belch.*"

No, thought Yula, *neither are you.*

She left the back room and wandered the station, weaving her way through a den of blue-scaled Voldari soldiers. Two of them stood on either side of the workshop entrance, guarding more provisions waiting to be sent to Karlik. She walked up to the soldiers, but they clashed their pikes together across the doorway, blocking her path. Other soldiers stopped talking and glared at her.

Yula stepped away from the doorway and went outside, planning to speak with the traders. But more soldiers slunk around the wagons and campfires. Some exchanged coin for food, ale or weapons. Other merchants received bags of coin and then started to pack their wagons, preparing to leave. Despite San-vessa claiming all the coin had been spent, it didn't appear that way.

While the mudgle station crew fed their bloated bellies, Voldari soldiers entrenched their authority in Karlik's most important line station.

Chapter 19

The fracturing

I tried to sleep. The exhaustion of past days demanded it. The world I once knew had fractured; its brittleness crushed beneath rock. Karlik's isolation had bred complacency. We believed events happening in the rest of Ostamp would never touch us. Our city in the Grauberge Mountains, surrounded by a fortress of snow and ice, would be our bastion. The flow of serpent oil brought wealth. Venting fires kept the horned wolves at bay while we worried about ash-snow and the occasional explosion. A reasonable trade-off, one mudgles had lived with for five generations.

But then the outside world came calling. The Voldari brought it in, arriving with machinations we failed to comprehend. We allowed their 'observers' into our offices of power. Saboteurs likely caused the mine explosion, cutting off the only road into Karlik. Now, Voldari soldiers controlled *Line Station 16*, the keystone to mudgle survival. The invaders could starve us to death with little resistance.

The next morning, I pulled across my bedroom curtain to find Rambleton holding open the front door.

"Almost stepped on baby floe bear," said the white mudgle.

I raced to Rambleton's side. A fetid Casca lay on the doorstep, covered in filth. The veneer of invincible immortality had been stripped away, leaving behind a frail boy whose shivering body pleaded for nurture. The arm braced across his chest fell aside, revealing a wound of ripped and bloodied flesh from his wrist to elbow. A mortal wound.

"You're hurt," I cried, kneeling beside him. "I thought...I thought you couldn't be."

"Wounds usually heal," whispered Casca. "But...."

Rambleton bent down and picked up Casca, carrying the blind boy inside. I checked the street in front of our house in case danger had followed. Anything that threatened an immortal would tear a mortal to shreds. Only ash-snow traversed the road bricks, skipping along with the uncertain winds that carried the demise of all I held dear.

I shut the door against the troubles and faced Rambleton. "Put him on my bed."

As we laid Casca on the quilt, I placed my hand against his cheek and flinched. Touching Casca's skin, which had turned as white as Rambleton's hair, felt like holding a ball of ice in my palm until my skin burned.

A sleepy Popa stumbled into my bedroom. "What's going on?"

"A warring sun melts eternal ice," said Rambleton. "And blood runs like water."

Popa shook himself awake. "It's too early for riddles."

"Casca's wound won't heal," I said.

"He should go to the Restoria."

Casca pushed my hand away. "No," he muttered. "Time will heal it."

"We can make a poultice," I said, then called to my sister, "Yula. Yula!"

"What?" came the muffle from behind her privacy curtain.

"Casca needs a poultice."

A half-naked Yula pulled across her curtain, yawned and ambled to the cookery.

Rambleton poked Casca's wound, then held a bloodied fingertip to his mouth and licked. "Blood real. The warring sun must have been strong. Why does the ice melt?"

"It...I shouldn't be," said Casca. "Melting. Bleeding. It's been generations since my last injury. But then, I've never been bitten by a weregrim before."

"A what?" I asked.

"A wolf crossed with a ravenous hound," said Popa. "According to the Book of Leaves, Volerdie used weregrims to guard his kingdom. He burned out their eyes to heighten the other senses until, eventually, through a travesty of dark magic, all offspring were born blind."

"Like Casca," muttered Rambleton. "A baby floe bear, maybe not. A baby weregrim instead."

"This is not the first time I've encountered the creatures," said Casca. "They shouldn't be able to hurt me, but this one...was different. It smelled...*infected*. Like poison flowed through its veins. And its growl...a scream of terror as it loped towards me."

"Have you been in the sewers?" I asked, wondering when to take Casca to the washroom.

He nodded. "A good way to travel the city undetected. I followed the Voldari. Discovered more of their plans."

"I've guessed the Voldari plans," said Popa. "They want oil for war and to rule Kogot. To do that, they must control Karlik."

"Control and conquer," said Rambleton, pacing around the bedroom. "Conquer and control."

Yula arrived with the poultice: flour, crushed linseed and dried athal herbs mixed with warm water. She spread the mash over a cloth bandage while we helped Casca sit up.

Blood dripped from the corrugations of pale, shredded flesh, onto the bed quilt as Yula wrapped the bandage around Casca's forearm.

He flinched with the pain but thanked her and then faced me. "I hope I wasn't followed, but I have nowhere else to go."

I clasped his hand. "How...how did this happen?"

"I've never known a weregrim so big," said Casca. "It trapped me in a dead-end street strewn with garbage. Two blind creatures trying to navigate their environment. But I've been without sight longer than the leagues of my memory, and that gave me an advantage. I tracked its inexorable sniffing. The shuffle of its paws over the road bricks as it stalked my scent with remorseless persistence. Someone had set its path to me, and it would relinquish its prey only to death.

"Remaining silent wouldn't help. Although already stained with the detritus of Karlik's sewers, I found a pile of half-frozen animal skins from freshly butchered carcasses. I rubbed the skins over my body to confuse the pursuer. Then I picked up a leg bone, woollydon I expect, slunk against a wall and waited.

"It crept towards me. I shuffled along the wall. One step, two steps. A macabre, sightless dance. Its hungering breath melted the frosty air. It tasted my scent beneath the mask. I brushed against its fur. It lunged, grabbing my forearm in its barbarous jaws. I bashed its skull with the bone. It squealed and squeezed tighter. I bashed again and again with blind fury. It released its grip. I burst from the creature and ran, not bothering to check if I'd killed it. The map of Karlik's streets drawn inside my head led me here." He squeezed my fingers. "I'm certain the Voldari want your skycart. They talked about finding the model-builder."

"Zurta? I have to warn her." I released Casca and turned to go.

Popa stepped in front of me. "It's dangerous out there. Especially for you. The Voldari will be watching."

"Zurta's in danger because of my invention."

"I'll go with you," said Yula.

"And me," said Casca.

"No," I said. "You should rest. Rambleton can bathe you. Then you and Popa should consult the Book of Leaves to see if it yields further clues. Voldari soldiers on our doorstep. Horned wolves roaming the mountains close to Karlik. Shadow men and weregrims. Fergutch?"

"I believe he's safe for now. If the Voldari knew about the workshop, they wouldn't bother with Zurta."

I nodded a vague acknowledgement, unable to process the pace of change swirling around me. Even my compulsion didn't have time to manifest its next obsessive sequence.

Yula and I dressed, then I took a paring knife from the cookery and slipped it into my coat pocket. While a pitiful excuse for a weapon, I'd lost my great, great grandmother's long knife and needed a crutch to help face the danger outside.

We left the safety of our home and marched down the street towards the Inventoria. An ash-snow blizzard battered Karlik. Venting fires raged with renewed and relentless purpose to consume every whiff of gas that might be hiding among the rocks, ready to cause another explosion. A northern gale whipped up the pollutant into a surging wall of devilry. I tugged my fur-lined hat lower and wrapped a scarf around my face to ward off the possession. But the alabaster demons attacked my defences with gritty flakes that felt like slivers of stone cut by witchery. They breached the gap between the top edge of my scarf and brim of my hat, stinging my eyes and blinding me.

"They want to open the balloon line today," cried Yula against the wind, using her hand to shield her face. "I'm supposed to be at work."

So am I, but everything else seems more important. "Balloons won't fly in this weather. At least the Voldari soldiers can't reach us."

"They will eventually. Greed and apathy will make sure of it."

The artifice of weather conjured by the raging ash-snow left Karlik's streets barren of life, everyone sheltering behind stone walls that couldn't protect them from the real threat. Still, I sensed a presence on the wind, driven into the worry of my faltering thoughts.

How far will my scent carry? Is a weregrim hunting me, too?

I panicked about the smells adorning my body. The animal-skin boots. The musty smoulder of my woollen coat. Lavender perfume sprinkled on my neck. Wafts of stale breath from a mouth that hadn't eaten properly in days.

I shoved fingers under my hat and rubbed at my hair, trying to expulse every fleck of lye soap trapped in the braids. Rubbed and rubbed and rubbed, comforted by the resurfacing of my compulsion.

No weregrim arrived on the wind. No Voldari braved the storm. Only Yula and I were mad enough to try. We pushed through the Inventoria doors and ran down the stairs with the doorkeepers calling after us as we shed ash-snow with abandon.

We burst through the basement door. I expected Zurta lived here. She'd never spoken of a home or family, the model inventions her only offspring. And someone had attacked her babies with vicious disregard. In the front room, fractured models lay strewn across the floor and tables, their parts flung to every corner or hanging together by bare and useless threads. Plans had been torn into strips and scattered like fallen leaves. Cabinets had been tipped over and broken open. Shelves swept clean of models. Oil lanterns smashed. Modelling tools crushed under granite.

In the corner, Willamay, the snergul, had been skewered on a metal spike, her dead body spreadeagled and gaping at the ceiling.

"Zurta!" I cried.

From the back room came a moan. We rushed there to find Zurta cowering under a table and covering her head with bloodied hands.

I crouched beside her. "It's me, Silveny."

"Silveny?" she whispered.

Zurta let her hands drop, and I gasped, my justice denounced by a battered face with bruised cheeks of violent purple, eyes barely able to open, and split lips crusted with blood.

"They killed Willamay," wept Zurta.

"The Voldari?"

She forced a broken scowl through the defacement. "I didn't tell them anything. I refused to give in to those...those...." Zurta passed out.

"We have to get her to the Restoria," I said to Yula.

She pushed passed me, knelt and pulled Zurta into her chest. My strong, reliable sister stood and marched to the doorway. I followed.

Vyrin Durk waited for us, a smile of fearful pleasure smudged over his deceitful face. "What have you done?"

"We haven't done anything," snapped Yula, brushing Vyrin aside and climbing the stairs.

But he trapped me with his accusation. "Is that you, Silveny? Hiding your crime behind a face mask?"

"We have to get Zurta to the Restoria," I urged.

He blocked the doorway with his weaselly frame. "Drudan wants to know where you are. Wants to know why you aren't inventing machines to move rubble. And the Voldari have been asking questions."

I tried to squeeze past. "Let me through."

But he ground his boot heels on the floorstones. "First, Jolia abandons her duty, and now you. Don't you care for your fellow mudgles? Are you happy for them to die under the rubble?"

I snarled at Vyrin and pushed my forearm into his throat, pressing him against the door jamb. "Shut up about Jolia. Shut up about…about everything."

I pressed harder. Vyrin's eyes bulged. He gasped for air and groped at my forearm, trying to pull it away. I surged one last time, then let him go. He staggered aside, clutching his throat.

I raced down the corridor with his rasping screams hounding me. "I'll tell the Voldari everything. Where you live. Who your friends are. You killed Zurta!"

Yula waited on the front steps outside, cradling Zurta in her arms. The wind-frenzied ash-snow pummelled our faces, trying to thwart any chance of saving Zurta's life. We trotted into the empty streets, heading for the Restoria. The whirling wind conjured menacing shapes around every corner. I longed to see another Curmudgle, wondering where they'd all gone.

In Fordun Park, bronze statues of Karlik's founders moved in my mind, shedding the brass skin trapping them in place and stepping from their granite pedestals to march into the storm, searching for another valley to call home. *If you value your life, run.*

We rushed inside the Restoria. In the reception area, a Voldari with a hedge of quills affixed to her scalp greeted us with a pointed stare.

"We need a healer," I announced.

The Voldari tilted her head, the bronze light from the oil lanterns refracting across her spiky head decoration. But she offered nothing more than spiny curiosity.

"Healer!" I yelled into the emptiness.

A mudgle with a blood-splattered apron trotted into reception.

"She's injured," I said, pulling the healer over to Zurta, still hanging in Yula's arms.

The healer checked Zurta's face, then pressed fingers against her neck and waited. And waited.

He shook his head. "No, sorry. She's dead. Take her to the Corpsehall. Around the back."

The healer left. No further explanation needed. No time for counsel or comfort. No place for respect or grief. Only callous disregard. *So many dead, life has become worthless.*

A raging vent fire of anger burned my chest. I didn't realise what my hand was doing until it released its grip. By then, it was too late. By then, I'd already slipped my fingers into my coat pocket and wrapped them around the paring knife's handle. By then, I'd already pulled the knife free and rushed at the quilled Voldari. By then, I'd already stabbed the invader in the stomach, preparing to gut her like any other trapped animal ready for the cooking pot.

But Yula grabbed me, and I let the knife go.

My sister pulled me back into the blizzard, leaving Zurta's body on the Restoria floor with a bleeding Voldari for company.

We chased the wind, hoping to catch a different future.

Chapter 20

Hiding from fate

"Stupid, Silveny. Stupid, stupid, stupid!" I slapped my hand against a bare thigh as I marched around the house. The sting crawled across the chastised skin but soon faded at the edges. Undeterred, I dug fingernails into my cheek, pressing hard on the little finger first, then the ring finger. Middle, index, thumb. One after the other. Rotating to the beginning and pressing harder the second time around. Third time. Fourth.

Blood trickled down my cheek. *Blood or tears? Both. Discharges of anger.*

I ground bare heels into the floorstones, searching for a rough edge that might cut me. That would stab the sole of my foot like I'd stabbed the Voldari. Punish me for inviting danger into our home. Threatening my family and friends.

I stopped pacing. "Where are my friends?!" I cried. "Barick, Gallan... J-Jolia. Where are my friends?"

"We're here," said Casca, stumbling up to me and pulling bloody fingernails away from my face.

His wound from the weregrim had healed. *Of course. Immortality protects him from the world.* But mortals like me had wounds that would never heal. Made mistakes that a lifetime of repentance could never correct.

Popa had fixed the blind boy's glasses, melding the broken obsidian lenses together such I could hardly see the joins. But I couldn't miss my reflection. The torment of a thoughtless, dangerous fool.

I balled the front of Casca's dirty jumper into my fist, pushed the blind boy up against the wall and snarled, "You're not my friend. I hardly know you. Ever since you arrived in Karlik, things have gone bad. We were happy before you came. Every second day, you disappear. I wish you'd disappear for good. You claim to be spying on the Voldari, but could be spying *for* them. Who are you? The ageless boy who sees without eyes. Who are you!?"

I shunted him against the wall, the back of his skull hammering into the stone.

Popa grabbed my shoulder and pulled me away. "Silveny. Please."

"You have to go," I snapped at him. "Get away from here. This is the first place the Statutoria will look. Anyone here will be accused of being my accomplice."

"We should all go."

"Flee," muttered Rambleton. "See we flee, to sky and sea." He ran around the room, flapping his arms.

"Escape Karlik," muttered Casca. "Board your skycart and fly out of here."

"It's not ready!" I screamed, then dropped to my knees, weeping. Popa rested his hand on my shoulder, and my muscles slumped. "T-t-the cart...w-w-won't be ready in time, Popa. We can't es-escape."

"Who else knows where the skycart is being built?" he asked.

I looked up at him, hoping the gaze of Popa's dulling eyes would reflect the wisdom I sorely lacked. "Only Casca and me. Even Yula doesn't know."

"Zurta knew," said Yula.

"She wouldn't have told the Voldari. That leaves Casca."

"I can be trusted," he said, pushing away from the wall and sitting on the bench seat.

"I trust Casca," said Popa.

I redirected my fingernails to my wrist and began to dig. "You know him less than I do."

"If the Voldari want the plans to your skycart, Casca could have delivered them long ago. He could have brought the invaders here. Or taken you to them."

"They're waiting for it to be built." *Press. Cut. Dig.* "That's it. They're waiting for the prototype." *Dig. Dig. Dig.* "Then Casca will lead them to the workshop, exposing his treachery." *Dig. Dig. Bleed.*

"Thousands of yarles yield many secrets," sighed Casca. "I can't share all of them with you. But the safety, the life of everyone here, I will not compromise. Not for the Voldari or anyone else. This I promise."

"I trust him," said Yula with a certainty that surprised me.

"We must trust the blind boy," lilted Rambleton. He stopped flapping, lifted me to my feet and squeezed Popa and me together in a hairy, white, shambling hug. "I'll protect you, Silveny. Like Popa Courtan I've protected all these yarles. I'll protect you both."

We held the embrace. Longer than we should, given peace officers could knock on the door at any moment. My weeping dried, and we broke apart. I thought about packing.

"I'll stay behind," said Yula. "I don't know where the skycart is, and I don't want you to tell me. I'll have nothing to offer them and say you went to Popa's cabin to visit him."

"You were at the Restoria," I said, clutching Yula's hand. "They saw you."

"I didn't stab anyone. I'll be reprimanded for running away, but they need me to work the balloon line."

"We should hurry," said Casca.

I didn't have time to argue. Didn't have time to let the renewed distrust of the blind boy fester. Something about him wasn't right, but every accusation I made, he deflected.

As I packed clothes into a rucksack, the idea of leaving my friends behind in a Karlik on the brink of upheaval eroded any moral justification for my actions. I couldn't help the city chart a more prosperous future with my inventions. I couldn't protect my friends. I had to survive. Nothing more. Escape. Get out. Flee. Leave everything behind. Start anew somewhere else and hope guilt didn't blacken any glimmer of happiness.

I stood on the doorstep, a bulging pack at my feet, and hugged Yula goodbye. "I wish you'd come with us. Please."

"They won't throw me in prison," said Yula. "I'm the best winch operator on the line."

"When the skycart's ready, I'll come back for you. I won't leave you behind."

She released me. "Go. The peace officers will be here soon. I'll head to work. They won't find me for a while."

I whispered in Yula's ear, "Where we used to play as pucks. The old workshop, west end of the market. Come there if you're in trouble."

I had to tell her. Yula deserved the opportunity to escape as much as anyone. I swept tears from my cheeks, gathered the rucksack and turned into a bleak day. Rambleton waited at the bottom of the steps, already harnessed to the sleigh. I stuffed my bag beside Popa, who sat up against the sleigh's backrest.

"I can help pull," I said to Rambleton.

"No need," he smiled. "Been long time doing this. Over rock and snow. Ice and moss. Here we go. Stones to cross."

Rambleton took off, and I scurried after him. Casca followed me. He didn't have to listen for my footsteps; the sleigh's wooden runners scraped and grated against the road bricks such that half of Karlik would hear us pass. But speed, not stealth, urged us forward. Once we reached Tablease, only the sewer cats and rats would notice the strange coupling of a blind boy, a white ball of hair, a failing old mudgle, and his obsessive daughter.

*   *   *   *   *

I banged on the workshop door, expecting Fergutch would already know we'd arrive. The bottom hatch opened, and Levan the snergul poked his snout outside, sniffed, then retreated inside. A lock clicked, and I expected the wooden door to swing open. Instead, the portcullis-like steel door screeched skywards but jammed at waist height from the ground.

"Levan!" cried Fergutch from inside. "Did you open that door?"

The snergul barked.

"Who?" asked Fergutch. "How many?"

Levan barked and yelped.

I bent over and called under the door, "It's Silveny."

"Not just you, by the sounds of it," grumped Fergutch. "You'll have to crawl under. Damn door's stuck."

I unstrapped Popa from the sleigh. "I can't walk much anymore," he said, "but I can crawl."

I got on my hands and knees and shuffled under the door beside Popa. Casca followed, and Rambleton unpacked the sleigh and began throwing bags inside.

"What's all this?" asked Fergutch. "This is a workshop, not a boarding house. Send these botherers home."

"No," I said, standing and brushing myself off before helping Popa to his feet. "We need a safe place to hide."

Fergutch squinted in interrogation. "Hide from who? What have you done?"

Popa placed his palms flat together and raised them to his chest. "Thank you, Eminent Lydan Fergutch, for granting us this sanctuary."

"Not been called that in an age."

"I remember when you were Eminent of the Inventoria. I'm Ardgal Courtan, once Literati Reader."

"*Hmph*," grumped Fergutch. "I vaguely recall. Think you're smarter than the rest of us. Never had time for books. I like to work with my hands."

Rambleton upended the empty sleigh and pushed it sideways under the workshop door, then crawled in after it.

"How many more out there?" asked Fergutch, waving his hand at Levan, who released a latch to let the door fall to the ground with a clang. "All these damn bags."

"This is all," I said. "We've come to protect the skycart."

"Haven't started building it. You were here only yesterday. I'm not a magician. Can't wave a stick...."

"Wand," interrupted Popa.

Fergutch sneered. "Can't wave a *stick* and have your damn skycart appear out of thin air. Anyway, plans are a mess. Model is nothing more than a puck's toy. How'd you expect me to work with such a misguided concept?"

"We must *make* it work," said Casca. "There's no other choice."

"What exactly are you protecting it from?"

"Who," I corrected. "The Voldari. They want to build their own skycarts."

"What in Grauberge for? I doubt the thing will fly."

"It'll fly," announced Casca with a certainty I didn't share. "The Voldari wish to be the only ones capable of building skycarts. It would give them an important strategic advantage."

"What does a boy know about strategy?" huffed Fergutch.

"He knows more than any of us," said Popa. "Possibly more than all the books and parchments in the Literati."

"The Voldari killed Zurta," I said. "They'll stop at nothing to get what they want."

"Zurta? She's d-dead?" Fergutch stood for a moment, a statue carved from grief, mouth parted in shock and a glisten of tears threatening to spill over. His shoulders slumped, and he turned away, dragging his boot soles back into the workshop depths.

Levan followed, his back hunched, head bowed and sagging on its neck, hands scraping the floor as if trying to collect his master's sorrow and secret it away to a special hiding place.

"Can we stay?" I called after Fergutch, but he didn't reply.

"Have to," said Rambleton. "No other places to hide."

"They won't find us here," said Casca. "The Voldari have never mentioned the workshop."

Is that the truth? I couldn't tell anymore. But I wanted Casca with us from now on. At least then, I'd know he wasn't scheming with the Voldari.

We carried our things into an adjoining room no larger than my bedroom. The plans for the skycart lay spread across a table and held in place by rocks at each corner. Snergul droppings and food scraps littered the parchments. I swept the waste onto the floor, determined to give my idea more respect.

Fergutch had scribbled over my notes and added to the sketches, sometimes with a manic flourish that illustrated his frustration.

"He's got hundreds of snerguls," I said to no-one. "All trained to work. He could have at least started the build."

"We'll help," said Popa. "I'm not completely incapacitated."

"And I'm not stupid," said Rambleton. "I'm strong in mind and body."

We'll start, but I don't know if we'll finish before fate comes calling.

*   *   *   *   *

Days passed. Five, ten, twenty. I thought about the world outside. About Barick, Gallan and Yula. My sister had sacrificed her safety for me. Her freedom. My distrust of Casca softened, and I asked him to check on her. Make sure she was safe. But he refused, fearful of another weregrim attack. For the first time since meeting him, I heard a tremble in his words. Sensed a terror crawling over his skin.

Immortality is his burden. Death his blessed release. But is there something in between that he fears more than anything? I felt sorry for him. Angered by my suspicion. *Paranoia has become my compulsion.*

We worked day and night on the skycart, sleeping when exhaustion demanded. Despite Fergutch's complaining, he gained renewed energy with us toiling beside him, and his snerguls wielded hammers, chisels, drills, and planers like they'd been born to it. We didn't need to leave the workshop. Fergutch had dug a cold store under the floor where he'd stacked enough food to last seasons. Wheels of cheese. Slabs of butter. Dried meats and vegetables. Grains. Beans. Flour. Barrels of ale. He hated going out in public. It suited us. Only the snerguls snuck out to gather chunks of ice to melt for freshwater.

Casca continued to keep his past close. Encumbrance weighed on his slight shoulders, but he approached each day with the vigour of someone who'd lived for ten yarles, not thousands. The boyish canvas on which the immortal portrait had been painted still showed through the brushstrokes laid down over an eternity. But I expected optimism took an enormous effort for Casca.

Rambleton, a foil to any fetters of pessimism, worked tirelessly with the snerguls, letting the industrious creatures climb all over him or make nests from his unruly white hair. He never wavered in his resolve to finish the job. Never complained of his lot. He'd been that way for as long as I could remember. I had no idea of Rambleton's age. Neither did he. I sometimes worried what would happen if he died before Popa. How Yula and I would care for my da'one with the same attention and affection as the white mudgle.

While Rambleton thrived, and Casca marked his tasks like notches in a belt of girded determination, Popa withered with each passing day. It had been the most time I'd spent with him for yarles, and he couldn't mask his struggle from me. For the one or two days a season I'd visited him in the cabin, he'd been able to disguise his decay. But he couldn't toil for more than an hour in the workshop without rest. He spent most days reading the Book of Leaves, yet it never offered the insight he promised it would. I wondered if the expectation provided comfort, despite the reality failing to deliver.

We couldn't build a full-sized carriage for the skycart. We didn't have the fabric to make a balloon large enough to carry the weight of the carriage, mudgles and cargo. And trying to procure more material would draw attention to us. So, we made a smaller carriage out of reeds, not timber, able to carry four mudgles and limited supplies. Any heavier, and we'd never get over the ridge between Mt Neasa and Mt Fachtna, the easiest way out of the Wyrm Valley.

Four mudgles meant someone had to be left behind. Fergutch ruled himself out, saying he was born in Karlik and would die here. Popa also refused to go because of his ailing condition, leaving room for me, Rambleton, Casca and Yula.

Popa's sacrifice wrenched at my heart, but I accepted the logic of his decision. We'd also be leaving Barick and Gallan behind. My absent friends. But I could see no other way.

* * * * *

On the 24th day since we arrived in the workshop, someone knocked on the timber door. I panicked, thinking the peace officers or Voldari had found us. Then I oscillated to expectation, wondering if Yula had come. Before I could counsel caution, Levan opened the door hatch and poked his head outside. He jumped back in just as quick, scurried to Fergutch and squawked.

"A stranger?" said Fergutch. "Don't need more of those."

"It might be my sister, Yula," I said.

"Male mudgle according to Levan. Strange shoe. Thick sole."

"Gallan?"

I strode to the door, dropped to my knees, slid the hatch across and peeked outside. The sight of a clumpy boot greeted me. "Gallan?"

"Silveny. Can you let me in?"

"How did you know we'd be here?"

"You told me."

Did I?

"I've been holding off coming," quickened Gallan. "Yula said it was better that way. But now...well, can you let me in? I might have been followed."

"Voldari?"

He didn't answer. I stood, unlocked the timber door and swung it open.

Gallan stepped into the workshop, listing from side to side like a ship in a roiling ocean. "Not only the Voldari we have to worry about," he stammered, eyes sending darts of panic left and right.

"What do you mean?"

"So much has changed." Gallan grabbed my hands and squeezed. "We need to save Yula."

Chapter 21

Gallan's aspirations

Gallan stood outside the door of his ma'one's Governant office, the weight of the oversized boot on his left leg dragging his world askew as it always did. His fathers would laugh when they told him stories of how he'd tumble over when learning to walk. When he was a puck, they'd strap a block of wood to the sole of his left foot to help Gallan balance. But he could never run. Whenever he tried, he fell forward, flat on his face. He remembered the day his da'one took him to the cobbler to have special boots made. The shoemaker said she'd never seen such a disparity in leg length. Such a *deformity*. Gallan steeled himself then never to let the burden rule his life. He carried it with resolve, promising himself to make a success of life regardless.

But is Governant scribe the best I can do? he wondered.

In the reception area, Voldari stalked the halls of power, acting like they'd always been there. They numbered more than a dozen now. Gallan kept a pictorial record in a journal, sketching the unique face and headdress of each Voldari he saw. So far, he'd noted twenty different visitors. Six of them confined themselves to the Governant, bending the will of decision makers through their intimidating presence or a quiet word in a sympathetic ear.

Days after the explosion at the Dragon Festival, Karlik had returned to its usual busyness, but not by the usual means. While the mines had reopened, miners worked double shifts, and scores of mudgles had been dragged from their other employment to fill critical shortages. The balloon line had been repaired, but while barrels of oil travelled out, few supplies came in. With *Death's Pass* still blocked by rubble, the balloon line had become more vital than ever, its unsatisfactory operation causing consternation among Karlik's citizens.

Gallan jumped when the office door flung open and Morry came out.

"She'll see you now," said Jilomain's assistant.

Gallan smiled at the sweet, pretty Morry, thinking he'd ask her for a drink in *The Dragon Bellows* one time. But not today. Today was for serious business, not frivolous wooing. He brushed past her and into his ma'one's office. Morry shut the door behind him as he stepped up to the imposing mahogany desk where, on the opposite side, Jilomain Stretten sat with her head bowed, scribbling on parchments with quill and ink. A lone chair had been placed in front of the desk. Gallan stood behind it, his hands resting across his groin. Jilomain didn't look up or acknowledge him. He sighed, in case his presence had gone unnoticed, but it had no impact.

He walked to the front of the chair, sat down and pulled a notebook and pencil from his shirt pocket.

"You won't be needing that," muttered Jilomain.

Gallan nodded to the top of his ma'one's head, then faced the lava-glass window, searching for a break in the clouds through the panel of beige-tinted indifference. A hazy pall had settled over Karlik, fed by the smoke from venting fires and chimneys. Yet, The Melt offered hope. Warmer air from the west replaced chill north winds, with promises carried on the breeze. Soon, much of the surrounding snow and ice would be gone, replaced by meadows of flowers, moss and lichen above the ash-snow line. In city parks, green shoots poked through the smothering of ash-snow, nature defying the ghastly by-product of mudgle industry with the fortitude of a young puck unwilling to let uneven legs slow him down.

I can run now, thought Gallan. *If I want to.*

Jilomain scribbled her last note, then plopped the quill back into the ink well. She looked up at Gallan with green eyes paled by her shock of red hair.

"What aspirations do you have?" she asked.

Taken aback, he jerked his head up. *Since when did she start caring for my aspirations?*

"I haven't given it much...." he stammered. "I'm happy being Governant scribe...."

"But you won't," interrupted Jilomain, "I mean, you *shouldn't* be happy with that for the rest of your life."

Gallan shrugged. "I guess not. I'm doing what I can...."

Jilomain raised her palm. "I see that. Your stories are well received." She clasped her hands beside her heart and leaned forward with serious yearning. "But you must desire more? Have unfulfilled dreams?"

Gallan had never spoken to his ma'one about his dreams. "I'd like to travel," he offered as a start.

She scoffed. "Whatever for? All you need is here. Karlik stands on the cusp of a glorious new future. Imagine the wonder we can build thanks to the rivers of oil being purchased by our Voldari friends. I've spoken with them about the world outside the Wyrm Valley. It doesn't sound appealing. Kogot is on the brink. Conflict threatens to spread across Nordland. We're much safer here."

"There are more stories beyond the mountains," he pressed. "Ones that could never be written in Karlik."

"Yes, but we're writing *this* story. You and me. We're recording this glorious history."

Gallan fell silent.

Jilomain unclasped her hands and softened her posture. "Don't you wish, my son, to be creating the headlines, not simply writing them? As scribe, you've attended many important meetings held in the Governant. You've seen how the Eminents work. Are privy to how they think. Have insights few others share." She stood, held her hands behind her back and walked over to the window, looking outside as if addressing the clouds. "You're scribe now, but could aspire to so much more. Soon, I'll need a new Governant Secretary."

Gallan's mouth turned dry. He enjoyed being a scribe. Meeting with mudgles across Karlik to record their tales. As Governant Secretary, he'd rarely leave this building. He'd always be under his ma'one's eye. Following her orders.

"After that," continued Jilomain, "the next step could be Vice Eminent, then Eminent."

A defiant flush warmed Gallan's cheeks. "All citizens vote on those positions. There's no guarantee I could hold them."

Jilomain spun on her heel and slapped him with a steely glare. "Don't underestimate my sphere of influence. I can make the arrangements. Citizens vote when there's a choice to be made, but if there's just one candidate...." She walked over to Gallan and hovered above him. "I expect my son, my sole offspring, to have aspirations." Jilomain stood there, looking down on him as he squirmed in his chair. Then she moved on, returning to sit behind her desk. "But all these wonderful opportunities are in your future. For the present, we have a serious matter to address. Your friend, the inventor...."

"Silveny?"

"*Hmm.* Yes, *her.* She attacked a Voldari. Stabbed her with a knife."

Gallan's cheeks drained of their defiant rouge. "She wouldn't do that. Silveny is kind. Gentle. She must have been provoked."

"That's for the Ceartais to decide."

"Ma'one, please."

"Stop. When at work, address me as Eminent Stretten."

When at work? thought Gallan. *You're never home.* He shrank in his chair, wondering if...why Silveny would do such a thing. Thinking about how he could protect her. About how that would get him in trouble.

"Eminent Drudan says Silveny Belarose hasn't been to work for days," said Jilomain. "I'm sure the Statutoria can find her, but I've asked Eminent Gardia to wait. The Voldari came straight to me for help. They trust me to sort this issue out, and now I'm trusting you. I want you to find your friend."

"Find her and do what?"

"Well, that is your test, Gallan Stretten. A test of your *aspirations.*"

Someone knocked on the office door.

"Enter," called Jilomain.

The door swung open, and in walked Morry pushing a cart topped with fresh food rarely seen in Karlik: rosy-red apples, blomgarnet fruit and vine berries, roasted boar surrounded by scarlet toms, yams, shiny green spaige, and sprigs of yellow Gallan couldn't name.

"The Voldari brought gifts," said Jilomain. "It would be an insult to refuse them." She faced Morry. "That will be all, thank you."

Morry left the office, closing the door and taking Gallan's desire for courtship with her.

Eminent Stretten smiled at him. "Eat with me, my son. You should ponder your aspirations with a full stomach."

After a meal garnished with guilt, Gallan returned to his closeted office with its smothering walls and planted himself behind the inadequate desk. Governant Secretary would warrant a bigger office. Possibly a window. He reached into the bottom drawer, emptied out the rolled parchments, unlatched a false base and lifted the lid to reveal a secret compartment. From the compartment, he retrieved the journal he'd kept to himself, where he'd sketched each Voldari visitor. It documented everything that had happened in Karlik since the Voldari arrived. A record free from the interference of those with different perspectives. Mudgles like his ma'one.

But now, he didn't know what to do with it. The words written inside threatened to undermine his *aspirations*. If the wrong mudgle discovered it, read it, he could say farewell to being Governant Secretary. Or the next Vice Eminent. Or Eminent.

He opened the journal to a blank page and pencilled in details of the meeting with his ma'one. Then he snapped the journal shut, placed it back inside the compartment, and covered his secret with parchments. He'd decide what to do with it later.

* * * * *

Gallan spent the day in his office, hoping no-one would knock on the door and ask why he hadn't gone to find Silveny. Six hours after high sun, he put on a hooded cloak and left, clumping up the stairs and through the Governant doors. Outside, venting fires fed clouds of ash-snow that swirled along the city streets, joining a woollydon and its driver who took a cart laden with oil barrels to *Line Station 1*. Two storeys above him, the lanterns in his ma'one's office still shone. She worked late, as usual, and he wondered if the Governant Secretary would be required to keep the same hours.

He considered finding Silveny. Jilomain's patience would eventually run out, and she'd ask Eminent Gardia to send peace officers. Gallan would miss the opportunity to display his loyalty and ambition. Fail the test his ma'one had set him. But he hadn't seen Silveny in days and worried something bad had already happened to her.

Must I betray a friendship for the sake of my aspirations? Aspirations he didn't realise he had until today. And if he urged Silveny to flee, the peace officers would eventually come for him. Gallan didn't expect his ma'one to stop them.

He wandered Karlik's streets, past huddled mudgles lined up outside a food store waiting for a delivery from the Governant-controlled stockpile. Hunched over, offering their backs to the ash-snow, the desperate clutched empty bags ready to fill. A female with a puck in tow pushed into the head of the line. A scuffle of citizens forced her out, dumping her and the young'un in a pile of ash-snow.

Inside, the store owner approached the lava-glass front door. Hunches straightened to expectation. Gallan could almost taste the salivation welling in hungry mouths. He sucked a piece of boar gristle out from between his teeth and swallowed it lest the crowd uncovered his secret feast.

The store owner shook her head, hung a 'Closed' sign inside the front door, then walked away. The starving mudgles wrestled with their displeasure. Some yelled abuse. Others banged on the door with demanding fists. The puck who'd been tossed aside stood from the ash-snow pile with a road brick in his hand. He hurled it at the shop window, shattering the lava-glass and spraying the crowd with rose-tinted anger.

Mudgles kicked the loose bits of glass away and started to climb inside. A whistle echoed down the street. Peace officers rushed to the disturbance, truncheons drawn, ready to deliver their justice.

Can't eat justice, thought Gallan, as he snuck away, not interested in writing stories about the city's despair.

Unable to decide what to do about Silveny, he ducked into *The Dragon Bellows,* hoping a black ale might clear his mind. After being decloaked and dusted for ash-snow by the doorkeepers, he limped through the maze of empty tables, inhaling the sombreness of a tavern barely a quarter full. A handful of dour miners, their faces covered in soot caked on by dried sweat, cupped gnarled hands around goblets of ale and stared at the alcohol as if the frothy swirl could tell their fortune. Peace Officer Crooshka sat alone by the door, slumped in his chair, his red coat unbuttoned to the waist, truncheon resting discarded on the floorstones. At the table beside Crooshka, a trio of artisans dressed in black huddled together, either whispering the merits of their latest creative triumph or delivering biting critiques of absent colleagues.

A Voldari hovered near the artisans, cocking his head sideways, attempting to capture an errant word with furred ears sliced on either side so they had a pointed top. A bushy brown tail with a black tip hung from the back of the Voldari's head and draped over the front of his shoulder. Gallan couldn't recall if he'd sketched this visitor, thinking he'd check his journal next time at work.

In the far corner of *Xeni*, the tavern's main room, sat Barick accompanied by the caged snergul, Sneckle. As Gallan approached, Barick didn't look up or acknowledge him, but Sneckle squawked a warning.

Gallan sat at the table and poked a finger into the snergul's cage to scratch her fur, but the animal snapped at his fingertip. "Damn," he said, jerking his hand away. "I'm not trying to feed you." He faced his friend. "I thought you'd be working or sleeping."

Barick shrugged, gulped a mouthful of alcohol, then held his empty cup aloft.

Horu, the waiter, ambled over. "Another one already?" he said, glancing at Barick, then Gallan.

"You keepin' count?" muttered Barick.

Horu smiled with condescending eyes. "You must know, waiters can't count." He faced Gallan. "What will you be having?"

"Whatever Barick's drinking."

"Two fire-rums. Where are the rest of your friends? I haven't seen them in ages."

"Got sick of you," mumbled Barick.

Horu stiffened his posture. "Lovely. Hardly a soul here, and those who have arrived are miserable and bitter."

"Why so quiet?" asked Gallan.

"Everyone's busy," said Horu. "Mining oil. Shipping oil. Building machines to mine or ship more oil. Serpent oil greases the wheels of Karlik commerce. Literally."

"You're still here," said Barick.

"Not for much longer," snapped Horu. "New opportunities emerging. The Voldari have turned things on their head. Recognised the valuable skills of people like me. One more night in this bog-hole and I'm done." He turned to go but stopped himself. "Oh, forgot. Don't bother ordering food. We're out. Until the balloon line is fixed properly."

"It is fixed," snapped Barick. "Damn Voldari are hoarding the food."

Horu glanced over his shoulder. "I wouldn't be cursing the Voldari if I were you. Won't end well."

Horu left, and Gallan returned his attention to Barick. "Have you seen Silveny or Yula?"

Barick looked up with sullen, hollow eyes. "Not since our last visit."

"I need to find Silveny."

"She'll be flitting around with that blind boy. Her new best friend."

"Don't know what to make of him."

"Immortal. It sounds unbelievable."

"You saw what happened when Yula stabbed his hand. The wound healed straight away."

"Could be black magic. He arrived when the Voldari did. They're all demons."

Gallan leaned in. "Keep your voice down. There's one over there."

Barick returned to staring at the tabletop. "Who cares? The pit bosses are working us into the ground. A few nights in the Statutoria gaol would be welcome."

"You don't mean that."

They sat quietly as the miners filed out of *The Dragon Bellows*. Horu returned with two cups of fire-rum.

"If that creature poops on the table," said the waiter, pointing at Sneckle, "one of you will have to clean it up."

Barick took his cup from the tray and downed a gulp. Gallan smiled and nodded as Horu placed the second cup on the table. He reached into his pants pocket and retrieved an amber token, flipping it to the waiter, who caught it with one hand.

"No more lousy tips," he muttered before walking off.

Barick traced a dirty finger around the rim of his tin cup, flecks of grit from under his fingernail falling into the alcohol. Speckles of ash-snow the doorkeepers had missed lined the crevices of his braided black hair like alabaster veins. He stank of oil, dirt and sweat, a pungent, musty, offensive odour that stung Gallan's throat.

"He's still there," croaked Barick, withdrawing his finger from the cup and flicking more dirt from under his nail.

"No," said Gallan. "Horu's gone."

"Not him," hissed Barick. "Shadow Man. He's still inside my head." He clutched his cup with a crush of bare hands. The youthful shine of his dark skin had paled. Grizzled wrinkles grew fingers from the corners of his eyes.

"Is he...is he speaking to you?" Gallan asked.

"You think I'm mad. Swallowed too much ash-snow. Breathed in too many oil fumes."

"I know you *believe* Shadow Man is there. I mean, I saw him too, remember. In the lava pits. There's something unnatural about him."

"He's not speaking to me. Not like he did when we met on *Death's Pass*. But he's loitering. Waiting in a corner of my mind. Waiting…for a weakness to exploit. Waiting to pounce." Barick finished his drink. "Why me? Why did he choose me?"

"You were unlucky to have crossed paths with him."

"He remembered me from the first encounter in the mine. Then we returned to find Jolia, and Da'one demanded I help him look for evidence of sabotage. It's like I'm drawn to Shadow Man." Barick's eyes grew wide. "Is he inside Da'one's head, too? Or Officer Crooshka's?" He nodded towards the door where Crooshka still sat slumped in his chair, then leaned forward and whispered to Gallan, "He's been watching me all night."

"You're imagining things." Gallan reached across the table, pulled one of Barick's hands from the empty cup, and clutched his fingers. "You're not mad. All of us are worried. Under pressure from everything that's happening to us. The explosion. The Voldari."

Barick pulled his hand away. "There's more of them," he whispered. "There must be. I see them everywhere."

Gallan nodded. "There's more. But the oil's flowing, and more supplies will enter Karlik once the balloon line…once things are sorted. I'm sure the food shortage is temporary. Soon, the Voldari will be gone, *Death's Pass* will be reopened, and things can return to normal."

They had another drink before Barick went home to bed. Gallan returned to his apartment, planning to find Silveny tomorrow.

*   *   *   *   *

The next morning, Gallan went to Silveny's house in Tork. No-one answered the door. He visited the Inventoria. They hadn't seen her, although one of her work colleagues, Vyrin Durk, swore she killed Zurta, the Inventoria model-maker. Vyrin expected Silveny had already fled Karlik to escape the Statutoria. Gallan didn't believe it.

He had one more mudgle to ask and left the Inventoria to begin the hike to *Line Station 3*. If anyone could tell him where Silveny was, it would be her sister, Yula.

Gallan lumbered up the narrow track to station three, dragging his burdensome boot across the marbly scree. Despite the impediment of uneven legs, he relished the climb above the ash-snow shroud masking Karlik, into a warming blanket of blue sky. Above him, a balloon floated its way up from station two, reeled in by the lead rope.

More barrels of serpent oil leaving the city, he thought, *but few returning to replenish dwindling supplies.*

A pair of Voldari in blue robes marched down the path. Gallan prepared his right hand for the accepted welcome: four fingers to the forehead, then heart. As the visitors approached, he raised his hand to his head. But they didn't look down to make eye contact, pushing past him like he didn't exist. An insect unworthy of their attention. He considered calling after them, 'I'm Eminent Stretten's son. She's head of the Governant.' *Soon*, he thought, *I might be Governant Secretary. Then Vice Eminent.* But he questioned if that mattered to the Voldari.

He climbed higher, wheezing with the effort of nursing his disfigured body up the ridgeline. On a rock ledge above station three, a shadow formed the silhouette of a horned wolf. Gallan stopped, waiting for the silhouette to move. Wolves rarely appeared during the day, and Karlik's venting fires held them off at night.

The silhouette wavered as if tousled by the wind, and then it transformed into the shape of a man. Towering, strong, ruthless. *Shadow Man?* Gallan almost turned back, worried he'd end up like poor Barick with a mind crippled by fear. But the sun shone across the rock ledge, and the silhouette vanished in a beam of blinding radiance.

Outside *Line Station 3*, Gallan waited for Yula to winch in the balloon from station two, her shoulder and arm muscles bulging with the effort. Sweat dripped from her forehead into her eyes, her mouth contorting in spasms of exertion. Knuckles threatened to burst the seams of leather gloves. Boot soles braced against the stone floor. As the balloon approached, one of the line crew pushed a stepped platform towards the docking post. Another prepared ropes and carabiners. It looked chaotic and treacherous, and Gallan thanked his ma'one for letting him be Governant scribe.

The line crew did their job, as they'd done many times before, and the station manager raised a blue flag to let station four know they had a balloon ready to be pulled up. Yula slumped onto a crate and swigged from a waterskin, her work over for now. Gallan limped into the station towards Silveny's sister.

A line crew member confronted Gallan. "You can't be in here."

"I know him," muttered Yula.

"Still needs permission," said the first mudgle. "Line stations are busy and dangerous places. Can't have a naïve, clumsy clot with a bung leg wandering into the machinery."

Yula dropped her waterskin, stood and grabbed Gallan by the arm, dragging him outside.

"What do you want?" she snapped.

"Where's Silveny? Everyone's looking for her."

"Everyone?"

"Well, the peace officers would be if my ma'one didn't intervene. They know about the stabbing."

"They've already been to our house. I didn't tell them anything. I'm not telling you."

"I'm Silveny's best friend," pleaded Gallan. "I can protect her. Ma'one will listen to me."

"Will she?" scowled Yula. "You're her finger puppet. You can't eat or shit without her approval."

A fist tightened in Gallan's chest. "That's not true. If I don't find Silveny, the peace officers will turn Karlik upside down. The Voldari are already threatening to withdraw their order for serpent oil."

"Might be for the best," said Yula. "We're shipping oil out, but the soldiers at *Line Station 16* aren't letting supplies come in."

"Soldiers?"

Yula squeezed Gallan's arm until he grimaced and pulled him further away from the station. "Voldari soldiers at station sixteen. Control everything."

"Have you told someone this?"

"Our station manager told the Statutoria and the Governant. I couldn't do it. They're already threatening to charge me with stabbing the Voldari if they can't find Silveny."

Gallan's world reeled. His ma'one had said nothing of Voldari soldiers anywhere near Karlik.

"The Voldari are holding us to ransom," said Yula. "Incoming supplies are a pittance of what's needed. Karlik will starve, and the Statutoria and Governant don't care."

What are your aspirations, Gallan? "I'll tell Ma'one, but I need to find Silveny."

"You can't help her." Yula went to walk off.

Gallan grabbed her wrist. "I'm the only one who *can* help."

Yula stopped, twitches across her face battling for a decision. "She's building her skycart. We're escaping."

Yula yanked her hand away and marched back into the line station.

Gallan stood there as bits of a puzzle fell into place. *Hiding in Tablease. The abandoned quarter, but not completely abandoned. Rumours of a workshop near the old market. Large enough to build a flying machine.*

* * * * *

Days passed. Gallan believed he knew Silveny's whereabouts but hadn't acted on it, frightened of what he would do if he found her. What his *aspirations* expected him to do. Karlik sank further into the abyss. Mobs gathered on the Governant steps, demanding Eminent Stretten release more food from the stockpile. But the stockpile had shrunk to a few bags of grain. Owners of near-empty shops boarded up doors and windows to ward off the harassment. The community fractured.

Those willing to pledge allegiance to the Voldari received preferential treatment. Access to more supplies. Protection from Voldari soldiers who'd begun coming down the balloon line.

Those who refused floundered. Oil mining had almost ground to a halt. Rumours spread that the Voldari would take over production and shipping. A resistance emerged, led by peace officers who wanted the Voldari to leave Karlik. But they numbered too few to fight the invaders' stranglehold.

The turmoil kept Eminent Stretten busy, and Gallan hoped she'd forgotten about his duty to find Silveny. But late one night, he woke to a knock on his apartment door. He opened it to find his agitated ma'one standing on the step. She'd only visited him once since he purchased the apartment a yarle ago. On the day he purchased it.

She pushed inside. "Did you find that inventor?"

"Not yet," yawned Gallan. "I will, though."

She grabbed his shoulders and shook him awake. "You better. The damn sister, Yula, killed a Voldari with a hunting bow."

"What?"

Jilomain released Gallan and sat on his bed. "I tried to intervene, but the Statutoria have her. She's in the gaol awaiting trial. The Voldari demand justice. Her death in exchange for the Voldari she killed. This, on top of what her sister did."

"Did you see the Voldari?" asked Gallan. "The dead one?"

"Yes, I saw him," hissed Jilomain. "Wrapped in a shroud with his bald head poking out. Stupid bird feathers plastered all over his scalp. They're going to take him back to Kogot. Imagine the smell by the time he gets there." She gagged. "But they're going, that's the main thing. They say once justice is served for their friend's death and the stabbing, they will finally leave Karlik."

"Are you sure they'll leave?"

His ma'one fell silent and scanned the single room where Gallan kept all his possessions. All the things his ambition had collected over the last two yarles. He wondered if she'd be disappointed that he had so little.

"I should visit you more often," said Jilomain with a wisp of longing. "Come for a meal. Can you cook?"

"Yes, but...I'm not thinking of food. I...."

She patted the bed quilt. "Sit beside me, Gallan. Sit with your ma'one."

He sat next to her. She pulled him across, pressed his head into her lap and stroked his braids. "Do you remember when you were a puck? We'd sit together for hours as I read you stories about wondrous lands and brave heroes. You loved those stories."

"Before you became Eminent."

She sighed. "That job has taken so much from me. Taken so much from my family. But I can give it back. Will you let me give something back, Gallan?"

He nodded, becoming drowsy as his ma'one's fingers caressed his scalp.

"Once we sort this mess out," she purred, "we can get rid of those Voldari. Ship them their damn oil and be done with it. But I need your help."

He closed his eyes, drifting with an affection he'd missed for so long.

"Now is the time to make Karlik a wonderful place again," she whispered. "Now is the time for heroes. I need you to be my hero, Gallan."

Chapter 22

The betrayal

"Yula goes on trial in a few days," whispered Gallan to the ground.

"We have to get her out of gaol." I turned from my friend, thinking to search the workshop for a weapon. I didn't know what I'd do with it. Or how I'd rescue Yula. But I couldn't leave her to face this madness alone.

Casca blocked my path. "It's much too dangerous for you." He faced Gallan. "Your ma'one sent you here to bring Silveny to justice."

Gallan nodded; the confession measured with teardrops. "It's true. They want Silveny for stabbing the Voldari. And there are questions about who killed Zurta. I avoided coming here. Hoped ma'one would forget. But now. Yula."

"She told you I'd be here," I said to Gallan.

"No," he urged. "Your sister didn't betray you. I worked it out myself."

Casca shook his head. "I don't like this."

"Yula will be executed," whined Gallan. "It's happened to others. Mudgles hanged for lesser crimes. Ma'one wanted me to be a hero. Saving Yula and helping you escape Karlik is the most heroic thing I can do."

I gritted my teeth to set a jaw of unbreakable courage. "I'm not leaving Karlik without my sister."

"If it's a trap," said Casca, "better I go. I've been sneaking around this city since I arrived. If anyone can rescue Yula, it's me."

"It's not a trap," said Gallan. "A resistance has formed. Those opposed to the Voldari. Barick is part of it. He'll get us into the gaol."

"He won't go against his da'one," I said. *He's a coward,* I thought.

"Warden Mulburat is a resistance leader. Barick will want to help." Gallan grabbed both my hands. "*I* want to help."

Casca yanked me away from Gallan and pulled me into a quiet corner. "This isn't right," he muttered. "You feel it, don't you?"

"Yula's in trouble. Gallan and Barick are her friends. *My* friends."

"Desperate times stretch the bonds of friendship thin."

"If you expect a trap, why are *you* prepared to go? I know you're scared of another weregrim attack. And if you're caught, they'll discover you're immortal. What will happen to you then? What macabre tortures might the Voldari conjure? They could give you to Shadow Man."

At the mention of Shadow Man, Casca flinched. Barely noticeable beneath his obsidian glasses – a twinge at the corner of his eye like someone had stuck a pin into his cheek.

"All I have left in this life is helping others," said Casca. "Only then do I discover the joy I long for."

"You can't do it alone. Yula is my sister. I should be the one to save her."

Casca leaned in and whispered, "Do you trust Gallan? Barick?"

Paranoia flared in my mind. Days ago, I didn't trust the blind boy. Now, he urged me to question my trust in everyone. But paranoia couldn't subdue the need to save Yula. Paranoia couldn't be my compulsion.

"I have no choice." I returned to Gallan. "You'll defy Eminent Stretten?"

He wiped tears from his cheeks. "My friendship with you is stronger than the bond I have with my ma'one. It's been that way for a long time. She cares only for her work. For her ambition. I want you and Yula to escape Karlik and find a better life. Finish the journey your parents started all those yarles ago."

"Is there a way?" I asked. "To keep us safe?"

"I'll talk to Barick. Is the skycart ready?" Gallan peered over my shoulder into the workshop.

"We're making progress. But this will have to be our sanctuary for a while longer. No-one else can know we're here."

"I'll keep it a secret." Gallan hugged me, then turned to go. "Be ready to leave tonight. I'll return then with a plan for Yula's rescue."

He left the workshop. I pushed past Popa, who blinked tormented eyes. His eldest daughter needed rescuing, but his youngest daughter would have to risk her life to do it.

"Casca and Rambleton...." Popa started.

"No," I bit. "Casca's still blind, despite all his magic. And stealth is not Rambleton's strong point. I won't have others face danger for my responsibility. Yula wouldn't be in this mess if it weren't for me. She would have killed that Voldari to protect us. There's no other explanation for it."

I found an empty rucksack and searched for things I might need for a rescue. A coil of rope. A hammer. A hand-axe. Random choices that lacked thought. I'd never broken into a gaol before.

"My special mouldewerp key will come in useful," said Casca.

"There will be guards," I muttered. "Peace officers. Voldari."

"I'll hear them long before they hear me."

"But will you kill if you have to? You told me you don't want to be a murderer."

"We'll pray it doesn't come to that."

"Prayers won't help us."

With my thoughts focussed on Yula, I urged Fergutch and his snerguls to work feverishly on the skycart. If we rescued my sister, we'd only be able to hide here briefly before the law found us. The cart needed to be ready within days.

As I waited for Gallan to return, Popa took me aside. "The skycart can carry four," he said. "If Gallan and Barick help rescue Yula, they'll be fugitives too. They'll also need an escape."

"Should I leave Casca behind?"

"He's immortal. I imagine he's survived worse than this."

"With Yula, Rambleton and me, that leaves room for one more."

"Rambleton won't leave my side."

"You'd sacrifice him...."

Popa squeezed my hand. "We love each other. We made a pact yarles ago that we'd go together if we could, into the arms of the mountain spirits."

I hugged Popa, still uncertain of the choices ahead.

Gallan returned that evening, bringing with him a plan to save Yula.

*   *   *   *   *

The mudgle with the clumpy boot led Casca and me through Karlik, streetlamps spotlighting an encore of ash-snow that drifted on the breeze. Trapped in the workshop for twenty-four days, I'd missed the comfort of the familiar, even if it threatened to smother me. The city was my home despite its problems and contradictions. Mudgles had traded their health for the wealth brought by serpent oil, and it appeared the black sludge would be our final undoing.

Maybe it was always going to be this way. Our fate sealed when mudgle explorers found the first cave with its pool of riches. The treasure left behind by mythical dragons and drakes marked, not in piles of gold and jewels, but fissures of bubbling, boiling oil.

But I had a choice. Be a part of this seemingly inescapable future or, indeed, escape.

No other mudgles walked the streets this night, our only companions the flakes of ash-snow that danced a welcome back. I didn't bother to put my hat on, a strange melancholy urging me to open my mouth and taste the gritty sleet. It may be my last chance. Atop the ridges surrounding Karlik, a handful of venting fires burned, not the usual dozens. As leaden clouds drifted in, the city grew darker, a tension suspended in the air. An expectation of a storm approaching.

We didn't speak. Words might betray us to the enemy. That's how I thought of the Voldari and those mudgles who had aligned with them. The visitors who came as friends offered nothing but despair.

Gallan led us along an alley squeezed between the Statutoria and the Inventoria. He then turned left and began descending stone steps.

"Is this a dead end?" asked Casca.

"It takes us to a door," said Gallan. "That leads to the gaol. It was built into the old mining tunnels that run beneath Karlik."

"You didn't answer my question. With just one way out, we're trapped like rats."

Rats. They crawled over the stairs, rising from the sewers in a revolting wave. I had to kick them aside as we walked. Gallan squashed one with his ungainly boot, pressing the heel down until the animal's eyeballs almost burst from its tiny skull. It squealed a final breath. I retched. Casca whimpered like he'd lost a friend.

We descended three flights of stairs into a moor of chilling air and ash-snow piled against the sandstone walls. Gallan stopped at a timber door with iron straps painted black. The light from the streetlamps barely reached us here.

Should have packed a lantern in my rescue kit.

"Barick will be here soon," said Gallan, as he knelt and dug ash-snow away from the door's base.

I crouched beside him and plunged my hands into the obstruction. Rats sniffed towards us. I tried to smack one away, but it latched onto my finger, biting through the glove. I cursed and swung it against the wall, a gush of air bursting from its mouth as it slammed into stone.

"Don't," said Casca. "We might need their help."

How are rats going to help us?

The blind boy stepped around Gallan and swept his hand over the door. "Is there a keyhole?"

I reached up and guided his fingers to the faceplate. With his other hand, he pulled the mouldewerp key from his pocket, fumbled around to feel the key's bit, and inserted it into the hole.

"Won't turn," said Casca.

"Magic key not so magic," mumbled Gallan.

"It doesn't always work," said Casca, returning the key to his pocket.

We cleared the ash-snow from the door. Casca stood beside us and chattered away in soft yips and squeals. The rats left us alone, and I wondered how far this skill of Casca's extended. *What can he get these creatures to do?* Being able to talk to animals didn't save him from the weregrim.

Behind us, feet scraped the stairs. Not the skitter-scatter of rats' feet, but the thud of boots and a pool of auburn light that announced the arrival.

"Damn it," said Gallan. "I told him not to use a lantern."

Barick appeared from the darkness, holding an oil lantern out front and kicking vermin aside as he went. "Where did all these rats come from?"

"Quiet," hissed Gallan. "You've already sent a beacon out to anyone wanting to foil us."

"Barick," I smiled. "I missed you."

He smiled back, placed the lantern on the ground and hugged me. "Glad to see you again. Things have turned so bad; friends are more important than ever."

"The key?" urged Gallan.

Barick pulled away and nodded, removing a ring of keys from his coat pocket.

"How did you get those?" I asked.

"From the resistance," he replied. "My da'one and dozens of peace officers are part of it. It wasn't hard getting keys to the gaol." Barick unshouldered his pack, uncinched the straps and pulled out a handclock. "The guards change at middle night, one hour away. Those on duty now are sympathetic to the resistance. They'll leave early, giving you time to rescue Yula."

"Are you coming with us?"

Barick shook his head. "I can't risk exposing the resistance. If we're caught, they'll know Warden Mulburat is involved. He'll be executed."

Paranoia asks: Why won't he take the same risk as you? I reply: Shut up and let me be. Let – me – be.

Barick unlocked the door. "You'll enter a passage hardly anyone uses. There's a gate, but the lock's broken. Follow the passage to the cellblock." He picked a different key from the ring and held it towards me. "This one opens cell seven, Yula's cell. Be prepared, Silveny. The gaol is overflowing with mudgles. Most will be asleep, but if they hear you, they'll cause a ruckus." He hugged me again. "Give me the door key. I'll wait here for your return. If a patrol comes down the stairs, I'll lock the door from the inside and find you. We either run or hide, or die together."

I slid the door key from the keyring and placed it in Barick's sturdy hand. He didn't shake or falter or shirk the danger. *He's a coward.* The slight stuck in my throat. At this moment, he proved to be everything but. He proved my paranoia wrong, and I might never repay his bravery.

I opened the door and stepped into the passage.

"We can't use a light in here," said Casca. "Let me lead the way."

Rope. I knew it. "Wait," I said, unshouldering my rucksack. "I have a rope. We should tie it around our waists."

I secured one end around Casca, looped the rope around my waist and went to tie the free end around Gallan.

He backed away. "I don't want to be tied up. We can't run if we're tied together."

"How will we follow each other in this darkness?"

"I'll hear you."

I shook my head and tied the rope around my waist, stuffing the rest into the top of my rucksack and shouldering it.

"Ready?" asked Casca.

"Yes," I replied.

He walked forward and the rope tugged. I followed him, hoping Gallan would stay close. We left behind the light from Barick's lantern, the dark passage swallowing us like a monster's throat. I pressed my hand against a wall of jagged rock. Dust kicked up into my nostrils from the dirt floor. A musty, cloying annoyance. At least we'd left the rats behind. No crawling squeaks, only Casca's searching breaths ahead and the stomp of Gallan's boot behind.

My compulsion fixated on the possibility of a fork in the passage. On the chance of getting lost. A minor worry given the circumstances, but compulsion and logic were rare bedfellows.

I pulled off my gloves and shoved them in a coat pocket. I ran my thumbnail against the edge of each fingernail, a favourite obsession. '*Click. Click. Click. Click. Click. Click. Cli....*'

"Stop it," whispered Casca.

You hear that? Of course he does.

As a distraction, I reached my left hand to the passage wall, rubbing fingers over the stone. We crept forward like thieves planning to steal dragon gold. Or oil. One slow and hesitant step after another. One scrape of rock wall followed by another followed by...nothing.

I waved my hand in the air. A squalid draft wafted from a side passage, and a gurgle of menacing darkness found my ears.

Should we turn here?

Casca pulled me ahead, not wanting to linger. I counted my steps from the junction, thinking we might need the side passage to hide in. A stupid thought, but the counting kept me from turning back. From abandoning Yula.

Casca stopped, and I bumped into him. "The gate," he said.

Gallan fumbled for my shoulder. "I'm still here."

A rattle of metal and a squeal of hinges, and we walked through the gate. We turned a corner into a passage lit by a single flaming torch bracketed to the brick wall. Casca led on, past a room to our right. I checked the room, worried about guards inside. But something more horrid lurked there. Implements laid out on a table. Whips and hooks and shackles. Spiked iron masks to wrap around heads. Clamps to crush bones. Pliers to pull teeth.

Torture devices. Wicked, horrible tools to do unspeakable things. Mudgles had not used them in generations. But here they were again, risen from the grave.

I shivered and scampered past the room.

We walked around another corner, pools of light ahead from oil lanterns hanging from the bricked roof. Casca stopped in the shadows.

"We're close," he said. "I can hear them breathing. Snoring. Dreaming."

"There's a stack of crates ahead," I said. "We can hide behind there and wait."

"Did you bring a handclock?" asked Gallan.

Damn it. I could've taken Barick's. Damn it! "No," I snapped and snuck up to the crates.

Gallan and Casca followed. I peered through a gap into a room with gaol cells on either side and two guards at the far end watching the door. They were dressed in shabby green coats, not the smart red uniforms of peace officers, and instead of truncheons, they held hooked pikes with polished blades.

"I hope we haven't missed the changing of the guard," whispered Casca.

I pulled the hand-axe from my belt, thinking of Philomine Belarose facing the might of King Faramund and his Erstürmen soldiers five generations ago. I tried to channel her strength and bravery, prepared to rush the guards and chop them to pieces. Prepared to do anything to save Yula.

I faced Gallan. "Did you bring a weapon?"

He shrugged. "Didn't think I'd need one. I don't want to be accused of being a traitor."

Isn't breaking a prisoner out of gaol already treason?

He placed a hand on my forearm. "We can trust these guards. They'll leave soon. That's our chance."

Unless we've already missed it. But I relaxed with Gallan's reassurance and waited, breathing in every wheeze and snore of the prisoners. Picturing every nightmare that must be torturing their minds. Hoping Yula had the strength to run with us. Or to fight.

"They're leaving," said Casca.

I wondered how he could tell.

The guards shut the door behind them, leaving only prisoners in the cellblock. I sprang out from behind the crates, not waiting for Casca or Gallan. Not wanting indecision to turn into cowardice.

I read the numbers above each cell. *Forty-two, forty, thirty-eight. Other side, thirty-seven, thirty-five. Yula's side.* In every cage slept a prisoner. Sometimes more than one. Slumped into a narrow cot or curled up on the stone floor. *Twenty-five, twenty-three, twenty-one.* A prisoner sat up in her bed, propped against the wall, staring out into the corridor. I faced her, my heart thudding louder than a hammer on wood. She smiled and placed her finger to her lips. I nodded and kept going. *Seventeen, fifteen, thirteen.* A prisoner sobbed with the pain of innocence stolen by injustice. *Eleven, nine, seven.*

Seven.

Inside the cell, Yula lay on a cot, dressed in prison rags and facing the back wall. I pulled the keyring from my pocket, fumbled for the right key, and then inserted it into the lock. Turned, and the lock clicked open. I slid the cell door across, cringing at the scrape of metal on stone.

Yula stirred as I ran into the cell. "It's me," I said as I knelt beside her.

She rolled over and whispered from a mouth bruised and bloody, "Silveny?"

"Can you walk?" I asked. "We're here to save you."

From swollen eyes, she squinted over my shoulder. "We?"

"Casca and...."

I tugged on the rope and turned at the same time. The rope went limp. I pulled until I held the loose end in my hand. Casca had vanished. Again. So had Gallan.

I'm alone. "We have to get out. New guards will come soon. Get up."

I dropped the hand-axe, forced my arms under my sister's side and tried to lift but fell forward with the failure. Yula pushed up from the cot and swung her legs to the floor, but they buckled when she tried to stand.

"Don't risk your life for me," she moaned. "I can't run."

"There's a way out. We'll go together."

I pulled Yula to standing and held her upright under the arms, thinking of escaping back down the passage. As I turned to face the cell door, it slammed shut, and the lock clicked. Outside stood my betrayal; Gallan with his ma'one, Eminent Stretten, beside him, and behind them the Voldari Urn-hasa, and two mudgle guards with green coats and pikes.

Gallan faced me with pleading, deceitful eyes. "I had no choice."

Eminent Stretten turned to him. "Where's the other one? The warden's son?"

"He's watching the door."

Stretten nodded to the guards, who took an oil lantern from the wall and raced back down the passage from where we'd come.

The Eminent faced me again, holding her hand through the cell bars. "Keys."

Yula collapsed back onto the cot. "Don't resist," she whispered. "Please."

I walked to the cell door and handed over the keys. Gallan turned away, unable to confront the consequences of his duplicity.

"So many traitors," said Eminent Stretten, shaking her head as she gave the keys to Urn-hasa. "Mudgles willing to disobey their leaders. Fools." She glared at her son. "Keep away from them."

He nodded, and they walked out. I sat beside Yula and cried.

Chapter 23

Cell seven

"**D**id you kill a Voldari?" I asked Yula.

She shook her head, rolled over to face the wall and pulled knees to her chest to shield her heart against this tragedy.

Urn-hasa lingered outside our cell, the tips of her feathered crown brushing the ceiling, her raisin eyes staring with menacing intent like an owl perched on a branch above a pair of dim-witted mice. She stepped aside to reveal a strange creature crouching behind her, balanced forward on knuckles at the ends of wiry arms, and thick legs supported by flat feet. Matted brown fur covered its entire body, except for a pale face with squinting, pebbly eyes and a flat, almost concave nose.

"Wu-epon," demanded Urn-hasa, her soulless eyes lost amid the tattooed black rings encircling them.

On four limbs, the creature shuffled forward, its spine horizontal, head level with its bottom, but still as tall as a mudgle. It shoved its hand through the bars.

I picked up the hand-axe and, for a fleeting moment, wondered how easy it would be to throw the axe between the cell bars and split Urn-hasa's skull. Splatter brains and blood across those snow-white owl feathers. But the violent flirtation vanished like a jilted lover. I held the axe by the blade and offered the wooden handle to the creature. It snatched the weapon and tossed it away with a grunt.

"Empty pack," ordered the Voldari.

I stood, opened the rucksack and tipped the contents onto the floor. Urn-hasa unlocked the cell door and slid it open, heralding another flirtation with escape. But the creature blocked my path, yawning with a cavernous mouth full of flesh-tearing canines. It loped inside, sat on its haunches and sorted through my belongings, tossing each item outside the cell, including the empty pack.

"Cu-lothes off," said Urn-hasa.

I paused in stagnant resistance, a whimper of defiance to the new order, and glowered at the invader. Behind me, a broken Yula offered no more than her back.

I waited too long. The creature reared up, as tall as its master, sprang forward and pawed at my clothes. I slapped its hands away. It dropped to all fours, pressed its nose to mine and snarled, spattering my skin with viscid saliva that reeked of Karlik's sewers.

"Alright," I said, unbuttoning my coat.

As I unshouldered the coat, the creature yanked it from my hands and tossed it outside the cell. It lost patience, ripping my shirt and undergarment over my head, then shoving me to the floor to unlace my boots. I unclasped my skirt and unwrapped it from my waist, not wanting the animal's hands violating me further.

"Stu-and," barked Urn-hasa.

I stood, naked.

"*Vek har*," she said to her servant, in the sharp bite of her language.

The creature dragged its calloused hands across my vulnerability. Lifted arms to check armpits. Pushed legs apart and debased my intimacy. Searched my hair, fingering and pulling at the braids.

It pressed down on my shoulders, compressing my spine and forcing me to squat above the pitiless stone floor. I closed my eyes, willing strained muscles to relax. *It'll hurt more if you're tense.* It hurt anyway, as the animal inserted groping fingers into my anus.

It faced Urn-hasa and shook its primitive head.

"*Mund*," said the Voldari.

The creature crouched in front of me and shoved its fingers into my mouth. I gagged at the taste of salty sweat seeping down the back of my throat. The animal wrenched my cheeks apart and peered into the void before shaking its head again.

"*Uit*," snapped Urn-hasa.

Her lackey gathered the rest of my clothes and loped from the cell.

With a molested ache, I stood, damming the flood of impotence rising behind my eyes. *Yula? Protect me. Save me from what comes next.*

Urn-hasa closed and locked the cell door as the guards sent to find Barick returned.

"Couldn't find him," said one.

Celebrate the moment. Barick is safe.

"Rags." Urn-hasa pointed at me, then marched off with her servant in tow.

The guards disappeared.

One returned soon after and tossed prison rags through the bars.

I clutched them to my nakedness and set accusing eyes on him. "What was that *thing*? With the Voldari."

"A gorvile," said the guard. "Don't make them angry. I've seen one tear a mudgle limb from limb."

"Why are you working for the invaders?" I asked, covering myself with a thin, filthy long shirt that reached to my knees.

"Better with them than locked in there with you."

He took his watch with his companion at the cellblock door. I slumped against the wall beside Yula, wondering if she'd noticed what had happened. Wondering if it had happened to her. Wondering if she cared.

"Talk to me, Yula," I groaned.

She rolled over to face me. "I'm so tired. They haven't let me sleep."

"Did they torture you?"

"I wouldn't tell them where you were."

"Gallan worked it out. He lied to me. About...about a lot of things. They'll find the skycart."

"They kept asking me when it would be finished."

"If they're waiting for Fergutch to complete the build before they move in, it might buy us time."

Yula scoffed. "Time for what? You see where we are. The charade is over. We're never leaving Karlik."

"Popa is waiting for you."

Disdain darkened my sister's face. "He's been gone for yarles. Hiding in that piteous mountain cabin with his simple friend. He could have lived here with us, but he chose not to. *Now* he's waiting? It's too late."

She rolled away again. I stilled shuddering arms by wrapping them around my legs and pulling knees to my chest. I rocked back and forth on my sit bones, counting each moment of unevenness inside my head, thinking the path of saviour would be revealed if I counted long enough.

*   *   *   *   *

I woke to door hinges groaning. It signalled a din of damnation, wails and curses from the incarcerated. Along the rows of cages, inmates thrust their arms out between prison bars, groping for freedom.

"Get back," yelled a guard.

I shook Yula's shoulder. "What's happening?"

"Morning meal. Only meal."

The mudgle guard pushed a cart down the corridor. She stood in front of our cell, dipped a ladle into a copper pot, then threw a serving of watery stew at my feet. "Have your bowl ready next time," she smirked.

"Bowl?" I queried. "I don't have a bowl."

The guard moved on.

I faced my sister. "Yula?"

"Under the bed," she muttered. "You can use the spoon to scrape it from the floor."

"I'm not.... Damn it, Yula, what's happened to you?"

She sat up and stared with uncaring vacancy. "Now you're here, the trial will be soon. Little point eating."

"I'm not quitting. There must be good mudgles left. Decent mudgles who'll fight to free us. Barick spoke of a resistance. Warden Mulburat and others. We can't give up."

"Waste!" cried another guard.

I stepped to the front of the cell. Prisoners tossed the contents of their waste bucket into the corridor. I pressed a hand over my face to mask the smell, a rotten, festering ooze trapped inside a windowless stone box. I lifted the wooden bucket from the front corner of our cell, pinched my nose, and tipped the waste outside. With a mop, the guard pushed the excrement along the sloping stones to an iron grate in the middle of the corridor. Another contribution to Karlik's sewers.

Karlik's sewers. Casca? Special mouldewerp key. Will he?

After another disappearance, when I needed him more than ever, my trust in Casca had waned again. I'd been a fool all along. Made a target of myself by inventing the skycart, a flying machine that could carry soldiers in war as easily as barrels of serpent oil. And I'd jeopardised the Voldari oil order by stabbing one of them. The visitors would demand their trial. They'd demand justice be done.

"Water comes next," said Yula. "Get the cup."

I slunk to the floor, reached under the bed and pulled out an empty tin cup, dented at the sides as if Yula had bashed it against the wall in frustration. The squeaky wheel of another cart ambled towards us. It stopped outside our cell, and someone familiar smiled.

"Who'd have thought?" said Horu. "Although you're a traitor, I'm still waiting on you."

"I'm not a traitor," I spat.

"Why are you here? Don't tell me you're innocent. Everyone in these cells claims innocence. It's tiresome."

"You quit *The Dragon Bellows* to work for the Voldari?"

"I work for Curmudgle prosperity. The only place I see that is in Voldari hands. Cup."

I handed the cup to Horu through the bars. Like the guards, he wore a green coat, shabby and hastily made with poor stitching and odd buttons that didn't match.

Horu went to tip a ladle of water into my cup, then stopped, smiling to himself. He placed the cup on the cart, unbuttoned his trousers, took out his penis, then held the cup underneath the tip and urinated.

I expected Yula to rush the bars and scream at him. But she hardly had the energy to roll over.

Horu placed the cup, brimming with frothy piss, on the ground. "As good as meduz," he said, then walked off, whistling to himself.

I crouched, pulled the cup into the cell and tipped the contents on the floor to let it seep into the sewers. A swollen tongue pined for moisture, but I wouldn't lower myself to drinking Horu's urine.

I stood and paced at the front of our cell, scraping my bare feet on the floorstones. My compulsion demanded restitution. A fixation to make amends for the unstimulating surrounds I'd trapped it in. Inmates moaned and cried around me, the unsettling drama of imprisonment. A prisoner across the corridor caught my eye.

"How long have you been here?" I asked.

He checked the wall. "Sixteen days."

"What did you do?"

He glanced up and down the corridor, then pressed his face to the bars. "Nothing. Voldari came to my store. Took what they wanted and left. I chased after them. For payment, you see. But they kept walking. I found a peace officer. She wouldn't do anything. I got, well, I got a bit heated with her. Shook her about. Ended up here. Rumour is you're getting a trial."

"You haven't had one?"

"Most here were arrested and then imprisoned. No talk of trials. But they claim they're going to organise work details. Get us into the oil mines. Better than sitting here waiting to die."

My companion's acceptance of his plight bothered me. "You've been gaoled with no trial? The authorities might find you innocent."

The prisoner shrugged. "Who decides innocence and guilt now?

Used to be the Assembly of Eminents. Most of them bow to the Voldari. If I got a trial, would it be fair? They only hold trials when they want to make an example of someone and for justice to be *seen* to be done."

The day dragged on, though I couldn't see its passing in this bleak, windowless place. While others slept or sat in stupefied silence, the gorvile returned without its Voldari master. It plonked down in front of our cell, sitting upright, left hand clenched and resting in its lap, the right scratching its furred chin, contemplating the strangeness of the creatures locked behind bars. A common mudgle like me had become exotic in this disorientating world.

I sat cross-legged on the cell floor, opposite the gorvile. It shuffled forward and opened its left hand, revealing a squashed bread crust. If I stretched an arm through the bars, I could reach the bread, but the gorvile might be using my hunger as a trap. As soon as my hand left the safety of the cell, I expected the creature to grab it and yank my shoulder into cold, hard steel.

"Put it on the ground," I said, pointing to the bread.

It tilted its head sideways, possibly trying to decipher my request. I acted out what I wanted, pretending I had bread in my hand and tipping the imaginary morsel to the floor. I'd be willing to swallow grit and slim to satiate my need and avoid the trap.

The gorvile shuffled closer and stretched its arm further towards me.

I shook my head. "Bread on ground."

The creature's shoulders relaxed, and it tipped the bread onto the floorstones. But it didn't retreat. It could still grab me if I reached for the food. Hunger beckoned, and a pointless trial waited like a pack of horned wolves on the hunt.

I'll be found guilty. Executed. Yula says no point eating. I say no point starving.

I reached my arm between the bars to snatch the bread. The gorvile pounced. I flinched, jerking my hand back. But the creature did something I didn't expect. It hugged its barrel chest and laughed, baring rows of glistening canines. It laughed so hard, it toppled over and rolled on the ground, staining its fur with the remnants of mudgle waste.

A futility washed over me, and I laughed, too. Laughed in the face of despair. Laughed because I refused to cry.

The gorvile deflated its buoyance, sat back up and pushed the bread closer to the cell with the back of its finger. I didn't hesitate this time, reaching out and taking the food. The creature smiled at me. At least, I think it smiled.

I brushed the grit and grossness from the crust. "Do you want bread, Yula?"

She moaned a rejection.

I sniffed the morsel. Not sure why. It smelled like urine. I tore off a piece and tossed it back through the bars towards the gorvile. *I could make a friend. If the creature can bring bread, it can bring keys.*

The gorvile picked up the scrap of crust and also sniffed it. Then it stared at me, holding the bread near its face.

I lifted my piece, held my breath and took a bite. The gorvile did the same, mirroring my action. We chewed the stale morsel together, prisoner and captor's pet, took another bite and sat staring at each other.

Then the gorvile stood and loped away.

"Come back," I said. "Can you get keys?"

But the creature disappeared, along with any hope of escape.

*　*　*　*　*

As the days passed, my compulsion demanded fulfilment, so I untwisted the waste bucket's wire handle and used the sharp tip to scrape mortar from the wall. Along each crevice between the hard-packed, rectangular stones I dug, satisfied when a fleck of mortar crumbled to the floor. I could do this for days and not loosen a single stone, most of them thicker than a loaf of bread, but my compulsion revelled in the distracting monotony.

Yula didn't help, but she didn't stop me. We'd been reduced to almost complete silence, searching for solace in our thoughts, not conversation. Trapped inside this depressing, barred square, both prisoners of injustice, should have brought us closer together. But it only accentuated our differences. Yula had unravelled all her braids, letting free a wild creature that sent its frizzy tentacles out from her scalp to search for a new homeland. Sometimes, I sat and combed my fingers through her frizz while she slept. When it was my turn on the bed cot, I dreamed of us escaping this horrible place. Of Yula rising like a flaming, ravaging phoenix and laying waste to all the compliant mudgles and their Voldari masters.

I never again forgot the food bowl or the cup. Meagre stew arrived every morning, not enough for one mudgle, let alone two, but it warmed my depression. Horu returned, but he'd had his joke and filled the cup with water. The gorvile, however, never returned with the keys, and desperation grew with my hunger such that I yearned for the trial. For the ordeal to end. I expected the Voldari had already stormed the workshop and taken the skycart. Or enslaved Fergutch and his snerguls to finish the build. Although I tried not to, I couldn't help but imagine the horrific fate of Popa and Rambleton.

My compulsion focussed on scraping away the mortar and didn't use the wire to mark the passing of days. So, I don't recall the exact day when a mudgle in black robes marched up to our cell and proclaimed, "Trial for the condemned!"

His pronouncement set off a cacophony of noise through the cellblock, inmates screaming at all the injustices of this new order. The promised work details had never eventuated, our captors content to let most prisoners simply starve to death.

Two mudgle guards in green coats joined their robed companion at the front of our cell.

"Hands out," snapped the female guard.

I faced Yula, hunched in the corner. She groaned to standing, then staggered to the front of the cell and jammed two hands together through a gap in the bars. The guard squeezed shackles around her wrists and snapped the lock shut. Yula tugged her hands back inside, the bars scraping against the shackles' outer edge.

"Now you," said the guard, glaring at me.

I followed Yula's lead. The guard slapped shackles on my wrists, catching loose skin in the hinge before she clamped them shut. I bit my lip and stood beside my sister.

The male guard unlocked the cell door and slid it across. Yula and I walked out together.

As the guards led us down the corridor, the inmates yelled abuse, spat at us, or tossed the waste inside their buckets at our bare feet. My blood boiled, thinking of the many days and nights I'd worked on inventions to improve mudgle life. To make things better for these heartless, thoughtless, cruel individuals. I decided then, they didn't deserve it. I decided then, only those I loved mattered.

Dragged by the guards, Yula and I stumbled together through the cellblock door and towards an unknown fate.

Chapter 24

Truth on trial

The guards led us along a corridor with oil lanterns hanging from the ceiling. I counted each lantern as we passed, the amber lights guiding us to inevitable doom. At the end of the corridor waited the Voldari, Run-targa, standing hunched below the ceiling in front of a steel door.

We stopped before him. "Justice has found you," he said, spit dribbling down the tusks that protruded from the corners of his mouth. He leaned in and whispered in my ear, "Tell me where the boy is, and I can save both of you."

Boy? Casca? Don't you want to know more about the skycart?

As Run-targa leaned back, Yula tensed beside me, throwing off the shackles of exhaustion. Her face burned under the lamplight, solid brick red building a fortified wall across her cheeks. Panting breaths flared from between her lips like dragon fire.

"Yula," I muttered. "Don't...." *Too late.*

She coiled her anger and slammed the tusked Voldari into the steel door. He staggered sideways and cowered before a mudgle half his size. Yula rushed him again, ramming her shoulder into his waist. A gush of air and spit exploded from his mouth. The guards fought to control my sister. I kicked one of them in the shins. He thumped the blunt end of his pike into the middle of my back. I doubled over, needles of pain shooting up and down my spine.

Run-targa gathered his courage, swaying his lithe torso away from Yula's swinging arms. He clamped a hand around the side of her neck, and her legs buckled. She collapsed to the floor, stunned like a battered fish.

The Voldari opened the door. The guards lifted Yula to her feet and dragged her up a flight of stairs. I stumbled after them, not able to consider a different path. At the top of the stairs, the leading guard knocked on a wooden door. It opened, and the guards threw us into a wall of curses and a flood of light. I crashed into Yula, grabbing her to stop us both from falling. Laughs rang out, followed by cries of 'Traitors!' and 'Thugs!'

My eyes adjusted to the blaze of hundreds of candles, melted to a dozen chandeliers hanging from a high, corniced ceiling. No lie or deception would escape this probing light of judgement. No shadow could hide a misdirection. We stood in the Ceartais, the Court of Justice, a hall built inside the Statutoria. The room bulged with rows and rows of mudgles seated on the edge of pews in eager anticipation of our demise. A desperate sliver inside me hoped to find friendly faces among the throng. Those who would decry this injustice and plead for our freedom.

Popa? Rambleton? Already dead. Barick? Too scared to show. Casca? Deceitful. Escaped, never to return. Eminent Drudan? Shamed by my absence.

The crowd offered naught but cold, blank faces or gleams of salivating retribution. The guards dragged us in front of a timber bench, longer than a wagon and taller than my head. Behind the bench, looking down on us, sat Eminent Stretten flanked by Urn-hasa and Hor-gnasher, the Voldari who helped Shadow Man sacrifice mudgles. Who helped kill my friend, Jolia.

Under normal circumstances, the Assembly of Eminents would sit in judgement in the Ceartais. But circumstances had deviated from the normal many days ago.

Gallan, a mudgle I once called friend, sat at the side of the bench. He didn't look at me, keeping his head bowed and scribbling a pencil across a notebook page as if writing a confession of broken friendship.

"String them up," said Stretten to the guards.

They hauled us to a timber structure that resembled gallows. Our hands still shackled out front, the guards lifted our arms above our heads and draped the chain of the shackles over a hook. We hung there, arms stretching to the ceiling, toes aching to reach the ground.

The crowd stilled to a dull murmur.

Vice Eminent Trotter Borke, dressed in a green uniform like the one Horu and the guards wore, appeared from the side of the hall and faced the bench. "Eminent Stretten, esteemed Voldari, our next case is one most grievous. Silveny Belarose is accused of assaulting a Voldari without provocation and of murdering a mudgle. Possibly two."

Murder? I didn't murder anyone.

"Her sister," continued Borke, "Yula Adermont, is accused of being an accomplice to these disturbing crimes."

"I didn't murder anyone," I squeaked out.

"Silence," growled Stretten. "You speak when asked." She addressed Borke. "Begin the case."

Borke nodded. "This won't take long, Eminent. As our first witness, I call on the healer, Punora Drayton."

A mudgle healer dressed in mauve robes walked over to the witness stand.

"You are the healer, Punora?" asked Borke.

Punora nodded.

"Are you willing to answer my questions truthfully?"

"Yes, I am."

Borke turned to me and Yula, who hung like slabs of meat. "Facing the judgement of the Ceartais this evening are the accused, Silveny Belarose and Yula Adermont. Do you recognise them?"

"Yes," said Punora. "They came to the Restoria more than thirty nights ago."

"For what reason?"

"They brought in a dead mudgle."

Some in the crowd gasped. A burning sting seeped down my arms, threatening to engulf my shoulders.

"Not any mudgle," clarified Borke. "They carried our most beloved model-maker, Zurta. You proclaimed her dead on arrival?"

"I did," said Punora. "The accused said she'd been beaten."

"Beaten to death," said Borke, facing the salivating crowd. "But beaten by who?"

"Voldari," I croaked. "Zurta told me...."

"There's no evidence of that," snapped Borke. "Our only *impartial* witness, Zurta, is dead, and the last mudgles to see her alive were Silveny Belarose and Yula Adermont." The Vice Eminent pointed his crooked finger of accusation at me, his hand shaking with the tremor of his conviction.

I turned my aching head to the crowd. "If we'd beaten Zurta, why would we take her to the Restoria?"

"Silence!" yelled Stretten. "You'll get a chance to defend yourself at the end."

"Defend the indefensible," sneered Borke. "I'll answer your question, Silveny Belarose. You took our irreplaceable model-maker to the Restoria out of guilt. You and your hateful sister beat her to the precipice of death, but then guilt overcame you." He faced the bench. "Eminent Stretten, esteemed Voldari, this is but one incident in a pattern of violence related to the accused. My evidence will show that carnage and death follow Silveny Belarose wherever she goes."

Why would I beat Zurta? It doesn't make any sense. Yula. Help. But my sister slumped beside me, head lolling to her chest, passed out from the Voldari neck pinch.

Borke stood in front of Punora. "After you pronounced Zurta dead, what happened next?"

"I told the accused to take the body to the Corpsehall, then left the reception area."

"But you heard something and returned straight away?"

He nodded. "A scream and a cry of pain. When I entered the reception area, the Voldari observer, Gil-hansa, had been stabbed in the stomach, and Zurta's body had been dumped on the floor. The accused had fled."

"Evil!" came a shout from the rumbling crowd.

"Monsters!"

"Murderers!"

"Traitors!"

Borke raised his palms to silence the mob, then faced Punora. "Did you see Silveny Belarose stab Gil-hansa?"

"No. But other than Yula Adermont, who else could it have been? They were the only ones in the reception area."

"Who else could it have been?" repeated Borke. "What happened next?"

"I treated Gil-hansa's wound and arranged for Zurta's body to be taken to the Corpsehall."

"And given the due care and respect it deserved."

Punora nodded.

"Thank you, Punora. That will be all."

The healer stepped down from the witness stand. As he walked past me, I offered pleading eyes to a fellow mudgle, hoping they'd evoke a change of heart. But he kept walking, disappearing back into the crowd of seedy faces eager for our downfall.

"I call on Gil-hansa as our second witness," said Borke.

The Voldari I recognised from the Restoria walked with careful, dainty steps up to the witness stand, holding her belly as if I'd stabbed her then and there. The quills on her scalp glistened like needles under the candle chandeliers. Frost-blue robes took on a sapphire sheen. Dark raisin eyes now resembled warm mulberry wine. She looked regal: a queen or princess.

A pang of guilt struck me.

Vice Eminent Borke faced the crowd. "Gil-hansa is not proficient in our language. Therefore, this court asks Run-targa to act as interpreter."

Run-targa strode from the corridor leading to the cellblock and stood beside the witness stand.

Borke addressed Gil-hansa. "Are you willing to answer my questions truthfully?"

Run-targa muttered into Gil-hansa's ear. She nodded to Borke.

"Good," he said. "You were the Restoria observer, learning Curmudgle ways of healing, is this correct?"

Run-targa whispered. Gil-hansa nodded.

The Vice Eminent continued, "While in the reception area, two Curmudgles burst in, carrying a dead mudgle in their arms."

She wasn't dead. Zurta wasn't dead. Not when we found her.

Run-targa whispered, received his answer, and replied, "That is true."

"As the healer, Punora, testified," said Borke, "Zurta was proclaimed dead, and the accused asked to take her body to the Corpsehall. But that didn't happen. What exactly *did* happen?"

The Voldari exchanged words in their language, guttural snipes that bit more than the shackles tearing at my wrists. Yula groaned beside me, a hint she might be coming to. Eminent Stretten and the Voldari judges glared at us with a ravenous hunger, like vultures waiting for an animal to die. The crowd enjoyed the entertainment. As I absorbed their moral supremacy, I noticed not a single peace officer among them. No red coats and truncheons, only green uniforms and frost-blue robes standing together on the perimeter of the spectacle.

Run-targa cleared his throat. "When Punora left the reception, the larger mudgle, the one I believe is called Yula, threw the corpse to the floor. The smaller mudgle, Silveny...," he smirked at me with delicious salivation, "...kicked the dead body in the face."

"No!" I cried, tears welling.

"Hang them!" a mudgle from the crowd yelled.

"Too quick, burn them!"

"I DIDN'T!" I screamed. "I w-w-wouldn't. I loved Zurta. I...."

"Silence!" yelled Eminent Stretten, jumping to her feet. "All of you. This is the Ceartais, not a tavern full of drunkards." She glared at me. "Silveny Belarose, keep interrupting, and you will be gagged."

No, I whimpered inside. *This isn't fair.*

"Continue," said Stretten to Run-targa before sitting back down.

"In a fit of uncontrollable rage, Silveny...."

"Can you please identify the attacker," interjected Borke.

After a whisper from Run-targa, Gil-hansa pointed at me with a long, delicate, noble finger that begged to be adorned with diamond rings.

Run-targa continued the story, "Silveny withdrew a sheathed dagger, rushed at me, and stabbed me."

It was a paring knife. From my pocket.

"Show the wound," demanded Borke.

Run-targa asked, and Gil-hansa opened her sapphire robes to reveal a stab wound in her stomach.

"Did you do anything to provoke this attack?"

Run-targa asked the witness. She replied, closing her robes. He interpreted. "Nothing at all. I was there merely to observe. The Curmudgle burned with rage."

"Uncontrollable rage," clarified Borke.

"Nothing would have stopped her. I feared for my life. She stabbed me, and they both ran from the building."

"But a good mudgle, a *loyal* mudgle, saved you. Treated your wounds."

"We are forever grateful to our true Curmudgle friends," said Run-targa.

"And we are grateful for your understanding and compassion in this awful matter. No further questions. You may stand down."

The two Voldari left the witness stand, joining their companions at the courtroom's side. The ache in my arms had reached my shoulders, twisting the joints as if my hands had been trapped inside a butter churn. I longed for my body to go numb to relieve the suffering. At the end of dangling legs, bare toes tapped the ground in a desperate, pathetic sequence. Despite impending death, my compulsion commanded a final performance.

"I call on Peace Office Kynil Crooshka as our third witness," announced Borke.

Who? Why? WHY?

Crooshka, dressed in a green uniform, not Statutoria red, took the witness stand.

"Peace Office Crooshka, are you willing to answer my questions truthfully?" asked Borke.

Crooshka nodded.

"Please explain to the court where you were thirty-four days ago."

"Warden Mulburat and I were ordered to search the mines for clues as to what might have caused the explosion during the Dragon Festival."

"There were others with you?"

"Yes. Mulburat's son, Barick Pulson, and the Voldari observer, Pul-ussa."

"What did you find?"

"Remnants of oil barrels, like they'd exploded. But we couldn't identify a complete serial number to discover where the barrels came from. Whether they'd been brought into the mine in an act of sabotage."

"We now know," said Borke, facing the crowd, "that evidence of sabotage was flimsy. The Assembly of Eminents have concluded that the explosion was caused by gas build-up." He returned his attention to Crooshka. "You found something else in the mines, didn't you?"

The peace officer bowed his head, muttering, "Yes."

"Speak up," said Borke.

"Yes. I found a body in the mines."

The crowd chattered in anticipation.

Borke faced the bench. "Eminent Stretten, esteemed Voldari, what happens next will be confronting and upsetting. But it's something we must endure so all can protect themselves against this murderous disease infecting our community." He called to the rear of the courtroom, "Bring in the evidence."

Along the centre corridor, lined on either side with the yearning crowd, a mudgle wheeled a stretcher with a white cotton sheet covering a body. Something stuck out from the chest, pushing the sheet up until it formed a tent. As the stretcher passed through the crowd, those closest to the corridor thrust hands over their gagging mouths or pinched their nose.

The whine of the stretcher's wheels set my head thumping. As it went past, an acid sting burned my nostrils. Bile rose in my throat. I would have vomited if my stomach had contained anything. Thoughts spiralled into madness. *What is this? What has this got to do with me?*

The evidence bearer stopped the stretcher in front of the bench and stepped aside.

Borke placed his fingers on the peak of the cotton tent. "Everyone should prepare themselves." He paused, scanned the crowd, pinched his fingers and removed the sheet with a flourish.

The throng erupted. Gasps. Wails. Shouts. Some fainted. Others cursed. A few rushed out, vomit dripping between fingers pressed over mouths.

My mind howled. It wept. *Jolia? Jolia. JOLIA!*

"My friend," I cried. "My friend."

Eminent Stretten nodded. The guards approached and tied a leather gag across my mouth. I gasped for air through my nose. Gulped, wept, muttered. Tapped my toes on the floorstones as if trying to squash thousands of deadly, stinging insects.

Vice Eminent Trotter Borke paced out front of the crowd, ringmaster to a vengeful circus. "Dear friends!" he called. "Dear friends, the body wasting away on this stretcher is Jolia Sojule, one of our most promising inventors." He waited for the din to subside before facing the witness. "Peace Officer Crooshka, can you confirm this?"

He nodded. "Yes. I recognise her from the Governant food court."

"Jolia worked at the Inventoria with Silveny Belarose." Borke faced the crowd. "Remember that. It's important." He returned to Crooshka. "And this is the body you found in the mine?"

The peace officer nodded.

"As you can see, Jolia has a blade sticking from her chest. A long knife. It looks ancient." Borke approached the body, holding his nose.

Jolia. What happened to you?

"Officer Crooshka," nasaled Borke before releasing his nose. "Was this blade in the body when you found it?"

"Yes. That long knife killed Jolia."

Borke leaned over the body and squinted at the knife. "There's an inscription on the handle."

"Philomine Belarose," offered Crooshka with compliant eagerness.

The crowd inhaled and held its collective breath.

"Indeed," announced Borke, "I confirm that the name inscribed in the bone handle of this long knife is Philomine Belarose."

"Those of you knowledgeable in mudgle history," began Stretten, "would remember that Philomine Belarose was a famous warrior who fought King Faramund during the Battle of the Under-road. She'd be struck with horror knowing her famous blade has been used to kill one of our own. Has been used by her great-great granddaughter to inflict murder."

None of this is true. Jolia was my friend. Crooshka knows it. Eminent Drudan knows it. Where is he? Where are the mudgles who can fight for me? Why have I been abandoned? I didn't kill Jolia. The last time I saw her, she stood beside the lava pit with Shadow Man. Waiting. Waiting to die. I didn't kill her, but I didn't save her either. All this...all this is a lie. Someone else used my knife after I lost it in the mine. Shadow Man used it. Or Hor-gnasher. Stretten! The murderer is sitting beside you! This isn't evidence; this is fabrication.

"There's more," said Crooshka, energised by the baying mob. "Silveny Belarose reported Jolia missing in a vain attempt to cover her tracks. To set us on a blind path. And...," cried the peace officer, barely able to contain his hateful excitement, "Belarose was the last one to visit Jolia's father before he died in the Restoria."

"Oh!" exclaimed Borke. "This is news to me. The horror is worse than I thought. It appears Silveny Belarose has a vendetta against the entire family."

With every skerrick of energy I had left, I forced myself to face Gallan. To confront him with this injustice. He could defend me. He could expose the lies of this sham court.

I moaned through my gag, trying to attract his attention. I bashed my toes into the floorstones. My mind begged him. But he never looked up. Never met my eyes. Only scribbled his creations in his notebook.

"You can step down," Borke said to Crooshka.

The peace officer left the witness stand as Borke continued, "Why would Silveny Belarose kill someone she calls 'friend'? We know she stabbed Gil-hansa in a fit of uncontrolled rage. Likely, she and Yula Adermont murdered Zurta, the model-maker. That also seems to be a conundrum until the last puzzle piece emerges. The court calls its final witness, Vyrin Durk."

Vyrin strutted to the witness stand, staring at me with a glee he couldn't mask. "Vyrin Durk, inventor," he spat out, eager to testify. "I promise to answer the questions truthfully."

Borke smiled. "You work with Silveny."

"Correct. Silveny and Jolia. At the Inventoria."

"They were close? Friends even?"

"I wouldn't say *friends*. Silveny latched onto Jolia. Followed her around all day. Jolia was the more experienced inventor. A *better* inventor."

Borke picked up a rolled parchment from a desk. He untied the ribbon, walked across to the witness stand and unrolled the parchment in front of Vyrin.

"Do you recognise these?" asked Borke.

"They're unfinished plans for a flying machine that uses refillable gas canisters. For the first time, a balloon could carry gas with it, keeping it afloat for days."

"Do you recognise the handwriting? The drawing technique?"

"Yes. These are Jolia Sojule's plans. We all knew she was working on something big. Something amazing. I didn't know what until I found the plans."

"Found them? After her death?"

Vyrin nodded so fiercely I thought his head would fall off. "Hidden under Silveny's workbench," he gleed. "There's a secret compartment. She'd stolen them."

"She'd stolen them," repeated Borke. "Stolen the plans to claim the invention for herself or destroy them so her own flying machine wasn't grounded before it could take off."

Vyrin chuckled. "Silveny's invention was a disaster from the beginning. It wouldn't fly. I tried to convince Eminent Drudan, but he ignored me. Thank goodness it was never built. Many mudgles would have died."

"Silveny would have known of Jolia's plans?"

"Definitely. They were always together. Always talking. Silveny stabbed Jolia in the back. Or the chest, it seems." Vyrin chortled again.

Borke faced the bench. "Silveny Belarose stole the plans for the sake of her own glory or to save herself from embarrassment. The only thing stopping her was her *friend*, Jolia Sojule. Either way, we have a motive for murder."

Embarrassment isn't a motive for murder. This doesn't make sense. Can't you see? Can't anyone see? Why would Jolia be in the mines? Why would I take her there, kill her, then get my friends to help find her? None of it makes sense. Shadow Man did it. Hor-gnasher did it. He should be on trial, not sitting on the judges' bench.

"You can step down," Borke said to Vyrin.

Vyrin Durk walked up to me and spat in my face. The crowd cheered.

Borke bowed to Eminent Stretten and the Voldari. "Our case is closed."

Stretten nodded. "The argument is compelling, demonstrating a clear pattern of violence by the accused. We may never know who attacked the model-builder, Zurta, but evidence suggests it was Silveny Belarose and her sister, Yula. Zurta likely knew about Jolia's plans, so Silveny had to shut her up lest she reveal the theft. Without question, the accused stabbed our Voldari friend, Gil-hansa, and almost certainly murdered Jolia Sojule and possibly Jolia's da'three, who may have also known about the plans. I'm surprised our loyal Eminent Drudan, Inventoria head, is still alive."

A few in the crowd chuckled.

"A despicable pattern of deception, theft and murder," continued Stretten. "And Silveny Belarose would have been brought to justice sooner if it weren't for the lies of Yula Adermont. She is as culpable as her sister. But protocol demands that the defendants get to plead their case." She motioned to a guard, who removed my gag. "It appears your sister can't speak," said Stretten, "so you must speak for both. Now is your chance to beg for mercy, Silveny Belarose."

Gallan finally lifted his eyes to me, tears streaming down his cheeks. Although I was about to die, I felt sorry for him. I stopped tapping my feet and arranged all the thoughts swirling in my head. *Shadow Man. Hor-gnasher helping sacrifice mudgles in the mine. Voldari taking over Karlik. Casca the blind immortal. Horned wolves circling the city. Weregrims. What should I tell them? How much will they believe?*

As I went to speak, a commotion broke out at the rear of the Ceartais. Doors burst open. Mudgles flooded in, many wearing the red uniform of Statutoria peace officers. Warden Mulburat led them, followed by Eminent Drudan and Eminent Leabaran from the Literati. Behind them came Barick, charging forward as if he'd never had a cowardly thought in his life.

The liberators arrived with axes, shovels, sledgehammers and swords. Any weapons they could find. They confronted the Voldari first.

"Attack!" yelled Stretten into the crowd. "Kill the traitors."

Those in green coats pulled truncheons from their belts or raised pikes and rushed at the liberators. Voldari soldiers in blue, serpent-scaled armour slithered from the corridor leading to the cellblocks. Eminent Stretten, Urn-hasa and Hor-gnasher fled.

From behind me, someone lifted my shackled hands off the metal hook. I collapsed to the floor.

Gallan lifted me into his arms. "I'm so sorry. Shadow Man is in my head, too."

"Yula," I croaked.

Gallan nodded and let me stand on shaking legs. He climbed on a chair and unhooked Yula, fighting to hold her upright.

Barick chopped his way through the madness with his mining pick. Peace Officer Crooshka, the dreamy Crooshka, confronted him with truncheon drawn. Barick froze, pick raised above his head. Crooshka swiped at Barick's face. Barick swung down, embedding his pick in

Crooshka's forearm. The peace officer screamed and dropped the truncheon. Barick yanked his weapon free and ran to us.

"We have to go," he gasped. "There's another way out."

Combatants in green, red or blue blocked the main doors, slashing, cutting, and smashing at each other. Gallan and Barick helped Yula stand and heaved her forward. I stumbled after them. Barick led us through a doorway, then down a corridor to a closed door. He banged on the timber. The door opened to a street. I tumbled outside, hands shackled in front.

Casca waited for us, holding his special key.

"Unlock the shackles," said Barick.

Casca freed me, then Yula, who staggered forward. Gallan caught her. We limped away, following Barick. I wanted to return to the workshop. To save Popa and Rambleton. That's all I cared about. The Voldari had the skycart. We couldn't escape. I needed to protect my family.

We lurched through Karlik's streets. Around us, mudgles in green coats fought mudgles in red ones. Voldari soldiers marched through the city, striking mudgles down whatever the colour of their clothes or skin. Everyone had an enemy. The city had turned on itself.

As dusk became night, we ducked into an alleyway with no street lanterns. The walls of the adjoining buildings enveloped us like a black shroud. On the ridges surrounding Karlik, not a single venting fire burned. We slowed in the darkness, tripping over gutters, rolling ankles on broken stones.

Casca gasped, and we stopped. A growl rumbled out from the night ahead and another from behind. A half dozen horned wolves encircled us. They stalked forward, pushing us together into a libation of easy prey.

"We're trapped," surrendered Barick. "I shouldn't have come this way."

"Not your fault," said Gallan.

The wolves crept forward. Noses to the ground. Ears pricked on either side of the swept horns crowning their skull. Lips curled so much their teeth shone through the darkness.

A bark snapped from the shadows, and the wolves stopped and slunk to their bellies. Another creature appeared, wolf-like, but taller and sleeker with no horns or eyes.

Casca sniffed at the threat. "A weregrim is here. It's come for me."

We crowded together, facing danger on all sides. Casca squealed a piercing shriek that set my nerves on fire.

"What are you doing?" I blurted.

"Calling for help," he said. "It may not work. His presence is strong."

"Who's presence?"

Casca didn't answer. The weregrim yipped, and a wolf launched at me. Gallan threw himself in front, and the wolf buried its teeth into Gallan's ribs. The other wolves attacked. Barick swung his mining pick with insane desperation, cracking one in the skull. Yula regained strength, gathering stones from the broken road and pelting the attackers.

Casca squealed again. A sewer hatch in the middle of the alley burst open, and out poured rats. Hundreds, thousands of rats. They swarmed the wolves, biting and gnawing at their legs.

Barick tore open the belly of Gallan's attacker, and the wolf thudded to the ground. We backed into a window at street level. I smashed the red lava-glass with a stone and kicked shards free of the jamb. Yula dragged Gallan across the footpath and shoved him through the window. She fell after him. I followed, tugging on Barick's coat to pull him away from danger.

We tumbled into a basement.

"Casca?" I hesitated.

"Not here," said Barick.

I pulled myself up to the windowsill. Outside, the weregrim snatched Casca away in its mouth. The blind boy screamed, then vanished into the night.

Chapter 25

A voice in the dark

Horned wolves jammed their heads through the basement window, snapping, biting and drooling. Barick clobbered them with his mining pick, splitting skulls as blood and bone showered the darkness. Sewer rats climbed through the wolves' fur, chewing at their eyes and noses. Yula and I staggered around the basement, looking for something to block the window. We found an old bookcase, empty, but tall enough, and pushed it across the floor. Barick cracked another skull. The wolves retreated. We shoved the bookcase in front of the window, bracing the barrier with timber beams we found on the floor.

It should hold, at least until the sewer rats eat the wolves alive. Rats?

In the pitch black, Yula panted beside me. Barick moaned, and Gallan whimpered.

"Are you alright, Yula?" I asked.

"That damn Voldari did something to my neck. Like he broke the connection between my head and the rest of my body. I knew what I needed to do, but couldn't do it. It seems to be wearing off."

"What happened out there?"

"Casca called the rats," said Barick. "He did it before. At the workshop."

"You've been to the workshop?"

"The Voldari were already there. Casca...did something. He can command animals, but the action pains him. Drains all his energy."

"The Voldari have the skycart?"

"I don't know. They drove us off. That was days ago."

"Did you see Popa? Rambleton?"

"No."

"Is Gallan...." I attempted.

"He needs help."

"He betrayed us," snapped Yula. "Let him die."

"Don't blame Gallan," said Barick. "The Voldari twisted everyone's sense of right and wrong."

"But you did the right thing," I said. "Despite the Voldari. Despite Shadow Man."

"My da'one wasn't going to let another fake trial go ahead. Watch as more innocent mudgles die. While greed blinded others, the resistance is fighting back."

"I have to find Popa and Rambleton."

"*Arrgh*," cried Gallan.

I fumbled in the dark, dipping my hand into a warm, sticky puddle. I sniffed my fingertips. *Blood.* "Gallan?"

"He's here," muttered Gallan in a dying stupor. "He's here."

"Who's here?" I asked, pawing at the blackness until I clasped his hand.

"He's here. He's here. He's here!" Gallan bolted upright and wrenched his hand from mine. "We must get out. We're trapped. We're trap...." He collapsed back to the floor.

"He's delusional," growled Yula.

"No," said Barick. "Gallan is right. He's in the basement with us."

"Who is?" I asked.

"Shadow Man."

A shocking heat washed over me like I'd been dropped into a boiling lava pit. Sliding on my buttocks, I pushed away from Gallan and slammed into a jagged stone wall, punching the air from my lungs.

"He's inside your head," said Yula. "You're both mad."

"The clever may use madness as a cloak," came a voice from the darkness.

"Who's that?" I piped, sliding further away. *Further away from what?*

Where is he? I jammed myself into a corner. "What do you want?"

"Who? I'm the same as I ever was, but never appear to be so. And I want what everyone wants, but few are willing to take."

"That's nonsense," bit Yula.

"Yula Adermont, do you claim to know the sense of everything?"

Inside the deepest, darkest corners of my mind, something, *someone*, probed. Tried to rip away the veils masking my thoughts. Tried to uncover my worst fears and stoke a rage that would never subside. *Shadow Man.*

"You feign strength, Yula," continued the voice, "but you are not strong enough to embrace your father. Not strong enough to forgive his misstep. Anger is easier. Hate is easier."

"Leave her alone," I cried. "Leave us alone."

"Silveny Belarose," cooed the voice. "I've longed to meet you after our first encounter in the mines when you trespassed in my home."

"Home? You were sacrificing mudgles." Shadow Man ripped a veil. "Stay out of my head," I spat.

"How did it feel?" he asked. "When you stabbed the Voldari. How much did you want her to die?"

"I didn't. I was angry. They've ruined our city. Our community."

"Did *they* ruin it, or was it Curmudgle greed?"

I ground my teeth together. "You won't get in. Yula, don't let him inside your head. Barick? Barick, where are you?"

"Barick and Gallan are indisposed," said Shadow Man. "Barick, trapped in glacial fear, and Gallan is dying. You must realise that, Silveny Belarose. There's little point taking him further. He will slow you down, and my horned wolves and weregrims will tear you apart. Don't risk your lives on a corpse."

He's playing with our heads. Toying with us. Fight it. "Why did the weregrim take Casca?" I asked, thinking I might catch Shadow Man off guard.

"What is Casca to you?"

"My...my friend."

Shadow Man scoffed. A cruel, mocking laugh that cut through my bones like a butcher's saw. "Casca is nobody's *friend*."

"The weregrim took him. Where?"

"Casca and I have unfinished matters."

He tore another veil protecting my secrets. I worried about what he was doing to my sister. "Yula, block your ears. Close your mind. Don't let him read your thoughts."

"He's trying," sobbed Yula. "He's hurting me."

I pushed away from the corner and scooted across the floorstones on my bottom. "Come to my voice. Find me." I waited, arms outstretched, reaching into the musty chill for the only family I could have left.

Something brushed my hands, and I grabbed at the air. Yula pulled me into a hug, the aroma of hungered despair and body waste from the gaol offering strange comfort. We sat on the basement floor, dressed in our prison rags, holding each other and shivering from the chilling unknown. I squeezed Yula tighter. Together, we could keep him out. Together, our love would be our shield.

"Your dead parents," snarled Shadow Man. "Trapped under the avalanche in a pocket of air. Hugging each other like you do now. But they became desperate. Gasping for life. One of them killed the others. Murdered his lovers so he could steal the last mouthfuls of air, hoping a rescue would come."

"Liar!" I screamed. "Liar, liar, liar."

"Do you not see, Silveny? Your inclination for violence is hereditary. You can't escape the burden of your ancestors. Poor little Casca will tell you."

"Get out!" I released Yula and stood, grinding bare feet into the floorstones. Then I charged into the darkness towards the voice. Towards Shadow Man. I wanted to knock him over. Strangle him. Kill him. *You can't escape the burden of your ancestors.* I floundered in the basement. Tripped over Gallan's prostrate body and crashed to my knees. I got up and lurched forward, sweeping the evil air as if my arms were scythes. But I couldn't find the torment.

"He's gone," whimpered Barick. "Stop, Silveny. He's gone."

I slumped to the ground and cried.

We sat in misery for an age. I should have helped Gallan. Instead, my mind searched for shapes in the obscurity. Faces. Anything that hinted of Shadow Man's presence. A target I could attack. A body I could stab with Barick's mining pick.

The icy fear eventually thawed, and I gained enough courage to explore the basement, discovering an empty rucksack and a lantern with serpent oil sloshing around in the tank. I prised open the drawer in the lantern's base, fingering a box of firesticks and a swatch of strike paper. I struck a firestick and lit the lantern's wick.

Within the amber halo, Yula appeared, slumped against the wall. Barick curled up in the corner like he'd been beaten. Gallan, lying face-up in the centre of the filthy floor, barely breathing and drowning in his blood.

I found a pile of old sheets, tearing one into strips to make dirty, pathetic bandages to wrap around Gallan's chest. I broke the handles off two brooms and used string and a piece of hooked wire to stitch the long end of another sheet to one of the poles. Yula helped, doing the same on the other side. When done, we'd made a stretcher.

Barick peeked behind the bookcase. "It's daylight outside."

"We have to wait until it's dark again," said Yula.

"That's when the wolves roam. And those other things."

"Yula's right," I said. "We'll be too easy to spot in the daylight." *Although Gallan might die here in the basement.*

* * * * *

At dusk, we pulled the bookcase away, climbed out the window and staggered down the alley, carrying a still-breathing Gallan on the stretcher. I led everyone to the workshop, the road bricks tearing at the soles of numbing feet. I didn't know what we'd find, but the workshop offered our only hope.

Behind us, a call rang out in the dark. A call of pursuit. We picked up the pace.

Chapter 26

Escape from Karlik

Inside the workshop, the staircase lowers from the ceiling and clangs to the ground.

Fergutch appears at the top. "We're on the roof," he calls.

"Come on," I say to Barick and Yula, shouldering the rucksack.

Yula limps to the stretcher, lifting the front end to carry Gallan up the stairs.

"I'll take it," I say, worrying about the blood seeping from the arrow still embedded in her thigh.

She grunts and hands me the stretcher. Barick takes the other end. Something hammers into the steel drum wedged in the door hole. The drum shunts forward.

I push up the first steps, facing away from the stretcher as it hangs low in my grip. My shoulders already burn. Barick pushes me forward, forcing me to take another step. Yula lags. We won't make the top before the drum is pushed out.

Hope scampers down the stairs as a dozen snerguls race past us and bolt to the door. They lean against the drum, forcing it back into the hole.

"Hurry up," snaps Fergutch. "Haven't got all night."

We're halfway up. Our raging pursuers smash another axe through the timber door. A snergul squeals and drops dead, riven in two. The drum is pushed in. Snerguls push out. Three-quarters of the way up the stairs. A clash louder than thunder rings against the drum, and it bursts into the workshop. Chaos ensues. Two horned wolves lunge through the hole in the door, ripping the snerguls to shreds. A mudgle follows, removing the door brace and opening it to the outside threat.

A Voldari strides in; Urn-hasa, my prison tormentor, come to finish the task. At the end of a leash, she drags a gorvile, already salivating at the thought of my demise.

We reach Fergutch. He takes the stretcher from me, and we clamber onto the flat roof. Barick follows. Yula limps up. Fergutch drops the stretcher and kicks closed a hatch as the unleashed gorvile bounds up the stairs.

Our saviour heaves a crate of bricks onto the hatch. "That should hold the bastards for a while," he grunts.

Popa and Rambleton run to me. Hug me. Then they hug Yula. We cry. With relief, terror, happiness. All bound in glistening drops tumbling from our eyes.

I pull away to marvel at the creation floating above the roof. The skycart, finished, it seems. Timber propellers fixed in stillness to the rear of the woven-reed carriage. Not meladoor, but it must do. Wings, nothing more than reedy skeletons covered in fabric, reach out from either side of the carriage, and floating above it, a glorious, promise-filled balloon. It's attached to a brass tube by a sleeve of fabric resembling a giant umbilical cord. A hiss of gas bleeds from the tube and inflates the balloon.

"How many passengers?" I ask Fergutch with naïve hope.

He shakes his head. "Still only four."

I unshoulder the rucksack and throw it into the carriage beside crates and loaded bags of supplies. Inside her cage, Sneckle the snergul hangs from a bracing timber and barks a welcome. Beneath us, the monsters smash against the hatch's underside, lifting the crate with dangerous ease.

"Bricks might not hold after all," grumps Fergutch.

He grabs a rusty pike, then throws another to Barick. Popa hands Yula a bow and quiver with a pittance of arrows.

The gas continues to pulse. The balloon fills, growing towards stars of liberated brilliance, their gleam freed from the dulling pollution of venting fires. But the stars can't match the beckoning shine of the two moons: Seena and Bargan. In Karlik, they never warranted names. Tonight, they deserve whatever accolade I can bestow. They deserve reverence as they light our path to freedom.

The web of ropes fixing the balloon to the carriage tighten. Those holding the carriage to the roof will strain soon.

"Help me get Gallan inside," I say to Rambleton.

The white mudgle glances at me with eyes bereft of dreams. We pick up the stretcher and stumble towards the entrance to the carriage, accessed by a drawbridge. Rambleton rolls Gallan off the stretcher, up the drawbridge and to the entranceway. But our friend won't fit through the gap. Rambleton pushes Gallan's legs into his chest and shoves him onto the carriage. It's awkward. Undignified. Painful. But it might save his life.

Balloon almost full. The four ropes tied to either corner of the carriage and looped through metal eyelets bolted to the slate roof begin to strain as the carriage lifts skyward.

'Crash!'

The bricks inside the crate, the only thing protecting us from death, shudder from a desperate force. I picture the gorvile bracing its legs against the stairs and ramming its broad shoulders into the underside of the roof hatch, and all the time, Urn-hasa is urging it on with her growling demands.

I snap at Barick, "Get in the carriage."

He stands beside the hatch, clutching the rusty pike and shaking, the bravery sucked from his veins. Waiting for the crate of bricks to fail.

I march over to him and grab his shoulders. "The steering wheel moves the rudder. It can help change direction. Fergutch might have made a sail. To catch the wind. Two cranks spin the propellers at the back. For bursts of speed. The thin white cords near the steering wheel open the balloon vents. Release gas when you need to come down. There's already ballast in the carriage...."

"Silveny," moans Barick. "Silveny. Why are you telling me this? You can drive the balloon."

I might not make it. "Better two of us know. Now, get in the carriage. Be ready to cut the ropes attaching it to the roof. Use your pike."

'*BOOM!*'

An almighty explosion from inside the workshop. The hatch bursts open, shattering the crate and sending bricks flying off into the night. Smoke seeps from a hole in the roof, ash-grey tendrils searching for a victim.

"Blown the damn hatch off its hinges," says Fergutch. "Everyone. Arm yourself."

I pull Barick's mining pick from his belt and scream at him, "Carriage! Now! Start cutting the ropes."

He nods and staggers away. A snarling horned wolf emerges from the smoke. Fergutch thrusts his pike, nicking the animal's side. Yula shoots an arrow. It lodges in the wolf's flank but only fuels its anger.

The creature leaps at Fergutch, wrapping its jaws around his throat. The old builder tumbles back, his pike clattering to the roof in surrender. Yula fires another arrow, hitting the wolf in the rump. Its jaws clench, and blood splatters over Fergutch's face. In the throes of death, a grim obstinacy sets beneath the blood. Fergutch braces his feet on the roof, lunges backwards, and tumbles over the edge, taking the wolf with him to the death waiting below.

Grasping a sword in one hand, the gorvile pulls itself through the hatch, then rears up, ready to fight. I squeeze the mining pick's handle, preparing to charge, wondering if I can. Rambleton senses my hesitation and jumps at the gorvile, knocking it over.

"Rambleton!" shrieks Popa. "Get away. You'll be hurt."

In a rolling maul, the gorvile slices Rambleton's chest. He cries out, blood staining his white hair with scarlet terror.

Popa weeps beside me. "Come away, Rambleton. Please."

Rambleton and the gorvile stagger to their feet. The white mudgle flings his body at the creature. The sword stabs him in the belly, but he pulls it ever closer, wrapping his arms around the gorvile and trying to crush its chest. Together, they fall back through the hatch and into the workshop.

"No!" screams Popa.

I clutch at thin air as he races to the hole.

Yula grabs his arm. "He's gone, Popa. We should get in the skycart."

The chaotic horror demands action. "Barick!" I yell. "Cut the ropes."

The balloon isn't full, but full enough. I undo the twine connecting the fabric sleeve to the gas tube and tie the sleeve off. I let the gas continue to seep.

"It'll carry five," I say to Yula, knowing it won't. But I can't leave Popa behind.

She drags him towards the carriage. That's when Urn-hasa, dressed for a fight in stupid, defenceless blue robes, thinking she's untouchable, climbs through the hole. She pulls a gold star from the robes and flings it at Popa. It lodges in his throat.

No! I'm the fool. I'm the fool.

Yula rests Popa on the roof, then fires an arrow at Urn-hasa. The Voldari sways out of danger as if the projectile flew as slow as a leaden cloud.

Out of arrows, Yula grabs Fergutch's discarded pike and lunges at Urn-hasa. The white owl moves with a grace and stealth that beguiles. She grabs the pike's handle above the blade and yanks Yula forward, tripping my sister onto her back. The pike wrenches free and spins in mid-air before the Voldari grasps the weapon and, with murderous serenity, thrusts the blade into Yula's side.

I rush at Urn-hasa, who's turned away. I spring onto the brass tube, still pulsing gas, and launch myself into the air at the Voldari monster. She swivels her owl-like head to me, dark eyes masking any fear, and tries to sway her torso from danger. I strain my arm as far as it will go and force my hand down, smashing the mining pick between the snow-white feathers on her scalp and cracking her skull like porcelain.

I fall on top of the invader. Her body twitches underneath me, trying to avert its demise. I roll away and clamber to my feet.

Yula crawls to Popa, and they embrace in loving resignation.

I stumble over to my family and tug on Yula's arm, ignoring the blood spilling from her side. "Please," I whimper. "We must go. Come on. Popa. You can both make it."

Yula shakes her head. "We're dying."

"Last rope!" yells Barick from the carriage.

I glare at him, angry at his competence when I need an excuse for delay. Then I weep lonely tears. "I c-c-can't…I can't lu-lu-leave you behind."

Yula's jaw tightens. "You must. Or we'll all die." She pushes me away and cradles her father. Her Popa.

Don't let sadness cause fatal delay. Sobbing, I jump into the carriage, pulling up and securing the drawbridge. Mudgles in green coats, imposters, climb onto the roof. One uses a hand-axe to chop into the side of the skycart carriage, splintering the woven reeds. Barick cuts the last rope, then heaves a sandbag at the mudgle, hitting her in the face. The balloon wills us higher. Barick launches more ballast, pelting a half-dozen mudgle pursuers. *Imposters.*

Yula reaches for a lantern, watching our ascent. Higher we climb, the two heroic moons claiming our escape. With the balloon out of reach, the mudgles turn on Yula and Popa. My sister, my unbelievably brave sister, throws the lantern at the brass tube of pulsing gas. The lantern's lava-glass shatters, and the little flame inside bursts into a venting fire larger than I've ever seen. It engulfs everyone on the roof. Yula, Popa and the imposters. Then, a cataclysmic roar shudders the streets of Karlik as the workshop explodes, showering the night with the flaming debris of the city's failure. *Our* failure to turn evil away before it took hold.

*　*　*　*　*

Me, Barick and a dying Gallan rise above our home. Now unrecognisable. Below us, shapes drift among the shadows, shunning the flames of the burning workshop. Sometimes, the shapes confront each other. Fight, maim and move on. Move on to become ghosts of what once was.

'Stop the haunting of Karlik,' warned Casca. But we didn't; the city overrun with ethereal demons longing for a life lost. They'd been unleashed by the Voldari, as if the visitors were necromancers conducting the haunting from behind a veil of alliance. It happened so suddenly; I couldn't stop it. I never had a hope. Neither did anyone else.

We drift past the serpent oil mines, forlorn holes without the venting fires to guard them, and the southerly breeze carries us above *Death's Pass*. I turn the steering wheel, moving the rudder to try to stop us from flying into cliffs on our right. We need a sail, but Fergutch didn't have the time or materials to make one. Barick spins the propellers, moving us away from danger.

We pass a cave mouth, the fullness of Seena and Bargan illuminating another ghost, stumbling on a ledge in a circle of disorientation as if searching for its lost soul.

"Someone down there," says Barick. "We could save them."

I lost Yula, Popa and Rambleton. I don't want anyone else. Especially not a ghost.

But the ghost throws off its shroud to reveal a boy. A blind boy.

"It's Casca," says Barick. He leans over the carriage's side and yells, "CASCA! CASCA!"

The blind boy faces the voices coming from the stars, and the moons glint in obsidian glass.

It is him. "CASCA!" I yell. "We're in the skycart."

"Can we reach him?" asks Barick. "This thing is impossible to steer."

"The breeze is taking us closer. Casca! I'm throwing a rope down."

I grab a coiled rope, tie one end to a cleat on the side of the carriage and toss the loose end over the edge. The rope's not long enough to reach Casca.

"Vent some gas," I say to Barick.

"Are you insane?" he snaps. "We won't get over the ridge."

"We only need to lose a little."

Barick mutters and shakes his head. He pulls on a release cord, opening a vent in the top of the balloon to let out gas. I take over the propellers, turning anticlockwise to hold the skycart in place.

"Walk straight ahead twenty paces!" I yell to Casca.

He follows my instructions. The balloon dips. The rope dangles above his head.

"Reach up! Reach!"

He reaches.

"Four paces to your left. Jump up!"

He jumps and grabs the rope.

"Close the vent," I say to Barick before leaning over the carriage's side.

Casca has pulled the rope down enough to loop it around his waist and tie it off. A gust of wind catches us and lifts Casca from the ledge.

"Help me pull him in," I urge Barick.

Together we heave. Hand over hand. Shoulders burning. Palms beginning to blister. Rope straining against the carriage's railing.

Eventually, Casca's head appears above the railing, and we pull him inside.

"I thought you were dead," I say to the blind boy before realising my stupidity.

"I could have been," replies Casca. "But fate has other plans for me."

Chapter 27

Casca

The weregrim carried me through Karlik's streets, its loping gait producing a distinct echo in the scuff of its paws over road bricks. It pays to remember that sound. We ran past warring Curmudgles, cursing and screaming as they battered each other into submission. Blades clashed. Blood spilled. Fear expelled bodily wastes. A female sobbed. I couldn't tell if Curmudgle or Voldari. An infant wailed. All lamented the end of something that would never be again.

We left the vexed sorrow of Karlik behind and began climbing, the rocky, unstable clink of scree shifting beneath our feet. Up a narrow chute, air cloying around me. Onto a road, flat, solid, dependable. Melting ice dripped into crystal pools. A mountain breeze swept away the lingering pollution from venting fires. The night air chilled.

The road led to a cave. Or a mine. Despite my broken eyes, I can sense subtle changes in light. We'd moved from the familiar comfort of moonlight to the oppressive, airless black of underground.

We travelled down. Down, around. Down, around. Over and over, following a burrowing path that spiralled its way to the bowels of the earth. With each corner, the air grew hotter, rising from below us.

The weregrim slowed, its panting breaths and vile drool washing me with exhaustion. Mucus ran from its nostrils. The clench of its jaw weakened. I wondered what would happen to me if the creature died on the path. If it never reached its destination.

My worry ended when the animal stopped and released me. Worry ended. Terror began.

You may think an immortal has nothing to fear. Or that fear is not an emotion we pay any mind to. I wish it were so. I wish immortal lives were full of joy and contentment. I've wished for many things over the thousands of yarles of my existence. Most remain ungranted.

The weregrim slunk away, leaving me alone with the darkness inside and out. I braced my hands on a dirt floor and pushed to standing. A seething, steaming pit bubbled nearby. Fire and brimstone. A few steps the wrong way and an eternal scorching more brutal than anyone could imagine awaited.

I stumbled away from the pit, reaching for a wall I could follow, thinking the path might soon lead up and return me to the surface. A cooler air drew me forward. Sucked me in like a vacuum. I should have realised the deceit of the enticement. It's what he does. Uses hope to crush spirit.

I entered an underground cathedral. A clap of my hands echoed through the chasm, a choral exclamation. Bounced from the walls like a wayward bird.

Not birds, I thought. *Bats.* Giant cave bats, each as large as a sewer cat. Their tinks and chattering squeaks, imperceptible to most ears, painted a soundscape across the cathedral roof.

As the bats swirled above me, I pirouetted with the calls, partners in a dance of exploration, sensing the world in ways few could understand. The bats settled, the chattering dimmed, and the scuff of my boots in the dirt sent a lonely echo searching for a mate.

I walked through the cathedral, not certain which way to go. A scent drew me closer. One I vaguely remember from generations ago. A smell of flesh and stone. Sulphur and ash. Blood and fire. I bumped into something that wasn't a rock. I discovered knuckles, bulging on thin, spidery fingers as a hand clutched a stone ball. But not stone. Definitely not. The hand rested on a knee, rendered in a coating that felt like shards of glass crushed into mortar set hard. I knelt, tracing my fingers along a rendered shin and calf, down to a right foot planted in the dirt.

My thoughts pulsed with the examination as they posed a possibility

I didn't want to accept. On my knees, I reached across with my right hand and found a left foot coated in the same cruel cement. Another leg. Knee. Fingers clutching a ball. I stood, feeling between the hands to find a seat. A seat with a face. Many faces. Set in stone. No. Not stone.

I dug my fingernail under a lip of crust and peeled away a fleck, revealing the flesh of a soft cheek.

"You must have known," said a male voice behind me.

I spun around. Thudding boots approached. Soles of steel. A ruffle of clothes. Breaths loud and searching, rattling my eardrums. While older than time, I felt young again. Vulnerable. A mischievous boy about to be scolded. A helpless, blind beggar.

The footsteps stopped. "You have aged," said the voice, rough and biting with a hint of superiority. "Immortality has not protected you from the weathering of time."

"Has it protected you?" I asked.

He laughed. "I seek the thrill of the violation."

"What a lonely journey that must be."

The voice hardened. "It didn't need to be so." He stepped closer. "Have you told your companions?"

"They call you Shadow Man."

He chuckled. "I've had worse names."

"They fear you."

"Why should my return be something to fear?"

"Because you're not who you once were. You're not the admired, benevolent leader who ruled Pergamos. Ambition and envy dragged you into an abyss. Cursed your subjects with a ruler of malice and spite. You watched, indifferent, as Pergamos crumbled to dust. You abandoned those who once loved you to pursue desires elsewhere."

"I have returned."

"It shouldn't be. The immortal sacrifice atop the great pyramid failed. Widukind died."

"Only for an instant. A moment of indecision on my part."

I backed away, thinking of a path to escape. I bumped into the stony chair. No, not a chair. A throne. The Throne of the Dead.

"You won't escape this time," he said.

"I'm no use to you. You don't need me."

"You're right, Casca, I don't need you. But I want you." His voice turned sombre, almost mournful.

I fought the sorrow welling inside me, understanding it as another sleight of emotion. Another ploy by Shadow Man to draw me to him. No, not Shadow Man. *Volerdie.*

"Why do you hide your eyes behind those glasses?" asked Volerdie.

"Others fear the scars of my blindness. Scars you inflicted."

"You're more than physically blind. Your mind is unable to see what is laid before you. As immortals both, we can share in the joy of exploitation."

"I don't want any of it." I dug my fingernails into the crust of the dead throne and tried to peel the layer of cutting render away as if that might weaken Volerdie's power.

"How did mortality feel?" he asked. "When my weregrim bit your arm."

"The wound healed."

"Ah, but it took time, didn't it? All that while you must have feared that you were immortal no longer."

"I don't want this!" I cried. "I'm not like you. Immortality was forced on me. You grasped it willingly."

Volerdie sighed. "You wanted it as much as I."

"Why are you hiding away here?" I growled. "You returned to Ostamp decades ago. Are you so weak from the travel between worlds?"

"Brave, Casca. Brave to think you could better me. It's true, the return was like a birth. At first, I was as weak as a babe and needed to regather my strength. But that journey is well advanced."

"You won't rule again. Most have forgotten you. Pergamos is no more. Enthilen is a land of peace. You will be shunned." I pulled another fleck of crust off, this one the size of my palm. The render on the dead throne had not hardened properly yet.

"The Voldari already worship me." Volerdie stepped closer, and a finger brushed my cheek. "Won't you sit beside me?" he asked. "Won't you share the joy that I will soon bring?"

"No." I reached inside my coat pocket and fingered the mouldewerp key.

"Then I should end it. Finally take your life."

Part of me wished that. Freed from the chains of immortality, the eternal torment would be over in a blink. But it was a coward's choice. If Volerdie was to be challenged, stopped, if the spread of evil could ever be stopped, I would have to play a part. I'd have to help those who stood in Volerdie's way.

His fingers groped around my neck and squeezed. With my right hand, I probed the exposed, fleshy part of the dead throne, looking for a weakness. I found an eyeball, soft and vulnerable. The irony made me smile. I yanked the key from my pocket with my left hand. Jammed the bow and shaft between my fingers and lashed out, smashing my fist down into the eyeball. Volerdie screamed. His fingers loosened their grip. I punched again, burying the key's bit into blood and bone, deep in the skull. Volerdie stumbled back.

'I was as weak as a babe.'

How much strength had he regathered? I didn't wait to find out. I pursed my lips and whistled a high-pitched whine unheard by most. But not giant cave bats. They left their roosts and whirled above me. Volerdie staggered, desperate to reach me before the escape. The bats descended in a cloud of urgency. Some swarmed around him. Others clawed at me with their feet. Grasped my clothes. Lifted my body from the cavern floor.

"What will he do, this boy!?" screamed Volerdie. "In the history of two worlds, evil has never been eliminated. It's entrenched in the hearts of women and men. How will you erase it, Casca? How will you build your utopia?"

His voice faded as I flew away, carried by the valorous bats. Away from eternal damnation. Away from the re-emergence of devilry in Ostamp. Up through the cathedrals of the underground and into the comforting moonlight.

Chapter 28

Into the unknown

"Volerdie?" I say. "Are you sure? I mean, you *are* blind."

"We've met before," replies Casca. "He's not someone you forget."

"He...he's Shadow Man?" asks Barick.

"Yes."

"You killed him?"

Casca offers a faint smile. "Malevolence has no end. Volerdie's power comes from the evil that others do. He grew in strength when Curmudgles turned on each other. Further acts of violence can't defeat him."

"How *can* he be defeated?" I ask.

Casca slumps to the floor of the skycart carriage. "It took all my energy to call the bats, and I could only do it because I'd distracted Volerdie with my attack. I need to rest."

He turns away to face the stars, ignoring my question. Although I already know the answer.

I shiver and search the crates and sacks piled in the middle of the carriage, hoping Fergutch packed clothes. I pry open a crate to find the Book of Leaves. Anger wells inside me, upset we've been carrying useless weight. Then, sadness overwhelms it. A painful loneliness deep in my chest. A longing for a past filled with Popa's love, Yula's strength, and smiles and hugs from Rambleton.

Inside a sack, I find a woollen coat and button it over my prison rags. Barick drapes a blanket across Gallan lying on the carriage floor, still breathing, then bursts into tears.

I wrap an arm around his shoulder.

"I'm leaving mu-mu-my family b-b-b-behind," he sobs. "Ta-ta-to the madness below."

"One day, we might return," I say, without believing it. I never want to return.

"All I thought a-a-about wu-was escape."

A wind change takes us back across the Wyrm Valley and over Karlik, the skycart offering a final farewell. Below us, dozens of Voldari soldiers march along *Death's Pass* towards Karlik, their reptilian armour glinting in the moons light. Four of them carry a chair at shoulder height. No, not a chair. The Throne of the Dead formed from contorted bodies encrusted in stone, the backrest crowned with the head of a horned wolf. A man sits on the throne, resting his chin on his chest. No, not a man. *Volerdie.*

Barick gathers his strength and grasps the skycart's steering wheel, moving the rudder to navigate us away from a rocky outcrop. I turn the propeller handles, trying to push us towards the balloon line and the ridge at *Line Station 16.* Once over the ridge, we can descend through valleys to the Nordland Plains. It will be a long, slow journey, made harder by the dark. But Seena and Bargan shine bright, guiding our way.

Comforting moonlight.

"I have to visit Revelé," mutters Casca.

"Why?" I ask.

"Volerdie's throne is not complete. He needs the eyes of lost souls and the *Infinitas.*"

"They're in Revelé?"

"Tom Anderson is their keeper. I must warn him."

Acknowledgements

Thanks to my wonderful beta readers Ian, Ness, Lori and Gayle for helping me start this new adventure.

About the author

G. W. Lücke shares a small part of Tasmania with his wife, a mischievous border collie, and a menagerie of animals and plants. When not writing, he fills his days with gardening, growing food, forest and beach walks, and being healed by nature.

Praise for The Relevation Trilogy

"There are brilliant lines and passages peppered across this novel, some so good they'll force you back for another read, while the action sequences and magical exchanges are exhilarating – a one-two punch that is rare in the world of fantasy writing. Lücke demonstrates a masterful use of language, bursts of unforgettable prose, a rich tapestry of characters, and a penchant for mythical history in this remarkably good second installment."

★★★★½ Self-publishing Review

"A fresh and intriguing fantasy...the author introduces an array of memorable characters... fantasy aficionados will...find themselves engrossed in the story from beginning to end."

'Get it'. Kirkus Reviews

"...an engrossing addition to the high fantasy catalogue. Lücke's characters have a vivid energy; the land and people of Enthilen are illuminated with care and detail, and the plot runs at a tight, satisfying pace."

Indi Reader (Approved)

"Lücke is a master of the cliffhanger, which he skillfully utilizes at the end of each chapter. Readers will be captivated to the very end."

US Review of Books (Recommended)

"Lücke strikes a perfect balance between stunning worldbuilding and layered narrative as his hero struggles against powerful enemies while on a journey of self-discovery. Lücke is a writer to watch for."

The Prairies Book Review

"Darkly real but classically fantastical...Packed with thematic descriptions and evocative prose, this fantasy is engaging, with many inspiring characters to root for."

Publishers Weekly (BookLife)